Traci Douglass is a *USA TODAY* bestselling romance author with Mills & Boon, Entangled Publishing and Tule Publishing, and has an MFA in writing popular fiction from Seton Hill University. She writes sometimes funny, usually awkward, always emotional stories about strong, quirky, wounded characters overcoming past adversity to find their forever person and heartfelt, healing happily-ever-afters. Connect with her through her website, tracidouglassbooks.com.

Deanne Anders was reading romance while her friends were still reading Nancy Drew, and she knew she'd hit the jackpot when she found a shelf of Mills & Boon Modern books in her local library. Years later she discovered the fun of writing her own. Deanne lives in Florida, with her husband and their spoiled Pomeranian. During the day she works as a nursing supervisor. With her love of everything medical and romance, writing for Mills & Boon Medical is a dream come true.

Also by Traci Douglass

A Single Dad to Heal Him

Wyckford General Hospital miniseries

Single Dad's Unexpected Reunion
An ER Nurse to Redeem Him
Her Forbidden Firefighter
Family of Three Under the Tree

US Search and Rescue miniseries

Risking His Heart for the ER Doc

Also by Deanne Anders

Festive Reunion with the Doctor

Nashville Midwives miniseries

Unbuttoning the Bachelor Doc
The Rebel Doctor's Secret Child
Single Dad's Fake Fiancée

Discover more at millsandboon.co.uk.

FOUND: THEIR FOREVER FAMILY

TRACI DOUGLASS

DR HART'S ROMANCE REMATCH

DEANNE ANDERS

MILLS & BOON

All rights reserved including the right of reproduction in whole or in part in any form. This edition is published by arrangement with Harlequin Enterprises ULC.

This is a work of fiction. Names, characters, places, locations and incidents are purely fictional and bear no relationship to any real life individuals, living or dead, or to any actual places, business establishments, locations, events or incidents. Any resemblance is entirely coincidental.

Without limiting the exclusive rights of any author, contributor or the publisher of this publication, any unauthorised use of this publication to train generative artificial intelligence (AI) technologies is expressly prohibited. HarperCollins also exercise their rights under Article 4(3) of the Digital Single Market Directive 2019/790 and expressly reserve this publication from the text and data mining exception.

® and TM are trademarks owned and used by the trademark owner and/or its licensee. Trademarks marked with ® are registered with the United Kingdom Patent Office and/or the Office for Harmonisation in the Internal Market and in other countries.

First published in Great Britain 2026
by Mills & Boon, an imprint of HarperCollins*Publishers* Ltd,
1 London Bridge Street, London, SE1 9GF

www.harpercollins.co.uk

HarperCollins*Publishers* Macken House, 39/40 Mayor Street Upper, Dublin 1, D01 C9W8, Ireland

Found: Their Forever Family © 2026 Traci Douglass

Dr Hart's Romance Rematch © 2026 Denise Chavers

ISBN: 978-0-263-41990-0

04/26

Printed and Bound in the UK using 100% Renewable Electricity
at CPI Group (UK) Ltd, Croydon, CR0 4YY

FOUND: THEIR FOREVER FAMILY

TRACI DOUGLASS

MILLS & BOON

To Sheila Hodgson,
former senior editor for the Medical line.

Thank you for everything, Sheila.
May you rest in peace and love.

You will be greatly missed. <3

CHAPTER ONE

THE WHIR OF helicopter blades sliced through mountain air as the helicopter Ezra "EZ" Benson was riding in banked hard left. From his place in the back, he glanced through the front seats into the cockpit to see the GPS coordinates flickering across the pilot's display. Below them, the granite peaks of the Teton Range jutted through snow like broken teeth, and somewhere in that maze of rock and ice, two climbers waited for rescue.

"Visual on the target," Nadja Haugen, the Backcountry Search and Rescue team's volunteer head pilot, said through the radio as she adjusted her grip on the controls. From past experience in heli rescues, EZ knew the wind shears at these altitudes could flip a chopper like a coin, but he trusted Nadja's expertise just like he trusted everyone else on the BSAR team. She was a veteran Swiss and Alpine rescue specialist from Norway with over a decade of service before moving to Jackson Hole with her family four years earlier. Not quite as much time as EZ, who had spent the last twenty years of his life first as a junior rescuer in high school, then as a combat medic in the military, then later—before joining this search-and-rescue team—on a weekly reality TV show called *Code Red Rescue*, where he helped save people from harrowing situations all over the world. Living life on the edge like that taught a person that panic wasn't an option when lives were on the line. Neither was failure.

Too bad that wasn't true when it mattered the most...

EZ squeezed his eyes shut and shook off the horrific memories that were never far from his mind since losing Sierra. Ice, snow, stormy skies, and the broken body of the woman he'd loved with all his heart—his wife, who'd been carrying their second child. Gone in an instant.

Gone and it's my fault. I failed again.

Stop. Get it together.

After a few deep, steadying breaths, EZ forced his eyes open again and leaned forward slightly to peer out the open doorway on the chopper's left side, where he could spot the climbers clinging to a ledge barely wide enough for a picnic blanket. One was moving. The other wasn't.

"This is gonna be tight," muttered Dave Morales, one of the team's volunteer medics, who was double-checking the supplies in his go kit while EZ got busy prepping the rescue litter.

EZ nodded, thanking God as a familiar calm settled over him once more. This was what he'd trained for, lived for—the razor's edge between control and catastrophe. The place where instinct and training converged into something approaching magic. When things went well, anyway.

Focus. Calculate. Execute.

As Nadja slowly brought down the helicopter atop a plateau as near to the ledge as they could find, fighting thermals that wanted to dash them against the cliff face, the rotors' wash scattered loose snow like confetti, revealing patches of black ice that made EZ's jaw clench. Ice.

Always the ice.

Another memory hit him like a slap—Sierra's laugh carrying across a snow-covered slope, her voice cutting through the current static on his radio. *See you tonight, hotshot. Don't let fame go to your head.*

But fame had gone to his head. EZ had agreed to shoot a special episode of *Code Red Rescue*, this time in Canada. It hadn't been part of his original contract, but he'd agreed to do it because his agent at the time had said it would be great for his career, and with the new baby on the way, EZ had wanted the extra money to put away for the future. And also, maybe a little bit, because he'd enjoyed the attention he got from being a hero to millions of loyal viewers. People walked up to him on the street to shake his hand, took selfies with him, and thanked him for his service. He'd been a young father, a blissfully happy husband, and at the top of his game them. Before everything had gone to hell in one fateful second. A second he should've been there for. Maybe he could've prevented it, spent time with Sierra instead of sending her off on a girls' ski weekend with her friends to Mammoth Mountain. He'd checked the conditions himself. It was a Level 1. The risk had been low, and he'd made sure that Sierra knew the safe runs to take. But while he'd been away on location halfway around the world, an unexpected snowstorm had hit just as the girls had arrived at their resort. Afterward, when the slopes were open again, they'd headed out for a day of fun, only to end up in a fight for their lives. The avalanche had come out of nowhere. Swift. Deadly. Merciless.

By the time he'd gotten the call, by the time he'd chartered the fastest plane back to Jackson—

"Okay, EZ?" Dave's voice snapped him back the present. "Ready to go?"

Right. He was here. Now. Not two years ago.

Chest tight as he nodded, they climbed out of the chopper then reached back in for their gear and equipment. Then he and Dave trekked through the knee-deep snow to the edge of the plateau and proceeded to set up their rigging. Once secured, EZ strapped on his harness and slowly rappelled down to the ledge where the climbers were stuck. Two young guys, in their twenties. The one still conscious, Todd, nearly wept with relief when EZ finally touched down on the rock. Then he kneeled to check vitals on the unconscious climber, Ben, before straightening. "Don't worry, Todd. We'll get you out of here. Your friend Ben is alive, but he's lost some blood from that cut on his head, and from the swelling around his right ankle it looks like it's at least a bad sprain, if not broken. Because of his condition, we'll take him up first in the basket, then I'll come back for you, okay?"

Todd swallowed hard, glancing from EZ to his friend then back again before nodding. "Okay."

EZ radioed up to Dave to lower the basket and then with Todd's help got Ben loaded onto the litter after putting a neck brace on him as a precaution. EZ rode up alongside Ben to make sure he made it to Dave okay, then went back down to bring up Todd. He got Todd strapped into a harness then hooked it to his own for the tandem ascent back to the top. They'd just made it to the top and removed their harnesses when the radios crackled to life again.

"EZ, this is base," Ruby Enapay, the team's coordinator and an RN, said. "We've got an emergency call. Personal. It's your daughter."

The world around him seemed to tunnel as his blood turned to slush. Oh, God. Not again.

"She's been injured at school," Ruby continued. "They took her to the ER at Teton Memorial."

The roar of helicopter blades in the distance faded as images of Maisy, his fearless, tree-climbing, adventure-seeking seven-year-old, overwhelmed him. They were too alike, she and him. Maisy thought the world was her personal jungle gym.

He managed to force words past his choked vocal cords. "How bad?"

"Unsure. They'll only release that information to a family member," Ruby said, the wince apparent in her tone. "I'm sorry, EZ. I know how scary this must be for you after…" Her voice trailed off and she cleared her throat. "But, hey. I'm sure she's okay. Kids that age hurt themselves all the time. Remember the incident at Yellowstone last summer? When she fell from that tree she'd climbed to get a better view of some elk? All she ended up with there were a few bumps and scrapes and a very bruised ego. This is probably the same sort of thing."

Or not.

Grim-faced, EZ helped Dave get a still-unconscious Ben loaded into the back of the heli along with Todd, then returned to gather their equipment and riggings before flying back to base, where an ambulance awaited the climbers. By the time they arrived, EZ had already been in contact with the ER and given consent for X-rays of his daughter's arm and any additional treatments needed to help her. Once they landed and got the climbers loaded into the ambulance, EZ followed them in his own truck, arriving at Teton Memorial in just six and a half minutes, when the ride usually took at least ten.

While the paramedics unloaded the climbers, EZ burst through the hospital's automatic doors still wearing his team flight suit, the antiseptic smell hitting him hard as it dragged up every medical nightmare he'd lived through in the last two years.

"Maisy Benson," he told the receptionist, probably too loudly. "I'm her father."

"Trauma two, just around—"

But he was already moving, following the familiar maze of hospital corridors until he heard Maisy's indignant voice.

"I don't like this itchy thing on my arm!" Maisy whined as EZ rounded the corner then stopped short in front the trauma-bay door.

There was his daughter, perched on the end of an examination table as a nurse finished putting a bright pink cast on her left arm. Standing nearby, scrolling calmly through the chart on a tablet, was someone he hadn't seen since high school.

Callie Dupree.

Callie looked up then and their eyes met, and for a moment the years collapsed. She looked...different. Older, obviously. More serious. But those intelligent green eyes were the same as he remembered, along with the way she tucked a strand of long blond hair behind her ear when she concentrated.

"Daddy!" Maisy jumped off the table and ran over to him. EZ caught her carefully, mindful of the cast.

"Hey, monkey. Heard you had another adventure."

"I did. I climbed the jungle gym superhigh! I had to because Johnny Keith dared me and you can't turn down a dare, right, Dr. Callie?" Maisy and EZ both looked at Callie, who apparently hadn't heard and just kept scrolling on her tablet. Maisy continued. "But then I fell all the way to the bottom, and it hurt so bad, and I cried a lot. Then they brought me here and Dr. Callie fixed me right up."

This time when Maisy turned to beam at Callie, Callie beamed right back and for a second EZ forgot to breathe. He shook it off quickly and chastised himself, focusing on something other than the fact that Callie was attractive. He didn't care about that anymore. His focus was raising his daughter—that's what was important now. He cleared his throat, his jaw tight. So Callie was a doctor, huh? Well, he supposed he shouldn't be surprised. She was always smarter than your average bear. Finally, when EZ realized he was just standing there like an idiot as both females stared at him, he said, "Dr. Dupree."

"Ezra Benson," she returned as carefully neutral as his voice had been. "It's been a long time."

"It has," he agreed, the seconds stretching awkwardly between them until he added. "Uh, thanks for treating my daughter."

"Of course." Callie gave a polite, cool smile. "Maisy's been very brave. The break was clean and should heal perfectly with proper care."

EZ nodded as a dozen inappropriate questions bombarded his brain. How long had Callie been back in Jackson? Where was she living? He remembered her parents putting their place on the market a few years back, so it couldn't be there. What had happened to the bright-eyed student who'd once tutored him through AP science back in the day and filled his hormonal teen self with all sorts of wicked fantasies that he'd never been brave enough to try and make real with her?

What. What?

Not what he should be thinking about right now. After what happened with Sierra, he was done with romance and relationships. He had more than enough on his plate to deal with already: raising Maisy on his own and running the Double B Ranch that he'd taken over from his dad after moving back to Jackson himself. He certainly didn't need to start thinking about Callie Dupree. Nope. Instead, he forced himself back to the topic at hand—Maisy's injury. "What are her restrictions?"

"No climbing for six weeks. Keep the cast dry. Follow-up appointment in two weeks in my office." Callie tapped a button on her tablet and papers printed out on a small machine in the corner. She grabbed them and handed them to him, their fingers brushing for half a second and sending unwanted tingles of awareness up his arm before he looked away to frown down at the list of instructions on his daughter's discharge papers. "The usual broken-arm protocol."

"No climbing?" Maisy's voice was pitched toward tragedy. "But, Daddy, what about my tree house?"

"The tree house will wait," EZ said firmly, then glanced back over at Callie. "Thank you, Dr. Dupree."

"You're welcome." She nodded as she turned to leave. "It was good to see you again, Ezra. And you take care, Maisy. Remember what we talked about—"

"Adventures are more fun when you're careful!" Maisy said, parroting Callie dutifully.

After she left, EZ took Maisy's good hand and walked out to find the discharge desk, wondering how he'd keep his adrenaline-junkie daughter out of trouble for the next six weeks.

"Daddy?" Maisy tugged on his hand. "Luka's here, too. He's in the waiting room. Can I say hi?"

EZ scrunched his nose. "Who's Luka?"

"My new best friend from first grade! He and his mom just moved here and—"

No. It couldn't be. But the sinking feeling in his gut told him that, yeah, it could be, as the pieces clicked together with uncomfortable precision. "Is he Dr. Dupree's son?"

"Yes!" Maisy started skipping. "Dr. Callie's really nice. And pretty. Don't you think she's pretty, Daddy?"

They stopped at the discharge desk so EZ could sign his life away in deductibles and co-pays. While he waited for the admin to run his credit card, he hazarded a glance into the adjacent waiting room through the glass doors nearby, where he saw Callie sitting with a small, dark-haired boy in the corner. Huh. Callie was a blonde, so the kid must take after her husband.

"Please, Daddy?" Maisy said, bouncing on her toes. "It won't take long, I promise."

The admin returned his insurance and credit cards, and EZ signed the forms with a sigh. Since the exit was through the waiting room, there really wasn't much choice in the matter. They could take the long way around the hospital but that was silly. And if they didn't stop, Callie would think he was rude, and Maisy would be upset. So, fine. They'd stop and he'd meet Luka, then say another quick goodbye to Callie and that would be that.

"Right. Let's go meet your Luka, monkey."

But as they stepped through the automatic doors into the waiting area and Callie looked up and their eyes locked again, EZ couldn't help feeling like his well-ordered world had been knocked off-kilter again.

Callie's day had started as it always did now, with her alarm going off at five thirty. She'd been back in Jackson for six months, and the routine still felt foreign—so different from the hustle and bustle of Chicago, where she'd lived since graduating from medical school.

"Mom, I can't find my dinosaur shirt," Luka called from down the hall, his voice already tinged with the anxiety that could derail their entire morning if she didn't handle it quickly.

"Check your bottom drawer, sweetie," she called back as she pulled on a fresh pair of scrubs and ran through the day ahead in her mind. Morning rounds at eight, clinic appointments at her pediatric office until two, afternoon rounds at three after picking up Luka from school, then hopefully be done in time to have dinner and spend quality time with her son before bed.

Once the dinosaur crisis had been averted, they managed their morning routine with the efficiency of a pit crew. Breakfast, teeth, backpack check, kiss goodbye at the elementary-school drop-off.

"Pick me up right here, okay?" Luka insisted, pointing to the exact spot by the flagpole. Only seven years old, he craved predictability, and uprooting him from everything familiar, when she'd decided Chicago held too many ghosts, and they'd moved back to her hometown of Jackson Hole six months ago hadn't helped.

"Right here," she promised, the same promise she made every morning.

The drive to Teton Memorial Hospital took her past the Double B Ranch, its sprawling fences and outbuildings a testament to old Jackson money and newer conservation efforts. She'd heard the Bensons still ran it, though she'd so far successfully avoided running into any of them. Especially—

She stopped herself. She'd been Ezra Benson's tutor during their senior year of high school. He'd been a popular jock and she'd been a science nerd. And sure, she'd had a secret crush on him, but then who hadn't? Wasn't like he knew or anything. At least she'd had enough presence of mind around him to not blurt it out like some lovelorn idiot back then. Even if just sitting close to him, his shoulder brushing against hers, meant the heat from is body sent shivers of awareness through her blood. The scents of his soap and musk aftershave were forever seared into her brain from her teenaged dreams...

Gah! She stopped abruptly for a red light she'd almost ran and shook her head. *Head in the game, girl.* She had a new life to build here, a practice to establish, a son to raise. The past could stay exactly where it belonged. In the past, along with her painful divorce.

Her morning rounds proceeded smoothly, as did her office hours. It wasn't until she arrived back at the hospital for her afternoon rounds with Luka in tow that her pager buzzed with an emergency notification. ER needed a pediatric consult, stat. She left Luka in the care of her favorite nurses, who said they loved watching him while they worked at their desks, and hurried toward the emergency room.

The ER was buzzing with activity, as usual, when she walked in and headed for the nurses' station there. "Hi, I was paged for a pediatric consult?"

"Yep," a nurse named Brenda said. She got up to walk Callie toward the trauma rooms and gave her the rundown on the case. "Nothing too difficult. We're just swamped right now, and the attending asked if Pediatrics had someone on call that we could get in to handle a kid's case. It's a seven-year-old female, fall from height, obvious forearm fracture," the nurse said, stopping outside one of the trauma-room doors. "Alert and oriented, vital signs stable. Parent en route."

"Okay, I'm on it." Callie took the tablet with the chart pulled up that the nurse handed her then walked inside, smiling at the nurse who was sitting with the child, then the child herself. She was a cute little thing with long red hair that was tangled in a lopsided ponytail. Beneath her right arm she clutched a stuffed elephant. Her left arm, the injured one according to the chart, was wrapped up in a makeshift sling. Even if she hadn't seen the girl's name on her chart, those hazel eyes—a trademark of the Benson family—gave her away immediately.

Callie set aside the tablet then pulled up a rolling stool in front of the exam table and sat down, smiling. "Hi there, Maisy. I'm Dr. Callie. I think you might be in the same class as my son, Luka."

"Yes! I know Luka. We're best friends now!" the girl said with remarkable composure for someone her age with a broken arm. "I climbed the jungle gym all the way to the top at recess because Johnny Keith dared me, but then I lost my balance and fell down."

Callie nodded as she stood and began gently examining Maisy's broken arm. "That must have been scary. Can you wiggle your fingers for me?"

Maisy obliged, chattering about her adventure as Callie palpated the fracture site. Clean break of the radius, no displacement. Straightforward.

"You were very brave, Maisy," Callie told her. "And I could never turn down a dare, either, growing up. But you know what my mom always told me? She told me that adventures are more fun when you're careful."

Maisy nodded, the light in her hazel eyes dimming as the corners of her mouth turned down. "My mom is dead."

"Oh, no." Callie sat down again, taking Maisy's good hand. "I'm so sorry to hear that, Maisy."

"She died two years ago, and now it's just me and my daddy."

Callie felt a lump start in the throat despite her usual professional demeanor. "That's tough. You know, it's just me and Luka now, too. Maybe it's good that you're best friends. He's here with me today. I can call the nurses and have them bring him down here to the waiting room if you'd like to say hello to him before you leave?"

"Oh, that would be great!" Maisy said, perking up again. "I'm glad I met you, Dr. Callie!"

"I'm glad I met you, too, Maisy," Callie said, unable to stop herself from grinning. She turned to the nurse who was waiting nearby and gave her the orders, then turned back to Maisy as the nurse went off to schedule the X-rays.

"Now, we're going to take some pictures of your arm with a special camera, then put a cast on it to help it heal. What color would you like?"

"Pink! No, purple! I like green, too. Can it be both?"

Callie explained she had to pick just one color and Maisy went with pink. Then the girl was rushed off to Imaging for her X-rays and Callie went out to the nurses' station to call upstairs to see of one of the nurses there could bring Luka down to her. By the time the X-rays were completed, and Callie had a chance to read the report, Maisy was back in the trauma room and the nurse was already applying her cast. Callie used the time to pull out her tablet and go through the rest of her cases at the hospital to make sure nothing had changed before she finished her rounds, but soon heard rapid footsteps echoing from out in the hallway, followed by a male voice that made her spine straighten despite herself. Deep, slightly rough, unmistakably familiar even after all these years.

Oh, boy.

Ezra Benson filled the doorway then, dressed in a flight suit, his dark auburn hair tousled, and his cheeks flushed. He'd filled out since she'd last seen him—broader shoulders, more muscular—and there were deeper lines around his eyes, and an edge of wariness that hadn't been there the last time Callie had seen him, when she'd left for college after high school. But given what Maisy had said about her mother, Callie wasn't surprised. Losing a loved one took a lot out of those left behind. She should know. And while divorce wasn't the same as death, the sentiment was the same in her case. Ezra's hazel eyes were one thing that was still the same, though, and when they landed on Callie, time seemed to stutter to a halt.

"Daddy!" Maisy launched herself at her father, who

caught her with practiced ease, his attention immediately focused on his daughter, giving Callie time to breathe again. She'd known this moment might come eventually. Jackson wasn't that big. She just hadn't expected it to feel like stepping on a live wire.

"Dr. Dupree," he said finally, his voice carefully neutral.

"Ezra Benson." She matched his tone, forcing her practiced professional demeanor back into place again. "It's been a long time."

"It has."

Get through this. Keep it professional. Don't think about the past, about your stupid crush.

She explained the injury, the treatment plan, the follow-up care. He asked good questions, but then he should with his experience. She knew that he'd volunteered with the local search-and-rescue team as a junior member even back in high school before joining the military after graduation, and she'd seen him on TV a couple of times over the years, when she'd had rare breaks in her schedule. He knew his way around a medical injury. When she was done, she printed out and handed him his paperwork, which he frowned down at like it was nuclear waste before his daughter tugged on his flight suit.

"But, Daddy, what will I do if I can't climb to my tree house?" Maisy whined.

"I'm sure you'll figure it out, monkey," Ezra said firmly, then glanced back over at Callie. "Thank you, Dr. Dupree."

There was something in his voice that made her wonder about his life now as a single father. Relief, maybe, or exhaustion. She could relate to both.

"You're welcome." She nodded as she turned to leave. "It was good to see you again, Ezra. And you take care, Maisy. Remember what we talked about—"

"Adventures are more fun when you're careful!" Maisy said, parroting her words dutifully.

Then she escaped into the hallway as quickly as professional decorum allowed, heart hammering against her ribs. All these years since she'd seen Ezra Benson, and her body's reaction was the same as it had been in high school—that electric awareness, the way her skin felt too tight, the stupid flutter in her stomach that had everything to do with—

The elevator nearby dinged and the doors swished open. "Mama!"

Luka ran out, tugging the nurse who'd brought him down with him. He launched himself at her legs, and she crouched to gather him close, inhaling the familiar scents of strawberry shampoo and playground dirt.

"Hey, baby. I've got a surprise for you."

"Mrs. Patterson called," the nurse said, and Callie's racing heart sank. Mrs. Patterson was Luka's first-grade teacher. "She left her number."

Callie straightened and thanked the nurse for bringing her son down. She grasped Luka's hand and led him out into the waiting room, then took a seat in a secluded corner before she pulled out her phone to call Mrs. Patterson back.

"Hello," the teacher answered a moment later, sounding harried. "Dr. Dupree. Thanks for calling me back. I know you're busy, but I thought you'd like to know that Luka had another disagreement today with a fellow student about playground rules. Except this time, it escalated to…pushing."

Callie closed her eyes and squeezed the bridge of her nose between her thumb and forefinger. "Okay. Thanks for letting me know, Mrs. Patterson. Luka's right here now, so I'll talk to him about it."

Callie ended the call and shoved her phone back into

her pocket before focusing on her son. "Luka, we've talked about using our words."

"But Johnny Keith was picking on Maisy, saying girls couldn't climb the monkey bars as high as boys, and he dared her to do it, and she did!"

"Yes, I know," Callie said. "And then she fell and hurt herself, so she came here where I helped her."

"You did? That's cool, Mom, because she's my best friend."

"That's what she told me," Callie said, steering the conversation back to the topic at hand. "Now, about that pushing..."

"Is Maisy here? Can I say hello?" Luka asked hopefully.

Before Callie could answer, Maisy's excited voice echoed through the nearby deserted waiting area.

"Luka, look! I got a pink cast!"

Ezra followed behind her, Maisy's stuffed elephant in one hand. When he reached Callie's side, he gave a crooked smile and shook his head. "So this is your son?"

"Yep."

They exchanged a look then, laced with amusement and something else—something filled with complexity, of shared history, of the strange circularity of small-town life.

"We should probably discuss playdate protocols," Ezra said carefully after a second, looking back at the kids, "since they're clearly going to be spending time together."

"Playdates?" Callie repeated, her brain still spinning from everything that had happened in the last few hours. "Uh, right. Yes. Playdates."

Maisy said, practically jumping up and down with excitement, "Can we have one now?"

"I don't think now is a good time. I need to get back to work, and you need to rest that arm," Callie said, slipping back into doctor mode. "But maybe in a few days, when you're feeling better and my schedule lets up."

Her phone buzzed then, as if in confirmation of her harried schedule, and Callie pulled it out to check her texts. "Sorry. That's one of my patients. I need to see them. C'mon, Luka. Let's go."

"Sure." Ezra stepped aside to let her pass, scrubbing a hand over the back of his neck. "I've got to get back to the ranch, anyway." He waited until Callie took Luka's hand and turned away, then added, "Thanks again, Dr. Dupree. For taking care of Maisy."

"Just doing my job," Callie said, then winced. It was silly for them to be so formal when obviously their kids would be playing together as much as possible. She turned back. "And please, call me Callie."

"Okay, Callie," he said, giving her another small, crooked smile. "And you call me Ezra. Or EZ."

EZ. All the popular kids had called him that in high school, but he'd always be Ezra to her. "See you around."

"See you."

As she walked away with Luka, she felt Ezra's eyes on her back, and when she reached the doors back into the ER, she couldn't help one last glance over her shoulder, where she found him still standing there, watching her with an expression she couldn't quite read.

Professional distance, she reminded herself firmly. *Ancient history.*

Except her son was best friends with his daughter, which meant ancient history was about to become very present reality.

CHAPTER TWO

THE GPS GUIDED Callie down a dirt road that seemed to stretch forever, past rolling fields dotted with cattle and horses that looked up lazily at her as her Honda Civic bounced over ruts.

"Is this where Maisy lives?" Luka pressed his nose to the window, fogging the glass with excitement as he took in the scenery around them. "It's huge!"

"Yes, it is," Callie agreed, slowing down to cross over a particularly rocky area.

The Double B Ranch sprawled around them like something from a Western movie—a main house with wraparound porches, red barns that looked like they'd been painted recently, and fencing stretching on for miles. Callie had known the Bensons owned land, but seeing it laid out like this made her feel small and more than a little awed. It made the knots in her stomach tighten more.

She'd finally been able to coordinate a playdate for Luka and Maisy within her busy schedule and today was it. After countless texts back and forth with Ezra Benson for about a week, it had been a relief to finally find something that worked for them both.

But now that she was here, her nerves were on edge at the thought of seeing him again. At least she had work as an excuse to leave quickly.

Just dropping off your kid. In and out. You've got charts to review at the office.

Her practice wasn't open on Sundays, but she had lots of paperwork to catch up on, so…

Then, up ahead, Ezra emerged from one of the barns, sleeves rolled up and hay in his auburn hair, and her breath caught. He moved with the same easy confidence she remembered from high school, born of playing sports and being outdoors a lot, but now there was something more grounded about him. Like the years had carved away the boy and left a solid man in his place.

Callie shook off her silly thoughts as she pulled to a stop in the curving driveway in front of the house and cut the engine. Luka was already squirming in his seat with anticipation. She unbuckled her seat belt and opened her door just as Ezra jogged up to the car. Callie did her best not to notice how well his well-worn jeans fit his muscled legs and backside.

"Callie," Ezra said as he reached her. "You're here."

Professional distance, Callie. Focus on the kid.

"I am," she said, closing her door and walking around to the passenger side to help Luka out. "I hope Maisy's feeling up to visitors."

"Are you kidding? She's been bouncing off the walls all morning. Cast or no cast, that kid doesn't know how to slow down."

As evidence, the front door flew open and Maisy ran out onto the front porch, then down the steps to race toward them, a purple backpack bouncing on her shoulders. Luka met her halfway and the reunion involved considerable squealing and careful hugging around the pink cast. Callie was glad to see him so happy again. It had been a while. Since before they'd left Chicago. Since before the divorce.

"Come on," Ezra said, falling into step beside her as they followed the kids down a path toward one of the barns. "Let me give you the grand tour of the place. Fair warning—it's pretty much controlled chaos around here."

He wasn't wrong. The ranch hummed with activity—horses in paddocks, chickens pecking around the yard, the distant sound of machinery from the fields. Lots of ranch hands running around. But it was organized chaos, with everything clearly in its place and well-maintained.

"How much land do you have here?" she asked, genuinely curious.

"About two thousand acres. We run cattle and horses mostly, some hay production. My great-great-grandfather started it, and I took over from my dad when I moved back to Jackson four years ago. Somehow I've managed not to screw it up yet."

They passed a corral where a massive black stallion paced restlessly. Ezra stopped and leaned against the rail with practiced ease.

"Someone's cranky today," he murmured, then whistled low. The horse's ears swiveled toward him, and after a moment's consideration, the animal walked over, shoving his enormous head over the fence for attention.

"This is Tornado," Ezra explained, scratching behind the horse's ears. "Rescued him from an abusive situation about three years ago. Took him six months to let anyone touch him."

Callie watched the way Ezra's hands moved with gentle certainty over the horse's neck, and something in her chest tightened. She'd forgotten how good he was with animals—the way he connected with living things, the patience he had with anything or anyone who was hurt or scared.

"He's beautiful," Callie murmured, only half talking about the horse.

"Pain in the ass," Ezra said fondly. "But, yeah. Beautiful."

Their eyes met then over the horse's head, and for a moment the years collapsed again. Seventeen-year-old Ezra had looked at her the same way once in one of the study rooms at the school. It had been late, and they'd been studying for his big chemistry final. She could still remember how the earth seemed to stand still and the air between them had vibrated with electric possibilities, and then he'd leaned in, and she'd leaned in, too, and…

A mechanical screech in the distance jarred her back to the present.

Cheeks hot, Callie looked away fast, pretending to watch the kids play nearby to cover her discombobulation.

"Ah, hell." Ezra turned to look over his shoulder at a building a bit farther down from where they were standing. "That's the hay elevator again. Thing's held together with prayer and baling wire. Hang on. I need to check it."

"Want help?" The offer slipped out before she could stop it.

He turned back to her, one dark auburn eyebrow raised. "Seriously?"

"Yes, seriously." She bristled at his surprise. "I grew up here too, remember? My dad had us out on his buddy's ranch every summer. Just because I've been living in Chicago for the last twelve years doesn't mean I've forgotten everything here."

"Right." Something shifted in his expression then—he was surprised, maybe. Mixed with a healthy dose of skepticism. "Good to know. Okay then, Doc. Let's see if you know which end of a wrench to hold."

The problem turned out to be a stripped bolt on the elevator's drive mechanism. Ezra disappeared into the bowels of the machine with a toolbox, muttering creative profanity, while Callie found herself oddly mesmerized by the competent way he diagnosed the issue.

"Hand me the socket wrench," he said from inside the machine, extending a grease-streaked hand out to her. She grabbed the first one she saw and slapped it into his palm. He drew it in then put his hand back out again. "No, the other one."

She passed it to him, peering into the shadows to see what he was doing, trying not to notice the way his broad shoulders flexed as he worked. When he emerged, covered in sweat and grease, and swearing, she bit back a smile.

"What?" Ezra growled, grabbing the towel she handed him to swipe over his face and arms.

"Nothing," Callie said, biting her lip to hide a smile. "Just…you've got a little something—" She gestured at his forehead.

"What? Where?" He frowned, scrubbing the towel over his face again. "Did I get it?"

"No. Here." Without thinking, she reached up to brush away the smudge of oil near his temple with her thumb. But the moment her skin touched his, the innocent moment seemed to turn into something else entirely. It was just like it was that long-ago night in the study room. Everything stopped. He went very still, his mesmerizing hazel eyes fixed on her face, and Callie realized how close they were suddenly standing.

Step back. Right now.

But instead of moving, she found herself watching him closely, cataloging the small changes since the last time she'd seen him. The laugh lines, a new scar along his jaw, the way his warm breath fanned the hair around her face, the heat of him. If she went up on tiptoe, she could discover if his lips felt as soft and firm as they looked and—

"Mom!" Luka ran in, shattering the spell. "Maisy says there's baby kittens in the other barn! Can we go see them?"

Callie pulled her hand back, fresh heat prickling her cheeks. "I should—we should check on the kids."

"Uh, yeah." Ezra scowled, stepping back and looking anywhere but at her. "We should."

They walked outside to find Maisy and Luka waiting outside the door to the main barn. Just beyond them was a box where a tabby cat was nursing four tiny kittens. Both children were whispering to each other, as if afraid they'd wake the babies.

"Aren't they perfect?" Maisy breathed as she kneeled down beside the box once Callie and Ezra reached them. "Cora says we can't touch them for another week, but we can look."

"Who's Cora?" Callie asked.

"Just the best housekeeper in Wyoming," said a voice from behind them. Callie turned to find a stout, spry woman with short white hair who looked to be in her mid-seventies approaching from the house, flour streaking her blue shirt and a warm smile on her tanned face. "Also, the only one who'll put up with the Benson men." She walked up to Callie and extended her hand. "Cora Wilkins."

"Callie Dupree," Callie said, shaking her hand. "And this is my son, Luka."

"Oh, I've heard all about Luka. Maisy can't stop talking about him." Cora studied Callie with the kind of thoroughness that suggested she missed nothing. "You're Don and Amy's girl, right? You're a doctor? Pediatrician?"

"Yep." Callie grinned. "Did you know my parents?"

"Sure did." Cora's smile widened. "Jackson's still a small

town at heart, despite all the bigwigs buying up the place. How are your parents liking Florida?"

"They love it. Sun, fun, and my dad has his own golf cart to drive around."

They both laughed then Cora turned to the kids again. "Maisy, have you shown your friend Luka the tree house yet?"

"How?" Maisy held up her cast dramatically. "I can't with my arm."

"You can look from the ground," Ezra said firmly. "But no climbing. We'll come along to make sure."

As they walked to an old oak tree behind the house, Cora fell into step beside Callie while Ezra went on ahead with the kids.

"I've known EZ since he was in diapers," Cora said conversationally. "Good man. Been through more than his share, but he's come out stronger."

Callie glanced at the older woman, but didn't respond. She wasn't sure where this was going.

"Just saying." The older woman shrugged. "Some folks think single parents have to stay that way, but I believe children need to see how love looks when it's working right."

As they neared the corner of the house, another car pulled up in the driveway, an SUV with Benson Veterinary Clinic emblazoned on the side in big green letters. Ezra's dad, Jeremiah, got out and waved to Callie and Cora. He started over toward them before spotting his son, and the warmth in his smile froze along with his steps.

Callie wasn't up on all the local gossip, but it didn't take much to see there was tension between father and son. Ezra said something to the kids Callie couldn't hear, then he turned around and stalked back to his dad in the driveway.

"Didn't know you had company," Jeremiah said, his gaze

darting to Callie before returning to his son. "I came to help with that bailer."

"It's fixed," Ezra said curtly. "You can go."

Jeremiah eyed Ezra for a moment, his jaw tight, then he crossed his arms. "Well, then. Maybe I'll check on that fence line in the south pasture instead. The one that's been giving us trouble."

"Already repaired it. Yesterday."

A muscle ticked in Jeremiah's cheek. "Right. Good. Guess you don't need me then."

"Guess not," Ezra said, his tone hard as granite.

"Family issues," Cora whispered to Callie. "Those two are complicated as calculus lately."

Then Jeremiah and Ezra's phones both alerted with texts at the same time. Both men pulled them out and looked at their screens. Jeremiah muttered something under his breath, then rushed back to his SUV and pulled away again in a spray of gravel while Ezra stalked back over to where Callie and Cora stood.

"It's a call from the BSAR team, code yellow. Possible missing hiker in Grand Teton. All available units report. I have to go." He'd already shifted into work mode—focused, decisive, already mentally gone by the time he looked at her again. She could relate. She did the same thing every day with patients. Ezra stuffed his phone back into his pocket and started toward his vehicle. "Sorry to cut out early—"

She needed to get to her office and tackle all that paperwork waiting for her. She needed to say goodbye. But still, she couldn't stop herself from asking… "Can I come along?"

He opened the door to his truck then looked back at her. "Sorry. You're not a certified member of the team."

"Just to observe then." Callie wasn't sure why she suddenly wanted to see Ezra work, but it felt as vital as breathing. "Please. I was raised here. I know my way around a trail. I'll stay out of the way, I promise."

Ezra took a deep breath as he stared at her, his expression a mix of thoughtfulness and urgency. Then he gave a curt nod. "Fine. But we'll have to get it cleared by Andy at headquarters first. No guarantees."

"Fine."

Giddy as a schoolgirl, Callie couldn't hold back a smile. She ran back over to kiss Luka, then asked Cora, "Are you okay with watching them until I get back?"

"Go," Cora said, waving her away. "You two do what you need to do. We'll be fine here. Don't worry."

"Yeah, Dad. Go save someone," Maisy called to Ezra, as if this was routine. Callie realized that for them, it probably was.

"Will do, monkey. You be good while I'm gone." Ezra climbed behind the wheel, and Callie rushed to the passenger side to get in and buckle up.

"Be good, Luka. I love you," Callie called to her son.

"Love you, too, Mommy. Be careful," Luka called back before she closed the door.

Then they took off fast out of the driveway and headed toward town.

"How often do you get called out?" Callie asked, gripping the door to keep from sliding around as Ezra sped through a curve.

"Often enough. No set hours with search-and-rescue. But I suppose being a doctor doesn't, either." Ezra glanced over at her. "Overall, we get around ninety call-outs a year, give or take. Everything from injured skiers and snowmobilers, to stranded hikers like today, water rescues, caves, stuff like that. The unpredictability can be hard when you're a single parent, but I can't imagine not being a part of the team."

"I feel the same about being a doctor," Callie said as they rushed down quiet country back roads toward the team's headquarters in a hangar near the base of the mountains. She'd looked up the hangar after getting home from her shift the day she'd first seen Ezra again in the ER. Not because she was interested in him or anything. Just normal curiosity. She wanted to see what it looked like now. Yep. That's all it was. She stared out the window at the scenery then, until they screeched to a halt in the hangar's parking lot five minutes later.

After cutting the engine, Ezra and Callie went inside, where the rest of the volunteer team members were assembling with their gear for a briefing before heading out on the call.

Immediately, Callie recognized several faces from growing up in the area. There was Dr. Andy MacDonald, a trauma surgeon at Teton Memorial, and Dr. Jules Fernandez. She and Callie had been friends in school and now worked together sometimes in the ER. Jules had been engaged to Andy for nearly two years now, but they still hadn't set a date yet, though both seemed blissfully in love. Callie wouldn't have imagined it—Andy was always quiet and reserved, and Jules was just the opposite—but it just went to show that no one could tell who might fall in love, and when. She hoped Jules and Andy had better luck in their marriage than she'd had in her own.

Next to Jules stood Jeremiah Benson, Ezra's dad and the local vet. He smiled when he spotted Callie and raised a hand in greeting before his gaze flicked to his son beside her and the smile melted into a stony frown. Callie felt Ezra stiffen beside her. Yep, definitely some bad blood there, but there was no time to worry about it now. Her mind switched into physician mode automatically as Andy gave the group the rundown on the situation while Ruby Enapay stood at the desk near the back at the hangar talking quietly on the radio with law enforcement to get more details about the situation. Callie couldn't hear exactly what she was saying at this distance but could hear the calm fortitude in Ruby's tone.

"Right." Andy glanced over as she and Ezra joined the circle of people gathered for the rescue. "Now that everyone's here, let's discuss what we're dealing with. Pete went up with Nadja to see if we could get a visual on the victim and he just radioed back that they spotted the injured hiker on the east side of Paintbrush Divide. From what Pete could tell from his location and the information he gathered from the injured hiker's partner, they were doing the Paintbrush-Cascade Canyon Loop when he slipped and fell approximately twelve hundred feet over snow fields and rock outcroppings toward Grizzly Bear Lake. Pete was unable to assess the patient's condition at this point, but said he could see the victim moving. Dave and I have gone over the situation and Dave thinks our best option is a short-haul extraction. Ezra, you and I will go on the first run to get the patient stabilized and assess his injuries, then the rest of the team can follow on a second run to help get him up and out of the divide. Any questions?"

No one raised a hand.

"Let's roll then. The clock is ticking, people," Andy said before everyone rushed away to grab their gear and whatever else they needed. It was controlled chaos, but Callie was used to that from the ER.

"Surprised to see you here," Andy said as he walked up to Callie. "Are you getting settled in town?"

"Yes, thanks. I was over at Ezra's ranch when he got the call, so I asked if I could come with him," she said. "You know I was always fascinated with this stuff growing up."

"I remember." Andy smiled. He looked more relaxed and happier than she had ever seen him and couldn't help thinking that had something to do with Jules. The gal was like a walking ray of sunshine. "Anyway, I don't want to get in the way."

Andy scoffed. "You're a native. You know this area as well as I do. You won't be in the way. But you'll have to sign a waiver if you want to observe. And you'll have to stay up top."

"No problem." She nodded. "I'm just excited to be here."

"Great." Andy glanced past her, his expression sobering again. "Time to go."

As Andy excused himself and walked away, Ezra came up beside Callie again, now dressed in a gray flight suit with orange reflective patches on the arms and legs. "Okay?" he asked her.

"Fine," Callie said. "He wants me to sign a waiver to observe with the second team and I have to stay up top."

"Sounds right," Ezra said, then guided her over to where Ruby stood at the desk, finishing up a radio call. She grinned when she turned and saw Ezra and Callie there.

"Hey, EZ," Ruby said. "Great to see you again, Callie. You joining our rebel force now?"

Callie laughed. "No. I took my son for a playdate at Ezra's ranch earlier and he got the call while I was there, so I asked to tag along. I remember hiking the Paintbrush-Cascade Loop when I was a kid. It was always my favorite. So pretty."

"It's still gorgeous," Ruby said. "And deadly if you don't know what you're doing or get off track like this poor kid. He's visiting from Poland with his partner. They were looking for a photo op and got a whole lot more instead."

"Ready?" Andy called to Ezra from the hangar doorway

as the whoosh of helicopter blades grew louder as Nadja came in for a landing on the pad off the parking lot. "Clock's ticking."

"Coming, Doc," Ezra said before turning back to Rudy. "Doc said she can come with the second team to observe, but she needs to sign a waiver."

"I'll get her all taken care of," Ruby said, shooing him away. "Go save another life!"

Ezra and Andy worked together to get all their gear loaded into the chopper then took off in another gust of wind and whirring.

"Okay, then," Ruby said, eyeing Callie up and down. "Your clothes are okay, but you'll need some climbing boots and a coat. It's cold up there on the top, even in October. What size shoe do you wear?"

"I remember. And an eight," Callie replied as she followed her back toward the lockers. Ruby opened one of the lockers and pulled up a pair of brown boots then handed them to Callie.

"We're the same size shoe so you can borrow mine. I'm stuck at the radio desk all day, so I won't need them." Ruby then walked over to a row of coats hanging on pegs on the wall. She grabbed a bright blue one with fur around the hood and gave it to Callie. "There, that should take care of you. And they won't miss you with that neon cobalt."

While Callie took a seat to change into the boots, Jeremiah came over with another man Callie didn't know. Jeremiah introduced him as Dave Morales, the team's helicopter rescue specialist. After handshakes and a bit of small talk, Callie was dressed and ready. "Anything I can help with?"

"We're just making sure all the packs are topped up with supplies. You can help with that if you want," Jeremiah said. "Come on."

She followed him over to an area where supplies were neatly stacked on metal shelving and began going the medical packs on the floor before them. "How are you, Jeremiah? We haven't really had a chance to talk since I moved back to town."

"Good. Busy as usual," he said, stuffing fresh gauze into the pack before him. "I delivered two calves and a litter of puppies today before coming here. But I love my work."

They worked side by side in silence, while Callie bit back the question she really wanted to ask about—what was up between him and his son—but it was none of her business, and eventually the truth would come out. It always did in a small town like Jackson.

Finally, the packs were ready, and Nadja had returned with the helicopter. Callie rushed outside with Jeremiah and Dave and the other members of the second team, then climbed aboard and strapped herself in. Callie had ridden in a helicopter before while shadowing a medic flight crew during medical school, but had forgotten the rush of adrenaline that came with liftoff. With her stomach dropping to her toes, she couldn't help grinning as they took to the air and the ground disappeared beneath them. Maybe Ezra was on to something with the whole risk-taking thing.

They flew toward the landing zone near Holly Lake. They'd have to hike up from there, but Callie was looking forward to the exercise. Between her busy shifts at the hospital, working to get Luka situated in his new life, and setting up their home after the move, she hadn't gotten to spend much time outside. She'd made this hike numerous times as a kid. It would be great to get back out there now.

They landed in an open field a few minutes later and Callie climbed out with the rest of the team, then crouched to avoid the rotors as Nadja took off again to head back to the accident site to get ready for the rescue lift with Andy and Ezra. The sun was out, and the blue sky above seemed to stretch out forever as they began to ascend to the top of Paintbrush Divide. Unfortunately, there was no way to hike from Holly Lake to Grizzly Bear Lake, where the injured hiker was located, otherwise this would've been a much easier prospect. So the plan was to reach the top, send Jeremiah and Dave down to help Andy and Ezra to help prep the patient for transport, then evacuate with the helicopter while Callie and the rest of the team at the top hiked back down to wait for transport back to the hangar. Having so many people waiting in the wings might seem like overkill, but better safe than sorry out here in the backcountry.

The hike to the top was longer and harder than Callie remembered, and by the time they reached, the summit she was sweating despite the colder temperatures. Snow covered the ground here, the vast white broken up by spots of brown and black where sharp rocks and boulders stuck up out of it. It was harsh and rugged and one of the most beautiful things Callie had ever seen.

While Jeremiah and Dave got suited up and set their rigging to rappel down to the injured victim, Callie joined the other team members, who were comforting the victim's partner while listening in on the action below through the team's two-way radio.

Though Callie couldn't see much from where they were, she'd been in medicine long enough to picture what was happening in her head. Outdoor rescues were never easy and frequently fatal, so the fact that the victim was still alive and semiconscious was a bit of luck, especially considering how far he'd fallen.

"We're ready to head down to you," Jeremiah said over the radio. "Status report?"

"Victim is a thirty-five-year-old male. He was knocked momentarily unconscious from the fall but is alert now. He sustained multiple cuts and bruises, a broken mandible, broken right femur and left humerus, possible spinal and neck fractures, and internal bleeding as well, but we can't tell without scans and X-rays," Andy said. "His vitals are holding steady and we've stabilized his neck with a brace and his body with a suck bag, but we'll need help getting him on the litter for evac."

"On our way," Dave said, then he and Jeremiah started down to the accident scene, pushing away from the cliff face with their feet. Then they let the ropes slide swiftly through their gear, until they landed on the rock below. After a few moments, the conversation on the radio started up again.

"Jozef," Andy said over the radio. "We're going you onto this litter so we can get you out of here. It may hurt a bit, but we'll do everything we can to mitigate that."

The victim gave a low, agonized groan, his response garbled as he tried to speak around his injured jaw, but Callie was able to decipher his words. "Hurry. My whole body's on fire."

"Oh, God!" Jozef's partner, Giselle, said beside her. "I didn't know. I thought he was just taking a picture, then his foot slipped and he was…gone. I'm so sorry."

"You couldn't have known," Callie said, putting an arm around the distraught woman. "And he's in the best hands now. They'll get him out and get him the help he needs, okay?"

Giselle sniffled and nodded, tears running down her cheeks. Stella, one of the other team members, got a tissue for her. "Okay."

Over the radio, a countdown sounded, followed by a sharp cry.

"Victim on litter," Ezra said. "I'm giving him another dose of pain meds to keep him as comfortable as possible during the evac."

"Nadja, we're ready for you," Andy said. "EZ, you ride up with the victim then the rest of us will follow one at a time."

Soon, the helicopter whooshed in again and this time hovered over the canyon, lowering a rope with a hook at the end to attach to the patient's litter. Ezra would attach his rigging clip to that and ride up alongside the litter to make sure the patient made it safely to the helicopter. Even knowing what was going to happen ahead of time, Callie's heart still tripped at the sight of Ezra and the litter rising out of the canyon, being towed toward the waiting copter like a phoenix from fire. An odd mix of excitement, pride, fear, and longing filled Callie before she tamped it down. Sure, Ezra was brave and smart, and looked so handsome just then she thought she might pass out. But that was not going to happen. She'd been there and done that with the whole "gorgeous daredevil who steals your heart then shatters it into a million pieces" and wasn't going there again.

Still, watching Ezra climbing into the helicopter then pull the victim's litter in and secure it made her pent-up breath release in a rush of relief. Wow. Just wow. He was impressive. So impressive.

Stop it.

Callie focused on Giselle, and definitely not Ezra, after that.

Once Jeremiah and Dave had been towed up to the helicopter and Nadja headed off toward the hangar again, Callie and the rest of the team headed back down the trail toward their transport point.

By the time they reached the bottom, Nadja was waiting to return them back to the hangar.

Jozef looked about as banged up as Callie expected given what he'd been through. Viewing him up close now, Callie could see that besides his jaw, several other bones in his face were also broken, including the orbit around his right eye, and his left eye was already too swollen to open more than just a slit. The poor guy had been through it, that's for sure.

The EMTs were getting him ready to load into the back of the ambulance to take him to Teton Memorial, and Callie stood with Giselle while they waited, arm around the crying, quivering woman. Giselle and Jozef were holding hands and exchanging words in Polish as best they could with Jozef's injuries. Callie didn't speak Polish, but it didn't take a rocket scientist to know they were words of love and thankfulness. The affection on Giselle's face was enough to confirm that.

Once the ambulance left with Jozef and Giselle, and the gear had been unloaded and packed away and the team had debriefed with Andy, Callie found herself alone with Ezra in his truck in the parking lot. The sun had set about an hour before, so only the greenish glow of the dashboard lights illuminated them. She would have that that after all they'd been through in the past few hours, things wouldn't be awkward between them anymore. But she'd be wrong.

Callie cleared her throat then stared out the window at the passing headlights of cars on the road in front of the hangar parking lot, wondering what to say. Finally, she said, "We should get back to your house. I need to get Luka to bed soon."

Ezra nodded, then started the engine and headed out of the lot without a word.

They stopped at a red light and Callie said, "You did good today."

"Yep." Ezra accelerated when the light turned green, his expression clouded. "What did you think?"

"I think I missed being out there more than I thought," she said, smiling as she gazed out the window beside her. "Maybe I should think about volunteering for the team next year."

"Maybe," Ezra mumbled under his breath. Something was clearly bothering him, but she didn't feel comfortable asking him. They drove on toward his house in silence. It wasn't until they turned into his driveway that he added, "You need to think about what would happen to Luka if you were gone."

Callie was taken aback by the abrupt turn of topic and blinked at him a moment. "That escalated quickly."

Ezra gave her an annoyed side-glance. "I just mean that if you volunteer, it's not all fun and games. It can be dangerous out there."

"And you don't think I know that?" Callie retorted, equally irritated now. She wasn't some kid, some dumb tourist who didn't know the terrain out here. She'd grown up here, just like Ezra. But it wasn't worth getting upset about, she told herself. She didn't care what Ezra Benson thought about her.

Do I?

No. No, she didn't.

"And what about you?" she challenged. "You're Maisy's only parent now. Shouldn't you watch yourself, too?"

Ezra shut up after that.

As soon as he parked the truck, she was out the door and heading up the porch steps toward the house to get her son. The sooner she put Ezra Benson and his dumb comments and his stupid handsome face out of her mind, the better.

By the time she'd gathered Luka and had him ready to

go, Ezra had come in and stood by the front door, Maisy dancing around his legs as she told him all about her time with Luka and how fun it had been.

"It was great to meet you, Callie," Cora said as she walked her to the front door. "Don't be a stranger."

"Thanks," Callie said, avoid Ezra's gaze. She could feel the weight of his stare on her and it made her heart do all sorts of silly things again—things that were better ignored. "I'm sure I'll see you again at the next playdate. My place next time."

"Sounds good." Cora shot Ezra a pointed stare before taking Maisy and heading for the kitchen, leaving Callie and Ezra alone with Luka.

"Well," Callie said at last. "Thanks for having Luka over today. And for letting me tag along on the call."

Ezra ran a hand through his short auburn hair then shook his head. "I'm sorry for what I said in the truck earlier. Sometimes, I say stuff without thinking and it gets me in trouble."

Callie chuckled. "Me, too. No worries." Then, suddenly self-conscious, she tucked her hair behind her ear. "Right. Well, we need to get home. I'll see you around, Ezra."

"Yeah, see you around, Callie," Ezra said, holding the door for her and Luka, then leaning his shoulder against the doorframe, crossing his arms and drawing her attention to his muscled forearms and those little veins that begged her to run her tongue along them and…

What? No.

She rushed down the porch steps with Luka like the hounds of hell were after them. By the time Ezra joined them in the driveway, she had her son secured in the car and was walking around to the driver's side. Ezra leaned his arms atop the car roof and watched her far too closely for Callie's comfort.

"See you next week."

Callie's brain was so scrambled at that point that she wasn't sure what he'd said. "I'm sorry?"

"To get Maisy's arm checked," he said, a small smile playing around his lips.

"Oh, right. Yes," Callie said as she fumbled her door open. Good Lord, what was wrong with her? She never got flustered like this. She tossed her purse in the back seat then hazarded a glance over at Ezra, who was still watching her, those hazel eyes of his unreadable in the gathering shadows. "Of course. See you then."

She got in, closed the door, and started the engine, pulling away after Ezra slapped the roof of her car then stepped back.

Yeah, if she was honest with herself, she knew exactly why she was so flustered, and it had everything to do with the man still standing in the driveway watching them as they departed.

"Mommy, why are your hands shaking?" Luka asked from the back seat, where he was strapped in.

She forced her attention away from the rearview mirror and to the road ahead, flexing her hands that were indeed shaking, more from adrenaline than anything else. This was ridiculous. "Nothing, honey," she said. "Mommy's just tired, that's all."

And she was tired. Of all her unwanted reactions to the last man on earth she should want that way. Her ex-husband, Owen, had been a daredevil, a survivalist, cut from the same adrenaline-fueled fabric as Ezra Benson. She knew the type as well as she knew her own reflection. Tough, smart, exciting. Reckless. And as dependable as they were in a crisis situation, when it came to the boring, day-to-day real-life things, like creating a home, raising a family, paying the bills, and making a life together…well, they were as fickle as tween-girl crushes on the latest K-pop band. Callie deserved better than that. Luka deserved better than that. Ezra Benson was not what they needed. And as of tonight, she vowed not react to him like that anymore.

As they turned onto the road in front of the ranch, she just hoped it was a vow she could keep.

CHAPTER THREE

EZ'S STEADY HANDS were on Maisy's shoulders as Callie went over the x-rays of his daughter's arm to make sure they were still on track with the healing, but his mind kept wandering to the incident at Paintbrush Divide. Specifically, the moment when he'd crested the top of the cliff on his way up to the helicopter with the victim, and he'd caught Callie watching him. It had been a long time since anyone had looked at him like that. Her expression had been full of rapt wonder and appreciation and…something he wasn't quite sure how to define. No. That wasn't true. He knew exactly what he'd seen on Callie's face because he'd felt the same thing when he'd watched her on his ranch earlier that day. More than attraction, more than awareness. Far more dangerous than lust.

What he'd seen that day was connection.

And under no circumstances was he ever going there again.

He had enough on his hands protecting Maisy, the ranch, and the rescue team. He wouldn't add another person to that list. Couldn't add them. Because if he did and he failed again and lost them, he wasn't sure *he'd* survive. And he had to be there, for Maisy, for all the others who depended on him.

So, yeah. He did his best to look anywhere but at the woman who was currently standing nearby, staring at a computer screen, close enough to him that he could smell the flowery scent from her shampoo, see how nicely shaped her hands were, wonder if her skin felt as soft as it looked…

Dammit.

Focus on your daughter, Benson.

"The films today look really good," Callie said, examining the X-rays the techs had taken right after they'd arrived at Callie's office. "Healing perfectly. Good work, Maisy!"

"Will I still be able to go trick-or-treating on Halloween?" his daughter asked hopefully.

"Of course! But I'll need to see you back in another couple of weeks to get that cast off, Maisy, so until then still no climbing, okay?" Callie turned back and kneeled in front of his daughter, carefully explaining why climbing too early wasn't a good idea and talking to her like a real person and not a dumb kid, like a lot of people did. EZ always did the same and he really liked that Callie did it, too. Honestly? He really liked a lot of things about her.

Gah!

Keeping her out of his head was not proving as easy as he'd thought and he really didn't like that at all. Nope. Not one bit.

"Right," Callie said, straightening. "That's if for today. I'll walk you out to the reception desk so you can schedule that follow-up appointment." The smile she beamed at EZ temporarily short-circuited his stupid brain again, rendering him a dopey dumbass who could do nothing but stand there and grin back at her like an idiot. Finally, when Callie turned and walked out with Maisy, holding her good hand, he snapped out of it enough to follow them.

Get a grip, dude.

He needed to get laid. That was all. It had been way too long since he'd had time to date anyone, let alone the desire to. What little free time he had was spent either sleeping or spending quality time with Maisy. Maybe he'd drive into Cheyenne on his next weekend off and take care of his needs with a woman who understood the rules. No strings, no emotions, just sex. He wasn't a monk after all. But casual hookups weren't really his style. Despite his risk-taking penchant at work, at home he preferred safety, security, and serenity.

As they walked down the hall, EZ walking behind the two gals, he glanced at the photos on the walls, more to keep himself from watching the sway of Callie's hips and backside in those light purple scrubs than anything else. Man, he was in a bad way, and that wasn't good.

Most of the photos were black-and-white shots of local landmarks, interspersed with photos of Callie with what he assumed were her patients and their families. Everyone looked so happy and satisfied. Callie was excellent at her job. He'd seen enough to know that the day Maisy had been hurt. She'd been calm, gentle, and competent, transforming his scared daughter into a chatterbox about cast colors and elk spotting. She was skipping along beside Callie now with her usual boundless energy.

When they arrived at the reception desk, the two medical assistants sitting behind it immediately zeroed in on EZ. He recognized the look—he'd been getting variations of it since high school. The taller one, probably in her fifties, elbowed her colleague. Her name tag read *Sally*. Her grin said she'd had practice flirting with younger men. "Well, hello there, Mr. Benson. How are you today?"

"We've heard so much about you," the second MA chimed in. Her name tag read *Sue*. "Callie told us all about your daring rescue. I think it's so brave what you do. Saving people like that."

He never quite knew how to answer those kinds of statements. To him, rescuing people was just his job, like being a lawyer or a pharmacist. But people always seemed impressed, so he just shrugged and gave a curt nod. "Thanks."

"Stop being so modest, Mr. Benson," her nurse Janet said. "Our Callie couldn't say enough about you. She was superimpressed. And she's seen things, you know? Moving back here from Chicago and all. Can't blame her for leaving the big city to come home, though, you know. Jackson is magical."

"It is," EZ said, glad to finally find something they agreed on.

Sue typed on her keyboard as she said, "Dr. Dupree's a single parent, too. Luka is just precious."

EZ hazarded a glance over at Callie and noticed she looked as uncomfortable as he felt. Before he could say anything, though, Maisy intervened.

"Luka's my best friend!" Maisy stood on tiptoe to see over the counter. "Can I have a lollipop?"

"Of course you can," Callie said, grabbing the jar then look at EZ. "If it's okay with your dad."

EZ gave another curt nod before signing off on the insurance paperwork Sally had just slid in front of him. He pulled out his wallet to hand her his card to pay for the visit. "Just one."

Maisy sorted through the candy in the jar to find the one she wanted, then held it up like a prize before unwrapping it and shoving it in her mouth. It was electric blue, and EZ fully expected her lips and tongue to be the same color in a few minutes.

"Daddy, can I have a sleepover with Luka this weekend?" Maisy asked hopefully around the lollipop.

"We'll see, monkey," EZ said as he fumbled his card back into his wallet before shoving the thing into the back pocket of his jeans again. "I'll have to check my schedule. And Luka might be busy."

"Actually," Callie said, "I think it's Luka's turn to have you over, Maisy."

After EZ finished scheduling his daughter's follow-up appointment, he followed Callie and Maisy to the exit doors. He imagined dropping off Maisy at Callie's place, maybe staying a bit to chat with Callie, having a drink, discussing their days, sharing dinner, sharing time and space, and how nice that might be to have again. The surge of longing inside him was a surprise and EZ was taken aback.

He cleared his throat as he folded the paperwork Sally had given him, then shoved it into his pocket. "We'll see."

The words came out rougher than he'd intended.

"Thanks again for everything you've done for Maisy," he said as he ushered his daughter out the door.

"My pleasure." Callie's arm brushed his as he passed her and an unexpected zing of electricity went through his nervous system before he could stop it. Great. Now, his head was flooded with images of her in his bed, moaning his name as he moved inside her, made her scream with ecstasy, tangled in his sheets, tangled with his body, tangled in his life…

"Let me know about the sleepover," she called after him as he rushed to his truck.

Do not think about sleeping with Callie. Do not think about sleeping with Callie.

But it was too late.

All the way home, the more he tried not to think about it, the more he did.

Things were getting out of hand and that was unacceptable.

He needed to figure out a way to get himself under control before he did something dumb, like kiss her silly.

That trip to Cheyenne was sounding better by the second.

Get it out of his system and get on with his life.

He just hoped it would be that easy.

* * *

It was not that easy.

Grumpily, EZ stared at the email on his phone, his coffee growing cold beside him in the early morning air. Winter Fundraiser Planning Committee—Mandatory Volunteer Assignment.

It had been sent at 3:30 a.m., a sure sign that whoever was behind it had anticipated the less-than-giddy reception it would get and had tried to avoid it as much as possible. It wasn't that he didn't want to help out at Maisy's school when he could. But things had been even busier than usually lately with the rescue team, since the winter tourist season has started earlier than usual with the early-November snowstorm, and now, it seemed everybody and their brother couldn't get out on the slopes fast enough, whether they knew what they were doing or not. Unfortunately for him—and them—people seemed to be falling into the "not" category more often these days.

Not to mention the fact his sleep had been less than stellar the past few weeks.

He'd made three trips to Cheyenne during that time, and it hadn't helped one bit. Probably because each time he went to the bar he liked there and started talking to a woman, eventually his mind drifted, wondering what Callie was doing, if she thought about him, too, if she'd say yes if he asked her to dinner…

Which he absolutely would not do. Nope. He'd been avoiding her as much as possible since Maisy's last appointment and he had no intention of changing that. Maybe he could get Cora to take his daughter to get her cast off? He made a note to ask her about it later. And thankfully, Maisy had been busy at school, too, so had seemed to forget about that sleepover with Luka. Which was great because he really didn't want to do that, either. Not because he didn't want his daughter hanging out with Luka. The kid was adorable. It was his mother that EZ was worried about.

Twice in less than a month he'd woken up in a sweat, breath fast and body hard as a rock, every cell in his being still locked in a dream of Callie, naked and wanton in his arms, needing him as much as he needed her. He couldn't fall back to sleep after that, so he'd get up, take a cold shower, and take care of business, the whole time wondering how the hell he'd suddenly become a randy teenager again.

It was stupid and irrational and infuriating.

Jaw clenched, he gripped the handle of his Wyoming Equal Rights mug tighter.

The state had been the first to grant women the right to vote and hold public office. EZ agreed with that concept wholeheartedly. Women could do anything that men could do, and usually better, including a specific woman driving him out of his mind with frustration.

But since he'd always been one to play his emotional cards close to his chest, EZ vented his frustration on the innocent email glowing on his phone screen instead of sharing it with anyone. People had enough on their plates. They didn't need his whining about his problems added to it.

"Mandatory volunteer," he muttered. "That's an oxymoron if I ever heard one."

"What's an oxey-mormon, Daddy?" Maisy asked around a mouthful of cereal.

He sighed and shut off his phone, setting it screen-down on the table before focusing on his daughter across from him. "Something that doesn't make sense, monkey. Like 'jumbo shrimp' or 'clearly confused.'"

"Or 'mandatory fun,'" Cora added dryly from the stove, where she was cooking up some fresh bacon that smelled like heaven. "Which is exactly what this fundraiser is going to be for you, Ezra Benson."

EZ shot her a look. "You knew about this?"

"Small town, sugar. Everyone knows about everything." She grinned over her shoulder at him. Since he'd lost his own mother to cancer ten years back, Cora had become his surrogate caretaker in more ways than one. "Besides, it's for Maisy's school. Which you always support."

"Exactly! I give them a generous donation every year. Isn't that enough?"

"Apparently not." Cora shrugged, sliding one batch of crispy bacon onto a plate before starting another. "Did you read it? What is it asking you to do?"

"No, and I don't know." He sat back, scowling and guzzling what was left of his cold coffee, then set down the mug firmly on the table, the weight of Cora's stare burning a hole through the back of his head. Fine. She wanted him to read it? Fine. Great. Wonderful. He'd never been a coward a day in his life, and he wasn't about to start now. After grabbing the phone with more force than necessary, he flipped it over and swiped the screen to open the email again.

But the more he read, the farther his stomach sank to his toes.

They had assigned him to the silent-auction committee. Which made sense since he had some experience with that, having helped Andy get the team's annual fundraiser set up last year to get their new helicopter. So it wasn't the assignment that bothered him. He could handle that in his sleep, if he got any. No, what bothered him was that the person they'd partnered him with was none other than the woman he'd been avoiding like trouble for weeks now. Dr. Callie Dupree.

Lord. It was like the universe was conspiring against him or something.

He took a deep breath and shook his head.

"What?" Cora asked as she finished with the bacon, then brought over a platter to the table and set it in the center. Maisy immediately grabbed two slices and ate them between bites of cereal. EZ reached over for one himself. He might be in an emotional quandary, but that was no reason to let amazing bacon go to waste. Cora filled a mug with coffee for herself, then sat down at the table and took a piece of bacon. "They ask you to run a kissing booth or something?"

"No," EZ said, frowning at her.

"Ew!" Maisy said. "Who'd want to kiss Daddy?"

"Gee, thanks, monkey," EZ said. Nothing like his kid to keep him grounded. Not that he needed it. He'd never really thought much about how he looked. It was what it was, and women seemed to like it, so whatever. He chuckled. "No. They put me in charge of a planning committee for the silent auction this year."

"Wow." Cora looked impressed. "That's a big deal. Lots of work. They give you any help?"

The last thing he wanted to do was to tell her. He loved Cora like his own mom, but the woman was an integral part of the local gossip machine and couldn't keep a secret to save her life. But he also didn't want to make it seem like a bigger deal than it was, either, so he said as casually as possible, "Yeah. It says Dr. Dupree and I will cochair the committee."

"Interesting." Cora tried to hide her smile by taking a sip of her coffee, but EZ saw it, anyway, making the knot of tension between his shoulder blades knot tighter.

Interesting was one word for it. He could think of others, but they weren't exactly fit for the morning breakfast table. He wasn't sure quite how, but the whole thing smacked of meddling. By whom, he didn't know, but he'd find out.

Eventually. For now, he needed to think of a rational, believable reason to say no. He got up to refill his coffee. "I think maybe I need to go out of town. Andy mentioned some training courses in California he wanted me to check out, so…"

"Ezra Joel Benson." Cora's voice carried the weight of thirty-five years of managing stubborn Benson men. "You will do no such thing! This is now your responsibility, and your mama—God rest her soul—taught you to always handle your responsibilities. Which means you will go to that meeting, you will be helpful, and you will stop acting like a skittish colt every time someone mentions Dr. Dupree's name."

The mention of Callie had him hesitating as he sat back down at the table. "Hey! I don't—"

"Yes, you do." Cora pointed a piece of bacon at him for emphasis. "Everyone can see it. Every time she's near you, you act like a fart in a skillet." She sat back and crossed her arms. "And it's getting ridiculous."

Maisy looked between them with the interest of a seven-year-old. "You fart in a skillet, Daddy?"

EZ choked on his coffee. "What? No. It's a saying." He gave Cora a pointed glance only to find her biting back a laugh, which did nothing to improve his mood. "Finish your breakfast, monkey, then—"

"Why don't you want to work with Dr. Dupree, Daddy?" Maisy asked after drinking the last of the milk out of her cereal bowl, then swiping the swiping the back of her hand across her mouth in lieu of the perfectly good napkin that was lying right there in front of her. EZ scrubbed his hands over his face. This conversation had taken a quick turn toward being out of control. "Because if you and Dr. Dupree work together then we'd spend more time together and Luka and I could have sleepovers every night, and—"

"Slow down, monkey." EZ summoned all the patience he had inside himself, while ignoring Cora's raised brow and knowing smirk. Dammit. He focused on his daughter instead, as she nibbled on another strip of bacon. "It's not that I don't want to work with Dr. Dupree. We're just both just really busy and that makes things difficult and—"

"But you make time for what's important," Maisy said, cutting him off. That seemed to happen a lot with the women in his house. "That's what you always say, Daddy. Isn't my school important?"

Well, didn't that just set him back on his heels. He opened his mouth, closed it, then opened it again, the right words deserting him. He had taught her that. A lesson he'd learned too well after losing Sierra. Time was a precious commodity that could never be recovered. So better to spend it on the things he valued the most in life. And at the top of his valuable list now was his daughter. Whatever mattered to her, mattered to him, too. And Maisy loved her school. Which meant he loved it, too. Which meant…

He tipped back his head and stared up at the ceiling.

He was going to have to do this. He didn't want to, but wasn't sure how he could get out of it without sending the wrong message to Maisy and giving credence to Cora's assertions about him and Callie that absolutely weren't true. Dammit.

So, two hours later, after dropping off Maisy at the school's front entrance, he made his way around the back to the entrance to the elementary school library, where a bunch of other antsy, overly caffeinated parents were waiting for their marching orders. A woman at the door directed him to a corner table bedecked with a handwritten sign—The Silent Auction Committee. Callie was there already, her blond hair pulled back, and was wearing lavender scrubs and a lab coat, suggesting she was headed to work right after this.

She looked tired, he noticed, but still as gorgeous as always. He wondered if she'd been having some sleepless nights, too.

Stop it.

"EZ!" Martha Hendricks, one of the teaching assistants at the school, waved him over with way too much enthusiasm for the task at hand. "We were just throwing out some ideas for the auction. Dr. Dupree has a great suggestion for themed baskets."

EZ took the only available seat, which happened to be beside Callie, and did his best to keep as much space between them as possible but was still hyperaware of her proximity all the same. She smelled like flowers and fabric softener and something slightly antiseptic—a combination that shouldn't have been appealing, but somehow was, anyway. To him, at least.

Ugh. Focus, dude.

"Ezra," Callie said, flashing him a polite smile. "Good to see you again."

"Dr. Dupree." He matched her professional tone, then caught Martha's interested expression as she watched them and tried to steer attention back to the topic at hand. "So… baskets?"

"Yes," Martha said, beaming at the two of them. "Dr. Dupree suggested medical-themed baskets for the auction. 'First aid for families,' 'wellness and self-care,' that sort of thing."

EZ nodded. "I like it. Practical but appealing."

"And maybe you could organize the adventure experiences," Callie said. "Helicopter tours, maybe some ranch activities?"

EZ thought it through. "Sure. I could talk to Andy about using the new heli to do a scenic flight, maybe offer a cattle-ranch-experience day."

"This is fabulous!" Martha said, clapping her hands. "I knew you two would be perfect for this."

So she was the one behind this. His suspicions grew. Martha just happened to be good friends with Cora.

Coincidence? He thought not.

Several other committee members arrived then, and while Martha was busy filling them in on their ideas so far, Callie leaned a little closer to him and whispered, "If you're not comfortable having people on your ranch, you don't have to—"

"It's fine," EZ interrupted, unable to stop himself for leaning into her warmth a little bit more. This close, he could see the tiny flecks of gold in her green eyes. If he moved an inch closer, he could kiss her and finally discover if those pink lips of hers felt as soft as they looked. The clearing of Martha's throat had him sitting back fast, and feeling like an errant schoolboy. "Uh, it's fine," he said, frowning down at his hands clasped on the table. "Whatever I can do to help."

That's the reason he was here. To help. The sooner he remembered that, the better.

"Great." Martha grinned. "As the cochairs, I'll let you two figure out the meeting schedule and how you want to communicate to your committee members. Email has worked the best in the past."

They all exchanged emails and then the meeting was over. As he and Callie walked out, she said, "How do you feel about you and I getting together once a week at first until we get plans finalized, and then we bring the others in?"

"Sounds reasonable." *Sounds like torture.* "What days and times work for you?"

"Pretty much any of them will work as long as it's after clinic hours and I'm not on call."

"Great. I'll check my schedule and we'll go from there."

They stopped near their cars, and EZ was battling the urge to duck into his car and lock himself away until he got his stupid brain back on track. Thankfully, an alert came over his phone, saving him an awkward goodbye with Callie.

He pulled out his phone and scanned the details. "Sorry. I need to go. Team call-out."

"Go," Callie said simply. "Someone needs you. We'll talk again soon."

Her understanding tone reminded him of how nice it was to be with someone who got it. The job, the responsibility, the way duty could interrupt dinner or meetings or anything else, and demand that you answer the call.

"I'll text you to work out the details of our first meeting," he said, backing toward his driver-side door.

"Okay. Be careful," Callie said, giving him a little wave before slipping into her own vehicle.

Her words stuck with him as he started his truck and pulled out of the lot, the sound of her voice mixing with the radio chatter filling the air with coordinates and medical codes.

The rescue sounded pretty routine—a broken leg on a backcountry trail, weather good, no complications. But as EZ drove toward the hangar, he found his focus was elsewhere, as he anticipated the next meeting with Callie way more than he should. And that worried him more than anything else.

CHAPTER FOUR

"Dr. Dupree, your last patient is ready."

"Thanks." Callie looked up from her patient charts and gave Janet a tired smile. It had been a long day. "Who is it?"

"Maisy Benson," Janet said with an entirely inappropriate grin. "Her dad's with her."

Of course he is.

Callie's pulse did something annoying. She sighed and closed out the file on her computer. The last few days had been beyond busy. She swallowed hard around a sudden lump of nervousness. How could she have forgotten Maisy's cast removal? Distracted, she walked down the hall to the exam room Janet had pointed her to. Through the open door she saw Ezra sitting on a chair next to the exam table Maisy was perched on, her legs swinging as she chattered about her day, while Ezra flipped through a magazine. He looked as handsome and broodingly intriguing as he always did. After smoothing a hand down the front of her lab coat and taking a deep breath to calm her racing heart, Callie pasted on what she hoped was a completely unaffected, polite smile and knocked lightly on the open door to announce her presence. "Maisy, ready to get that cast off?"

"Yep, Dr. Callie. It's itchy. I got to leave school early today just to come here!"

"How exciting!" Callie walked over to the counter to put

on some gloves and grab the tools Janet had set out for her when she'd prepped the exam room earlier. She sat on a wheeled stool and rolled over to sit in front of Maisy, doing her best to ignore the weight of Ezra's stare on her as she got to work on Maisy's cast, and wondering what to say to the man. He looked like he wanted to be here about as much as she did, but it wasn't like she could get away with not talking to him at all. That would be weird. But her mind was blank as to what to say. Thankfully, he made the decision himself.

"Speaking of school," Ezra asked, tossing the magazine back on the small table beside him. "Did you get the latest update text about the fundraiser?"

Right. The fundraiser. Yes. Okay. She could talk about that. It was safe territory. She knew how to deal with him regarding the fundraiser. The school had sent a small avalanche of messages recently about tweaks and changes to the auction events. Mostly updates about the baskets or other special committee meetings. "Yes," she said cautiously, hazarding a glance over at him. "Why?"

His lips pressed together and a muscle ticked near his jaw before he exhaled slow, seeming to come to some kind of decision inside himself. He sat back and crossed his arms, shaking his head. "No reason. I just wish they'd make up their minds and quit changes things." He sighed and scrubbed a hand over his face then said, "Maisy's still bugging me about Luka sleeping over."

Maisy practically vibrated with excitement. "Yes, please, Dr. Callie. We'll have so much fun!"

"I'm sure you will," Callie said, unable to keep from smiling. "Luka's been asking me about it, too. Whenever your dad says it's okay, we'll get it set up."

"So the responsibility's on me then?" Ezra said, brow raised. "How convenient."

Callie finished removing Maisy's cast then stood and walked over to dispose of it in the biohazard bin against the opposite wall. He sounded irritated by the fact she'd put the ball firmly in his court. Typical. She'd always had to be the one making all the decisions with her ex-husband, Owen, because he couldn't be bothered with such trivial things. All his energy had to be saved for the next thrill. As she washed her hands with more vigor than necessary, she couldn't help snipping back. "Oh, I'm sorry. I thought you'd want input into your daughter's schedule. My bad."

"What's that supposed to mean?" he asked, getting up and walking over to stand near her, close enough for her to feel the heat of his body, catch the scent of soap and spice from his skin. Her whole right side prickled with awareness against her will.

Stop reacting to him. What happened to your vow?

"For your information," he said, lowering his voice and leaning in a bit closer, his gravelly tone doing all sorts of naughty things to her insides as she dried her hands with paper towels from the dispenser, "I am very much concerned about my daughter's schedule. I just have a lot going on right now at the ranch and with BSAR team training, so it was one thing I hoped you'd help with."

"Are you two fighting?" Maisy asked from behind them, sounding worried. "Please don't fight."

Right. And now, she felt horrible.

Callie turned around and said in unison with Ezra, "We're not fighting."

After throwing away her paper towels, Callie walked over to Maisy and put her hands on the little girl's shoulders. "We weren't fighting, honey. We were just discussing some things."

Maisy looked skeptical. "Really?"

"Really," Ezra said, moving in beside Callie, his voice gentler now, melting Callie's annoyance like butter.

"Hey, I think Janet has some special treats at her desk for patients who are extra good on their visits. Why don't you go ask her about them? Tell her I sent you," Callie said as she lifted Maisy off the table and set her on her feet. "It's just down the hall there."

Bouncing on the balls of her feet, Maisy turned to her dad. "Can I, please?"

Ezra took another deep breath. "Yes, monkey. Go. Dr. Callie and I have a couple things left to discuss before we leave."

Maisy took off down the hall, leaving them alone. Since it was the end of the day and most of the staff and all of the patients had left, an odd sense of intimacy settled over the room.

Oh, God.

Fumbling with the keyboard of the computer on the counter, Callie did her best to focus on Maisy's file and not the man beside her, and the unbidden images that flooded her traitorous brain—of him leaning in closer and kissing her, touching her, pulling her closer and slipping his hands inside her lab coat, under the hem of her scrub top, the edge of danger, the fear of being caught adding a jolt of intensity and excitement.

Ugh.

She shook it off and deleted a whole line of nothing but *x's* she'd inadvertently typed.

She was lonely, that was all. She hadn't been with anyone since the divorce over a year ago and craved adult company, that's all. That explained why she was having totally inappropriate fantasies about Ezra Benson. Yep. That was it. Could have been anyone at all she was thinking about. Not just him.

Get it together, girl.

But as she finished her documentation, hands trembling slightly, the room suddenly felt smaller with him in it. Why did he have to be so rugged and masculine and infinitely attractive? It wasn't fair. Even in his dark jeans and button-down shirt, he looked like he'd walked off the set of some sexy cowboy ad with those broad shoulders and long, strong legs. She stepped away from the counter and him, hoping to put as much space between them as possible. "So…the fundraiser."

"Right." He took a seat in the chair across from her desk, the word emerging rougher than normal, as if he was affected by her, too. He crossed his legs, one booted ankle resting on his knee. "In the last text they wanted up to come up with some additional ideas for prizes to raise more money. What auction packages do you think bring in the highest donations? I've been wracking my brain and came up with scenic helicopter tours, ranch experience packages, and wilderness survival lessons."

Grateful for something to think about besides him, she nodded. "All of those sound great."

"Good." Ezra uncrossed his legs and leaned forward, resting his elbows on his knees, his hands relaxed and clasped between them. "Oh, and I also talked to Andy right before I came here about offering a BSAR demonstration."

"That should be a popular item too." Callie crossed her arms and leaned her hips back against the wall behind her. "I was thinking we could add some medical baskets, too. First-aid supplies, wellness gift certificates, maybe get a donation from one of the luxury spas in Cheyenne for a day of pampering."

"Good idea," he said, then pursed his lips. Now, all she could think about was kissing him.

Bad, Callie. Bad. Remember your vow.

"That'll be popular," he continued as if he hadn't noticed her sudden fixation on his mouth.

Awkward silence descended for a moment, and Callie found herself cataloging small details—the way he fidgeted with his watch, the small scar on his knuckles she'd noticed before but never asked about.

Say something, idiot.

Flustered, she began, "Well, Ezra—" at the same time he said, "Well, Callie—"

They both stopped and chuckled, the tension in the room lessening slightly.

"Sorry," Callie said. "You go first."

Ezra sat back, looking as wary and confused as she felt. He scratched his jaw, then said, "We should probably get on that sleepover thing, too, while we're here, so Maisy will stop bugging me about it." One side of his lips quirked as he glanced at her. "And you did say it was up to me, so…"

Damn. Touché.

Callie opened her mouth to answer, but was saved from further embarrassing herself when Maisy called from down the hall, "Daddy, look what I got from Janet!"

Her footsteps pounded the tile floor as she approached, then Maisy filled the doorway once more, holding up an enormous blue lollipop nearly the size of her head. "Can I eat it now?"

"Not yet, monkey," Ezra said, standing as Callie bit her lip to keep from laughing. "Cora's making dinner for us at home."

"Oh. I forgot." Maisy's disappointed tone matched the slump of her shoulders. Then she perked up suddenly. "Hey, maybe Dr. Callie and Luka can come back to the ranch this weekend to see the new baby horses."

Ezra glanced at Callie then shrugged. "We do have two

new foals. Born last week. So, if you and Luka want to come by and see them…"

"Please, Dr. Callie?" Maisy said. "I've already told Luka about them and he's so excited to meet them."

Callie's heart squeezed at her pleading stare. Luka had been asking about going back to the ranch again, so shouldn't she do what would make her son happy? "Well, I suppose we could stop by for a short time this weekend." She glanced at Ezra. "Will Saturday afternoon work for you?"

"Saturday afternoon works," Ezra said.

"Yay!" Maisy did a little happy dance.

"Uh, great then." Callie straightened and walked them down the hall to the entrance. She needed to get Ezra out of there before she did something stupid, like climb him like a tree. "I guess we'll see you Saturday then. And I think we're on the right track for the auction, too. Your ideas are perfect."

"Thanks." He and Maisy stepped outside, then Ezra turned back. "See you later then."

"See you Saturday," she said past her constricted vocal cords.

Going to the ranch again was stupid. Totally the opposite of what she should be doing, but it was for the kids. And there's be plenty of other people around to keep her out of trouble where Ezra was concerned. She wasn't looking for love, wasn't interested in romance, especially with a man who seemed more like her ex-husband than she'd expected. But still, as she finished up and left the office to go pick up Luka from school, Callie found her looking forward to Saturday more than was wise.

Callie barely glanced at the GPS this time as she drove down the same winding dirt road she remembered from their previous visit, past rolling pastures where cattle grazed in the afternoon sun. From his car seat in the back, Luka practically vibrated with excitement.

"Are we almost there? Can I see the baby horses first thing? Do you think Cora remembers me?"

"Sweetie, how could Cora forget you?" Callie chuckled as she watched her son in the rearview mirror, his whole face lighting up as they approached ranch.

It's been so long since I've seen him like this.

It's all she'd hoped for when she'd moved back here. To see Luka happy again. To see him come out of his shell and thrive. She was thrilled he'd found Maisy and was embracing life again. She just wished all that wonderfulness didn't come with Ezra Benson attached. Not because she didn't like him. She did. Too much. And that was a problem because she'd already learned the hard way what happened when she let yourself depend on someone who lived for the thrills, who ran toward danger instead of away from it, when she'd built her happiness around another person's presence in her life. Because adrenaline was a drug and as soon as those thrills went away, so did the person she'd depended on. Owen had taught her that painful lesson. Callie had no illusions about who and what she was. A mother, a pediatrician, a solid, strong, dependable woman.

She couldn't compete with jumping out of helicopters or scaling mountains or racing cars.

And she refused to ever try again. If someone didn't want her for herself, they could move on.

She took a deep breath and flexed her stiff fingers on the steering wheel. It was silly to get so worked up about the visit today. But EZ wasn't Owen. And they weren't involved. Not like that. She didn't want him that way. She wasn't looking for love. She was fine with the way things were.

Then they crested a small hill, and the ranch came into view, sprawling and picturesque in the golden afternoon light. It really was breathtakingly lovely here. Her own heartbeat kicked up a notch as they turned onto the long driveway and headed toward the main house, where she spotted EZ's dusty truck out front, then the man himself unloading stuff from the back, muscles rippling beneath the black T-shirt, his long legs encased in soft denim, highlighting his strong thighs and perfect butt.

She swallowed hard and pulled to a stop alongside his truck, then cut the engine, feeling flushed and flustered.

Are you fine, though?

She wanted to say yes, she really did, but then EZ straightened from where he'd been reaching for something in the bed of his truck and spotted her, a slow smile growing on his lips, her stomach doing flips and her mind racing with all sorts of inappropriate thoughts.

Get a grip, Dupree. You're thirty-two, not sixteen.

Thankfully, before Ezra reached her, Maisy flew out the front door of the house and raced down the steps to where Luka had unbuckled himself from his car seat and was now scrambling out of the vehicle to see his best friend. Ezra had stopped to watch them, his mussed auburn hair blowing in the slight breeze and his smile growing into a full-blown grin, and something shifted inside Callie, softened, unfurled, like a tightly clenched fist finally letting go.

"Dr. Callie!" Maisy called once she'd let Luka go. She clambered up onto the running board on the passenger side as Callie put the windows down. "I'm so glad you're here! We're just getting ready to feed the horses. The babies are so cute and one of them is really fuzzy and I can't wait to show you and Luka and—"

"Monkey," Ezra said, his voice low and deep, and suddenly much closer than Callie had expected, sending a shiver of awareness through her. He was at her open window, resting one beefy forearm on the door as he leaned in slightly to see his daughter in the other window past Callie. "Give them a chance to settle in first. Those colts aren't going anywhere."

Callie felt trapped in her seat in the best possible way, all Ezra's warmth and his scent enveloping her, and if she leaned in ever so slightly, she could kiss him and—

What the—

She couldn't get out without hitting him with the door and she didn't want to make this situation any more awkward than it already was, so she focused on Maisy instead, surprised by how normal her voice sounded when her insides were shaking. Not with fear, but with something else entirely. Something hot and molten and definitely forbidden. "It's okay, Maisy," Callie said gently. "I bet Luka's just as excited to see them as you are. Why don't you two go ahead over there while I get out of the car?"

Ezra seemed to get the hint and moved back to open her door for her. "Go on, kids," he called as they raced away. "We'll be right behind you." He waited until Callie was out of the vehicle, then closed the door behind her before leading her toward the front of the house. "She's been talking about you two since we were in your office on Thursday. According to her, you and Luka are the second coming."

"Wow." Callie laughed, doing her best to tamp down the warmth spreading through her chest at his nearness. This was ridiculous. She wasn't some silly schoolgirl crushing on a boy. She was a grown adult with a successful career and a child and a whole life and history of her own. She didn't need a man. Even if right now, she really wanted one. One man in particular.

Stop it.

As they rounded the side of the house and started down the path toward the horse pens she remembered from their first visit, she hazarded a glance over at Ezra, noting the shadows under his hazel eyes, like he hadn't been sleeping well. She wondered if he'd been having some restless nights, too.

"Mom, hurry!" Luka called, jarring her out of her thoughts. "Come see the babies. They're so cute!"

"We're coming, buddy," Ezra called back before Callie could. "Takes us adults longer to get there."

When they finally reached the pens, the horses were back inside, along with Maisy and Luka. In the shadowed interior, the temperature was cooler and smelled of hay and horse, and she felt hyperaware of Ezra beside her—the way he moved with unconscious confidence, the way his arm brushed hers as he pointed to where they were headed, the last stall on the right.

Focus on the kids. Focus on anything except the gorgeous guy beside you.

"So," Ezra began as they walked down the wide, straw-covered hallway. "How was your Friday?"

"Busy. Three cases of strep, two ear infections, and one very dramatic splinter removal." She found herself relaxing a little as he distracted her from her raging hormones. Work was a safe zone. Always had been for her. "You know, the usual life-or-death pediatric emergencies."

"Sounds harrowing."

"You have no idea. The splinter patient was convinced he was going to lose his entire finger."

"How old?"

"Fourteen."

Ezra laughed, the sound rich and warm. "Sounds about

right. At that age they're all bravado until they're hurt, then they become big babies. Ask me how I know."

Now, it was her turn to laugh. "I have a hard time ever imagining you as a big baby."

"It's true. I once cried when I broke my little toe playing soccer. Not that I'd ever admit to it then. And honestly, it never stops. I remember once in combat medic training, one of the guys passed out during his own blood draw."

They were both chuckling when they reached the stall where Maisy and Luka were standing on tiptoe to peer over the door, their voices quiet and reverent at they watched the new foals with their mothers.

"Oh, my gosh," Callie breathed, moving closer to join them. "They're beautiful."

Two foals, maybe a week old, stood near their mothers in the spacious stall—one a rich chestnut color, all legs and curiosity; the other darker, with a white blaze down his face and white socks that made him look like he was decked out in formal wear.

"We named the chestnut Honey," Maisy whispered importantly. "And the dark one is Bandit because he looks like he's wearing a mask."

"Perfect names," Callie agreed, watching as Honey took tentative steps toward the stall door, drawn by the children's voices.

"Can we pet them?" Luka asked Ezra.

"Not yet, buddy," Ezra said, moving in closer behind Callie to see into the stall, his warm chest brushing her back. "They're still too young. But in a few weeks, when they're stronger, maybe you can come back and help me and Maisy start getting them used to people."

"Really?" Luka's blue eyes went wide. "I can help train baby horses?"

"If your mom says it's okay."

Both children turned to look up at Callie with identical expressions of hope. Far too aware of Ezra behind her, she swallowed hard and answered cautiously, "We'll see. It depends on the schedule. Between my work and your school, and then with the fundraiser coming up, we've got a lot on our plate."

Thankfully, Ezra went to check on one of the other stalls then, allowing her to breathe again.

They spent the next thirty minutes watching the horses before going to look at the chicken coop, where Luka became enchanted by how the hens clucked and fussed over their chicks. Then they visited the cattle in the far pasture, Maisy explaining the difference between Herefords and Angus with the authority of someone who'd grown up around livestock.

Callie checked her watch and saw the time, and was just about to tell Luka they had to go, when shouts erupted from near the main house. Even from this distance, she heard the urgent panic in the man's tone. "Help! Please, somebody help us!"

She and Ezra ran over to find a man in work clothes waving frantically from the direction of a large shed. Ezra cursed under his breath, and shifted immediately into a different mode—focused, alert. "That's Miguel, one of our seasonal guys."

As they got closer, she saw that there was someone on the ground behind Miguel—another ranch hand from the way he was dressed—lying very still. Her heart tripped and her mind raced with all the medical reasons for why that might be. A fall, a heart attack, worse…

"What happened?" Ezra asked when they finally reached the area and kneeled beside the man on the ground, Callie on one side, Ezra on the other.

"Carlos was up on the ladder fixing the roof trim," Miguel said, his accent thick with stress. "The ladder slipped, and he fell. Hit his head on the concrete step there. He's been unconscious for maybe two minutes."

Callie was already assessing the man's condition. Carlos looked young, maybe mid-twenties, and was breathing but unresponsive. Blood pooled under his head where it had struck the concrete.

"Ezra, call nine-one-one," she said, her voice calm and professional. "Tell them we have a head trauma, unconscious male, possible skull fracture."

"Already on it," EZ said, phone to his ear.

As Callie carefully palpated Carlos's neck, checking for obvious spinal injuries, she asked Miguel, "How far did he fall?"

"Maybe eight feet? The ladder just…gave way."

Significant height. Head impact on concrete. Definitely serious.

"Carlos?" Callie called loudly, checking his pupils with the flashlight from her keychain. "Can you hear me?"

No response. His breathing remained steady, but his pupils were unequal.

"Ambulance on the way," Ezra said, ending his call and kneeling beside Callie again. "What's his status?"

She kept her voice low to avoid upsetting an already stricken-looking Miguel. "Unequal pupils, unresponsive to verbal stimuli. Significant head trauma." She caught Ezra's gaze, seeing her same concern reflected in his eyes. "We need to stabilize his head and neck until paramedics arrive. Do you have a cervical collar?"

"In my truck. Let me grab my first-aid kit."

As he got up to rush toward the driveway, she instructed, "And bring whatever medical supplies you have."

Callie continued her assessment and was glad that the kids were still far enough away to not see this. She vaguely registered Ezra talking to Cora, then the housekeeper going over to the kids to keep them occupied. "Miguel," she said, "I need you to help me manually stabilize Carlos's head and neck."

"Of course," he said, crouching down near Carlos's head. "Whatever you need."

Ezra returned with his first-aid kit—one that was more comprehensive than the standard ranch emergency supplies because of his background and work with the rescue team. As he kneeled beside her once more, their hands brushed as they worked together to carefully position the cervical collar.

"Once we get this on, we need to roll him to check for other injuries." Ezra's voice was steady and professional as he snapped the collar into place. "Careful—maintain spinal alignment."

They worked in perfect synchronization, Ezra seeming to anticipate her needs before Callie voiced them. He held Carlos's head steady while she examined his back for obvious injuries, then helped position him in the recovery position when she was satisfied there were no spinal fractures.

"Vitals are still stable," she reported, checking Carlos's pulse again. "But he's still unresponsive. They'll need to order a CT scan once he gets to the hospital."

"Should I go wait for the ambulance?" Miguel asked.

"Yeah," Ezra said, glancing at his watch. "They're coming from town so it'll take them about twelve minutes to get here."

Callie gave Miguel a reassuring smile. "We'll keep him stable until they arrive."

As the man ran toward the ranch entrance, a weak but audible voice said, "What happened?"

She looked down to fine Carlos looking up at her with glassy, half-lidded eyes. "You had a fall, Carlos, and you hit your head. Please stay still, okay. My name is Dr. Dupree. Can you tell me your full name?"

"Carlos… Carlos Mendoza." His eyes opened a little more now, though they were still unfocused. "My head hurts like hell."

"I'll bet it does," Ezra said. "Can you wiggle your fingers and toes for me?"

Carlos complied, though slowly. Better than nothing.

"What year is it, Carlos?" Callie asked.

A pause. "Twenty twenty-five?"

"Good. Do you remember what you were doing before you fell?"

"Fixing…the roof trim on the shed. The ladder…" He started to raise his hand toward his head, then stopped when Ezra caught it and put it back down at his side again. "Did I crack my skull open?"

"You have a head injury, but you're going to be okay," Callie assured him. "The ambulance is almost here. We're going to get you to the hospital for some tests."

In the distance, the wail of sirens grew louder. She and Ezra remained with Carlos until Miguel returned, this time with a pair of EMTs from Teton Memorial.

"Hey, Doc. EZ," the lead paramedic said as they prepared to transport Carlos. Callie had seen him in the ER. "Thanks for keeping him stable until we arrived. Textbook head injury?"

"Looks like it," she said, then relayed the patient's vitals and history to him before standing beside Ezra. "Hopefully, he'll be okay."

The EMT nodded, glancing between her and Ezra. "We'll do everything we can. But having you both here definitely ups his odds for a full recovery. You guys make a good team."

A good team.

That sounded nicer than Callie cared to admit.

After the ambulance left, with Miguel riding with Carlos to the hospital, Callie found herself standing alone with EZ in the sudden quiet of the ranch yard. The kids must've gone off somewhere with Cora and now that the adrenaline was wearing off, she felt slightly shaky.

"Well, that was…" she began.

"Intense?" Ezra said, finishing her sentence and giving her a small smile. "Nice work, Doc."

"Same to you."

They looked at each other across the space of a few feet, and the late autumn air between them seemed to shimmer with possibilities. Afternoon sun filtered through the leaves of a nearby oak tree, casting everything in golden light. Ezra stepped closer as if drawn by the same invisible string that was tugging her nearer to him as well, close enough that his scent, his warmth, surrounded her once more.

"Callie," he said, his voice soft, intense. "Callie, this is complicated. I don't want to get involved with anyone. Not after… I told myself never again, but I can't stop thinking about you. No matter how hard I try."

Callie's breath caught. "Ezra…"

He stepped closer then, close enough that she had to tilt her head back to meet his eyes. "Tell me I'm crazy."

"You're crazy." The words came out softer than she'd intended. "I don't want to get involved, either."

"So what are we doing here then?" His question was barely a whisper as he cupped her face gently with one hand, his thumb tracing along her cheekbone, making her lean into him and shiver all at the same time. It had been so long—too long—since someone had touched her like this, looked at her like this. "Tell me to stop. Tell me to leave you alone and I will, I swear. Even if it kills me."

It was her chance. Her moment to walk away and continue in the life she'd said she'd wanted. Alone. Safe. Secure. But instead, she found herself clutching the front of his T-shirt as she went up on her toes and pressed her lips to his.

The kiss was soft at first, tentative, like they were both testing the waters. Then Ezra groaned low in his throat and his arms wrapped around her waist, and Callie suddenly found herself pressed against the tree trunk, kissing him just as desperately as he was kissing her. And, oh, boy. It was good. So good.

Seemed Ezra Benson kissed like he did everything else—with complete focus, full of intense passion, like she was the only thing in the world that mattered. His hands were tangled in her hair now, angling her head so he could deepen the kiss, and Callie's knees wobbled. If he hadn't been holding her up with his body, she'd have melted into a puddle of goo at his feet.

She was just beginning to wonder why she'd avoided this for so long, beginning to think she could stay in this moment forever, when voices drifted over to them.

"Mom, where are you?" Luka's voice called from the front of the house, and it hit Callie like a bucket of ice water to the face.

They sprang apart like teenagers caught by their parents, both breathing hard, staring at each other with something between amazement and panic, warning bells clanging loud in Callie's head.

Oh, God. What did you just do?

Ezra looked as flummoxed as she felt, his chest heaving and his gaze focused on her mouth.

Callie forced herself to turn away and swiped a hand across her mouth, then straightened her shirt and her hair before her son and Maisy came tearing around the corner and over to where they stood.

She felt breathless and dizzy and completely out of her depth as she raised a shaky hand to check the time on her smartwatch. Throat dry, she forced out squeaky words. "We should, uh, probably get going, sweetie. I'm on call tomorrow, and I need to be at the hospital early for rounds."

It was a cowardly move, but she had to get out of here. She needed space, time to think about what had just happened without Ezra's overwhelming presence scrambling her brain.

The walk back to her car was filled with chatter from the children, talking over each other about the baby horses, the chicken coop, the cattle in the field. Callie made what she hoped were appropriate nods with Ezra walking beside her, at a careful distance now, her lips still tingling from his kiss.

After getting Luka into the car, Callie wiped her palms on the legs of her jeans, looking anywhere but at Ezra. "Uh, thank you for having us over again today," she said, her voice more formal than before to put more distance between them. "Luka had a wonderful time. And thank you for your help with Carlos."

"Of course," Ezra said quietly, staring off into the distance. "Guess we'll talk about it at the next committee meeting."

"Guess so." She tucked her hair behind her ear. The fundraiser was in three weeks. They had two more meetings between now and then, but they were virtual, so thank the Lord for that. Time and space would definitely help her get whatever this was under control. "See you then."

Callie fled for the safety of her vehicle then, barely acknowledging Ezra as he called, "Drive carefully."

Coward.

As they pulled away from the ranch, Callie couldn't stop herself from watching Ezra's slowly shrinking form in the rearview mirror until he disappeared completely as they turned onto the road back to town. Driving home through the approaching dusk, Callie couldn't forget how well they fit together, how he seemed to know what she needed before she even knew herself. But that wasn't what she wanted.

Was it?

Honestly, she didn't know what she wanted anymore.

CHAPTER FIVE

BY THE TIME of the Jackson Elementary Winter Fundraiser, EZ felt much more in control of himself where Callie was concerned. The kiss had been a mistake, an aberration, something not to be repeated. And staying busy with work and the BSAR team had helped tremendously. As had getting all the auction packages ready to go.

Now, as he stood in the transformed school gymnasium, which resembled something between a country fair and an upscale auction house, he felt contented. They'd handled what needed to be handled. Gotten through it. Moved on. As he followed the signs directing traffic between the silent auction tables, ring-toss games, and a photo booth complete with props that included cowboy hats and fake mustaches, he felt pretty proud of himself.

EZ adjusted the helicopter pilot headset that someone had insisted he wear for "atmosphere" and approached the Adventure Experiences table, which displayed everything from scenic flight vouchers to ranch-day packages, where he and Callie had been assigned to work together.

"You look ridiculous," Callie said, shaking her head. He'd been concerned that things between them would be weird after their ill-advised kiss several weeks ago, but thankfully, Callie seemed unfazed by it. He wanted to ask her how she'd seemed to forget it so completely because if he was honest, those moments still snuck into his dreams sometimes—how she'd felt, how she'd tasted, how she'd sounded, those tiny moans she'd made as if she couldn't get enough of him. He took a deep breath and grabbed a glass of punch off a tray of a passing server, then chugged it down completely to quench the low burn inside him. He needed to get over it. Benson men put duty before desire, and he'd be damned if that would change tonight. Callie obviously wanted to keep things platonic, and he did, too, despite his earlier actions. And if they never discussed that kiss again, it would be too soon for him.

"Thank you. So helpful," he said sarcastically as he tossed his empty plastic cup in a nearby trash can while doing his best to stare at how lovely she looked tonight. And it wasn't even like the attire for this thing was formal. She'd dressed appropriately for the occasion in soft-looking faded jeans, boots, and a cream-colored sweater that made her skin glow. Professional but approachable. That sweater looked silky, and he found his fingers eager to touch her and find out, but he clenched his hands and jaw tighter until the feeling passed, and watched the bidders milling around to the different tables.

What the hell is wrong with me?

He'd never had a problem controlling his reaction to a woman before.

That's not true.

Okay. Fine. This had happened to him once before. With Sierra. But that was totally different, and he was absolutely not going there again. Not with Callie, not with anyone. He'd failed Sierra. Not been there when she'd needed him most and it had cost her everything. He never should have gone off to film another episode of his show instead of being with his family, protecting them. How could a man trust himself after that? Forgive himself after such a huge failure?

"How are we doing on bids?" Callie asked as she flipped through the auction sheets, jarring him from his thoughts.

He shrugged and swallowed hard to lubricate his dry throat, then answered, "Uh, better than expected, I think. The helicopter tour is up to eight hundred dollars."

"Really? That's amazing."

"Yeah. Amazing enough to make me slightly terrified about what people expect from a 'romantic sunset flight.'" He gestured at the description on the sign for the prize that someone had apparently embellished without consulting him.

"You didn't write that?"

"I wrote 'scenic helicopter tour.' Martha must've enhanced it." He scowled at the flowing script that promised "sweeping mountain vistas" and "unforgettable moments above the clouds." "Does that sound like something I'd say?"

Callie laughed—the first genuine laugh he'd heard from her all evening. It wrapped around him like a warm hug. "Well, now that you mention it, no. But since it's doing so well, you'll just have to live up to the marketing."

"Great." He exhaled slowly. "No pressure."

The table got busy again and they fell into an easy rhythm, taking turns greeting potential bidders and explaining the various packages. EZ covertly watched Callie interact with the other parents from beneath his lashes, noting how she remembered everyone's names, asked after their kids, made them feel seen and important. She was really good at that.

"She's good at this," said a voice beside him, echoing his thoughts so precisely it made him jump. He turned to find Linda Martinez, whose son was in Maisy's class.

He forced a polite smile for them. "She is. But then I'm sure she's had lots of practice, being a doctor and all," he said carefully.

"You seeing anyone right now, EZ?" Linda asked, bold as brass, continuing the town's tradition of prying into everyone else's business. He thought maybe if he ignored her or pretended like he hadn't heard, she'd take the hint and leave, but she didn't. She just waited there, watching him with a raised brow.

EZ sighed inwardly, seeing where this was heading already. "No. Why?"

"Oh, I just wondered." Linda gave him a smile chock-full of meddling matchmaker. "Callie is divorced and newly back in town, too. Maybe you could be neighborly and show her how things have changed around here since she's been gone."

He wasn't going to ask Callie out on a date because that way madness lurked. Thankfully, before he could respond, Linda's kid dragged her off to look at some dolls for auction that were supposedly the new hot thing on social media. The toys looked possessed to him, but the kids were crazy about them, and Maisy was no exception. She'd already specified which ones she'd like for Christmas, so he was going to have to bite the bullet and hunt one down for her soon. Maybe he should put in a bid himself on one of them as a solution to his problem.

"Everything okay?" Callie asked, appearing at his elbow, her sweet, flowery scent wafting around him and reminding him of things better left forgotten. "The way you were concentrating on those toys over there, I'd have thought they were made of solid gold."

"For the prices and scarcity of the things, they should be," he grumbled, but smiled. Callie was a parent, too. Maybe she could advise him one way or another. "I was thinking maybe I should go bid on one of those ugly things for my daughter for Christmas. She's over the moon about them. No idea why. They'd give me nightmares."

Callie laughed again, her pretty face brightening. "Yeah, they aren't exactly what we played with, are they?"

"No!" He gaped at her. "Remember those talking teddy bears?"

"Yes!" Callie grinned. "I used to talk to mine every night before I fell asleep."

"Same." But the rush of nostalgia had made his decision for him. "Hey, can you cover the table by yourself for a second while I run over to put a bid in on one of those toys?"

"No problem." She shooed him away. "Better make it a good one. It's getting pretty cutthroat from what I hear."

He made his way over to the table and ended up putting in three bids on three different toys, thinking at least one of them should pan out for him. Then, after greeting a couple of volunteers with the rescue team who were making the rounds at the auction tables, he headed back to Callie, just in time to catch her talking to Luka and Maisy. They'd raced over from the ring-toss game in the corner. Maisy was clutching a stuffed bear under one arm.

"Daddy, look what I won!" Maisy said, holding up her toy to him. "It's for the new baby when the stork comes."

EZ's brain stuttered, his gaze flying to Callie, who looked like she was trying not to giggle. "What?"

"Tommy said his mom's getting a baby from a stork," Maisy explained, as if he was slow. "So I thought this would be a nice gift for them."

His pent-up breath rushed out in a huff of relief. He nodded. "That's real nice of you, monkey."

Before he could say anything else, the microphone at the

front of the room squeaked in a shrill hiss of feedback, followed by Martha's voice booming over the din of conversation in the gym. "Ladies and gentlemen, the live auction will begin in fifteen minutes in the cafeteria. Please finish your silent auction bids here then make your way down the hall to join us for more exciting items!"

"Right. We should check the final bids here at our table," Callie said, turning to the locked wooden box at the front of their table. "If we each do half, it shouldn't take long."

They worked through the bid forms, tallying final numbers and making notes for the winners. When they both reached for the final bid, their hands got tangled and there was that familiar jolt of awareness again. The one he'd vowed to ignore. The one he couldn't seem to ignore if his life depended on it.

Get it together, Benson.

"Wow. The winning bid for your helicopter tour is fifteen hundred dollars," Callie said and showed him the tally sheet she was keeping. He didn't miss the sudden blush of pink on her cheeks that told him maybe he wasn't the only one feeling that buzz of attraction from such an innocent touch. And maybe he should forget about it if he knew what was good for him. "Incredible work, Ezra."

"Thanks." An unaccountable flush of pride spread through him like wildfire. He shouldn't care what she thought about him and his stupid tour, but he did. Man, he so did. He tried to focus on the numbers instead of how close she was standing. "And that one medical basket of yours, the one with all the spa stuff and the gift card for massages, went for nearly a thousand. So good work to you, too!"

She gave him a demure smile and a slight bow. "Thank you. We make a pretty good team, huh?"

Time seemed to slow as her words hung between them

and EZ knew from the flash of heat in her eyes that he wasn't the only one who was now reliving that kiss in his backyard. It had been good. Better than good. Sweet and sexy and sinful enough to make a man sell his soul for more.

And it would never, ever happen again.

But as they cleaned up their table before heading down to the cafeteria to join the others, EZ couldn't shake the feeling that they'd somehow crossed a line that he wasn't sure he could never uncross.

Worse, he wasn't sure he wanted to. And that spooked him most of all.

The live auction was in full swing by the time he and Callie found seats near the back of the cafeteria. The auctioneer—a local rancher with a voice that could project to the next county—was working the crowd into a bidding frenzy over a week-long cabin rental.

"This is insane," Callie murmured as the citizens of Jackson bid against each other with increasing determination.

"Just wait until they get to the big-ticket items," EZ said. "Last year someone paid three thousand for dinner with the mayor."

"Three thousand? For dinner?"

"Open bar included," he said, winking.

Callie laughed and several people around them turned to look. Right. They were still being watched, analyzed, whispered about. Part of EZ wanted to sink down in his chair and disappear. The other part considered pulling Callie into his lap and really giving them something to look at.

Yeah, none of that.

He cleared his throat and sat up straighter, crossing his arms.

The auction continued with various services—lawn care,

house cleaning, a year of snowplowing. Then moved on to one of the most coveted items of the night, besides the dolls in the other room.

"Next up is a handmade quilt from the Jackson Quilting Circle, featuring our beautiful mountain landscape."

"That is so pretty," Callie said, her voice soft and full of wonder.

He tore his eyes away from her to glance at the quilt. She wasn't wrong. It was gorgeous—blues and greens and whites that captured the essence of the Tetons, stitched with obvious care and skill.

But it didn't hold a candle to Callie herself in EZ's opinion. He swallowed hard.

"Starting bid is five hundred dollars," the auctioneer announced.

Hands went up around the room. Six hundred. Seven hundred. Eight hundred.

EZ ran a finger under the collar of his shirt and wondered when it had gotten so hot in there. Next thing he knew, the auctioneer pointed at him and said, "We have fourteen hundred from the man in the back."

Callie turned to him, wide-eyed. "What are you doing?"

EZ didn't know himself. It had been a mistake. He hadn't been bidding. But seeing her glowing, gorgeous face and the sparkle in her green eyes had him reconsidering his decisions.

The bidding continued. Sixteen hundred. Seventeen fifty. Two thousand.

"Twenty-five hundred," EZ called, loud and clear. Hey, he could afford it. And even if he had to pay twice that for the quilt, it would be worth it to have her keep looking at him like that, full of delight and joy and adoration. Forget crack, Callie was the most addictive drug in the world to him right now.

"EZ, what—" Callie began.

"Going once…going twice…" The auctioneer's gavel hung in the air.

"Three thousand!" someone shouted from the front at the last second.

EZ hesitated for a moment, his heart racing as fast as it did during the most harrowing rescue. Adrenaline sizzled through him, urging him to bid again, keep bidding until he won, but he forced himself to shake his head slightly. He wasn't a daredevil anymore. He'd learned that painful lesson too well with Sierra. Better to be safe than sorry.

Applause filled the room and Callie turned to him once more. "Why did you do that?"

EZ looked embarrassed. *Because I'm an idiot*. Rather than saying that, though, he replied, "You liked it and I thought… I don't know what I thought."

He hadn't been thinking. That was the problem. Or he'd been thinking with something other than his brain. Either way, this whole thing he had for Callie was getting ridiculous and he needed to get a grip on it before it got even more complicated. Bad enough he'd kissed her under that oak tree. And if the kids hadn't interrupted them, who knows how far things would have gone, they'd both been so lost in the moment. He didn't want to lose control like that ever again. Bad things happened when he did.

The auction wrapped up with a dinner package at a fancy French fusion restaurant that had just opened in town that went for an astronomical sum. Then, the live auction was over and gradually people began to filter out and head back to the gym, where a DJ had set up and was now pumping out tunes for everyone to dance to in the middle of the open floor.

As they made their way down a hallway lined with student artwork and motivational posters, Callie finally said, "Thank you. For trying. The quilt, I mean."

"No problem." EZ stopped walking and turned to face her. Even the harsh fluorescent lighting in the hallway did nothing to dim her loveliness. "Like I said, you looked at it like it mattered. So I thought you should have it."

Her gaze was far too perceptive for his comfort. They were standing close to avoid blocking the hallway, close enough that he could see the flecks of gold in her eyes, see a tiny copper freckle near the corner of her mouth. A mouth he'd very much like to kiss again and…

"We need to talk about it," she said suddenly, breaking him out of his erotic haze.

Dammit. What the hell is wrong with me?

He stumbled over his feet as she pulled him into an alcove out of the main path of traffic. "Talk about what?"

"The kiss," she said, then glanced around to make sure they weren't being overheard. "What it meant."

He frowned, his brain still catching up to the present moment. "Meant?"

"Daddy!" Maisy careened into the alcove with Luka close behind her. "They're dancing in the gym! Can we stay and dance?"

EZ glanced over at Callie then ran a hand through his hair, feeling rumpled and restless and ridiculously on edge for some reason. "Uh, yeah. Fine, I suppose." Then he added, "For a little while."

Maisy squealed with happiness then ran off with Luka in tow back toward the gym. EZ and Callie followed. The DJ was playing a popular country tune by Luke Bryan, and some parents had already claimed dance-floor space as kids raced around the edges. They'd lowered the overhead lights and the DJ had set up some colored lights around the edges, the spinning kind that made the place look like a giant kaleidoscope.

"Dance with me, Daddy?" Maisy asked, tugging on EZ's hand.

"Of course, monkey."

He probably looked ridiculous but he let his seven-year-old lead him through something that might generously be called dancing. Luka and Callie were off to the side with another group attempting some kind of line dance that bore no resemblance to the actual music.

Once the song ended, he and Maisy made their way over to where Callie and Luka stood, both breathing hard and grinning. The DJ started another song—this time something slow and romantic that made several teenage couples around them sigh dramatically. The kids ran off to get more punch while he and Callie stood there awkwardly trying not to look at each other.

Finally, EZ had had enough. She obviously wanted to discuss what had happened between them and he needed to not be surrounded by half the town when they did it, so he extended a hand. "Dance?"

Callie looked up at him, her expression slightly startled. "Oh, I don't think—"

"You wanted to talk, Callie. Let's talk. Out there, where these people can't hear us."

She took a deep breath and his hand. "Fine."

He led her to a relatively quiet corner of the floor, settling on arm around her waist, their joined hands finding a comfortable position. They moved carefully at first, finding a rhythm that worked.

"You're a good dancer," she said, surprising him.

EZ shrugged. "Sierra insisted I learn. Said she wasn't going to marry someone who couldn't hold his own at weddings."

The mention of his wife should have created distance, but somehow, it didn't. Another couple moved past them, forcing them a bit closer together.

"She sounds like an incredible woman," Callie said, looking up at him.

"Yeah. She was."

They swayed together as he tried to figure out a way into the subject they were both avoiding. Finally, he figured straightforward was the best way. He lowered his voice for privacy. "About that kiss."

"Yes." Callie looked as uncomfortable as he felt. "We shouldn't have done that."

"No," he agreed, despite every cell in his being vibrating at the nearness of her. "We shouldn't have."

She stared at the center of his chest and said, "It's not that I don't like you. I do. Too much. But I just got out of a messy situation and I don't ever want to deal with that again. You're a wonderful man, Ezra, and a really great kisser, but—"

"You think I'm a great kisser?" he said, his brain snagging on those words. It made him feel inordinately proud for reasons he didn't want to think about too much. Best to change the subject, considering she looked like she wished the earth would swallow her whole. "And why do you call me Ezra when everyone else calls me EZ?"

"Oh, I, uh…" She inhaled deeply, then said, "I like your full name. Sounds very solid, strong."

He snorted. "I think the word you're looking for is biblical."

The tension in her body eased as she relaxed in EZ's

arms. "Was your family very religious? I don't remember that."

"Not really. But my mom was raised Catholic and always liked those old names from when she was a kid, so that's what I got."

"I see." Callie smiled up at him then, making his stumble over his own feet before he quickly caught himself. "Well, I like your name. And I guess maybe I like using it because then you'll remember me."

Like he could ever forget her.

Heat prickled up his neck and into his cheeks and he couldn't help smiling down at her. "Fair enough. I like your name, too, Callie. Always did. You kept the Dupree, huh?"

"I did." The stiffness was back in her spine, and he regretted bringing it up immediately, but it was out there now, so... "Good thing, too, considering how things turned out."

"He didn't deserve you," EZ said, feeling defensive on her behalf.

"I agree," Callie said, flashing a small smile. "That's why I'm not with him anymore."

"A woman who knows her worth and what she wants. I love that."

"You do?"

Then she was looking at him again and the rest of the world fell away as he found himself lost in her green eyes, wondering what she'd do if he bent and kissed her again in front of God and all these people. She felt so good in his arms, like she fit there, like she was supposed to be there, even if he knew she wasn't.

The song ended too soon, and they stepped apart as the other parents began collecting children, gathering coats, making plans for car pools and babysitting exchanges.

"I guess we should probably—" Callie gestured toward where Luka was yawning against the wall beside Maisy.

"Yeah."

They said their goodbyes, the earlier tension replaced by something softer as they led the kids out into the parking lot. Callie got Luka into his car seat and EZ did the same with Maisy in his truck, then they met in front of their vehicles again, breath frosting in the cool night air.

"So," he said, for lack of anything better.

"So," Callie responded, not moving. "We never did finish talking about that kiss."

"No, we didn't."

A car across from them flicked on its headlights, spotlighting them and ruining the intimate moment.

"Guess I should get home then."

"Same." He stayed where he was as she backed to her driver-side door, only moving once she'd gotten in and started her vehicle. She waved as she pulled away, leaving EZ staring after her red taillights, wondering why he couldn't seem to get Callie Dupree and the way she'd felt as they'd danced out of his mind.

CHAPTER SIX

EZ STARED AT the ceiling of his bedroom, watching dawn light creep across the walls. He'd been awake for two hours, replaying last night on an endless loop. The way Callie's beautiful face had lit up when she'd seen that quilt, like the sun coming out from behind the clouds. The dance. The way she'd felt in his arms, like she belonged there.

Which was exactly the problem.

The conflict was ripping him apart. His guilt told him no one belonged with him. That he didn't deserve to have love, a marriage, a future filled with happiness and joy and togetherness, because he couldn't protect it. He'd lost it once. He refused to ever put himself through it again.

No matter how tempting Callie might make it.

With a resigned sigh, he rolled out of bed and pulled on running gear, needing to move, to shake the thoughts and forbidden yearnings that had been circling his brain like vultures. The ranch was quiet at this hour—even Cora wouldn't be up for another thirty minutes.

His feet hit the dirt road with steady rhythm, but his mind refused to settle. He'd spent the two years since Sierra's death building walls around his heart high and strong, learning to live with the guilt and the loneliness.

And now, Callie Dupree had waltzed back into his life

and made those barriers feel as substantial as a wet paper towel.

It makes no sense.

He'd been raised to be self-sufficient, he'd been trained in the military to be guarded and steadfast, yet all it took was one pretty blond doctor and her adorable son to send all that flying out the window.

What the hell is wrong with me?

By the time he made it back to the house, EZ still didn't have an answer to that last question. Luckily, he didn't have long to continue brooding about it because Maisy was up by then and bouncing around the kitchen in her unicorn pajamas while Cora made pancakes.

"Ew, Daddy!" Maisy said, all wrinkled nose and disdain. "You're all sweaty and gross!"

"Thanks, monkey. Very observant." He ruffled her already messy red hair as he passed her on the way to grab a towel from the laundry basket atop the washer in the laundry room off the kitchen, deliberating ignoring Cora's pointed stare tracking his ever step.

He had a face full of towel when he heard Cora, from her spot in front of the stove, as she said, "Dr. Dupree called while you were out. Something about forgetting to talk to you about something last night."

EZ's stomach did something acrobatic as he cursed inside his head. With both females now staring him down with obvious curiosity, he had to say something. "Did she leave a message?"

Cora shook her head as she flipped another pancake in her pan. "Said she'd try your cell."

Sure enough, as soon as he pulled it out of his pocket there was her number with a voice-mail notification. He'd had it on do-not-disturb mode during his run, so it hadn't alerted him to the call. Now, he felt torn and twisted about what to do, the spike in his pulse having nothing to do with the strenuous run he'd just had and everything to do with the woman who'd left that message.

Listen to it. Don't listen to it. Grow up and grow a pair.

Then his phone buzzed with another incoming call from her, making the decision for him because there was no way he could avoid answering under the watchful gaze of Pecos Pancake and her deputy, Nosy Nelly. After a deep breath for patience, he hit the accept button, proud of himself for how normal he sounded when he said, "Morning."

"Hi. I hope I'm not calling too early," Callie said, her voice polite and professional, way different than the softer, more relaxed and intimate tone she'd had last night with him while they danced. It should've made him happy that perhaps he was off the hook for the whole kiss debacle, because no way would she have sounded like this for that conversation. But instead of being relieved, he felt annoyed. Had she brushed it off so easily? How? Why? And, worse, why the hell couldn't he do the same? Troubled, he did his best to focus on what she was saying and not the new knot of tension in his stomach. "The reason I called was we forgot to discuss wrap-up details for the fundraiser committee last night. It's part of our duties."

Right. Of course. Business. Duty. Both things he knew inside out. Safe territory.

The stiffness in his shoulder blades released a bit. "Sure. What do you need? Can we handle it now?"

She sighed, the soft sound hitting him in an entirely different way, and he had to tamp down tightening in an entirely off-limits area of his body now before things got out of hand. "Unfortunately, I think it'll be quicker and easier to just do it in person, if you're okay with that. What does your schedule look like? Today isn't good for me as I'm on call, but what about tomorrow evening? Martha emailed all the final numbers we have to sign off on, and we need to coordinate thank-you notes for the donors, that kind of thing."

Numbers. Notes. Sure. Fine. Sounded very dry and boring.

He could do this. He would do this. Then put this whole silly infatuation he had with Callie Dupree behind him once and for all. He put her on speakerphone as he pulled up his calendar, then frowned down at his screen. "Uh, looks like tomorrow evening should work for me. Say five thirty? Or do you need later?"

"Five thirty is great," Callie said, sounded as determined as he felt. "Let's meet at the school entrance. Martha said they'd leave it open for us along with one of the classrooms to use."

EZ gave a curt nod even though she couldn't see him. "I'll be there."

"Okay." The line went quiet for a moment, then… "See you then."

She hung up before he could say anything else, leaving him staring at his phone and wondering why doing the right thing felt so much like running away. He fixed himself a cup of coffee as he stewed over it.

"Are you gonna marry Dr. Callie, Daddy?" Maisy asked, syrup-covered fork halfway to her mouth.

EZ nearly choked on the gulp of hot brew he'd just taken. "Monkey—"

Maisy continued as if he hadn't answered, talking around a mouthful of pancakes like they hadn't taught her any manners at all. Which they had. "Because I really think you should. She's really nice, and Luka's my best friend, and then we could all live together and have ponies."

He just blinked at her, the simple logic of a child cutting right to the chase. If only life could be that easy. "It's not that simple, sweetheart."

"Why not?" Maisy frowned, looking genuinely confused.

"Because..." He ran a hand though his hair then took a seat at the table, directly across from a suspiciously silent Cora. "Because grown-up relationships are complicated."

"Everything's so complicated when you're old," Maisy observed, sounding disgusted by it all. EZ knew the feeling. "I don't ever want to get old."

Thankfully, the topic of conversation switched from his impending decrepitude to some new project she and Luka were working on at school, and things flowed after that. EZ felt a lot more at peace when he finally went upstairs to shower and dress for another day of ranch work.

He spent the next few hours fixing things that didn't need fixing, moving cattle that were perfectly happy where they were. Anything to keep his hands busy and his mind off tomorrow's meeting.

He was in the middle of repairing a fence that was probably fine when his phone buzzed to life with a BSAR team text asking all available volunteers to respond immediately. A code red. Missing climber in the Dunraven Pass area. It was going to be particularly tricky because according to the local weather reports, severe weather was moving in later.

EZ was already jogging toward his truck before the transmission finished. This was what he was good at. This was what made sense. Saving people he didn't know, people whose lives weren't tangled up with his own complicated history.

Twenty minutes later, he and Andy, Jules, and Dave were airborne, along with Stella and a couple of the new probationary volunteers who were still learning the ropes and putting in the hours until they could be eligible to become regular members of the BSAR team after passing this final test. Nadja was flying them in, as usual, toward some of the most challenging terrain in the area. Dave had been keeping track of the weather reports, and they weren't encouraging—snow squalls moving in from the west and visibility dropping fast.

EZ checked out his window again, searching the ground below for any sign of their victim, then called in an update on the radio. "Benson to base. Approaching target area. No visual yet."

"Copy that, EZ," Ruby responded. "Be advised, we've lost radio contact with the climbing party. Last known position approximately half a mile southeast of your current location."

Nadja, who was listening in on the call, banked the helicopter, giving EZ the opportunity to scan a new area of the white expanse below. Somewhere down there, someone was in trouble. Cold, probably injured, most definitely scared.

Just like Sierra was.

The thought hit him out of the blue and stole his breath for a second before he shook it off. It had been a while since he'd been plagued with memories from that time, and he had a pretty good idea why they were surfacing now. One more reason to get over this whole mess with Callie and get his head back on straight. He squinted down at the search area once more, looking for any signs of life in the rapidly deteriorating conditions. But as the snow began to fall harder, obscuring his vision, more flashbacks to that awful day flooded back.

Sierra backcountry-skiing with friends. A perfect day that turned deadly when an unexpected avalanche swept them down the mountain. By the time rescue teams reached them, she'd been gone for hours. And EZ had been away in Canada, sitting atop a glacier with the reality show's directors and cast, rescuing people for TV while his wife died alone in the snow.

Regret burned like a hot coal through his gut, threatening to pull him under again, but then a flash of color caught his eye in the snowstorm—bright orange against white. Nadja dropped altitude at his direction, fighting a wind shear that threatened to slam them into the mountainside.

There. Two figures huddled against a rock face, one waving frantically.

From there, the team kicked into gear quickly, their hours of training making each move second nature. Lower the basket, haul up the injured climber then return for the other hiker, stabilize in flight, transport to hospital. Nothing he hadn't done a hundred times before.

But as they flew back toward base, the climber—a woman about Callie's age—grabbed his arm, tears streaming down her face as she said, "Thank you. I thought I was going to die up there."

"You're safe now." EZ covered her hand with his own, giving her a reassuring smile.

"My husband—he didn't know I was climbing today," the young woman continued, glancing at her friend as she added, "I didn't tell him because he worries, you know? But I could have died, and he wouldn't have known where I was, and—"

She cried harder then, and EZ's chest constricted in sympathy. He knew those feelings, too. The what-ifs. The guilt. The crushing weight of responsibility.

What if he'd been there with Sierra that day instead of Canada? What if he'd made different choices? Would things have turned out differently?

But that way was madness. He knew that. Just like he knew that he never wanted to feel that out of control again.

By the time he landed at the base, EZ was determined to get himself back on track. He went through the postflight checks, paperwork, debriefing with Andy and the team, all without thinking about Callie. Proof that it could be done. He could put a kibosh on any unwanted emotions he might be developing for her if he just tried hard enough.

He was feeling pretty good about himself when he finally made it home as the sun was setting, his body exhausted and sore. Maisy was getting ready for bed, and Cora had a plate of something that smelled like comfort food waiting for him on the table.

"Rough one?" she asked as he took off his coat and hung it on a peg by the door before sitting down at the table, starving, not bothering to clean up first.

"Yeah. Young woman. Hypothermia. Broken arm and concussion. Close call."

"But you got her."

"We did."

Cora sat in the chair across from him, studying him. "You know, EZ. Sierra wouldn't want you to be alone. And Callie is such a lovely person. She—"

"Stop right there," he said, holding up his hand with the fork in it. "Callie and I worked on a committee together at the school where our kids are best friends. That's it. Nothing more is going to happen there, okay?"

And maybe the more I repeat that, the more it will become true.

"Fine." Cora shrugged then sat back, crossing her arms, every bit as stubborn as that bull out in his fields that refused to move until he wanted to. "Stay alone. Suffer. Not my business. But what about Maisy? What she needs?"

Here we go again.

They'd had this same conversation so many times he'd lost count. It always ended the same, with Cora mad and him feeling like an idiot for being lured in again. But he'd walked right into it this time, so there was no excuse. No escaping it, either, apparently.

"What Maisy needs is a father who takes care of her and protects her."

Cora seemed to consider that for a long moment, then leaned forward to let him have it. "You know what I think? I think you're scared. And I think you're using Sierra's death as an excuse to avoid taking a chance on being happy again."

EZ looked up sharply. "How dare you—"

"Oh, don't give me that, sonny. I've known you since you were in diapers and your bluster doesn't bother me at all. What I see is you blaming yourself for something that was beyond your control and punishing yourself for it by pushing away the first woman you've cared about in a while."

"I don't care about Callie that way!"

"Uh-huh. Sure. And water isn't wet," Cora said. "Anyone with one good eye can see that's not true."

Pissed off, more at himself than anyone else for being so obvious about the whole thing with Callie, he left half his dinner uneaten and went upstairs to take a shower. Fine. Maybe he had been drooling after Callie like a lovesick puppy, but all that stopped tomorrow. He'd meet her and they'd wrap up the fundraiser business, and whatever was happening between them would end before anyone got hurt.

It was the smart way to handle things.

Too bad he wasn't exactly feeling like a genius right now.

The next day at 5:30 p.m. sharp, Callie stood outside the elementary school's entrance, her nerves wound tight as piano wire. She'd spent the time since her phone call with Ezra alternating between relief that she'd finally have a chance to tell him how she felt about that kiss and terror over how he'd react. Which was silly. They were both adults. Both with lives and responsibilities and way too much going on to worry about one silly kiss. Taking things any further between them would be way too complicated, too risky, too... everything. It made no sense and went against everything she'd moved back here to find—peace, quiet, space for herself and Luka to be free. Safety. Security.

Ezra pulled into the parking lot then and stepped out of his truck, all long legs and confident swagger, and her heart did a flip without her consent. Honestly, no man should be allowed to be that effortlessly sexy. It was unfair.

"Hey," he said, flashing her an easy smile as he held the door for her and they went inside. The hallway smelled like disinfectant and childhood—crayon shavings, playground dirt, the lingering sweetness of juice boxes. They followed the handwritten signs Martha had taped to the lockers and ended up in the library again, where they'd first met as a committee. They sat at one of the small tables, their knees brushing as they got situated. She hazarded a glance at him from beneath her lashes, noting the dark circles under his eyes. She wondered if he'd been part of the rescue the day before. She'd been working with another patient when they'd brought the woman into Teton Memorial's ER. She was fine, thank goodness, but those missions had to take a toll on the team members.

"So," Callie said, pulling a folder of stuff she'd printed out from Martha's email from the tote bag she'd brought. She set it between them on the table like a shield. "Thanks for meeting me."

"Of course. It's our duty, right?" His tone matched hers—

polite, distant. Nothing like the man who'd held her while they danced, who'd kissed her senseless beneath that oak tree.

They spent the next fifteen minutes going over the final tallies from their tables, handing out thank-you-note assignments, and reviewing the committee disbandment logistics. When it was over, an awkward silence descended, both of them looking anywhere but at each other until finally, Callie couldn't take it anymore. *Time to get this over with.*

"Ezra, I like you. As a person. I think you're a great rescue team member and rancher, and a wonderful father to Maisy, but I don't think we should pursue that kiss any further."

He looked up at her, his hazel gaze intense as he focused on her. "Go on."

"I just… I'm not looking to get involved with anyone that way." She clasped her hands atop the table to keep them from trembling. *Why am I so nervous? This is what I want. Isn't it?*

One moment stretched into two as she collected her scattered thoughts, feeling oddly obligated to justify her decision to him when she knew darn well she didn't have to justify her decisions to anyone. "It isn't you," she said, wincing internally at the clichéd words. "I mean, my marriage was a train wreck. My husband was constantly chasing the next big thrill, the next adrenaline rush. He put that ahead of everything else, including me and Luka. I couldn't take that anymore. Luka deserved better. I deserved better. I came back here to Jackson to start over, start fresh. And while I admire you and everything you do with your BSAR team, that's basically everything I left behind. I won't go back to Luka and I being second to anyone or anything again. I won't spend half my life worrying if the person I love will come home to me safe and sound and alive. That's no way to live. I want a quiet, comfortable, risk-free life from here on out. Which means you and I aren't compatible."

Ezra watched her for a long moment, so long that she had to look away for fear he'd see into her very soul. Finally, he sat back in his chair and scrubbed his hands over his face, his shoulders shaking. At first, she thought he might be crying, and she felt awful. Then she realized he was laughing. At her, most likely, and then she felt irritated.

"What's so funny?" she asked.

"This whole situation."

Callie felt her stomach clench. Maybe she'd misread the whole thing and made herself look ridiculous, but no. That kiss they'd shared had been real. Passionate, heartfelt, hot. No one could fake that. "Why?"

"Because we've both been dancing around this subject for so long, not realizing that we're in sync."

Oh. Right. Well, that was good then. No hurt feelings, no messy emotions.

It made her feel more deflated than she'd expected.

"I came here tonight to tell you the same thing." His words came out in a relieved rush, like he'd been holding them back for a while now. "We can't do this. I can't do this." He gestured between them. "I can't let myself care about you. It's not fair to you or to Maisy."

"Why not?" she asked before she could stop herself. She knew she should just leave it as it was. She'd gotten what she wanted, a clean break. But for some reason she couldn't. "Why is you caring about someone not fair?"

A small muscle worked in Ezra's cheek, his jaw tight. Maybe she'd pushed it too far, but it was too late now. He looked away from her, then back, his hazel eyes dark now with what looked like a mix of anger and pain. "What happened to Sierra was my fault. I wasn't there. Didn't protect her when she needed me the most. And I wouldn't be able to protect you, either. Because that's what I do. I fail the people who matter most to me. And I have my hands full now just making sure Maisy is safe."

"I didn't ask you to protect me." She should stop, she knew that, yet something deep inside her compelled her to keep going. "I don't want you to protect me. Maisy probably doesn't, either. She just wants a dad who loves her." She shook her head. "Look, I understand your guilt. I think its misplaced, but I understand it. I felt guilty, too, divorcing my husband and uprooting Luka's life, but I knew it was for the best. You acting like a martyr because you think you're protecting everyone else by sacrificing any chance at a new love makes no sense. Especially when it clearly only makes you miserable."

Stop it. Stop making this worse. You got what you wanted. Get up and go home.

Yet her body refused to move, keeping her there, keeping her engaged in this conversation that was only digging deeper and becoming more personal, more intimate by the second.

He snorted. "Like you're one to talk, Callie Dupree." His voice was rougher now, more honest. "What about you and your fears? You divorced your ex because he was a self-absorbed adrenaline junkie, but now, you're saying you won't get involved with me or anyone like me because my missions with the team are dangerous. I mean, I get it, but don't kid yourself. I saw your face that day you came out with me to watch. Saw the war between condemnation and craving. You say you hate risk, but you miss having a little bit of it in your life, I think."

The accuracy of that hit like a physical blow. The truth

was he was spot on. And Callie felt her defensive walls slam back into place. They stared at each other across the small space, breathing hard like they'd been running instead of arguing. The air between them crackled with anger and attraction and something deeper, more painful.

"Fine," Callie said finally. "Maybe we're both too broken for love. But that's good because we're not going down that road, anyway, right? Isn't that what we just agreed?"

"It is. You're right," Ezra said, pushing to his feet.

Callie stood too, not realizing how close they were until she bumped into him, and he put a hand on her arm to steady her and suddenly every inch of her felt electrified. It was like they were right back under than oak tree, his face so close to hers that she could see the exhaustion warring with desire in his eyes, feel the warmth of his body, smell the soap and fabric softener from his skin. Neither of them moved.

"We should leave," she whispered. "This is a terrible idea, and we should walk away."

"We should," he agreed, his gaze locked on her mouth as his hands came up to frame her face, gentle despite everything the tension pulsing between them. His thumb traced along her cheekbone, and she leaned into the touch, unable to stop herself, as her eyes slid closed. "But I can't seem to stay away from you, Callie."

"Ezra—" she murmured, trying to force herself to pull away, walk out the door and never look back, and losing the battle completely.

"I'm going to hurt you," he said quietly. "Disappoint you. Let you down when you need me most. I'm the walking definition of risk."

"I know. And I'm going to panic and push you away the first time you put yourself in danger," she replied. "We're both disasters waiting to happen."

He exhaled slowly, his warm breath fanning her lips. One of them needed to end this before it went any further. Neither of them moved.

"This would be the worst idea either of us has ever had," Ezra agreed.

Then his lips touched hers, softly and tentatively, tasting like regret and possibility, and Callie's brain short-circuited. All those reasons why this could never happen, should never happen, drowned under a tsunami of endorphins and sinful pleasure. The kiss was brief, careful, loaded with everything they'd tried to deny. When they broke apart, both were breathing unsteadily.

"I, uh, I should go," Callie said, not moving.

"Probably."

"Before we do something even more stupid."

"Good plan."

Forcing herself to step back at last, Callie picked up the folder off the table and shoved it back in her tote bag, her hands shaking slightly. Ezra stayed where he was, watching her, his expression unreadable. She made it all the way to the door before she heard him call her name softly.

"Callie—"

"Don't." She paused, not trusting herself to look at him. "Just...don't."

She made it to her car then sat in the school parking lot as the sun set, all the emotions she'd been holding back so tightly breaking free, crashing over her in waves. She wanted Ezra Benson. Against her wishes, against all logic, against every self-preservation instinct screaming at her to run.

Thankfully, by the time she made it home, she'd pulled herself together enough to get through dinner and bedtime routines with Luka. But later, after her son was asleep, she sat on her small back patio with a cup of tea and stared out at the mountains.

She'd come back to Jackson for a fresh start. For stability. For the chance to build a quiet, predictable life for herself and Luka.

Getting involved with Ezra Benson would be the opposite of everything she'd planned.

Then don't. It's not too late to tell him it won't work.

But as she went to bed that night, she could still feel his hands on her face, his kiss on her lips, and knew with sinking certainty, that it was already too late for her. Telling herself to stop caring about him was about as effective as telling her heart to stop beating.

Apparently, she'd crossed some line along the way and now this thing between them had a momentum all its own, and threatened to sweep them both away if they weren't careful.

CHAPTER SEVEN

EZ ADJUSTED HIS tie for the third time, catching his reflection in the hallway mirror. The navy blue suit had been hanging in his closet for two years, bought for funerals and weddings that never seemed to come. Tonight, it felt like armor.

How the hell did I get here?

Oh, right. He'd gotten here because he'd kissed Callie Dupree in the school library instead of ending things like he'd planned. Then, to top it all off, the other day he'd texted her and asked her out for dinner. Worse still, she'd said yes. So now, they were going out. On a real date.

It had been late, and he'd been lonely and unable to sleep, as memories of their kisses ate away at his good intentions. He'd hit Send then regretted it immediately. But it was too late to back out now. Callie had become a drug he couldn't seem to resist no matter how awful the aftereffects might be.

It shouldn't be a big deal, he told himself for the umpteenth time. Adult people went to dinner together all the time. People dated. So what? Have a nice dinner, some nice adult conversation with someone who didn't work for him or wasn't on the BSAR team. Eat some good food, then go home. End of story.

Except it felt like a really big deal to him, probably because this was first time he'd dated since Sierra. And no matter how many times he told himself it wasn't important, his gut told him this wasn't just some casual fling like what he did in Cheyenne. There was nothing casual about what was happening between him and Callie at all.

What the hell am I doing?

He just hoped he didn't do anything too dumb.

After fiddling with his stupid tie yet again, he sighed and smoothed his damp palms down the front of his suit coat.

Maisy bounced into the hallway, pigtails flying. "Daddy, you look fancy!"

"Thank you, monkey."

"Are you nervous?"

Terrified. "A little."

"That's silly. Dr. Callie likes you. I can tell because she gets that smiley look when she sees you."

"Smiley look?"

"Like when I see ice cream." Maisy nodded sagely. "It's a good look."

Before EZ could process that particular piece of kid wisdom, the doorbell rang. After a deep breath for courage, he opened it to find Callie holding Luka's hand. The kids were finally having that sleepover they'd wanted, but the thought quickly left him as his brain went temporarily offline.

The dark green dress she wore hugged her curves and fell to just above her knees, with heels that brought her closer to his height. Her long blond hair was down, falling in soft waves around her shoulders, and she'd done something with makeup that made her eyes look even more luminous.

Breathe, Benson. Form words.

"Hi," he finally said, notching one mark on his mental dumb list already and they weren't even out the door. Not good.

"Hello." Her cheeks pinkened slightly and he realized he'd been staring. Notch number two.

"You look…wow."

"Thank you," she said, tucking her hair behind her hair and looking away demurely. "You, too. Uh, I mean, you look handsome in your suit. Really handsome."

Behind him, he heard Maisy giggle and heat prickled up from beneath the collar of his dress shirt. He hadn't felt this gawky and gangly since high school.

Realizing he was being rude, he quickly stepped aside and gestured for them to come in. "Cora's busy in the kitchen making dinner for the kids, and I hear there might be a movie involved."

"With popcorn?" Luka asked hopefully.

"Lots of popcorn," Cora confirmed from the kitchen. Moments later, she peeked her head around the corner to smile at them all. "Now, go on, you two. The reservations won't wait."

EZ had chosen the restaurant carefully, with advice from his trusted BSAR teammates. Jules and Andy had both suggested something upscale enough to feel special, but not so fancy that they'd feel like they were on display, because obviously once the town figured they were out on a date everyone would be watching. It almost reminded him of when he was working in LA and people would recognize him from the show and ask for autographs when he and the other guys were just out and about, living their lives. It was flattering, sure, but also made him feel like he was in a fishbowl, on display.

Maybe that's why he was still on edge as he drove them into town in his freshly cleaned and polished truck. Maybe they should have gone to Cheyenne instead for this first foray, somewhere without the added pressure of public scrutiny on top of the regular first-date jitters. Except it was too late now.

Gah. Stop questioning every decision, Benson.

"You okay?" Callie asked in the quiet shadows of the truck interior. "You seem tense."

"Just overthinking things, as usual."

She snorted. "Welcome to the club." After looking out the passenger window for a moment, she added, "This is the first time I've gone on a date since the divorce."

"Same. I mean, since Sierra." He glanced at her, then back at the road.

They fell into comfortable silence, but EZ could feel the weight of anticipation between them building as he parked the truck in the lot behind the restaurant, then walked around to open her door, her sweet floral scent surrounding him as they entered the restaurant. It was a new place that had opened not long ago called the Moonlit Hearth. He'd checked their website when making the reservation and it was described at cozy and quiet, and served a variety of French and American cuisine, including vegan options, if Callie was into that. Once they stepped inside, he was relieved to find dim lighting and lots of booths, the kind of place where they could talk without having to shout. The hostess seated them in the corner with a view of the mountains, candlelight flickering of the table.

"This is nice," Callie said, looking around. "I've been wanting to try this place since I moved back."

"Well, it's good we're here then," he said, picking up his menu to have something to do with his hands beside fidget.

Their server came and they ordered wine, appetizers, and entrées based on the server's suggestions. If the food tasted half as good as the smells wafting out from the kitchen, he'd be happy. Not that he'd probably notice much, considering how distracted he was by the woman across the table from him. After a couple of sips of wine, Callie seemed to relax a little more, talking about her week at the hospital, and he in turn told her all about Maisy's latest adventures, delighted when she laughed at his stories, captivated by how her whole face lit up with happiness in a way that made his chest tight. He stopped himself form rubbing the area over his heart...barely.

Slow down there, cowboy. This is one date, not a lifelong commitment.

"Penny for your thoughts," Callie said, watching him over the rim of her wineglass.

"Nothing," he said, taking a gulp of his own chardonnay then shrugging, trying to act casual when he felt anything but. "I was thinking about how nice it is just to sit and talk with someone like this. Not that I don't have other adults to talk to, but they either work for me or on BSAR or—as Cora likes to remind me—have known me since I was in diapers."

Callie giggled, the sound shimmering around him like a favorite song. "Cora has a way with words."

"That she does." He grinned. "But she takes good care of me and Maisy, so I can't complain too much."

Something shifted in her expression, the light in her eyes dimming slightly with something he couldn't quite name. Sadness, maybe. No. Loneliness. The recognition resonated deep inside him.

"It's good to have people around who take care of us."

"Who takes care of you, Callie?" he asked before he could stop himself. "Your parents are down in Florida now, right? I remembered when their house went on the market. Have you reconnected with any of your old friends here since you've been back?"

She shrugged, not looking at him. "Yeah, my parents have a place in St. Petersburg now. And sure. I see people at the hospital, catch up with them there, but it's hard, you know? I don't have a lot of time between work and being a single parent. I'm sure you understand."

"More than you know." He finished off his first glass of wine then poured them both a refill. "Maisy's great and I'm sure Luka is, too, but sometimes you just need another grown up to talk to."

"Exactly." Callie exhaled slowly, her shoulders visibly relaxing as the server brought their appetizer, the house smoked Idaho trout dip with grilled flatbread and pita. They each fixed a plate then dug in. EZ was starving. He hadn't eaten since lunch, at first because he was too busy, then later because he was too nervous for tonight. "I mean, don't get me wrong," she said between bites. "Luka always gives me a fresh perspective on things. Kids see things differently than adults do. Less complicated."

"True." He studied her face in the candlelight. "Maisy does the same thing for me. Always straight to the point, always honest. Even when it's brutal." They both chuckled. "But it's refreshing, too. I get stuck in my own head sometimes and forget that what I think about myself and the world isn't always true. Maisy's my antidote to that."

They chatted more about their kids and Callie shared more with him about her life in Chicago and soon dinner arrived—local Wyoming prime rib for him and red bird half chicken for her—and his nerves gradually dissolved away as they ate slowly and talked about everything and nothing. He watched Callie's hands move as she talked, memorizing the sound of her voice.

This is what normal feels like. What good feels like.

Then, all too soon, they'd finished dessert—a slice of the restaurant's famous carrot cake, which they shared—and it was time to go. He hadn't really planned for anything past dinner, not knowing how it would go, but now, he was certain he wasn't ready for the evening to end yet. After paying the bill and giving the server a generous tip, he smiled over at Callie. "Want to get out of here?"

"Where did you have in mind?"

"Trust me?"

Callie was quiet for a moment, watching him closely, then nodded. "Yeah. I trust you."

As they drove through the quiet streets of Jackson, past the town square with its iconic elk-antler arches, toward the valley's north side, Callie watched the landscape change from commercial to residential to increasingly rural, her curiosity building.

"Are you kidnapping me?" she asked lightly.

"Would it help if I said it was for your own good?"

"That's exactly what a kidnapper would say."

He laughed, the sound deep and rich and downright dangerous to her composure. She'd spent the entire dinner trying not to spend too much time watching him, fighting the urge to trace the line of his jaw with her fingertips, or smooth the small furrow between his eyebrows when he was thinking.

Get a grip, Dupree. It's just dinner.

But it didn't seem like just dinner, and she was pretty sure he felt it, too.

At last, EZ pulled into a small parking area she didn't recognize, near what looked like a trailhead. In the darkness, she saw the outline of mountains against the star-filled sky.

"It's beautiful here," she said when he came around to open her door for her, helped her out and into her coat before putting on his own. Such a gentleman. "But I'm not exactly dressed for hiking."

"No hiking required. Promise." He went to the back of his truck and pulled out a blanket and what looked like a thermos. "Just a short walk to one of my favorite places."

The path was flat and well-maintained, leading through a grove of aspens toward an open meadow. Even in the dark, Callie sensed the vastness of the space around them, the way the land opened up to embrace the sky.

"Here we are," EZ said, spreading the blanket near the center of the meadow.

They settled down beside each other, a tapestry of stars in the heavens above them, more brilliant than anything Callie had seen in years of city living. The Milky Way stretched overhead like a river of light.

"This is so beautiful," she breathed. "Thank you for bringing me here."

"One of the benefits of living in the middle of nowhere." EZ opened the thermos and poured her a cup of hot coffee, then took a swig straight from the thermos himself. "I used to come here a lot after Sierra died. When the house felt too big and too quiet."

"Does it still? Feel too big?" she asked before she could stop herself. Thankfully, the darkness hid her wince. Regardless of how curious she was about his past, she hadn't planned on bringing it up tonight.

At first, she didn't think he'd answer, because he just stared up at the sky. Then, finally, he glanced over at her, smiling, his teeth white in the darkness. "Not as much lately, to be honest. Not since you and Luka came back to town."

Callie's breath caught in her chest and her heart did something complicated. They were sitting close enough that his warmth surrounded her as did the scent of his cologne—musk and pine and a hint of something purely Ezra. Silence stretched between them, comfortable but charged.

"Callie," he said at last as he set aside the thermos, then shifted slightly to face her. "About the night in the library. I'm not sure—"

She faced him, too, her coffee forgotten beside her now. "I'm not sure, either, Ezra. I'm not sure what we're doing here, not sure if it's good or bad, or right or wrong. All I do know is that it seems inevitable, somehow. It terrifies me and comforts me at the same time. Does that make sense?"

He nodded then leaned in slowly and she met him halfway.

This time, it wasn't careful or hesitant. This time, she poured months of longing and confusion and hope into the contact, and he responded with equal intensity. His hands tangled in her hair, hers fisted in his shirt, and for a moment the world narrowed to just this—the taste of him, the feel of his mouth on hers, the way he said her name against her lips like a prayer.

When they finally broke apart, both breathing hard, Callie felt breathless and brazen and beautiful for the first time in a long time, thanks to the man who was looking at her like she was the most wonderful thing he'd ever seen.

"Wow," EZ said unsteadily, his gaze still locked on her mouth.

"Yeah. Wow." Her words were soft and shaky.

They settled in again, the blanket around them, Ezra's arm around her shoulders, keeping her close to his side, his chin resting about her head as they sat quietly, just taking it all in.

"Callie, I never expected you. Never expected to feel the things I'm feeling again. This is moving fast and I think we're both scared, and there are a dozen reasons why this is complicated, and we should walk away." He shook his head, his hazel eyes full of conflict. "But I also think I can't.

Not yet." He cupped her face in his hands, thumbs tracing her cheekbones. "You should probably be the responsible adult here."

"Probably," she agreed, clasping his wrists, but otherwise not moving. "We should slow down, though. Not rush into anything we might regret."

"Yes." He nodded, leaning his forehead against hers. "We need to be responsible."

"Agreed." She took a shuddering breath. "Except I'm not feeling particularly responsible right now."

"So what should we do?" he asked. "Because my house is full of Cora and kids."

"My place is empty," she suggested, shocked at herself, but also feeling more alive than she had in years. Maybe there was something to risk taking after all. At least for this one night.

"Yeah?" he asked, pulling back to look in her eyes. "Are you sure?"

"Absolutely," she said, then kissed him again, like she'd been wanting to do since the meadow.

Callie didn't remember much about the drive to her house in town, didn't remember getting out of the truck and in through the front door, which took her three times to unlock because her hands were shaking so bad and she dropped the keys twice. Once in her living room, she glanced around, suddenly nervous because she hadn't planned on having anyone here, but they weren't really there for the interior design, so…

"Coffee?" she asked, for lack of anything better as Ezra Benson stood in her home, looking bigger and stronger and much more masculine than he had before, making her pulse pound and her blood sing in her veins. She hadn't wanted someone this much in a long, long time, maybe ever.

"I don't think either of us wants coffee," he said, stepping closer to her in a way that made her want to climb him like a tree. And from the way he was looking at her—like she was something precious and fierce and necessary—the feeling was mutual.

"Callie." He moved closer still, walking her backward until she was pressed against the wall, his hands coming up to rest beside her, caging her in in the best possible way. "Are you sure about this?"

Instead of answering with words, she reached up and loosened his tie, then slid it off around his neck and let it fall to the floor, not missing how his breath hissed between his teeth and the tightness in his muscles.

"I'm sure," she said softly, resting her hand on his chest, feeling his heart race beneath her palm. "Are you?"

"God, yes!"

This time when he kissed her, it was with the full weight of his restraint breaking apart. He picked her up, carried her into the open kitchen, and set her atop the granite island, the stone cold beneath her as she wrapped her legs around his heat, pulling him closer.

Eventually, they fumbled their way to her bedroom between kisses, leaving a trail of clothing and whispered endearments in their wake.

Making love with Ezra was like nothing she'd ever experienced before. His hands mapped every inch of her skin like he was memorizing her, his voice reverent when he whispered her name against her throat. And those walls she'd built around her heart after the divorce began to crack and crumble despite her wishes, despite knowing that this was one night, not forever.

And afterward, as Ezra gathered her against him after taking her over the edge of ecstasy and back again, her head on his chest, his heart steady under her ear, Callie forgot about the risk, forgot about everything except this moment with this man. She might regret it tomorrow, but she couldn't bring herself to do it tonight.

They talked quietly for hours, and when Callie finally fell asleep in his arms, she felt more satisfied than she had in years.

And that's what worried her most.

CHAPTER EIGHT

EZ WOKE A few hours later, disoriented for a moment by the unfamiliar room, the soft breathing beside him, the weight of an arm across his chest. Then memory flooded back—dinner, stargazing, the way Callie had kissed him like she was drowning, and he was air.

What did I do?

Not the making-love part. That had been...pretty damn wonderful. Sweet, hot, intense. More than just the physical. He wasn't going overboard, he knew they weren't in a "relationship." But to him it felt like they'd...connected on a deeper level. More than sex, more than just a biological urge. He'd almost forgotten that was possible.

Which was probably why he was waking up in a panic now.

In all the time he'd driven up to Cheyenne in the last two years to take care of things, he'd never once spent the night. And now, he was with Callie Dupree. In her bed. In her life. He turned his head slightly to see her sleeping face—soft and peaceful and trusting—and, oh, boy. That was bad.

Because all he could think now was how Sierra used to look exactly like that in the morning.

Before he'd failed her.

Carefully, EZ slipped out of bed, gathered his clothes, and dressed in the living room. He needed to get out of here. Needed to get home. Needed to get some space to think.

Needed to remember why he'd spent two years avoiding exactly this situation.

He left a brief note on the kitchen counter saying he'd drive her car back over to her house later when he brought Luka home that day because he didn't want to leave her stranded and because he didn't want to be rude. Well, ruder than he already was. Which only made him feel worse. Then he let himself out into the predawn quiet.

The drive back to the ranch gave him twenty minutes to spiral into all the ways this could go horribly wrong. All the ways he could fail again. All the ways in which life could step in and destroy everything again in the blink of an eye.

Except you don't love Callie Dupree, he reminded himself. *Right?*

He scowled and stepped on the brakes as a raccoon ran across the road in front of his truck.

No, he didn't love Callie. It was way safer for everyone if he didn't. Because when he loved someone, he lost them. He failed them.

What about Maisy?

His daughter was different. And he lived with a constant fear that if he didn't keep everything under control, he could lose her, too. So, yeah. No. He didn't love Callie. He couldn't.

The ranch was quiet when he arrived. For a second, he thought maybe he'd gotten lucky and he could sneak in before Cora got up. But, no. He didn't get more than three steps from the kitchen door, before she called to him from the walk-in pantry. "Good morning! How was your night? Must've been pretty good considering the time you're getting home," she said, sticking her head out with a grin, which quickly fell. "What's wrong?"

"Nothing," he grumbled, walking over to pour himself

a cup of the fresh coffee in the pot on the counter. "Everything." He sank down in a chair at the table and scrubbed a hand over his face. "I don't know."

Cora emerged from the pantry and gave him a flat stare and a sigh. "I do. You're doing what you always do."

"And what's that?" he asked testily.

"Borrowing trouble from tomorrow instead of enjoying what you've got today."

He ground his teeth. The last thing he needed right now was a bunch of folksy advice from his housekeeper. "It's complicated, Cora."

"Usually is." She studied him with knowing eyes. "But running away isn't the answer, either."

"I'm not running!"

"Sure." She made a show of checking the smartwatch he'd bought her for Christmas last year. "And that's why you're sitting in my kitchen at six thirty on Saturday morning wearing yesterday's clothes and looking like someone kicked your favorite dog. If that's not running, I don't know what is."

He wanted to tell her that it wasn't her kitchen—it was his and he didn't need her advice—but dammit, she was right. Just as well, because before he could say anything, Maisy appeared in the doorway in her dinosaur flannel pajamas, her auburn hair sticking up at impossible angles.

Bleary-eyed, she frowned at him. "Why are you fighting with Cora, Daddy?"

The question hit him like a bullet. "I'm not fighting with Cora, monkey. We were just talking."

Maisy did not look convinced. "Where's Callie?"

"She's at home," he said past his constricted vocal cords. He should've slept in his truck until everyone cleared out. Saved himself a bunch of questions.

"Why?" Maisy's face fell. "Luka's here so she's all by herself."

"She's probably tired," he said, ignoring Cora's pointed look at his answer. He cleared his throat and tried again. "Adults need their sleep."

"But—"

"How about we make pancakes for when Luka wakes up?" Cora interrupted smoothly. "You can help me crack the eggs."

As Maisy bounced off to wash her hands, EZ stood, thinking this might be a good time to escape, only to find his way blocked by Cora.

"You know what your problem is?" she said, tapping the tip of the spatula against his chest. "You think happiness is something that gets taken away instead of something you choose every day."

"Cora—"

"Sierra would be furious with you right now. That woman loved you enough to want you to be happy, even without her."

The words hit like a physical blow and that was it. It was one thing to take him to task. It was another to bring his dead wife into this. Anger prickling up his neck, he said lowly to avoid Maisy hearing from down the hall, "That is none of your business. You don't know what she would think about my life now."

"I know she wouldn't want you punishing yourself for the rest of your life because she died."

Outraged, more because she was right than because she was wrong, EZ opened his mouth to respond, only to be cut off again, this time by Luka, who stood in the doorway, rubbing his sleepy eyes.

"Mr. EZ? Is my mom okay? Maisy said you came home without her."

Great. Now, I have to explain to a seven-year-old why I ran away from his mother.

"She's fine, buddy," he said, forcing his tense shoulders to relax. "She's at home sleeping. I'll take you home later in her car."

"Oh." Luka climbed onto a kitchen stool. "You didn't have a sleepover with her?"

EZ choked on his coffee. "What?"

Thankfully, Maisy returned then and the kids and Cora got busy making breakfast, allowing him to flee upstairs to his room. After a nice long shower, he climbed into bed to try and get a little more shut-eye, only to have his nightmares return full force. Always the same—snow, ice, the sound of Sierra calling his name, the crushing weight of being too late.

He woke up gasping, reaching for Callie, only to remember she wasn't there. That he hadn't let her be there.

Later that day, the sleep deprivation made him irritable, unfocused. He'd snapped at Dave during a training exercise with the BSAR team, then made a spotting error that could have been dangerous if Andy hadn't caught it in time.

Once they'd returned to the hangar, Andy pulled him aside. "Everything okay?"

"Fine," he growled, shoving his gear into his locker then slamming the door shut. "I just didn't sleep well last night is all. Sorry about the mistakes. They won't happen again."

Andy watched him closely. The guy was quiet, so when he said something, it was usually powerful. "I'm not worried about the mistakes. I'm worried about you. Jules said you were out with Callie Dupree last night."

EZ started to ask how Jules knew about that but stopped himself. Of course everyone knew. Jackson, despite all its fancy homes and rich vacationers, was just a small town at heart. He should know better. He did know better. Still, having everyone up in his business didn't sit well with him. He shook his head and stepped around Andy. "I'm fine. Everything's fine. Don't worry about me."

But EZ was starting to worry about himself. He'd thought by putting some distance between them after last night, things would go back to normal. That she'd be out of his system. But it wasn't turning out that way. He kept thinking about her, about last night, about how she'd felt and sounded and tasted. About how he really wanted to go back over there and take her back to bed again, but he couldn't do that because he couldn't get attached. He had to protect her and Luka by staying away. He didn't deserve nice, normal things like love and happiness and a future with someone.

And maybe if he repeated that enough times, his stupid heart would get on board with it.

It didn't seem to work, though, which was why he sat on his front porch at midnight that night, staring at his phone, torn between returning the calls she'd made to his phone that day, or facing the voice mails he'd been too scared to listen to.

Such a coward.

One more reason she deserved better than him. Better than someone who carried so much guilt and fear that he could barely function emotionally.

He sighed and stared up at the starry sky until his phone vibrated in his hand again and Callie's name glowed on the screen. After a deep breath, he straightened and hit the answer button because enough was enough.

"Hi," he answered, his voice rougher than he'd intended.

"Hey," Callie said, sounding cautious. "Just wanted to make sure you were okay. You left in a hurry this morning, so…"

Straight to the point. One of the many things he liked about her.

"I left a note," he said, knowing it was lame.

"Yeah, I saw it." She hesitated and EZ lived and died in those few seconds. Finally, she asked in a quiet voice, "Do you regret it? What we did. Because if you so, just say so. I'm a big girl. I can handle it."

"No. God, no. That's not—" He scrubbed a hand over his face. "Last night was perfect. You're perfect."

"Then what's wrong?"

Everything. Nothing. Me.

"I'm not good at this," he said at last, knowing it was an excuse, but it was the best he had just then. "The relationship thing. The letting someone in."

"I know. Neither am I. Not anymore." She sighed. "But I thought we both understood that."

He exhaled slowly. "It's late. You should get some sleep."

A long pause. Then she said in a cooler tone, "Right. Sleep. Okay."

"Callie—"

But she'd already hung up.

EZ sat on the porch until sunrise, staring at his phone, knowing he'd just thrown away what was probably the best chance he'd had at a new future in years.

Better to hurt her a little now than destroy her completely later.

But as the sun crested the mountains, painting the sky in shades of pink and gold, he couldn't shake the feeling that he'd just lost something precious and rare in his life.

The ER at Teton Memorial was having what the staff diplomatically called "a Sunday." Which meant chaos barely contained by computers and caffeine.

Callie finished suturing an eight-year-old's chin—courtesy of an ill-advised skateboard trick—and was washing her hands when one of the nurses poked his head around the curtain.

"Dr. Dupree? We've got a four-year-old in bay three with a LEGO stuck up his nose, a six-year-old in bay five who may have eaten her grandmother's blood-pressure medication, and twins in bay two who superglued their hands together."

Just another day in paradise.

At least staying busy kept her from thinking about last night with Ezra and the fact he'd bolted this morning before she'd woken up and what that might mean. He'd left a short note in the kitchen, which made it all about as clear as mud.

With a sigh, Callie pulled paper towels from the dispenser on the wall, then said, "Okay. Get poison control on the line for bay five, stat. I'll take the twins first since that's probably the quickest, then the LEGO situation."

"You're the boss," the nurse said, giving her a grin and a cheeky wink before leaving.

If she was the boss around here today, then they were all in trouble.

After taking care of the discharge paperwork for her current patient, Callie made her way to bay two, where identical ten-year-old boys sat on the exam table, their right hands firmly adhered to each other at the palms. They looked significantly less pleased with their science experiment than they probably had an hour ago.

"So," Callie said, pulling up a stool. "Want to tell me how this happened?"

"We were testing if superglue really works," the one on the left said.

"Spoiler alert—it does," added his brother.

"I can see that. I'm Dr. Dupree. Which one of you is which?"

"I'm Mason," said the one on the left. "He's Dixon."

"Your parents named you Mason and Dixon?"

"They thought it was funny," Dixon said with the weary tone of someone who'd had this conversation many times.

"They have a unique sense of humor." Callie examined their glued hands, noting that at least they'd had the sense not to use their fingers—just palm to palm. "Good news— we can fix this. Bad news—it's going to take some time and a lot of acetone. And you're both going to smell like a nail salon for a while."

"Will it hurt?" Mason asked, eyes wide.

"Nope. But it'll be boring. You'll be sitting here while we dissolve the glue bit by bit."

"Can we at least get Popsicles?" Dixon asked hopefully.

"We'll see how cooperative you are during the removal process."

Callie left a PA instructions and plenty of acetone-soaked cotton pads, then moved on to bay three, where a miserable-looking little boy sat with his mother hovering anxiously.

"Hi there. I'm Dr. Dupree. I hear you've got something that doesn't belong in your nose?"

The boy nodded, his eyes red from crying.

"It's a LEGO," his mother said. "The little round one? He was—" She glanced at her son. "We're not entirely sure what he was doing."

"Seeing if it would fit," the boy mumbled.

"And the answer is yes," Callie said matter-of-factly. "Which you now know. What's your name?"

"Noah"

"Okay, Noah. Here's what's going to happen. I'm going to look up your nose with this very bright light to see exactly where our LEGO friend ended up. Then we're going to get him out. It might be uncomfortable, but it shouldn't hurt. Sound good?"

Noah nodded, looking slightly less nervous now.

The extraction took all of three minutes with the right tools. Callie held up the offending LEGO piece—a small yellow cylinder—triumphantly.

"Ta-da! Want to keep it as a souvenir?"

"No," Noah said emphatically.

"Fair enough. Now, Noah, buddy, let me give you some advice—your nose is for breathing and smelling, not for storage. If you want to hide LEGOs from your sister, I suggest a shoebox under your bed like everyone else."

His mother gave her a grateful look as Callie left to give the nurses discharge instructions for him, then headed to bay five for the most serious case, the six-year-old who had indeed ingested her grandmother's medication, but poison control confirmed it was a small enough dose that monitoring and activated charcoal would be sufficient. Callie spent twenty minutes soothing both the terrified little girl and her equally terrified grandmother, explaining exactly what they were doing and why.

By the time she'd checked on all her patients and updated their charts, two hours had passed in what felt like twenty minutes. Time for her fifteen-minute break.

She washed up then headed to the staff break room and pulled out the hasty lunch she'd packed for herself before leaving her house. In his note, Ezra had said he'd bring her car back along with Luka when she was ready, but since she'd been called in for an unexpected shift it had worked out well to have her son at the ranch. She'd caught a ride in to work with one of the ER nurses who lived nearby.

After pulling her container of soup from the microwave,

Callie took a seat at one of the small tables against the wall and pulled out her phone to check her emails in the otherwise deserted break room. Considering the noise she'd left behind in the ER, the quiet was a little bit of bliss.

As she ate, however, her thoughts circled back to Ezra and how he'd slipped out before dawn without waking her after their night together, how he'd answered her texts about Luka. But that was it, nothing about last night at all. It all felt too familiar. The avoidance.

Just like her ex-husband, Owen, who'd pulled away whenever their marriage required actual emotional investment. Who'd used his pursuit of the next adrenaline rush as an excuse to run away from anything that truly scared him.

Stop. He isn't Owen.

But there were similarities. The emotional walls. The way he shut down when she tried to get close.

She'd just finished her last spoonful of soup when her phone buzzed. For a crazy second, she thought it might be Ezra texting to tell her he'd made the worst mistake of his life and wanted to spend the night with her again tonight, but no. It was only a text from her sister in Denver. Callie had mentioned her date with Ezra to her and now wished she hadn't.

How's the cowboy? Was he good?

Callie groaned, shook her head, and squeezed her eyes shut. Thank goodness, she was alone. If the rest of the hospital knew she and Ezra Benson had slept together there would be no end to the gossip.

It's complicated, she texted back.

Everything's complicated with you. Just be happy for once.

Easy for you to say. You married your college sweetheart.

After dating three other guys who broke my heart. Happiness isn't about avoiding pain, Cal. You know that. It's about finding someone worth the hurt.

Callie turned off her phone before Ashley could send more unsolicited wisdom. She didn't need relationship advice. She needed to figure out where things were going from here with Ezra. It wasn't like they could avoid each other. Their kids were best friends. They were going to see each other again and it was most definitely going to be awkward if they didn't handle it the right way.

She was still thinking about it later when she had her nurse friend drop her off at the ranch so she could pick up Luka and get her car. Cora met her on the porch, but Ezra was nowhere in sight. She wasn't sure if she was relieved or frustrated by that. The situation was awkward enough that even the kids noticed it.

"Mom, why are you and Mr. EZ being weird?" Luka asked her that night over dinner.

"What do you mean, honey?" she asked, trying to sound as clueless as possible.

"He used to smile a lot, but now he just looks grumpy."

He's not the only one. "I don't know, honey. Maybe he's got a lot of things going on at the ranch."

"Like what?"

"I don't know. The ponies? I'm sure it's nothing for you to worry about."

But Luka had always been far too observant for his own good. "He didn't act that way before you guys went to dinner together. Did you have a fight?"

"No," she said, shoving a forkful of instant mashed potatoes in her mouth to give her a chance to think of an answer. "Not exactly."

"Did you talk to him? That's what you tell me to do when I'm mad at someone."

"It's more complicated than that, sweetheart."

"Everything's always complicated with grown-ups," Luka sighed, sounding exactly like Maisy. "I never want to be an adult."

Callie could sympathize. She wasn't having a great time right now, either.

Honestly, she should just forget about it. It wasn't like they'd been in a relationship. It wasn't like her heart was involved here.

Was it?

No. It wasn't because she'd promised herself that she wouldn't do this again. Wouldn't be with another man who was afraid of his feelings, a man who chose to leave instead of doing the hard work to make things better.

So, if Ezra Benson didn't want a relationship with her that was fine.

Completely fine.

So fine that she'd show him exactly how fine it was with her tomorrow, when they were both assigned to be chaperones on the annual first-grade school field trip to the nature center.

CHAPTER NINE

Signing the permission slip for this field trip had seemed like a good idea to EZ at the time. A nature center visit, educational programming about local wildlife, a chance for Maisy to learn something outside the classroom. Early December in Jackson meant fewer outdoor opportunities during school hours when the weather was bad, and the kids had been bouncing off the walls for weeks. So when they had a brief warm-up and the school had asked him if he wanted to chaperone a final, impromptu excursion to the nature center for Maisy's class, he'd figured why not.

Of course, that had been before he'd slept with Callie and screwed everything up.

He'd luckily managed to avoid speaking to her in the few days since that fateful night, but today, his luck ran out.

They stood at opposite ends of the school bus with other parents and the teacher, Mrs. Patterson, in the middle, helping to supervise twenty-five first graders, who were vibrating with excitement about seeing "real animals" and "maybe…bears."

"Remember, we stay together," announced Mrs. Patterson over the cacophony of chatter. "Buddy system at all times. And if you see a bear, do *not* try to pet it."

"Even if it's really fluffy?" asked Tommy Martinez.

"Especially if it's fluffy."

EZ caught Callie's eye across the distance and swore she was trying to bite back a smile, same as him. For a moment, the knot of tension in his chest eased a bit, at just the sight of her, before he forced himself to look away again.

No more of that.

They'd made it about twenty minutes down the trail, keeping a good distance between each other, with Callie up ahead and EZ bringing up the rear of the group, trying to keep the herd of cats impersonating kids in line and doing his level best not to admire the sway of Callie's hips and how her jeans hugged her superb behind to perfection, when his phone buzzed in his pocket. His stomach sank as he pulled it out to find a team callout on the screen.

BSAR: we have reports of an injured climber on the north face of Mount Glory. Heli rescue. All available team members requested.

They'd stopped so the guide could point out some native plant species to the kids, and now, every head in the group turned to look at him as his phone continued to buzz as team members responded.

Wincing inwardly, he shoved his phone back in his pocket. "Sorry, I've got a callout with the search-and-rescue team and need to go." He put his hands on Maisy's shoulders as she stood in front of him. "Sorry, guys. I have to go help someone who's hurt."

"In the helicopter?" Maisy asked once he'd crouched in front of her, pride evident in her voice.

"Yes, monkey. In the helicopter."

"Will you be back to see the wolves?" Luka asked hopefully from where he stood in front of Callie.

EZ glanced over to them and found Callie watching him with an expression he couldn't quite read. "I'll try, buddy."

He kissed the top of Maisy's head then straightened. "Be good for Dr. Callie and Mrs. Patterson."

"I'm always good," Maisy protested.

He rushed back to the bus to ask the driver to take him back to the school so he could get his truck. On the way, he gathered more information about the injured victim. Solo climber, fall from height, unable to self-rescue. And the weather window was closing fast with an early winter-storm system moving in sooner than predicted.

The morning had started clear, but he saw the dark line of clouds building over the western peaks. The weather report had called for snow later tonight, but mountain weather was notoriously unpredictable.

The rescue took about two hours and went about as well as could be expected, considering they were pulling someone off a cliff face in deteriorating weather. Nadja flew expertly, as always, and he and Andy and Dave managed to get the poor hiker lifted into the chopper and back to base without issue. The climber's vitals stabilized on their way back to the hanger, while the storm clouds continued to build with alarming speed.

They'd barely started their team debrief afterward inside the hangar when Ruby's radio crackled to life again with a new call, this one sending EZ's heart nosediving to his toes.

"School group at Eagle Creek Nature Center reporting they can't reach one of their hiking parties. Group of five—two parent chaperones, and three kids—went on the Moose Ponds Trail two hours ago and should have been back by now."

"What?" EZ choked out past his tight vocal cords. What the hell were they doing out on the Moose Ponds Trail? The teacher had been clear that the entire group needed to stay together. And, sure, they were short one chaperone because he'd been called out for the team, but they should have been able to cope without him.

It's your fault.

Oh, God.

"We need to go!" he said, hurrying to grab his gear once again.

"EZ, wait," Andy said, trying to take his arm to stop him. "The weather is—"

"I don't give a damn about the weather!" he retorted, pulling free. "If Maisy is out there, along with Callie and Luka, I have to help them. If anything happens to any of them, I will never forgive myself. I have to find them and make sure they're safe."

"I'll help," Dave volunteered. "We can take my truck."

"Wait for me," Pete called, running after them out in the parking lot.

From what Callie remembered from her childhood, the Moose Ponds Trail was supposed to be easy. Forty-five minutes round-trip through gentle terrain, with educational stops along the way. She'd figured there was no harm in veering off a bit since she was familiar with the territory. Of course, that was before Tommy Martinez spotted what he insisted was a "baby bear" fifteen minutes into the hike.

"It's not a bear, sweetie," Callie had assured him, but Tommy had already bolted off in pursuit of what turned out to be a particularly tubby porcupine. Tommy's mother, Sara, had slipped on some wet leaves and twisted her ankle chasing after her son, so Callie had helped her over to a fallen log where she could sit and rest for a bit while Callie wrangled the three kids with them.

"I'm fine," Sara insisted, though Callie could see Sara's ankle was clearly swelling. Hopefully, it was just a bad sprain and not anything worse. She should have brought a med kit with her just in case, but hadn't thought there wouldn't be any need. Famous last words apparently.

"Just give me a few minutes," Sara said, wincing.

But the few minutes had now stretched into an hour as they waited for Sara's pain to subside enough that she could hobble back with them to find the rest of the main group. And now, as Callie looked up at the sky as they stood in an open field in front of Jenny Lake, the clear morning had given way to gathering storm clouds.

"Dr. Callie," Maisy said, tugging on her jacket. "Is it going to snow?"

"Maybe a little. Nothing to worry about," she said, trying to sound far more optimistic than she felt currently.

"I think I'm ready," Sara said, trying to stand but then giving a painful gasp as she tried to put weight on her ankle and sank back down onto the log. "Sorry. I just need a little more time."

Callie pulled out her phone again, hoping Mrs. Patterson might have received her earlier texts about their situation, but nope. Still no signal and her texts hadn't been delivered yet. Not uncommon in the mountains, but not helpful, either, in their current situation. She could head back on her own with the kids, but that would leave poor Sara out here by herself, so that wasn't an option, either. Okay. She could handle this. After all, she was a local. She'd spent endless hours in this terrain as a kid.

Figure it out, Callie.

"Right. Change of plans. Since we haven't made it back to the rest of the group yet, I think we should find some cover in case the weather gets bad." She looked over at the dark line of the pine forest ahead. Judging from her past treks around here when she was a kid, they were about two thirds of the way through the 3.2-mile trail, and it would take longer to get Sara back to the nature center in her current condition than it would to shelter in place until the storm was over. And there might be a place just up ahead, if it hadn't collapsed into ruin in the years she'd been gone. "I think there's an old, decommissioned ranger station just past the tree line in the forest, or there used to be, anyway. But if it's gone, at least the trees will provide some cover for us."

She managed to get Sara up and wrapped an arm around her waist to help support her weight, forming a human crutch while the kids carried their backpacks, chattering nervously as the first snowflakes began to fall.

"Look! Snow!" Luka proclaimed.

"It is pretty," Sara added.

Yeah. Like a fairy tale. But the temperature was also dropping, and the light flakes were already becoming heavier. Callie had watched the weather reports earlier that morning before leaving the house with Luka and they had said it could get tricky later that night, but it looked like the system had moved in earlier than expected. Not uncommon around here. But being out in the backcountry during a storm was different than being in town, and things could go south quickly.

It took another twenty minutes because of Sara's injury, but they finally found the old ranger station Callie had remembered—still standing, thankfully. A small, weathered structure that looked like it hadn't been used in years but was at least still intact. The door wasn't locked and Callie shouldered it open to reveal a single room with a dusty woodstove in one corner. After getting Sara settled atop an old crate someone had left behind, Callie inspected the rest of the space and managed to find an old storage chest filled with some shabby, abandoned supplies—a couple of tin cans with the labels removed, four granola bars of unknown age, and three unopened bottles of water. There was an old sleeping bag and one blanket, both stained and torn, and a two-way radio that looked older than Callie herself and didn't work at all when she tried to get it turned on.

"This is like camping!" Maisy declared, trying to inject cheer into a situation that was becoming worse by the minute.

Callie checked Sara's ankle again and saw some bruising now in addition to the swelling, which indicated it might well be a fracture instead of just a bad sprain. The woman needed medical attention, but that wasn't happening anytime soon.

Outside, the snow fell harder, and the wind had picked up now, too, whistling through the cracks in the old ranger station. Through the small, dirty window, Callie saw the nearby tree branches beginning to bend under the growing force of the storm.

Yeah, they weren't going anywhere for a while.

"Mommy?" Luka appeared at her elbow, his voice small. "Will EZ come rescue us?"

Callie's heart squeezed and she kneeled in front of him. "I don't know, honey. I'm sure everyone is worried and Mrs. Patterson has already let someone know we're missing, so hopefully they're looking for us now."

She remembered Ezra's calm confidence and easy manner on the team rescues she'd observed and how competently he'd assisted her with Carlos's head injury and hoped that he would be on their trail.

Out of desperation, she checked her phone again but still no signal.

They were on their own for the time being.

"Okay, kids. We're going to have an adventure. Like camping, but in a building instead of a tent."

"Will we roast marshmallows?" Tommy asked hopefully.

"Sorry, buddy. No marshmallows," Callie said, handing out a granola bar each to the kids and one to Sara. Callie could stand to miss a meal. Then she handed a bottled water to Sara to split with Tommy and divided up another bottle between herself and Maisy and Luka, saving one for later in case they needed it.

The wind howled harder now, making her think of the wolves in this area. Or worse.

If Ezra was out there, she hoped he was being careful. Because if something happened to him while he was trying to rescue them, after how they'd left things, she'd never forgive herself.

"Dr. Callie?" Maisy's voice was quiet, uncertain. "Do you think my daddy's alright?"

Callie sat down and pulled Maisy onto her lap, then unzipped her parka to wrap it around them both. "I bet your daddy is just fine, sweetheart. If anyone can find us, it's him."

Please let that be true.

CHAPTER TEN

SEARCH AND RESCUE during a blizzard was like navigating inside a washing machine. EZ braced himself against the side of the helicopter as a wind shear tried to flip them sideways, snow pelting the windows so hard they could barely see ten feet ahead.

This is insane. You should be grounded. You're going to get yourself and everyone else killed.

But somewhere down in this white hell, Callie and Luka and his daughter were lost. Along with another kid and one of the other chaperones. They'd managed to get ahold of Mrs. Patterson before leaving the hangar, so they knew how many people to search for, at least. And regardless of who was down there, he'd be damned if he was going to sit on the ground while they faced this alone. He had to do this. He owed it to Callie. He owed it to Sierra. He owed it to himself.

And he could not fail this time.

"BSAR base," Nadja said from the cockpit. "We're approaching the last known coordinates, but visibility is near zero." She glanced back at EZ, Dave, and Pete, who all shook their heads. "So far no signs of the missing group."

"The weather is deteriorating rapidly," Andy said. "Return to base."

"No!" EZ shouted, jolting everyone. "Lower me down

then you guys can head back, but I'm staying out here until I find them."

Andy's curt tone came through clearly despite the static. "Negative, EZ. I'm ordering you back. Now. This is beyond rescue protocol. You're risking more lives by staying out there than you'd be saving."

Nadja fought the helicopter through another brutal gust, instruments spinning as she struggled to maintain altitude. Below, the forest looked like an ocean of white, all landmarks obliterated by the storm.

In his mind the same thoughts spiraled over and over.

This is exactly what happened to Sierra. Storm, terrain, impossible conditions. And now, you're putting all your friends at risk, too.

"EZ." Andy's voice again. "Come back to the hangar. We'll launch ground teams instead. Multiple search parties with GPS and emergency gear."

"Ground teams can't get through this weather," EZ replied. "That's why it's best if I go alone. I'm trained for this. I can do it."

"Doubtful," Nadja interjected, pointing toward the fuel gauge.

EZ squinted to see it and his stomach dropped. Yeah, they'd been in such a hurry to get here they hadn't taken the time to top off the fuel tank, and now, they were running dangerously low. Maybe twenty minutes left, not including the reserve needed to make it back to the hangar safely.

Dammit. The conditions were getting worse by the second. Another gust hit the helicopter, and this time an ominous creak echoed through the cabin as the tail rotor shuddered. The helicopter's controls lit up like Christmas Day with warning lights.

"Nadja, what's your status?" Andy's voice was sharp with concern over the radio.

"Possible rotor damage. Handling feels off."

"That's it. You're coming back in. Now."

EZ didn't argue this time as they circled over the forest one more time and he scanned desperately for any sign of the missing group. Nothing but trees and snow and the growing darkness of late afternoon.

I'm sorry, Callie. I'm sorry, Maisy. I'm sorry, Luka. But I'll be back.

"Returning to base," Nadja finally said into the radio as they turned toward home.

The flight back was harrowing, the damaged rotor making control increasingly difficult. It was a testament to Nadja's talent as a pilot that she handled it as well as she did. By the time they set down at the hangar again, EZ felt exhausted, defeated, and frozen to the bone.

Andy waited in the parking lot for them with what looked like half the BSAR team. Nadja shut down the engines, and they waited for the rotors to slow before getting out.

"You did the right thing," Andy said as EZ approached him.

"Did we? They're still out there."

"We've got enough people here to mobilize six ground teams." Andy gripped his shoulder. "Search-and-rescue dogs. The transportation department is sending a team with specialized equipment to keep the roads open for us. We're going to find them."

EZ wished he felt as optimistic.

They could be anywhere. Injured, lost, hypothermic. Dead.

EZ shook away the thought. No. Callie was smart, capable, medically trained. She'd grown up here. Had the protocol drilled into her. She'd find shelter, keep the kids warm, keep everyone alive until help arrived.

There was the nature center itself, but obviously they hadn't made it back there. So...the abandoned ranger station. It was pretty rough and not regularly restocked with supplies, but it would give shelter from the storm. Clean water, blankets, maybe a bit of food.

"I know where they are," EZ said, confident now. Callie was smart and a local—she'd remember the station was there. He felt it in his bones. "The abandoned ranger station near Jenny Lake."

The team split into three groups, one headed to the ranger station, the other two searching the surrounding area just in case they'd gone elsewhere. The plan was to canvas as much of the area as possible as quickly as possible, with all the teams eventually converging on the same central rendezvous point if they hadn't found anything.

EZ was in team one with Dave, Andy, and Jules. They started off into the frigid weather as the last of the day's light dwindled. Soon they needed flashlights to see five steps in front of them as the storm raged. What should have taken an hour to complete took twice as long to get halfway down the trail, each team radioing in periodically with updates. Each one another blow as they found nothing yet.

Finally, the shadow of the tree line was in sight through the torrent of snow. Not far to the ranger station now. EZ's heart tripped in his chest. *Please let them be there.*

Andy held his gaze as he radioed in. "We're at the tree line. Heading into the forest to the ranger station now. We may lose contact for a while. Over."

EZ shook his head. "Let me go on ahead. I can move faster on my own."

Andy watched him closely for a long moment, clearly

weighing options. Finally, he nodded. "Fine. You've got emergency gear, thermal blankets, medical supplies. Radio contact every thirty minutes, if possible. If not, you wait for the ground teams to help with evacuation. No heroics."

"Got it," EZ agreed, but in his heart he knew he'd do whatever was necessary to bring everyone home safe.

"You're not going alone," Pete said, stepping up beside him.

"No, you're not," Dave agreed, moving to EZ's other side. "We're a team, remember? Andy can run incident command from out here, right?"

"Agreed. I like that plan much better." Andy gave a curt nod. "Be safe."

The abandoned ranger station felt like a cage made of ice and fear.

Callie had managed to gather enough trash and dry kindling to start a small fire in the old woodstove in the corner, but it barely pushed back the cold creeping through every crack in the walls. Outside, the storm howled like something alive and angry.

Sara had developed a fever. Not high but concerning, given her injured ankle and their isolation. Callie had used a scarf from one of the kids to create a makeshift compression bandage, but without proper medical supplies, there was only so much she could do.

The kids were holding up remarkably well, considering. Maisy had appointed herself "cabin commander," and insisted they take turns telling stories to "keep our minds off the scary stuff."

"Once upon a time," Tommy said from his nest under the blanket with his mom, "there was a superhero named Captain Marshmallow—"

"Marshmallows aren't superheroes," Maisy interrupted.

"This one was. He could fly and shoot marshmallows at bad guys and make really good s'mores."

"Did he have a cape?" Luka asked.

"The best cape. Made of graham crackers."

Callie smiled despite everything. Children's resilience never ceased to amaze her. While she was cataloging worst-case scenarios—how long their emergency food would last, whether Sara's ankle was broken, what would happen if the storm didn't clear by morning—the kids were creating imaginary worlds where marshmallows saved the day.

Please let Ezra be okay out there and not stuck like we are.

"Don't worry. My daddy always finds people," Maisy said with seven-year-old certainty, as though reading Callie's mind. "He's really good at rescuing."

"Yes, he is."

"He rescued me once. From the scary closet monster."

"Scary closet monster?"

Maisy nodded solemnly. "After my mom died I kept having bad dreams about things in my closet. Daddy didn't just tell me monsters weren't real. He brought his big flashlight, and we looked in every corner until I could see there was nothing there."

Callie chest ached with sweetness. She could picture Ezra, patient and thorough, not dismissing his daughter's fears but helping her face them.

"He's good at making the scary stuff not scary anymore," Maisy continued. "He'll make this not scary, too."

"I hope so, sweetheart."

"Are you scared?"

Terrified. "A little. But being a little scared is okay. It helps us be careful."

"Daddy says being scared means you're still being smart."

Smart. Yes. Let's all be very smart about this.

Callie checked her phone again—still no signal.

The storm seemed to be getting worse. Through the small, dirty window, she could barely see the trees outside now. Everything was a swirl of violent white.

How is anyone supposed to find us in this?

Around ten o'clock, according to her smartwatch, Luka started crying.

Not the dramatic tears of a kid who didn't get his way, but the quiet, exhausted sobs of a child who'd been brave for as long as he could manage.

"I want to go home," he whispered against Callie's shoulder. "I want my own bed. I want morning cartoons."

"I know, baby. Me, too."

"What if we can't find our way out?"

"We will. Ezra will find us," Callie said firmly, pushing aside her own fears. "Maisy's daddy and all the other team members are very good at finding lost people."

"Promise?"

How can I promise something like that?

"I promise we're going to get through this together," she said carefully. "All of us."

Sara and Tommy huddled closer in one corner, and Callie settled in with Maisy and Luka in another, a tangle of small arms and worried faces. Even brave Maisy looked tinier than usual.

"Dr. Callie?" Tommy's small voice asked from across the tiny space. "Can you tell us a story? A good one?"

"What kind of story?"

"About brave people. Who save other people."

Callie thought for a moment, then began. "Once upon a time, there was a rancher who was also a superhero…"

She told them about a man who could fly through any weather, who never gave up on people who needed help, who could find anyone, anywhere. She told them about his daughter, who was brave and smart and never met an adventure she didn't like. About a doctor who could fix anything that was broken, and a little boy who could make anyone feel better just by being kind.

As she spoke, one by one the kids drifted off to sleep, exhausted by fear and cold and the strange adventure none of them had asked for. Sara, too. But Callie stayed awake, checking on Sara, listening to the storm.

Because somewhere between the storytelling and trying to hold everything together while the world raged outside, Callie had realized something that terrified her more than the storm:

She'd let EZ in. Into her life. Into her heart. Even though she'd sworn not to. Even though it made no sense whatsoever for her to fall for a man who risked his life nearly every single day.

And now, if he died trying to rescue them, she'd never get the chance to tell him.

She snuggled farther down in the sleeping bag, holding Maisy and Luka closer.

We're going to make it through this. All of us. I refused to have things end this way.

But as the wind howled and the building around them creaked under the storm's assault, Callie couldn't shake the feeling that was growing with each passing minute. The next few hours would determine whether they all went home together, or whether someone didn't go home at all.

CHAPTER ELEVEN

THE TREK THROUGH the blizzard was like walking through a living nightmare. EZ, Dave, and Pete moved through knee-deep snow, connected to each other by a climbing rope strung between them, their headlamps cutting weak beams through the swirling white chaos. Each step forward was a battle against wind that wanted to knock them sideways and cold that bit through every layer of gear.

Under normal conditions, the three-mile lollipop loop that followed the south shore of Jenny Lake took about two hours, give or take time to stop and sightsee. In this mess, he doubted they'd covered more than three quarters of a mile in the hour they'd been out here so far. Of course, it didn't help that they were presently in the Lupine Meadows area, which was open and flat, allowing the snow and wind to pelt them at full force. The abandoned ranger station where EZ hoped to find them was in a wooded area just past the meadows. All they had to do was get there.

"How much farther?" Dave shouted over the wind, though he was only three feet behind EZ.

EZ checked his GPS, wiping snow from the screen with a gloved hand. "Mile, maybe."

They trudged onward, legs burning with each step, lungs aching from breathing the frigid air, but EZ pushed forward with single-minded determination.

Callie. Maisy. Luka. They're counting on you. Don't you dare fail them, too.

With every step, the voice in his head grew louder, cataloging every mistake, every moment of poor judgment that had led to this disaster.

"EZ!" Pete's voice called from the back of their line, carrying a note of alarm. "Watch it!"

He turned to see Pete pointing to an area just to EZ's left. They'd gotten closer to the edge of the frozen lake than EZ had thought and if he wasn't careful, he'd walk right into it. It was still too early in the season for it to have frozen over, but the water was still cold. Just what he didn't need. Hypothermia on top of everything else.

Perfect. Pay attention, Benson. People are depending on you. Don't let them down. Not again.

"Thanks," EZ said, his voice flat with exhaustion and self-recrimination.

"No worries," Pete said, positive as always. "It happens in weather like this."

"Let's keep moving," EZ growled, frustration and fear making his voice harsh as they turned away from the lake and headed farther inland. "Every minute we're out here, their situation gets worse."

They pressed on, the pines in the distance gradually getting bigger the closer they got, but rather than encouraging EZ, his mind had continued to spiral deeper into the dark place where every slip in the snow, every moment of disorientation, every minute of delay was evidence of his fundamental inadequacy.

What the hell are you doing out here? You can't save anyone. You couldn't save Sierra. You can't save Callie. At this rate, you won't even find them before they freeze to death.

It took another thirty minutes of brutal hiking to finally

locate the abandoned station, barely visible through the snow, just a dark outline through the trees.

But as they started toward it, Dave slipped on a hidden patch of ice and went down hard.

By the time EZ reached him, Dave's face was grim with pain. "My knee. Think I tweaked it again."

EZ palpated the injury through Dave's snowsuit as best he could. Swollen, probably sprained. Another person hurt because he'd dragged them into danger.

He and Pete got on either side of Dave and helped him toward the ranger station. It felt like one of those nightmares where he was desperately trying to reach something that seemed to get farther away with every step. But finally, they made it, and while Pete helped Dave lean against the wall of the dilapidated cabin, EZ pounded on the door.

"Callie! Maisy! Hello? Anybody in there?"

For a terrifying moment, nothing. Then—

"Daddy?"

Maisy. His relief was so overwhelming his legs threatened to go out from under him.

"Yes, monkey! It's Daddy! Open the door!"

But it wasn't his daughter who let him in, it was Callie. She looked pale, exhausted, beautiful, and—most importantly—alive.

"Ezra." She stared at him like he'd hung the moon and stars even with all the drama between them. He didn't think he'd ever tire of seeing that expression on her face. "Thank God, you're here."

"Are you okay?" he asked Callie roughly at he hugged his daughter close, his throat tight with emotion. "Is the rest of the group with you?"

Please tell me I got here in time. Please tell me I didn't fail completely.

"Yes, they're here. Sara, Tommy's mom, has a sprained ankle and mild fever. The kids are scared and cold but fine."

EZ nodded and stepped aside to allow Pete and Dave in before closing the door behind them. Now that they were out of the weather and his adrenaline high started to burn off, awkwardness set in before he reminded himself that this was work. Get in, help the injured, get out again.

But even as he and Pete began treating Sara's ankle and Dave's knee with their medical supplies while Dave passed out fresh protein bars and bottled water from his pack to the kids and Callie, he couldn't quite keep his guilt at bay.

You put them in danger by not being there. You put everyone else in danger during unsafe conditions. You're a walking disaster.

From across the cabin, while she kept the kids occupied so Ezra and the others could deal with the injured, Callie watched Ezra from beneath her lashes.

He still had issues where she was concerned. It was obvious in the rigid line of his shoulders, the way he avoided her gaze, the distance he kept between them even as he diligently made sure they were all safe. Andy had confirmed the rest of the BSAR team would not be able to reach them until the storm let up in the morning.

Some of the tension inside Callie relaxed. Not ideal, but at least they knew they'd be getting out of there soon.

Once they'd got Sara's ankle stabilized and a brace on Dave's injured knee, Ezra radioed the hanger to report their status, but his expression said that emotionally, he was somewhere else entirely, locked behind walls that seemed higher than ever.

After things had settled down and the kids snuggled down in the sleeping bags again, snoozing away, along with

Sara, Callie finally worked up the courage to talk to Ezra about what was happening between them. She managed to find a bit of privacy as they sat in front of the small fire in the stove while Pete and Dave went outside to check the perimeter.

She clutched her bottled water in her hands as she stared at the flickering flames. "Are you okay?"

"Fine," he said, not looking at her. "Just tired."

Liar.

The turmoil inside him all but radiated from him like heat from the stove. As difficult as this situation was already, it had to be so much worse for him, considering how he'd lost his wife. She wanted to talk to him about that, get him to open up to her, share with her, depend on her to have his back, but wasn't sure how to even begin at that point.

"Thank you for saving us," she said after a moment.

He shook his head, his expression one of disgust. "I didn't save you. I didn't save anyone. You wouldn't even be in this situation if it wasn't for me."

"That's not true."

"Isn't it?" He glanced at her then, his hazel eyes burning with self-recrimination. "I never should have left the group at the nature center. I should have stayed with you and the kids instead of chasing after another rescue. Should have—"

"Stop it." Callie put a hand on his arm, forcing him to look at her. "Stop doing this to yourself."

"Doing what? Acknowledging reality?" He sounded bitter, resigned. "I put all of you in danger. Then I put my own team in danger trying to find you. I made bad decisions when it mattered."

"That's not—"

"It is." He pulled free, turning away. "It's exactly what it is."

The hours passed slowly. Sara's fever stabilized, Dave's knee pain seemed manageable, the children slept fitfully but safely. Through it all, Callie and Ezra stayed awake, with Callie watching Ezra and Ezra staring into the fire with the expression of a man cataloging his failures.

As dawn began to gray the small windows, Callie had had enough. She leaned closer to him and whispered, "Talk to me."

He was quiet for so long she thought he wasn't going to answer. Then he shook his head. "There's nothing to say, Callie. I can't do this."

Her pulse faltered. "Do what?"

"This. Us." He gestured vaguely between them. "I can't keep pretending I'm the kind of man you deserve. I'm not good for you, Callie. I'm not good for anyone that way anymore."

"Ezra, we need to talk about what happened—"

"No, we don't." He met her gaze then, the pain in his eyes so raw it took her breath away. "Sierra died because I wasn't there when she needed me. And now, I almost let the same thing happen to you. To Maisy. To all these people here. I'm toxic, Callie. I don't deserve love because I can't protect it."

"But you did protect us. You found us despite the horrible weather."

He gave a derisive snort. "This time. What about next time? What about the time after that? Because you know me. You know rescuing is in my blood. There will be a next time. And you already lived through that once with your ex. I can't ask you to do it again with me."

Callie felt like he'd physically struck her, a mix of outrage, anger, and desperation boiling inside her. "And who says you get to make that decision for me?"

"Me. I'm making that decision for both of us, because I

know myself. We never should have..." He glanced around before continuing, lowering his voice even more in case there were any other ears listening in, which in a cabin the size of theirs was a distinct possibility. "Sleeping together was a mistake. I know it. And sooner or later, you'll know it, too. It was my mistake. Thinking I could do this again. Have a normal life, a normal relationship. Thinking I could be what you and Luka need."

"You are what we need—"

"No." His voice was firm, final. "I'm not. What you deserve is someone who doesn't carry the kind of baggage that gets people killed. Someone who doesn't put his job before his family. Someone who's there when you need him."

"You're here now."

"Only because I made bad choices that could have gotten everyone killed." Ezra glanced at Dave, who was dozing fitfully against the wall. "I'm not the man you think I am, Callie. I destroy the things I love."

His words flowed like ice in her veins. "You don't mean that."

"I do." He stood carefully, moving away from the circle of warmth. "When we get out of here, whatever this was between us is over."

"Ezra—"

"Don't." He held up a hand. "Please."

Callie stared at him in the growing dawn light, at this man she'd fallen in love with despite all her best efforts. She should have known better. She knew the kind of man he was, knew he was addicted to the adrenaline, the rush of rescue. A hero. But not for her. She'd let him into her life, into her heart, into her son's life. And now, it was over. Just like it always was for her.

I should have known better.

She'd fooled herself into thinking this time was different, that Ezra wasn't like Owen. That he wouldn't hurt her like he had. That this time, the man she loved would choose her, choose Luka. But no.

And now, she had to deal with the aftermath. Pick up the pieces. At least she had practice with that part.

"Fine," she said quietly, her voice steely despite the world crumbling around her. "If that's what you want." She refused to beg a man to be with her if he didn't want to be there.

"It's what's best—"

"Sure. Because you're the arbiter of what's best for everyone you know, yeah?" The anger finally came, hot and bright and burning away the ache inside her. "Well, you don't get to decide what's best. And don't you ever think you make that choice for me or Luka, okay? I make those choices. And if you're too blind to see what a blessing our connection was then you're right. You don't deserve it."

"Callie—"

"No. You said your piece now I get to say mine." She stood, still keeping her voice low though her tone turned vicious out of pain and regret. "You're right about one thing, Ezra. You're not the man I thought you were. I thought you were brave. Turns out you're just another man who runs when things get real."

She saw him flinch and had to clench her fists at her sides to keep from reaching for him, from apologizing. Because he needed to hurt, as much as he'd hurt her. Needed to feel a fraction of what she felt at that moment. Then she walked away. Pulled on her coat and went outside to wait for the rescue team to arrive because she couldn't stay in there with him for one more second. Couldn't let him see her cry.

By the time the BSAR team found them an hour later, she had herself together again. As they were evacuated by snowmobile, checked by paramedics, transported back to safety, Callie maintained a careful distance from Ezra. If someone was just seeing them for the first time, they'd think they were professional. Polite. Strangers.

Once they were back at the school parking lot, Luka kept asking her why her eyes were red, why everything felt different than it had in the cabin.

But Callie had been down this road before.

Been abandoned. Left behind. By a man who claimed it was for her own good, who wrapped his fear and guilt in noble intentions. At least this time she hadn't been stupid enough to marry him first.

As she and Luka pulled out of the school lot, driving past Ezra's solitary vehicle still in its spot, she made herself a promise. This was the last time. The last time she made the mistake of loving the wrong man. The last time she opened her heart to someone who handed it back the minute things got real and difficult. The last time she learned this lesson because, apparently it took her more than once.

But this was it. The last time she'd let herself be broken by someone else's inability to stay.

CHAPTER TWELVE

Today, the Teton Memorial emergency room smelled like disinfectant and regret.

Ezra stood outside the door to trauma room two, watching through the small window as Jules examined Sara's ankle. The woman would be fine—sprained ankle, mild dehydration, nothing that wouldn't heal. Everyone was fine, medically speaking. Physically, they'd all survived.

So why does this feel like another failure of your life?

He'd debriefed the mission with Andy already and everyone called it a success. Textbook rescue. No casualties, minimal injuries, all missing persons accounted for.

But EZ had seen Callie's stricken expression in the dim firelight when he'd told her it was over. Noticed the way she wouldn't look at him now, wouldn't let him near Luka on the ride to the hospital. Heard the careful distance in her voice when she'd answered the paramedic's questions.

No, we're not together. He's just...a friend.

It had cut deeper than any blade.

Which made no sense because this was that he'd wanted, what he'd explicitly asked for. What he knew was for the best for everyone. For him to wall himself off to protect everyone else.

Wasn't it?

"EZ?" Andy leaned against the wall in the hallway beside him. "How are you holding up?"

"Fine."

"You don't look fine." Andy studied him with the kind of thoroughness that came from knowing someone since being kids. "You saved them, you know. All of them."

"Did I? Or did I put them in danger in the first place by not being there when they needed me?"

Andy gave a beleaguered sigh. "You can't be everywhere at once, EZ. It's physically impossible. Believe me, I've tried. You were on a rescue call yesterday—doing your job. Saving lives."

EZ didn't respond. How could he explain it to Andy? The self-loathing, knowing Sierra's blood was on his hands. All he knew was that logic didn't matter when guilt lived in your bones. When every success felt hollow when measured against the one failure that mattered most?

"Where's Callie?" Andy asked after a moment.

"Gone." The word tasted like ashes. "Took Luka home about an hour ago."

"And?"

"And what?"

Andy was quiet for a moment, then looked like it pained him as he asked, "You two were involved, weren't you?"

EZ gave him a side-glance before staring at the wall across from him. No way would Andy have asked that on his own. The guy kept his emotions more suppressed than EZ. At least he had until he'd gotten engaged. "Did Jules tell you that?"

"No." Andy frowned at his toes. "Okay, yes. But that doesn't mean I'm not concerned about you and Callie. She and Jules are good friends, and my fiancée is the best judge of people I know." He shrugged. "Look, believe me, I understand wanting to lock yourself away from the world, how it feels to be that isolated, but thinking it's the best thing, the noble thing to do. I'd hate to see you stuck in that place, too, just because you're too stubborn to see beyond your own past."

Too late.

Andy's words hung over him like a shroud as the awkward silence stretched taut. Finally, EZ straightened. "I need to check on Maisy."

He found his daughter in another trauma room at the other end of the hall, sitting on a hospital bed that dwarfed her small frame. She wore a hospital gown decorated with cartoon animals while her clothes were being cleaned after their night in the cabin. Cora sat on a chair in the corner, looking older than EZ had ever seen her.

"Daddy!" Maisy's face lit up when he walked in. "The doctor says I'm fine. Just cold and tired."

"Good." He kissed the top of her head. "How are you feeling, monkey?"

"I'm okay. But..." Her face scrunched with confusion. "Where's Dr. Callie? And Luka? I thought they were coming to see me."

EZ's chest tightened. "They had to go home, sweetheart."

"But they didn't say goodbye." Maisy's voice got smaller. "Are they mad at us?"

No, baby. They're mad at me.

"Dr. Callie wanted to get Luka home so they could both change and get warmed up."

"Oh." Maisy seemed to accept this, but something in her eyes suggested otherwise. "Did you and Dr. Callie have a fight?"

EZ looked at his daughter—this bright, perceptive little

person who saw too much and understood things far beyond her years.

"No, we didn't fight."

Which was true. He'd told Callie it was over and she'd accepted it, point-blank.

"Then why isn't she here?" Maisy sighed.

"Sometimes things don't work out the way we want them to," he said carefully.

"But why not?"

Because I'm cursed. A failure. I destroy everything I touch.

"Sometimes they just don't."

Maisy seemed to consider that for a moment, then said, "I think that's really dumb."

"Maisy—"

"Dr. Callie makes you happy. You smile more when she's around. And she makes me happy, too. And Luka's my best friend. And now it's all messed up because of some dumb grown-up thing."

EZ stared at his daughter, shocked by the accuracy of her assessment.

"It's not dumb, monkey. It's—"

But he didn't get to finish that sentence because Maisy burst into tears and it was probably just as well because he wasn't sure what he'd have said, anyway. Honestly, it did seem kind of stupid looking back on it now, but that didn't negate the fact it had been the right thing to do. EZ pulled his daughter into his arms, feeling her small body shake with sobs. Over her head, he met Cora's eyes and saw deep disapproval there. Seemed he'd screwed up things with everyone today.

"Sometimes we can't have what we want," he said quietly

before one of the nurses returned with discharge papers, and EZ focused on the logistics of getting Maisy home.

But as they left the hospital—his daughter back into her own clothes, Cora driving in complete silence—EZ couldn't shake Andy's words from earlier.

You're too stubborn to see beyond your own past...

Maybe Andy was right. Maybe he was being stubborn. Because giving up was easier than risking everything and failing again. Because walking away hurt less than being left behind. Because some things were too broken to fix.

And maybe he was just in his own head too much to know up from down presently.

The icy situation didn't improve when they got home. Without a word, Cora took Maisy upstairs, leaving him alone to stew in his own mistakes at the kitchen table.

He'd been beating himself to a pulp over and over since Sierra died. Closing himself off from everyone and everything because he wanted to protect them. Like he was doing them a favor somehow. But Andy was right. He couldn't control the future. Hell, he couldn't control anything, and all he'd really done was make himself miserable. He remembered being a kid and his mom sitting him down and talking to him about brooding too much, and man, she'd be so angry at him now.

He scrubbed his hands over his weary face as the consequences of his actions that Sierra's death had pushed down hard on him.

If he was truly honest with himself, he knew Andy was right. He'd kept everyone away emotionally because he was too much of a coward to love fiercely again. Truthfully, he'd thought he was saving Callie and Luka by walking away. Thought he was protecting Maisy from future heartbreak.

But that wasn't what he was doing at all. He was just making sure he got to decide when the pain happened.

The realization hit him like a sledgehammer as he looked up to see Cora in the doorway.

"I don't know exactly what was going on between you and Callie," she said. "But I do know that both of you lit up like Fourth of July fireworks whenever you were around each other. That kind of chemistry is rare and precious. And if you throw it away just because you're afraid, you're not the man I thought you were. Not the man Sierra thought you were, either."

She turned on her heel and left, and EZ stayed where he was, head in his hands as memories crashed over him like a tsunami. The look in Callie's eyes when he'd ended things. Maisy's tears in the hospital. The emptiness of his own house without Luka's laughter.

She'll never forgive me.

But you won't know unless you try.

He picked up his phone, then set it down again. Picked it up, set it down.

Finally, he typed a simple message: I was wrong. About everything. Can we talk?

He stared at the words for ten minutes before deleting them.

Best to sleep on it. Decide in the morning.

He went to bed torn and twisted, a little niggling hope echoing in his head.

Maybe it wasn't too late. Maybe there was still time to fight for what mattered.

Maybe it's time to stop being a coward.

Callie's house felt too small and too quiet since coming home from the hospital earlier. She'd tried distracting herself by catching up on her emails and cleaning, anything to keep her mind occupied.

It wasn't working.

"Mom?" Luka appeared in her bedroom doorway, clutching his stuffed dinosaur. "I can't sleep."

She looked at her own bedside clock—11:00 p.m. Well past his bedtime, but she hadn't been sleeping, either.

"Bad dreams?"

He nodded and climbed onto her bed without invitation. "About the storm. And being cold. And..." He hesitated. "Why are you mad at Maisy's dad?"

Callie's chest tightened. "I'm not mad, sweetie. We're just spending some time apart."

More like he decided, and you just went along with it, but whatever.

"Did he do something bad?" Luka's voice was small, confused.

Yes. She took a deep breath. "No, sweetheart. It's just sometimes people...can't make things work. No matter how much they might want to."

"But why not?"

Because happy isn't enough for some people. Because when things get scary, some people run.

"I don't know, Luka. I wish I did."

He snuggled closer, warm and solid and the one constant in a life that felt like it was falling apart.

"I miss Maisy," he said quietly.

"I know. I miss her, too."

"Mr. EZ was gonna teach me to ride horses."

Callie closed her eyes, remembering their last ranch visit. Before everything had gone to hell. Before she'd let herself believe they could have a future together.

"Can I sleep with you tonight?" Luka asked.

"Of course."

They lay in the dark together, Luka's breathing eventually evening out into sleep. But Callie stared at the ceiling, replaying his words from the cabin.

I made bad choices that could have gotten everyone killed.

I'm not the man you think I am, Callie. I destroy the things I love.

When we get out of here, whatever this was between us is over.

That wasn't the worst part, honestly. It was recognizing the pattern of her choices—Owen's excuses wrapped in different packaging.

She'd thought EZ was different. Thought he was brave enough to fight for them when things got difficult. Instead, he'd proven to be just another man who walked away when love required courage.

Callie's phone buzzed on the nightstand. It was late. After midnight now, and for a moment, her heart clogged her throat. Good news never came at this hour. But then, maybe EZ had come to his senses, maybe he'd realized what he'd thrown away.

But it was just her sister, Ashley, texting again from Denver: Haven't heard from you in days. You okay?

Callie stared at the message for a long time, then typed back: No, not really.

Her phone rang immediately.

"What happened?" Ashley's voice was sharp with concern.

"He ended it before it ever really got started."

"Why?"

Trying not to wake Luka, Callie quietly gave her sister

the abbreviated version—the storm, the rescue, EZ's decision that loving her was too dangerous.

"That's the stupidest thing I've ever heard," Ashley said when she finished. "He saves you and then decides you're not worth saving again?"

"Essentially."

"Oh, honey, I know this hurts. But maybe—"

"No." The word emerged sharper than she intended. "Don't make excuses for him. Don't tell me he was just scared, or that he'll come around, or that I should fight for him."

"But—"

"I am done fighting for men who don't want to be fought for. Done making myself smaller to accommodate their fears. Done believing that if I just love someone enough, they'll choose to stay."

Ashley was quiet for a moment. "Okay. You're right. I'm sorry."

"Look, I'm fine," Callie lied. "Luka and I are fine. We don't need him."

We just thought we did.

After hanging up, Callie eased out of bed, careful not to wake her son, and went to the kitchen. She made tea she didn't want in a desperate attempt to feel normal. The house felt different now—like a fortress. Like all she needed or wanted.

Liar.

She never should have started imagining a different life. Sunday mornings at the ranch, Luka learning to ride horses, family dinners around Cora's big table. She'd let herself picture Christmas mornings and birthday parties and all the ordinary moments that made a family.

And then reality stepped in. Like it always does.

The next morning, Callie dropped Luka at school and noticed him scanning the playground hopefully. Looking for Maisy, probably. She considered talking to his teacher about arranging a playdate—the kids shouldn't have to suffer for the adults' failures.

But what was the point? It would only make things harder.

Better to make a clean break. For everyone.

At work, she threw herself into patient care with even more intensity than usual. Every child she treated was a reminder of what she was good at, what mattered. She was a doctor. A mother. That was enough.

During lunch, standing in the break room stirring coffee she couldn't taste, Callie stared out the window toward the mountains, knowing somewhere out there EZ was going about his life without them. Probably relieved he'd escaped before things got too complicated.

Good for him. Good for us. We're better off.

She almost believed it.

But later in her office, surrounded by the trappings of her successful, independent life, Callie couldn't shake the memory of Sunday morning pancakes at the ranch. Of EZ's hands fixing the hay elevator while she watched. Of the way Maisy's eyes had lit up when she and Luka talked about something they were both excited about.

You made the mistake of wanting more. Of believing someone when they said you mattered.

Her last patient of the day was Emma, a twelve-year-old with a sprained wrist from playground gymnastics. As Callie examined the injury, the girl chattered about her family, her pets, her best friend, who was also named Emma, which was "superconfusing but also supercool."

"Dr. Dupree?" the girl asked as Callie finished the exam. "How come you look sad?"

Callie forced a smile. "I'm not sad, sweetheart. Just concentrating."

That evening, after Luka went to bed, Callie sat on her small back patio with a glass of wine. The mountains were silhouetted against the star-filled sky, and for a moment she could almost pretend it was her first day back in Jackson, before everything had gone wrong.

Enough. No more feeling sorry for yourself.

She made herself a promise: no more looking back. No more missing what she'd never really had. No more hoping that EZ would come to his senses and fight for them.

She had Luka, her career, a life that was good enough.

But her dreams later were filled with helicopter rescues and mountain meadows and an auburn-haired hero who'd walked away when things got too tough.

CHAPTER THIRTEEN

THE CALL CAME at four the next morning, shattering EZ's restless sleep.

Bleary-eyed, he fumbled to grab his phone from the nightstand in the dark and squinted at the text onscreen. BSAR team alert: massive mudslide in valley northwest of Jackson. Multiple structures affected, unknown casualties. All available volunteers respond immediately.

EZ was out of bed, showered, and dressed within ten minutes. After the freak blizzard, the temperatures had shot right back up into the mid-fifties, causing a quick meltdown. The yo-yo weather had surprised everyone. It wasn't normally that bad this early in the season, and now, the town was paying the price for it.

He stopped in the kitchen to grab a protein bar and energy drink, then was in his truck and on the way to the hangar. He'd slept like crap, tossing and turning all night in a haze of regret and self-recrimination, so he needed any external help he could get to stay alert and ready. At least he'd be lost in duty and adrenaline for the next few hours while he dealt with the aftermath of the mudslide and wouldn't have time to dwell on what had happened with Callie like he'd done pretty much 24/7 lately. It was exhausting and demoralizing. But mostly it hurt, more than anything had since losing Sierra.

Twenty minutes later, EZ was airborne with Andy, Jules, Pete, and Stella, flying toward a scene that looked like something from a disaster movie. The rapid snowmelt had destabilized the entire hillside above Cedar Creek Ranch, sending a wall of mud, rocks, and debris sweeping down the mountainside, taking out everything in its path.

"Damn," Pete muttered over the intercom. "Look at that."

Below them, what had been a thriving ranch operation six hours ago was now a wasteland of thick, chocolate-colored mud. Buildings were buried up to their rooflines. Vehicles had been tossed like toys. And somewhere in that mess, people were trapped.

"Ruby, this is EZ," he said over the radio. "We have visual on the slide area. It's extensive—at least half a mile wide, maybe more. Structures are completely buried."

"Copy," Ruby said. "State police and local law enforcement are on their way on the ground, as are fire and EMS. They're setting up command at the highway junction. Can you do an aerial assessment, look for signs of life?"

"Roger."

Nadja nodded and flew them in a grid pattern over the disaster zone, while Pete used FLIR thermal imaging to look for heat signatures, scanning for any sign of movement or trapped survivors. The scale of destruction was overwhelming, but their training kept them focused.

"There!" Pete said, pointing at a red blob on the screen. "Heat signature in what looks like a barn."

EZ radioed it in. "Ruby, we've got possible survivors in a structure about two hundred meters southeast of the main house. Requesting immediate ground-team support."

"The ground teams are having trouble getting close enough to the slide zone," Ruby said. "They want to know if our team can attempt another extraction."

EZ assessed the landing zone—thick mud, unstable terrain, debris everywhere. He glanced over at Andy and Pete, who both gave curt nods. "Nadja, can we attempt a landing?"

Nadja did her own assessment then said, "It's tricky, but doable."

"Affirmative. We can fit one more patient in here now, then return for more after returning to the hangar," EZ told Ruby over the radio. "Team attempting touchdown now."

Nadja brought the helicopter down carefully, and EZ felt the landing gear sink into the soft earth. The rest of the team was already prepping the medical basket and emergency gear.

"Jules, you and Stella stay with the heli," Andy ordered. "Nadja, keep her ready for immediate takeoff."

"Roger that," Nadja said.

EZ, Andy, and Pete got out and waded through knee-deep mud toward the heat signature, carrying rope and rescue equipment. The barn was tilted at a crazy angle, with one wall completely caved in, but the roof was still intact. The closer they got, the more EZ could hear voices inside—weak, but definitely human.

"Hello?" he called. "Can you hear me? This is Jackson Hole Search-and-Rescue!"

"Here!" A woman's voice, strained with exhaustion. "We're trapped in the tack room!"

They followed her voice to a small door barely visible above the mud line. The frame was twisted, the door jammed shut. At least three voices were audible inside by EZ's count—an adult woman and what sounded like two children.

"Ma'am," Andy called, "we're going to get you out of there. Are any of you injured?"

"Yes," the woman called back. "I think my daughter's

arm might be broken. And my son is having trouble breathing—he has asthma and his inhaler was in the house."

Dammit.

EZ keyed his radio. "Ruby, let ground rescue know we've got three trapped civilians in a partially collapsed barn. Adult and two children. One child with a possible broken arm, and one child with asthma in respiratory distress. We need immediate medical evacuation."

"Roger that," Ruby said. "FYI, radar is tracking another rain system moving in fast from the west."

He glanced at the ridgeline in the distance, noting the dark clouds building over the mountains. *Of course rain was coming in. Because the situation wasn't complicated enough already.*

"How long until ground medical evac can get here?"

"Thirty minutes minimum. They finally reached the slide zone. Maybe longer if the weather closes in."

Thirty minutes. A kid having an asthma attack doesn't have thirty minutes.

EZ studied the jammed door, calculated the risk of trying to extract them now versus waiting for the ground team. The sound of labored breathing from inside the makeshift shelter seemed to make the decision for Andy.

"We're going in," Andy said. "Tell Ruby."

After twenty minutes of cutting, prying, and creative engineering to get the door open far enough to squeeze through, they got inside, where they found a woman in her thirties with two kids, maybe seven and nine years old. The little girl was cradling her left arm, clearly in pain but trying to be brave. The boy was sitting against the wall, wheezing with each breath.

"Ma'am, my name is Ezra Benson, but please call me EZ. We're here to get you all out of here."

"Thank God," the woman breathed. "And I know who you are. You're Dr. Benson's son. He was just out here yesterday before the rain inoculating my cows." She gave him a weak smile. "This is my daughter, Maia, and my son, Joshua."

"Hi, Maia," Pete said, kneeling beside the little girl to carefully examine her injured arm while Andy crouched near the boy. Even from where EZ was beside the mother, he could see the blue tinge around the boy's lips despite the oxygen they were giving him.

Andy checked Joshua's vitals, and tried to distract him when he asked, "Have you ever ridden in a helicopter?"

The boy shook his head, his eyes wide.

"Well, you'll get to today." Andy smiled, pulling a quick-acting albuterol inhaler and spacer out of his medical pack and administering an initial four puffs to the boy. He then waited another minute and a half before reassessing and administering a fifth puff. "Just as soon as we get you all out of here."

By the time they got the woman and kids out of the barn and back to the helicopter, Stella and Jules were ready and waiting for them. As Nadja took off again, Andy radioed in directly to Teton Memorial ER.

"This is Dr. Andy MacDonald of BSAR. We are en route to the hospital directly with three mudslide victims. One adult, two children. Please have Pediatrics ready to assist with triage."

EZ's breath caught. *Callie.*

He had any contact with her since the cabin incident, thinking it would be easier for them both that way, but obviously that wasn't true. Not for him, anyway. Callie seemed fine with it, though.

Grow up, Benson. This is what you wanted. You're not the

priority here, anyway. Your patients are. You're a professional. Act like one. Besides, she might not even be on call.

Joshua's breathing became more labored again as they flew through increasingly rough weather toward the hospital. Fifteen minutes later they landed at Teton Memorial in wind and rain, the storm having caught up with them during the flight. Medical staff rushed out to meet them, including—

Callie arrived in the chaos of medical personnel, wearing scrubs and a jacket, hair whipping in the wind as she ran alongside the gurneys the medical staff pushed toward the helicopter. She was in full doctor mode, professional and focused, but when her eyes met EZ's across Joshua's gurney, time stopped for a heartbeat.

Then poor Joshua went into full respiratory distress, and everything else became secondary.

"Seven-year-old male, severe asthma attack, I've administered a quick-action albuterol inhaler. Eight puffs, point-six-three milligrams each," Andy reported as they rushed toward the ER with the boy on a gurney between them.

One of the techs attached a pulse finger-oximeter to Joshua's finger. "Oxygen sats dropping, increasing respiratory distress."

"Trauma two," Callie called, taking charge of Joshua's care as they rushed through the automatic doors into the bright, busy ER. "I need a pediatric crash cart and respiratory therapy stat."

EZ and the rest of the team stepped back as Callie and the ER staff took over. Then they went back to the helicopter to return to search-and-rescue operations. The one place where he was still in control, still wanted, still important.

Callie worked in the thick of it for three hours with helicopters and ambulances arriving regularly with more mudslide victims. The ER was in disaster mode, everyone on deck, every available bed prepped for incoming patients.

She'd thought she'd been ready for it, ready for the kind of focused medical challenge that kept her mind occupied and her hands steady. Then she'd seen EZ again. She'd imagined what it would be like when they met again, because, of course, they would in a town this size. She'd imagined herself being cordial but distant, proving to him that she didn't need him, didn't need anyone to fulfill her.

Then she'd locked eyes with him on that windswept helipad and her heart had done something complicated against her will and all her good intentions had vanished in the storm. She'd recovered quickly, though, as her patient had gone into full respiratory distress and her focus had zeroed in on the most important priority at present, her patients. Everything else could wait.

Once she and her team had finally gotten little Joshua stabilized, she returned to the nurses' desk to pick up her next case, half expecting to see Ezra waiting there for her. Which was dumb because why would he? He'd made it clear things were over between them, so, of course, he'd go back to work.

After that, Callie had thrown herself into treating the steady stream of mudslide casualties until the ER finally began to quiet down again.

She was just on her way to the break room to grab a much-needed snack when an announcement came over the hospital PA system.

"Code blue, BSAR helicopter landing pad. Code blue, BSAR helicopter landing pad."

Cursing under her breath, Callie veered right and ran toward the automatic doors leading out to the helipad where the BSAR chopper was touching down. She joined the other staff running out into the rain and wind toward the aircraft, pulling a gurney and emergency resuscitation equipment along between then, wondering who the poor patient was in life-threatening condition, then nearly stumbled over her own feet when she saw a familiar face being unloaded from the heli.

Ezra.

Oh, God. No.

On autopilot, Callie worked alongside the other docs as they ran through the doors into the ER and straight to trauma room one, her heart hammering against her ribs. *Please let him be okay. Please don't let me lose him before I've figured out if I can forgive him.*

Ezra was unconscious, blood trickling from his head, his breathing shallow but steady. As if in a long tunnel, she vaguely heard the other ER doc in charge of his case calling out his assessment and orders.

Head trauma. Possible internal injuries. Get him to trauma, get a CT scan, assess for—

Callie stepped back so as not to get in the way as more techs rushed in to help. Pete stood near the doorway, blood on his forehead but otherwise seemingly okay.

"What happened?" Callie asked, her gaze trained on Ezra.

"Secondary slide," Pete said grimly. "Came down while we were evacuating survivors. Caught the edge of it. EZ took the worst of the debris impact. Luckily Nadja kept the bird airborne long enough to get clear."

From the room, she caught the call of one of the ER docs treating Ezra again. "Vitals are stable, but he took a significant blow to the head. Possible concussion, possible more serious trauma."

Then they rushed his gurney out, hurrying toward CT

for an emergency scan, and Callie found herself relegated to the waiting room with Pete and the growing crowd of BSAR personnel.

All she could do was wait.

And pray.

And realize that maybe some things were more important than the risk of getting hurt again.

Please be okay, she thought, staring at the trauma-room doors. *Please wake up so I can tell you I was wrong to give up so easily. So I can tell you that maybe we were worth fighting for after all.*

CHAPTER FOURTEEN

CALLIE TRIED TO go back to work. She checked on her patients and monitored Ezra's condition surreptitiously as much as possible. She wasn't an ER doc, so wasn't allowed to treat her own loved ones or family members, anyway. Though, technically, Ezra wasn't either to her any longer, but...

Oh, who was she kidding. She still cared. More than she should. More than she ever wanted to. More than she'd even been willing to admit to herself before now.

Somewhere, against all odds and her own wishes, she'd fallen for Ezra Benson, and now, she might lose him all over again. All because she'd let her old hurts decide her future decisions. So dumb. So—

"Dr. Dupree?"

Startled, Callie looked up to find Andy MacDonald approaching, still in his muddy rescue gear, exhaustion written in every line of his face. She'd been so lost in her thoughts she hadn't even seen him come into the ER.

"How is he?" Andy asked, his expression one of concern.

"They're running tests—CT scan, MRI, the works. Last time I asked, Dr. Chen said he's stable, but they won't know the extent of his injuries until he regains consciousness."

Andy sank down into an empty chair along the wall, looking exhausted and exasperated. "I probably shouldn't tell you this, because it's not my place to intervene, but in all the years I've known EZ, I've never seen him as happy as he was these past few months."

Callie took a deep breath and a seat beside him. "And?"

"And then I've never seen him as miserable as he's been these past few days, since the cabin rescue." Andy leaned back in his chair. "Walking around like a ghost. Doing his job but just going through the motions. I don't know what happened out there or what was going on between the two of you prior to that, but…" He sighed and scrubbed a hand over his stubble-covered fact. "Look, I am the last person to pry into other peoples' business, but Jules said I should talk to you and see if you can—"

"I can't," Callie snapped, then shook her head, softening her tone. "I mean. There was something happening with us, but then he ended it and I've been honoring his wishes, so…"

Andy nodded, taking that in a moment before responding. "Well, I am no relationship expert at all. Just ask Jules." Callie snorted and he smiled. "But EZ has been through a lot and…he's a good man. Stubborn as hell, blaming himself for things that are out of his control, but a good man. And as someone who tried his darndest to avoid anything resembling love for as long as humanly possible, only to discover in the end that that was the stupidest move ever, I just hate to see people making the same mistakes I did when the opportunity is right there in front of them. And, yes, Jules did coach me on this speech beforehand because I'm still an idiot when it comes to emotions. But then, maybe EZ is, too."

"Maybe," Callie said, smiling for the first time in what felt like forever. Before she could say more, the door to trauma room one opened and Dr. Chen emerged, looking tired but relieved.

"He's stable," Dr. Chen said to them. "Moderate concussion, some bruised ribs, a nasty gash on his forehead that took sixteen stitches. But no signs of internal bleeding, no skull fracture, no spinal damage. He got lucky. He's still unconscious, but you can see him now. Family first, then friends. One at a time, please."

Family. Callie wasn't family. She wasn't even sure if she classified as a friend anymore after he'd broken things off.

"Oh, and Dr. Dupree?" Dr. Chen said. "He's in and out. But every time he surfaces, he says your name."

My name? Her pulse tripped. Maybe he did still care. Maybe it wasn't too late.

Callie nodded, not trusting her voice.

"Don't expect much conversation—he's pretty groggy from the pain medication."

Andy went out to tell the rest of BSAR team in the waiting room while Callie made her way to trauma room one on unsteady legs, hands trembling. She paused outside the door, taking a deep breath, trying to prepare herself for—

For what? For seeing the man you love hooked up to machines? For facing the fact that you almost lost him before you could tell him how much you care?

She bit her lip and pushed open the door to find Ezra in his hospital bed, looking pale and younger than his thirty-two years. His head was bandaged, a brace around his neck, his auburn hair sticking up in disarray, monitors beeping steadily beside him. Then his hazel eyes flickered open and locked on her.

"Callie?" he croaked.

"Hi." She moved to his bedside, hesitant. "How are you feeling?"

"Like I got hit by a mountain. Which, technically, I did." His chuckle was hoarse, tired, but firm. He closed his eyes for a moment, and she thought he'd fallen asleep once more, but then he looked at her again. "You came. Even though you hate me."

"I don't hate you, Ezra." The words came out softer than she'd intended. "I never hated you."

"You should. I'm a coward. I threw away the best thing that's happened to me in years because I was too scared to fight for it."

Tears pricked Callie's eyes. "Ezra—"

"I know I made a mess of everything, and I don't deserve—"

"Stop." She took his hand carefully, mindful of the IV. "Just…stop talking and let me say something."

He went quiet, watching her with the hazel eyes that had been haunting her dreams.

"When you ended things that night in the cabin I was angry," she began. "Furious. I felt like you'd thrown me away the moment things got hard, just like Owen did."

"Callie—"

She tightened her grip on his hand. "But then I realized that you risk your life to save people you've never met. You fly into dangerous conditions because people need you. Not like Owen did, just for the thrill of it. And I realized something else."

"What?"

"You didn't end things because you didn't care. You ended them because you cared too much. Because you were so terrified of failing me, failing Luka, that you decided it was better to fail us on purpose."

Ezra frowned, squeezing his eyes shut. "That doesn't make it right."

"No, it doesn't. But it makes it understandable. And it makes it…" She paused, searching for the right word. "Forgivable."

The silence stretched between them, filled with the beeping of monitors and the distant sounds of hospital life, their gazes locked.

"What are you saying?" Ezra said quietly after a moment, looking like a little boy who was both hopeful and terrified of what the outcome might be.

"I'm saying I was scared, too. Am scared. Terrified of losing someone I love again, terrified of watching my son get attached to someone who might leave. But what happened today, when I thought I might lose you for good..." She took a shaky breath. "I realized that being afraid of loss isn't a reason to avoid love. It's a reason to fight for it."

Ezra's fingers tightened around hers. "Callie—"

"I'm saying that against my better judgment—I love you, you stubborn, self-destructive, heroic idiot. I love you, and I love the man you are when you're with us, and I love the father you could be to Luka, and I love—"

She was crying now, and Ezra reached up with his free hand to wipe the tears from her cheek with his thumb, wincing slightly at the effort.

"I love you, too, Callie," he whispered. "God, I love you so much. I'm sorry I was such a coward. I'm sorry I hurt you, hurt Luka. I'm sorry—"

"Shh." She leaned down to kiss his forehead, then pulled back slightly to meet his gaze. "We both made mistakes. We were both scared. But we're here now."

"Are we? Are we really going to try this again?"

Callie smiled, seeing the same hope and fear and love all mixed together that swirled inside her. "Yes. But this time, we do it right. We take it slow, steady. No running when things get hard. No letting fear make our decisions for us. No matter what happens, we face it together."

"Together," he agreed softly.

"Together. You, me, Luka, Maisy. A family."

"A family," he repeated, like the words were a prayer.

They stayed like that for a while, holding hands, planning a future that finally felt possible. And when Maisy burst through the door an hour later, Cora trailing behind her, the little girl's face lit up with joy.

"Dr. Callie! You're here! Does this mean you guys aren't fighting anymore?"

Callie looked at Ezra, saw the question and hope in his eyes, and grinned. "No, sweetheart. We're not fighting anymore."

"Yay!" Maisy launched herself carefully onto the bed beside her father, then wrapped her small arms around both adults. "Best day ever," she declared. "Even with Daddy being hurt."

"Even with me being hurt," Ezra agreed, looking at Callie over their daughter's head.

Their daughter.
Their family.
Finally.

Three days in the hospital gave EZ plenty of time to think. Time to plan. Time to realize that almost dying had a way of clarifying what really mattered.

When they finally released him with a stack of discharge instructions and orders to take it easy, he had a plan. Not a grand gesture—just a simple, honest conversation about the future.

Callie, Luka, and Maisy picked him up from the hospital, and EZ's chest tightened at the sight of them together. Luka had been to visit every day, bringing drawings and stories and chatter about school. The recent distance between them replaced by the easy affection that had developed before EZ had nearly ruined everything.

"Ready to go home?" Callie asked as she got him settled gingerly into the passenger seat.

Home. Such a simple word, but it meant something different now. Not just the ranch, but anywhere the four of them were together.

"Yeah. Ready."

They drove in comfortable silence, Luka and Maisy chattering from the back seat about their latest school project while Callie navigated the familiar roads toward the ranch. EZ watched her profile, still slightly amazed that she was here, that they were trying again, that she'd forgiven him for being such a colossal fool.

When they pulled up to the ranch house, EZ noticed several extra cars in the driveway.

"What's all this?"

Callie smiled, looking slightly nervous. "A welcome-home party. Cora may have gotten a little carried away with the planning."

They walked into the house to find it full of people—BSAR team members, what looked like half of Maisy's first-grade class with their parents, several of Callie's colleagues from the hospital. Even his father, Jeremiah, was there. A banner reading "Welcome Home!" hung across the living room, and the smell of Cora's cooking filled the air.

"Surprise!" Maisy shouted, running toward the house once she'd gotten out of her car seat in the back. "Do you like it?"

"I love it, monkey." EZ caught her once he'd limped up onto the porch with Callie's help, and pulled his daughter into a careful hug, mindful of his still-healing ribs. He smiled as Cora joined them, then gave her a chiding look. "Though I thought we talked about not overdoing things."

"Figured it was time this family celebrated something instead of surviving it."

This family. Including Callie and Luka without question, without awkwardness. As if they'd always belonged.

The party was perfect—low-key, full of laughter, people genuinely happy to see him alive and well. But what struck EZ most was watching Callie navigate the crowd with ease, chatting with everyone, helping Cora in the kitchen, settling seamlessly into the role of cohost.

Like she belongs here. Like this is where she was always meant to be.

Later, after the guests had gone and the dishes were done, after Maisy and Luka had fallen asleep on the couch watching a movie, EZ found himself alone with Callie on the front porch.

"Thank you," he said, settling beside her on the swing. "For today. For everything."

"Don't thank me yet. I haven't told you my conditions."

EZ swallowed hard. "Conditions?"

"For us trying again. For making this work long-term." Callie turned to face him in the moonlight, expression serious. "I need you to promise me something."

"Anything."

"Promise me you'll talk to someone. A counselor, a therapist, someone who can help you work through the guilt about Sierra. Because I can't live with someone who runs every time he thinks he might fail me."

EZ started to protest, then stopped. Maybe she was right. He'd tried all this time to deal with the guilt, the fear, the self-destructive patterns—and yet they were all still there, just under the surface. One near-death experience hadn't magically fixed years of trauma. "Okay. I promise."

"And promise me you'll let me help carry the burden sometimes. That you won't shut me out when things get hard."

"I promise."

"And promise me you'll let Luka be your son, really be your son, not just your girlfriend's kid you're nice to."

EZ looked through the window at Luka sleeping on the couch, dark hair falling across his face, looking young and peaceful and perfect.

"He already is my son," EZ said quietly, knowing in his heart it was true. "I love that boy like my own."

"Good." Callie's voice was soft, emotional. "Because he loves you, too. Talks about you constantly. Wants to be just like you when he grows up."

He snorted. "Poor kid's got terrible role models then."

"Stop." Callie nudged him gently. "You're going to be an amazing father to him. You already are."

They sat in comfortable silence for a while, just the creak of the swing filling the air as they watched the stars emerge over the mountains. His arm around her, her head on his shoulder, his fingers toying with her hair.

Finally, EZ asked, "What about us? What about the scary parts, the unknown parts?"

"We figure it out as we go. Together." Callie looked up at him, her green eyes fathomless in the dark. "I'm not saying it will be easy. I'm not saying we won't fight or disagree or have moments where we want to throttle each other."

"But?"

"But we stay and work through it, because this—us, the kids, this family we're building—is worth fighting for."

EZ pressed a kiss to the top of her head, breathing in the

scent of her shampoo, still slightly amazed that she was here, that they got this second chance.

"What about logistics? Two households, one…"

Callie smiled. "Home is wherever you and the kids are."

Family. Home. Forever.

"Marry me."

The words slipped out before EZ could think about them, raw and honest and completely unplanned.

"What?" Callie sat up, blinking at him.

"Marry me. I know we're just figuring this out, and we have a lot to work through still. But I don't want to waste any more time. I want to marry you, be a father figure for Luka if he'll let me, give Maisy the mother she wants, give all of us the family we deserve."

"Ezra—"

"I don't have a ring. Hell, I can barely sit up straight without my ribs screaming. This is probably the worst proposal in history. But I love you, Callie, and I want to spend the rest of my life proving it."

Callie was quiet for a long moment, and EZ felt panic rise. *Dammit. You blew it. Too much, too fast.*

"Yes."

"Yes?" Now, it was his turn to blink at her, shocked.

"Yes, I'll marry you. Yes to all of it." Her eyes were bright with unshed tears. "But I have one more condition."

"Name it."

"The wedding planning. That's all Cora and Maisy. I'm not getting in the middle of that."

EZ laughed, pulling her closer despite the protest from his ribs. "Deal."

They sat there planning their future, talking about wedding dates and living arrangements, and how to tell the kids in the morning. And as the night grew later and the mountain air grew colder, EZ felt something he'd thought was lost forever:

Peace. Contentment. The bone-deep certainty that he was exactly where he was supposed to be.

This is what happiness feels like, he thought as they headed inside, checking on the kids, moving through the house that already felt like it belonged to all of them.

This is what home feels like.

This is what love looks like when you're brave enough to fight for it.

And as he fell asleep that night with Callie curled against his good side, EZ knew that whatever challenges lay ahead, they'd face them together.

All of them. One stubborn, imperfect, absolutely perfect family.

* * * * *

*Look out for the next story in
the US Search and Rescue miniseries*

Coming soon!

*And if you enjoyed this story,
check out these other great reads
from Traci Douglass*

Risking His Heart for the ER Doc
A Doctor to Heal the Best Man
A Single Dad to Heal Him

All available now!

DR HART'S ROMANCE REMATCH

DEANNE ANDERS

MILLS & BOON

This book is dedicated to the physical therapy staff
at the Andrews Institute Rehabilitation center
located in Jay, Florida. My sincere thanks
for all your patience and kindness.

CHAPTER ONE

Not for the first time, RN Devon Campbell questioned her decision to interview for the position of manager of surgical services at the Hart Sports Institute. As the pounding of her heart matched the clicking of her heels, she reluctantly followed the HR manager down the hallway to a suite of exam rooms. There was no doubt that she needed this job. And it was perfect for her. Since graduating from nursing school, she'd had experience in both the operating room as a circulator and as an assistant, along with experience in presurgery and recovery. This surgical center had only been open for a few months and she'd researched it enough to know that it showed all the signs of becoming a world-class orthopedics center with many well-known athletes already giving it rave reviews. Being able to be a part of the foundation of an institution like this would be very rewarding.

Also, the position of manager would give her not only the financial security she needed, but also the flexibility to be there for her seven-year-old son, something she hadn't had at her last surgical job with its twelve-hour shifts and on-call nights. The long hours and childcare were why, after the death of her husband, Zachary, she'd had no choice but to resign from her position. Then there had been the move from California, where her husband had been stationed in the navy. While she had been excited to move back to Florida and the home in the little beach town of Silver Sands that she'd inherited from her grandmother, the closest hospitals were thirty minutes away and the commute wasn't something she'd wanted to make. She knew she could sell her grandmother's home and move closer to the city, but the last year had been hard, and being in the place where she had grown up made her feel less alone. She wanted this job. She needed this job. Shalonda, the HR manager, had all but said she would be offered the position when they'd talked on the phone.

Yes, the job was perfect in every way. If only that was the real reason she was there. Her heart sank at the thought.

They turned a corner and the real reason she was determined to get this job stood in front of them. Michael Hart, former professional football star and now orthopedic surgeon and founder of the Hart Sports Institute, dressed in a tailored suit that Devon knew had cost more than her monthly food budget, was heading down the hall toward them. At six and a half feet tall, he'd lost none of the muscular build he'd had when he was plowing through a line of defenders during one of the quarterback-sneak plays for which he had once been so renowned.

As he looked up from the clipboard in his hand, Devon's steps slowed. Unfortunately, the beat of her heart was paying no attention, and chose to speed up as if she was running a marathon instead. It was the eyes. Those beautiful pale green eyes that had always made her react this way. She would have thought that she would be used to them after seeing them every time she looked at her son.

"Dr. Hart, do you have a moment?" Shalonda asked as they stopped in front of him. "I wanted to introduce the applicant for the surgical services manager that I told you about, Devon Campbell."

Devon held her breath as Michael looked over at her. This was it. The moment she'd dreaded. Time stood still for a moment, and at first she thought he didn't recognize her. Was that really possible? After all, it had been over eight years since the last time he'd seen her. She was no longer the young, innocent college student she'd been back then. Surprisingly, the thought of him not recognizing her hurt. But why? She'd gotten over her childish crush years ago.

Then she saw something in those eyes of his change and the hurt was replaced with the fear of remembering the promise she'd made to Zach before he had died and the reason she had come home to Silver Sands.

"Sunshine?" he asked, his eyes widening and the firm line of his lips beginning to turn up in a smile.

Sunshine. For a moment the nickname made her smile. No one had called her Sunshine in years. It was a name her grandmother had called her, and later a few childhood friends. It brought back memories of lazy days on the beach after all her chores were done. The sand, the sun, and the warm emerald gulf waters had been her playground then. It had been a long time since she'd been that girl. She could barely even remember her.

"Hi, Mickey," she said, for a moment letting happier memories replace all of her fear of this meeting. She remembered that crooked smile of his that he'd used to charm her grandmother into baking his favorite chocolate chip cookies. She remembered the way his eyes would light up when the two of them stood on his balcony and spotted a herd of dolphins playing off the shore. And she remembered the way his lips had felt on hers, gentle and sweet, the first time he'd kissed her.

Her memories screeched to a halt and her body went rigid. It wasn't just her grandmother who this man had been able to charm. She'd been a victim of his charm one too many times. Not that she could blame him for either occasion, as the first had been on the night he'd lost his parents and the second time had led to her getting pregnant with her son, when she'd been only too willing to fall for the charming man he'd become.

"So you've moved back home? Last I heard, your husband was stationed in California," he said as he studied her with an intensity that made her want to squirm.

But then, Michael Hart had always been intense about everything in his life. It was how he'd made it to the NFL and how after the injury that had ended his football career he'd pivoted into the medical field.

It didn't surprise her that he knew about her marriage. Silver Sands was a small beach town mostly made up of long-term residents, and her grandmother had been a large part of the community until she'd passed away. What was surprising was that he hadn't heard the latest news about her life. "My husband passed away last year."

"I'm so sorry," he said. There was shock, then sympathy in his eyes. "I didn't know. Have you moved into your grandmother's house? I know it's been empty for quite a while."

"It's home," she said, knowing that he would understand. He'd known her grandmother and, like the rest of the town, he knew that the only real home Devon had ever had as a child had been that little cottage across from the beach.

A nurse stepped out of one of the exam rooms and smiled at the three of them. "I'm going to put in an order for Ms. Hughes's pre-op lab work and I was about to go over the postsurgery instructions. Is there anything else you need?"

"No, thank you, Jesse. I think we have everything covered. I went over the consent and I just put it on the chart. Let me know if she has any more questions," Michael said. The woman nodded, then returned to the patient's exam room. "Why don't you tell me what makes you right for this job, Devon?"

The change in subject stunned her for a moment, then she remembered she wasn't there to reminisce about the past—she was there for an interview. "I have a bachelor degree in nursing and worked as an OR assistant while in school. I've worked as a circulator for two years. I did pre- and postsurgery at the navy hospital where we were stationed. And my last position was manager of the postanesthesia unit at the Fresno County hospital. I have a copy of my résumé if you would like to see it."

"That's not necessary. If you weren't highly qualified for this post, Shalonda wouldn't have given you an interview or brought you here to meet me. We're not a large surgical center. We specialize in orthopedic and sports medicine. While we are quickly becoming known for treating celebrity athletes, I founded the clinic to provide excellent service for not just the famous, but also for anyone suffering from an injury. We treat everyone equally and respect everyone's privacy." He began to walk down the hall and they followed him. "That being said, we also recognize that some of our patients, because of their celebrity status, require us to take more precautions to keep them protected from the media. I don't think that will be something you will have a personal problem with, but as manager it will be something that you will have to make sure is enforced in your department."

They stopped at an open door and Devon knew by the large oak desk that sat against a bank of large windows that it must be Michael's office.

"Give me a moment to make a call and I'll be right back to give you a tour of the place." Michael said.

As Michael stepped inside the office, Devon looked over at Shalonda and realized that the woman hadn't said a word since she'd introduced Devon to Michael. "My grandmother used to be Dr. Hart's parents' housekeeper here in Silver Sands, and I would tag along with her when I was a kid."

There. That sounded innocent enough. The woman didn't need to know how close she'd once been to his family. Though it didn't explain the use of each other's nicknames. Most housekeepers probably weren't friendly enough to call their employers' children by their nicknames. But then, her grandmother had been more than just a housekeeper to Michael and his brother, Matthew.

Instead of questioning Devon further, Shalonda just smiled and nodded her head. "It sounds like this has been a good surprise for Dr. Hart. The two of you should work well together."

"Do you really think he's going to offer me the job?" She knew she should be happy that it looked like she would be getting what she wanted, yet she couldn't help but worry about how easily her memories had rushed back to a happier time, when their lives had been so tangled together.

"Well, he wants to give you a personal tour. Of course, that could be him wanting the two of you to catch up. Or it could be he wants to show off a bit. This place is spectacular," Shalonda said. "It looks to me like this will all work out great. I'm going to get back to my office. Just have Dr. Hart bring you back to me when he finishes showing you around." With that, the woman turned on her heel and left Devon standing in the hallway alone.

A few moments later, Michael came out of his office. "Sorry, I needed to check on one of my patients."

"I don't want to hold you up. I know you must be busy." And though she knew it was the perfect time for her to start executing her plan to find out if Michael was someone she wanted in her son's life, she really wasn't prepared to spend this time alone with him right now. But then, would she ever really be prepared for this?

When her husband had asked her to find Michael and explain to him about Conner, she'd been unable to refuse. Zach had been sick for almost a year by then and he'd suffered too much for Devon to deny him anything. But even now, after making the move back to Silver Sands and standing here beside Michael, she had her doubts about Zach's reasoning. She knew Zach had only been doing what he thought was best for Conner, but her husband had never experienced the teasing and embarrassment she'd suffered as a child. He didn't know what it was like to have people call his mother names. Having it come out that Conner was Michael's son instead of Zach's in her small town would cause a lot of talk. And when the parents talked, the children would hear every word. Somehow, she had to protect her son while also keeping her promise to Zach.

When she'd seen the advertisement for the surgical manager position she'd immediately come up with the idea to use the job as a way to get to know Michael again and make sure that Zach was right in thinking that it would be good for their son to have his biological father in his life. Now, she was seeing that this wasn't going to be as easy as she had thought. She couldn't seem to look at Michael without old memories returning.

"I'm really sorry to hear about your husband," Michael said again as they left his office suite and headed back down the hall toward the front entrance.

"Thank you," Devon said. It always felt awkward to have people tell her they were sorry to hear about Zach's passing, especially people who hadn't known him. "He was a good man. A wonderful husband and father, too."

"Your grandmother told me that you had a little boy," Michael said as they took another hallway, this one labeled with a Staff Only sign.

"You saw my grandmother before she passed?" Devon said, hoping Michael couldn't hear the wobble in her voice.

"I came home briefly, right before I began my residency. She was very proud of you. She showed me a picture of you and your husband and your son. She said you'd just moved to California then. You looked happy."

Devon knew the picture he was talking about. She'd found it among her grandmother's things when she'd come home for her funeral. It had been taken right after Zach had just joined the military and Conner had still been a newborn. Looking back now, her world had been perfect.

They came to a stop at a set of double doors with a sign stating that surgical attire was necessary to enter and she looked up into Michael's face. "I was very happy."

"I'm glad you were happy," Michael said, his voice low and earnest. Something passed between the two of them then as he once again studied her face. Neither one of them spoke about it—that night they'd shared—but she knew they were both thinking about it.

For a moment, they just stood there. She wasn't sure if he'd thought she'd spend her life being miserable, because he'd never called her after that night, or if he truly just meant he was glad she had been happy. Either way, she'd had enough of the past. It was time to get back to the here and now.

"So how many operating rooms do you run a day?" she asked.

"We only run four at a time right now, but we have the ability to run two more." Since they were unable to enter the ORs, as neither of them was dressed in their scrubs, Michael explained a little about the operating room setups and the staffing, then led her into the recovery room and through to the presurgery areas. As he explained the reasoning behind each department layout, she could hear the pride in his voice. It was easy to see that he had found his place in the medical world, even though it was far from the future he'd planned when they were growing up.

"This place is amazing. The technology is first-rate and I can already tell the layout works perfectly," she said, though what she really wanted was to ask him how he'd managed to accomplish all of this in such a short time. But she couldn't let herself do that. The only way she could do what Zach had asked was to keep things strictly impersonal between her and Michael.

"I'm glad you think so," Michael said as they made their way back to the small HR department, where Shalonda was waiting for her. His phone went off and he paused to read a message before looking back up. "I'm sorry, I need to make a call so I'm going to leave you with Shalonda now. I hope you decide to join us here. As you can tell, the staff here are friendly and I think you'd be a great addition to the team."

An hour later, Devon walked out of the sleek entrance to the surgical center with an offer for a job that more than met her needs. Shalonda had told her to think about it overnight, but she'd also told her not to take too long. There were other candidates interested in the position and they wanted to get it filled as soon as possible.

Devon knew that the woman had to think she was crazy for not accepting the position immediately. After all, it was the position that she had applied for. But after seeing Michael again after all these years, she wasn't sure that she was doing the right thing.

She'd planned on basically infiltrating Michael's business to see what type of man he'd become. After seeing him and talking to him, she now felt unsure about her plan. She'd known Michael since she was thirteen. What more did she hope to learn about him?

Or was she just trying to postpone the moment that she knew would change everything? The moment she had to tell Michael that she'd had their child and never told him.

By the time she hurried home and changed her clothes, then drove to the football field, where she'd dropped off Conner that morning for camp, she was feeling better. For a moment, she'd let her guard down and forgotten the reason she was there. It wasn't to relive old times with Michael. She was there for her son.

Feeling better now, she locked her car and walked

over to the bleachers, where the other parents were watching from the small stands that had been set up. She spotted Conner the moment she sat down, his hair a little more copper than her own strawberry blond, making it easy to pick him out. His face was flushed as he concentrated on the exercise they were doing. And when he looked over at the boy next to him and smiled, Devon thought her heart would explode. It had been so long since she'd seen a genuine smile on her son's face. Maybe this was a sign that coming back to her small hometown was the right thing to do. And maybe, no matter how things turned out with Michael, she'd found the perfect place for the two of them to begin to heal after losing Zach.

Michael headed to his truck at a trot. His last surgery had run longer than he had expected and then he'd gotten so caught up in all his new CEO responsibilities that now, he was going to be late. He knew he was wearing too many hats but at the moment, he had no choice. His plan to slowly open the sports institute six months ago hadn't gone quite like he'd planned. In the months leading up to its opening, he'd received so many requests from orthopedic doctors in the neighboring area to perform surgery in the new surgical center that they'd opened up with almost a full schedule. Of course, he'd vetted each surgeon. The failure of his football career just made it more important that this center was a success. He couldn't afford to have less than the best working here.

But while he was thrilled that his idea of a sports-centered surgical center had been received so well, after six months the workload was starting to get to him. He needed help. That thought reminded him that he hadn't heard from his brother in several days.

"Call Matt," he ordered his car system, then waited as the phone rang several times.

"Hey, bro. What's up?" his little brother asked. He could hear voices and the ringing of call bells in the background.

"Just checking in. What's going on there?" Michael asked. The guilt he felt about those first few years after their parents had died still haunted him. Even though it had been years since they'd repaired their relationship, he knew he had let his brother down. He'd never forget, never wanted to forget, how he'd let himself get too caught up in his own life to think about the brother he'd left behind with grandparents who'd never wanted the responsibility of caring for a teenage boy. He could take the easy way out and blame it on being busy with college and his football career, but the truth was that he'd been so self-absorbed that he hadn't given his brother's situation that much thought. Yet it had been his little brother, the one that his grandparents called irresponsible, who had been there for him after his football injury. He'd helped Michael navigate through the surgeries and the rehab that had followed, handled the media storm, and had even taken time off from his own college courses. Michael knew he wouldn't be where he was now if it hadn't been for his brother.

Michael would never be able to make up for the way he'd let Matt down, but he knew he'd never let it happen again. His brother was family. The only family he had besides his grandparents, who had only ever seen the two of them as a responsibility they didn't want.

"Nothing now. I assisted Dr. Davis with two total knee surgeries and was attending for two more. But I did get called in last night for a trauma, an open ankle fracture, which took three trauma nails to repair." His brother's voice was getting faster as he talked about the trauma case. Matt was destined to be a great orthotrauma surgeon. Pride filled Michael. They'd both lost their way for a short time, but now they were on a path that he knew would have made their parents proud.

"How's it going there? One of the other residents saw an article on the clinic that came out last week. You're getting good media coverage after that tennis star raved about how well he's doing after you did his ACL repair," Matthew said.

"First, the media coverage is great for the surgical center, which is good for both of us, not just me. That patient's recovery was remarkable and he worked hard with physical therapy to help make that happen. But I think that new femoral fixation I told you about helped with his knee stabilization, too. I'm seeing it make a big difference in the way my patients are recovering. As soon as you get here, I'm going to set you up with the vendor representative to be trained with it. Her name is Rachel and she's been extremely helpful."

"I'm looking forward to that. Anything else going on? Did you get that new surgical manager hired who was supposed to interview today?" his brother asked.

"I think so, and you're not going to believe who

it is. Do you remember Devon Fitzpatrick?" Michael still couldn't believe that Devon had showed up today. He'd thought of her many times over the last few years. Like a lot of occasions in his life, things between them hadn't ended the way he would have liked.

"Sunshine? Ms. Donna's granddaughter? Of course, I remember her. It seemed she had a hard life before she came to live with her grandmother. She was so quiet when she first started coming to the house. It took months before she said more than two words to us."

"Mom said that Ms. Donna had taken custody of her because Devon's mom had let some guy move in with them and he'd get drunk and beat on the two of them."

"Yeah, that was the rumor around school, too. I never could understand why some of the kids teased her about her mom when everyone knew none of it was her fault. Remember when you threatened to beat up that kid at the high school for making fun of her? You were her hero after that. She had such a big crush on you that year, though I was definitely the best-looking of the two of us."

Michael knew his brother was teasing. It had been a joke between the two of them since they were teenagers, each one of them declaring they were the better-looking Hart brother. But Michael didn't bother to argue with him now. Scars littered his body from all the surgeries he'd had after the injuries he'd received when two defensive linemen had tackled him, crushing him into the ground and ending his pro football career. But most of his scars couldn't be seen from the outside. Even after several surgeries on his right leg and arm, his body sometimes creaked and popped, letting him know that it had been changed forever.

And as far as the crush Matt claimed Sunshine once had on him, Michael had always thought of her as more of a little sister...until the night his parents had died. It had been that night, the night she'd found him walking on the beach, which had changed things between them. Her sitting down with him right there in the sand while he cried over the loss of his parents with her arms wrapped around him had been more than his grandparents had ever done for him. They'd talked for hours about his parents without him feeling embarrassed or judged. They'd both cried and laughed, and when the sun had just started to come up, he'd found himself kissing her. It had only been one kiss, but there had been nothing brotherly about it. Then there had been the night a few years later when they'd run into each other at the hotel in Tallahassee. That night had been an eye-opener for both of them. Seeing Devon—and he'd definitely thought of her as Devon instead of the girl he'd known as Sunshine—dressed up in a short black dress, with her strawberry blond hair up in some fancy knot on top of her head, and her long legs walking toward him in those crazy high heels, had erased all his memories of the teenage girl he'd once known.

He'd never told Matthew about that night in Tallahassee. He'd treated it as a guarded secret, one too precious to share. She'd left her number on a piece of paper that he'd found lying on top of his suitcase the next morning when he was packing to leave. He could have called her then, but he'd put it off. Something to do later, when his mind wasn't so filled with getting ready for the next game. Then he'd woken up in the hospital to find out his life had been changed forever. He could have made a comeback after the concussion he'd received, maybe even made it back after he'd recovered from the broken femur. But the complete detached bicep and rotator-cuff injury wasn't something a quarterback could bounce back from. His career had been over, and he'd been surprised to find that without football, he didn't have much of a life left.

But all of that was in the past now. The injuries had happened. He had never made that phone call. And Devon had apparently moved on quite quickly to someone else.

"Her name is Campbell now. Her husband died recently and she's moved back home to live in Ms. Donna's house."

"I hate to hear that about her husband. You know she called you the day after your injuries," Matt said, his voice becoming muffled.

"What? What did you say?" Michael asked as the background sounds on the phone went silent. Had he heard his brother right? She'd called him? "Matt? Did you say she called me?"

"Sorry," Matt said as his voice suddenly came back across the phone line, "I got on the elevator."

"Did you say that Devon called me while I was in the hospital?" Michael asked again, his voice a little more inpatient now.

"Yeah, she called several times. A lot of people called that first day, you must have gotten at least a hundred calls after people watched you get injured. It was horrific seeing you carried off the field. The media was camped outside the hospital for almost twenty-four hours. The vice president of the United States even made a call to wish you well on behalf of the president. It was crazy."

"But you said Devon called several times?" Michael asked, still surprised that he hadn't been told, though it wasn't like he'd been in any condition to take the calls those first few days. But what if he had? Would it really have made any difference?

"Yeah, after I gave your phone to your agent to handle, Devon even called my phone a couple times. Said she'd got my number from Grandpa Hart. She seemed really worried about you, but I told her you were going to be okay. It was before the team announced just how bad your injuries were, though," Matt admitted.

The announcement that he wouldn't ever be returning to his former career hadn't come until a month later. Not until after the last surgery, when the poor prognosis for a full recovery, or at least one that would make him able to return to playing football, had been determined.

"Hey, you okay?" Matt asked. "I didn't mean to bring all that up again." Matt was the only one who knew that Michael still struggled with how his dream of playing pro football had come to an end.

"No, it's fine. I was just surprised to hear Devon had called. It was nice of her to do it. I'll have to thank her." Once again, he wondered what might have happened if he'd just found time to make that one call after the night they'd shared.

"You sure?" Matt asked.

"Yes," Michael replied.

"Well, if she's as right for the manager job as you say, hire her. It would be great to work with her when I make it down there. Besides, you need the help. All you've done is work since that place opened. You have no work-life balance. It's not good for you."

"Says the brother who's working day and night in his residency," Michael teased, his brother's words hitting a little too close to home.

"It's residency. I'm supposed to have no life. Besides, I'm the youngest brother. You're getting old, bro. It's time for you to start thinking about starting a family," Matt said. This wasn't the first time that his brother had brought up the subject of Michael settling down.

"I have a family. I have you," Michael said firmly.

"Hey, hold on a moment," Matt said. Michael could hear someone in the background talking to his brother. "Hey, Mickey, I've got to go. Patients to see and all that."

Michael told his brother goodbye and ended the call as he pulled into the community sports complex. He parked near the football field, where the town's youth played everything from Tiny-Mites to high school football, with kids starting at age five going up until graduation. The complex had needed a lot of work when he'd played there as a kid. Fortunately, he'd finally been able to get the town board to see that the community needed a safe place for the kids to enjoy sports and recreation. Now, there was talk of a public pool where people could cool off during those hot summer days and a splash pad for the younger children, too.

He'd come back to town hoping to make a difference in the community where he could. Today he was there to help his best friend, Bryan, with the summer football camp that they put on every year for the kids registered for that year's recreation teams.

After getting out of his truck, he looked up in the stands at all the eager parents, watching their offspring. He remembered looking up into those stands and seeing his own mom and dad rooting for him. He hoped every parent up there was as supportive of their kid's dreams as his parents had been.

Then he saw her. She'd changed since he'd seen her earlier that day. Now dressed in jeans and a simple white T-shirt, she looked like any other sports mom, except for that beautiful blond hair with those pale red highlights that shone bright in the sunlight. He'd always thought that was where she had gotten the nickname Sunshine. Though he knew he needed to join Bryan, he couldn't stop himself from climbing up the steps to join her on the bleachers. After seeing her today at work and then the call with his brother, he found himself wanting to know more about the woman Devon Fitzgerald had grown up to be.

"I wasn't expecting to see you again today," he said as he took a seat beside her. Then he realized the reason she was probably up in these stands. Devon had a son. "Is your son out there?"

For a moment, she didn't answer him—didn't even look at him as her eyes started darting around the stands as if looking for an escape. She seemed nervous. He looked around to see what had her so upset.

A whistle went off on the field, bringing their attention back to where Bryan was having all the players fall in around him. Michael looked back at Devon, who took what seemed to be a very deep breath, as if she was about to face something painful.

"Yes. My son, Conner, is out there. He's on the Mitey-Mite team," she said, still staring at where all the kids stood listening to Bryan's first-day-of-camp speech that Michael had heard so often he could almost recite it himself.

"A Mitey-Mite? That's the team Bryan and I coach." He looked over to where Devon was staring and saw a boy with hair only a shade darker than hers. Who would have ever thought that someday he would be coaching Sunshine's son?

CHAPTER TWO

Devon couldn't believe it. What were the chances that she'd come back to town and enroll her son into football only to find that his biological father was going to be the coach? She'd never even considered the possibility. Michael had once been a big-time football star, but she would have thought he'd be too busy with his new career to take time out to coach a team of seven-year-olds.

Devon stared down at the field, where she could see her son concentrating on every word his coach was saying. Conner had been fascinated with the sport since the first time Zach had taken him to a college game at their alumni weekend. Devon had gone along, thinking the five-year-old would tire and get restless during the long game. But instead, Conner had listened to his father explain everything that was happening on the field. Zach, being an IT guy, had always been interested in the strategy of the game and he'd passed his interest onto their son.

Zach had been such a good dad, so patient and caring. Yet that day she couldn't help but think about Michael and the fact that he should have been the one explaining the game he loved so much to Conner. Of course, then the guilt had set in, as it always did when she thought of Michael. But how could she be thinking about Michael being there with her son when Zach had been such a good husband and father to them both?

Yet here she was now, with Michael sitting beside her, telling her he was going to be their son's new coach.

But Conner had never been Michael's son. He was Zach's son in every way that counted. Her college friend and roommate had made that commitment to her and the child she'd carried when they'd taken their vows. And if what had grown between them hadn't been her childhood dream of love, it had been something even better. Their friendship had grown into something more real than anything she had ever known before. There never could have been a better father than Zach. Her only regret was that the two of them had never been able to have another child. But they'd both known that the radiation treatment Zach had received when he was young had meant there would no more children. And, yes, she knew that was one of the reasons Zach had been so willing to marry Devon when she'd found out that she was alone and pregnant. He'd wanted children. But that had never mattered to her. He'd been there for her when she'd needed him. Because of Zach, Conner had never had to face the childhood teasing she'd been subjected to when people had asked her where her dad was. Devon would always be thankful for that. Zach had always been there for Conner. He would always be her son's father.

It was because of Zach that she was here. He had made her promise to tell Michael about Conner. He could have been selfish and kept Conner thinking that he was their son's only father. But he hadn't wanted that. He'd wanted Conner to have someone to be there, if not to replace him, at least to fill in for him. It had been the most loving thing Devon had ever experienced. Yet here she stood, not able to do what she'd been asked to do. Not yet. Not until she was sure that Michael was someone she wanted to share her son with.

Clearing her throat, she tried to calm herself before continuing, but her emotions had been all over the place today. She needed to go home. Or maybe she just needed to change the subject. "Thank you for showing me around the surgical center today. It was amazing."

"Opening a new surgical unit was risky and we couldn't take a chance of it not taking off. Our goal was for the Hart Sports Institute to be the premier surgical unit for professional athletes. We needed the draw that would have to help bring in the local, everyday athletes. But I also wanted to offer something for the professionals that I didn't have when I was injured," Michael said.

"What's that?" Devon asked, turning to look at him. She found herself interested in this part of him, the businessman she had never known. It was just one more piece of the puzzle that she needed to understand about him.

She'd always thought of Michael as a jock. Not that he wasn't smart. He was very intelligent. He'd never had any trouble in school. Still, she'd never imagined him going to medical school and becoming a doctor, let alone building something like the surgical center. For as long as she could remember, he'd been totally consumed with his dream of playing professional football. But now, he was not only a well-known orthopedic surgeon, but also the founder of an impressive surgical institution.

"Privacy and confidentiality, things that are hard to find these days between the media and the internet, were two of the most important things we considered when we designed the clinic. We wanted a way for someone who preferred to keep their visit totally private to get into the clinic and out again without the public being aware. So we created areas in the hospital where we can treat our patients on a one-to-one basis when needed," Michael said.

"So that's what the private recovery rooms I saw are for," she said, thinking about the layout of the surgical center in a whole new light.

"Yes. It's also one of the reasons I knew Silver Sands was the perfect place for the clinic. We're a small town. Family-oriented. We're not full of tourists. There are no five-star restaurants or even a water park within miles. This isn't a place where you're going to have a bunch of paparazzi hanging around. While it is known that some athletes and some celebrities have used the clinic, it's unlikely that they'll run into anyone here looking for a story. It's the perfect place for someone to not only recover, but they can also go through rehab with our physical therapist, if they choose. I'm in the process of leasing a couple condos where they can have our physical therapist come to them for the first few days after recovery."

"It sounds like you've thought of everything," Devon said. She couldn't help but be impressed.

"I had a lot of time to think about it when I was in rehab myself. It was a nightmare for the first few months with the media hounding me every time I had to go out in public. It was the whole experience, the good and the bad, that made me want to go into orthopedics and open a place where professional athletes could feel at home."

He stood and waved to one of the coaches, someone Devon had known almost as long as she'd known Michael. "It looks like Bryan is ready for me. Stick around after we finish here, and we can talk more. There's something I'd like to talk to you about besides the job."

And with that, he headed down the steps and then across the field to where the young boys were waiting. She held her breath when he joined the group and she saw Conner move to the front, almost directly in front of Michael. Would he see Conner and recognize him? Would he notice the way his eyes were the same green color as his own? Would he notice that crooked smile that the two of them shared? Her brain told her he wouldn't see the similarities. But in her heart, where she'd let fear of this moment grow, she just knew that it was possible. All it would take was for him to start putting a few small things together, like Conner's age, and exactly when they'd spent their one night with one another, and he would know that Devon had kept one of the biggest secrets in her life from him.

She knew that she'd need to tell him, but she couldn't bring herself to do it. Not yet. Not until she was absolutely sure that her son wouldn't be hurt.

It wasn't that she thought Michael would ever physically harm Conner. Michael was nothing like the men her mother used to move in with them. He'd never think that it was okay to backhand a child because they were in their way, nor would he ever lock a child in their room for hours without food. It wasn't the physical abuse she was afraid of. Instead, it was the emotional trauma that could come from this situation. The kind her mother had inflicted when she'd abandoned Devon for days without calling, never thinking about how that made Devon feel unloved and unwanted. Would Michael want to know Conner, or would it make her son feel rejected if he didn't?

Besides, what was the hurry? Maybe having Michael coaching Conner's team was a great opportunity for her to see how he and her son got along together.

And what could it be that he wanted to talk to her about besides the job? Was it about that night they'd spent together? It could be considered an uncomfortable situation between the two of them if she went to work for him. But more than likely it was so deep in his past that he wouldn't even be thinking about that now, let alone bother to mention it. Would he? And if so, what would she say to him?

One-night stands were probably common for someone like Michael, but her? She'd only had the one, and to her it hadn't been as much a one-night stand as it had been one night that she had been waiting for since she was sixteen and had lost her heart to the first boy who had kissed her. Now, she realized that the first kiss they'd shared had been the action of a young boy reaching out for comfort. He'd just found out his parents had been killed in a car crash and they'd spent the night grieving together. But she'd been too young to understand that then. After that night, she'd believed that at some point Michael would see that the two of them were meant for each other. But after he'd gone to college and she'd never heard from him, she'd accepted that it hadn't meant as much to him as it had to her.

That was until the night they'd run into each other in the foyer of that hotel in Tallahassee. It wasn't like she'd gone to that hotel expecting to see him. They had both been a long way from home, her attending college there and him only in town to give a speech. It had seemed like fate had set everything up to finally bring the two of them together. It had only been after Michael had fallen asleep without one word of love or even a mention of seeing her again that the doubts had begun to form in her mind.

She'd left her phone number in the hotel so that he could call her, making it plain that she was interested in more than just that one night. She'd been a naive fool to think that Michael had intended for their encounter to become anything more.

Later, she'd spent hours searching for articles on Michael as she'd tried to figure out if he was really the man she thought she knew or if he had become someone else. Someone who would never give her another thought. She'd found several articles mentioning parties he'd attended and pictures of the women he'd escorted to them. Beautiful, sophisticated women who would not have a problem spending the night with a man without their heart being involved. She'd decided then and there that wasn't the kind of woman she wanted to be. That would never be her. She'd had one night with a man she'd built up in her imagination, but the truth was she hadn't even known the man he was then. The fact that it reminded her of something her mother would have done didn't make her feel any better.

So when he didn't call her the next day, she'd forced herself to accept she'd made a mistake in letting her heart get involved so easily and promised herself she'd never do that again. Even after she found out about his injury, she'd called him multiple times. Yet he'd never reached out to her. Then, three weeks later, there was a surprise. One that came with a test and two pink lines.

A whistle blew and she realized she'd been so lost in her thoughts that she hadn't even noticed the coaches were winding down that day's camp. She stood and waited for Conner to gather his shoulder pads and water bottle, then she saw Michael headed back her way. And right behind him was her son.

After remembering how she'd felt that day, sitting all alone on the floor of her dorm bathroom holding that pregnancy test, she wanted to run and grab Conner, then rush the two of them out to her car before Michael made it to her. She never wanted her son to feel as abandoned as she had felt that day. "Of course, that wouldn't look suspicious at all," she muttered as she forced herself to slow down. She made herself take careful steps down the bleachers and then met the two of them with a smile that she was sure was too bright.

"I saw that catch you made. Way to go, buddy," she said as she stepped around Michael and took her son's water bottle, holding it tight against her chest as if it was armor or, even better, a weapon. This was the moment she'd dreaded. The moment her son and Michael would first meet. Maybe it was better that it happen now, when they were surrounded by all the other parents and kids rushing around them. Maybe it was best to get it over with.

So before she let her nerves get the best of her and she did something crazy, like bolt off the field dragging her son behind her, she turned to Michael. "Mickey, this is my son, Conner."

"Mom, his name isn't Mickey—it's Michael Hart. You know, number sixteen," Conner said in a too-loud whisper to Devon then pointed to where there was a *16* posted on the back fence behind a goalpost. Devon remembered when she'd first seen the sign designating the number for their hometown football hero after Michael had led his team to the college football playoffs.

"But your mom has known me for a long time, so she calls me the name my parents and her grandmother used to call me," Michael said as he stretched out his hand to Conner.

As Conner reached out and shook Michael's hand, Devon held her breath. She'd never imagined this moment would ever happen. But Zach's death and her promise to him had changed everything.

"Really? You know my mom?" Conner said, looking up at Michael with eyes as wide as saucers.

"I do. We grew up together right her in Silver Sands. I played ball on this field, just like you will," Michael said, then looked over at her. "And I'm hoping your mom is going to work with me."

Conner looked over at Devon then, and studied her

like he'd never seen her before. "You're going to help the coach with our team?"

Before she could answer her son, Michael's arm came around Conner's shoulders. "I just coach part of the time. I gave up football and became a doctor. I hear your mom is a good nurse so I'm hoping she'll come work with me where I do surgery."

"Why did you want to give up football? My dad said that the football players make lots of money and they don't have to work but one day a week," Conner said, his face so earnest as he insulted athletes around the world without even knowing it. "Didn't you want to make lots of money?"

"I think we've taken up enough of the coach's time for now," Devon said, taking her son's hand and pulling him beside her before turning back to Michael. "I'm sorry. He's at the age where he never runs out of questions."

"Well, of course he asks questions. If he doesn't ask he'll never know the answer. Right, Conner?" Michael said as Bryan walked up behind him and Devon finally saw her chance to escape.

She had just turned toward the parking lot when she heard Bryan call out to her. "Devon, are you meeting us at the Pizza Shack? Most of the boys are going."

She pretended she didn't hear him, but Conner had heard the word *pizza* and dug his heels into the ground. "Mom, can we go? Can we? You like pizza and this way you won't have to cook supper."

Devon looked down at her son's face and felt all her fears melt away. Since they'd lost Zach, Conner had been just as lost as she had been. He'd had some friends, both from his school and families of some military friends of Devon and Zach's, but he'd insisted on staying close to her whenever possible. He'd turned down sleepovers and playdates each time he'd been invited. Devon had even considered taking him to a therapist until she'd realized that it wasn't really depression as much as Conner didn't want to leave her alone. It was her depression that he was responding to. Her withdrawal from her own friends that caused him to want to stay close by her side. So instead of Conner being taken to a therapist, it had been her who had sought one out.

But here was Conner wanting to be a part of something. She'd hoped that once they'd gotten settled in town and he began to meet new people that this would happen. If she said no now, he might not want to go next time. She knew she had to set an example for him and also help him start flying on his own again. And wasn't this the perfect opportunity for that? In a town this size, the boys on his team would also be the boys in his school classes from now until graduation.

So although she wanted nothing more than to put some miles between her and Michael right now, she turned to her son and nodded her head, then turned to where Bryan and Michael stood waiting for her answer. "Pizza sounds good. We'd love to go."

"Thanks, Mom," her son said with a smile, "and don't worry. I still have some of my birthday money so I can pay for it."

Devon felt her face go red, but she didn't say anything, knowing that her denying that she needed her son's money just to buy a pizza would make it look even worse. Her son had always been too attentive for his age, constantly asking questions about anything he didn't understand. And after a few times of her telling him that they couldn't buy some luxuries, like a new game for his gaming system or the fancy tennis shoes he'd seen on TV, she'd had to sit him down and explain that they had to be careful how they spent their money until she found a new job. Since then, he'd requested very few things from her, another reason that going out tonight would be good for him.

"We'll meet you there," she said, then took her son's hand in hers and headed to her car.

Michael waited at a table for two that had been placed close to where the team's players and their parents were sitting at several tables thrown together by their waitress. He usually avoided most of the spontaneous team outings, both because of his job and the fact that he felt like the odd one out as all the other coaches had families. He was the only coach of the Mitey-Mites team who didn't have a son playing.

But tonight, he'd changed his plans from going back to the office to finish up paperwork so that he could talk to Devon. He told himself that it was because he wanted to talk to her about the job, but he was afraid it was more than that. Ever since they'd spent that one night together, he'd often thought of her. Even when her grandmother had told him that she had married, he'd felt that things had been left unsaid between the two of them. He had told himself that it was his conscience that had bothered him all these years, after not calling her. But today, as they'd talked, he'd wondered if there was more to it than that.

So here he sat, watching the door and waiting for Devon and her son to come in. He'd seen her through the front glass windows pulling up in a little SUV more than five minutes ago, but neither she nor Conner had gotten out. From what the little boy had said, he couldn't help but wonder if she was inside the vehicle counting out her change to see if they could afford to come inside and join them.

Michael had always known that his family was well off. His father had been a successful neurosurgeon in Atlanta before he'd retired and moved his family down to the beach. His mother had done well also, working as a news anchor for one of the local television channels before he had been born. Both of his parents had been older when they'd met, his mother turning forty just after his birth. Not long after his brother had been born, the two of them had decided to retire to the beach. They'd searched for a small town where they could raise their sons and had bought a large home that was only a few feet from the warm gulf waters.

Then his parents had been killed after a car had run their vehicle off the road and into a parked car. They'd died instantly, the police officers had said, as if that would make an eighteen-year-old boy who'd just learned his parents were gone feel better. There had been a large settlement from the accident that had been put in a trust for him and his brother by his grandparents. His college had been covered with scholarships, even though he hadn't needed them, so his trust had been mostly untouched. Then he'd been drafted to play football, and he'd made enough money on media and television sponsorships, along with the money from his contract during his one year playing at a professional level, that he had more money than he would ever need in his lifetime if he handled it well.

Thinking that Devon might be sitting there counting out change to buy a piece of pizza for her son made him feel sick to his stomach.

The door to the SUV opened and he relaxed when he saw both mom and son smiling as they walked, hand in hand, toward him. The bell over the door rang as it swung open and Devon's son pulled away from her and ran to a group of boys sitting at the end of one of the tables. When Devon looked around for a seat, he raised a hand and waved her over to him. He saw the hesitancy in her steps, but then she slowly walked over to the only empty chair on that side of the room. The one he'd so carefully saved for her.

"I was beginning to think that you weren't going to show," he said, and then wished he could take the words back, not wanting her to think he'd been sitting there worried that she didn't have the money to afford to join them.

"Sorry. I just needed to have a talk with Conner. He... I think he got the wrong idea about a few things." Her eyes didn't meet his and he could see that she was embarrassed.

He wasn't really sure what her situation was as far as her finances went, but he did know a way to help that wouldn't be embarrassing for either of them. Actually, it would help him out as much as it seemed it could help her out. "I wanted to talk to you about the job. Shalonda sent me a message saying that she had offered you the position and you were considering it. What can I do to help make up your mind?"

For a moment she looked taken back, her eyes a little wild, as if he'd cornered her. "Is it the hours? The money? I know we're a new facility without any type of financial history, but I can guarantee that we are financially stable. We are almost at capacity when it comes to our office space being rented out and our daily surgical schedules are getting filled up faster every day."

For a moment all she did was stare at him, her mouth half-open and a deep crease forming between her eyes. Then she started laughing, and both her hands came up to cover her face. He was afraid she might be crying, but when she let her hands fall, there was nothing but a broad smile on her face. "Are you trying to convince me to take a job with you because my son had some misguided belief that I couldn't afford to buy a pizza?"

"No, I mean…" He wasn't sure what to say. "No, not really. Though it did cross my mind. I had planned to talk to you about the job, anyway. That's why I had asked you to stick around after the game. I just thought…"

"You thought I was desperate for money and you wanted to help me out," she said, now sounding a little annoyed at him. "Yes, I need a job for the money, Mickey. It is why most people apply for jobs, you know. But I'm not destitute, if that was what you were thinking."

"I didn't mean to insult you." He looked around the room as if he could find some way out of the hole he'd dug for himself, because right now, she reminded him of her grandmother. If there was one thing Ms. Donna had it was a strong sense of pride.

"I really do want to hire you. I need a good manager. The one we had originally hired had to move not two months after we opened when her husband got transferred to Texas."

"Oh, I know you need me. But I'll bet you a whole pizza that you were sitting here about to offer me more money than what Shalonda and I had already discussed, just because you thought I was broke."

He didn't say anything, unable to deny that the thought had crossed his mind.

"Well, no matter what you might think, I don't need anyone's charity," she said, her deep green eyes narrowing at him.

The server, who Michael planned on giving a generous tip, picked that moment to interrupt them, taking Devon's order for a soft drink and assuring Michael that the pizza he had ordered, for the two of them, would be out momentarily. Devon tilted her head toward him and her eyebrows went up with her unspoken question.

"Yes, I ordered a pizza for both of us. The one with all the meats and vegetables that you use to love. I've also ordered for all the kids." It was definitely time for him to change the subject. He could circle back to the job after she got over being mad at him. "I spoke with Matt today. I told him you'd interviewed for the job. He was really excited to hear you had moved back to town. He said you'd called him a few times after I was injured."

"He only told you today, after all this time, that I had

called you after you were hurt?" she said, then took a drink of the water that had been provided. "You didn't know I'd called?"

"No, I didn't. Don't be mad at him. Things were crazy then, with the media, my coach, my agent. I don't know what I would have done if Matt hadn't showed up to help out." It had been called "the Great Tragedy" by the media. There had been so much hype about him being the number one draft pick. Then the games that the team had won that season had just doubled the amount of press coverage he'd received. He'd felt lost during those first days, weeks, and months. It had been a lot like the loss he'd felt when his parents had been killed. He'd felt alone and vulnerable, something that a six-foot-six, two-hundred-and-thirty-pound pro quarterback could never let anyone see. But Matt, barely twenty, had plowed through all the people surrounding Michael and taken over. He was the one person who Michael had known he could trust when the pain and medication had left his grasp of his surroundings a bit tenuous.

"I'm not mad," Devon said slowly. "I'm just surprised you didn't know I'd called until now."

Their pizza came and neither of them spoke much as they ate, with just a few comments about the deliciousness of all the pizza's cheesy goodness.

Then Michael felt a tug on his shirt and looked over to see that Devon's son stood beside him. "Excuse me, Coach Hart. I just wanted you to know that I'm sorry if I said something that might have given you the—" the boy paused and took a breath "—m-press-on that my mom doesn't have any money. I didn't mean to embarrass her. She does have some money. We just have to be careful with it until she gets a job. Until then, we have to save all our money so we don't get our electricity turned off, because then I won't be able to play any of my video games."

The boy left their table then and ran back over to join the boys from his team as they all tucked into the pizza Michael had bought. He looked over at Devon, whose mouth was open, a piece of stringy, melted cheese clinging to her lips. "I can't believe he just did that. He... I just tried to explain to him that we had to pay the bills first before we spent anything on extras. I thought he understood."

Michael couldn't help but smile. "He's a kid. Give him a break. I think it was very nice the way he was trying to help you."

"If he helps me any more I'm going to start finding casseroles at the front door." She shook her head as if she couldn't believe her child's behavior, then looked up at him. "So tell me more about this job, because it looks like I need to get one before my son has Child Services over at the house checking out my cabinets for food."

So he told her about the job, most of which he was sure Shalonda had already gone over. Then he told her about his and Matthew's dream for the place, their hopes that the surgical center could grow and provide more rehabilitation services for the community as well as professional athletes. "I don't want to make you take this job if it's not what you're looking for. It's going to take time to build the practice here, even though we're off to a great start. But if you decide you do want the job, come in Monday morning. Shalonda will do the paperwork then and you can start right away."

She nodded her head at him, but he didn't miss the fact that she didn't actually say she'd be there Monday. He wanted to ask her just what it was that was holding her back, but he didn't want to push too hard.

While they finished their pizza, Michael told her more about his and Matt's plans, and she gave him suggestions that were helpful. A few minutes later, he watched as Devon and Conner walked across the parking lot, once more hand in hand. For a moment he wondered what would have happened if he hadn't been so tied up in that dream of his to play football at the highest level. Or better yet, what would have happened if he hadn't been injured two days after the night they'd spent together? Could they have had more than just that night together? Could they have taken the friendship they'd had for years and built something more out of it? If he had called her and arranged to see her again, would the two of them perhaps even have had a family? Would it be him buckling their son or daughter into the car right now, getting ready to head home together?

He shook his head. He'd quit wondering about what life would have been like if he hadn't been injured many years ago. What had happened between them all those years ago was in the past. Devon had gone on to marry and have a son. She had probably not given that night another thought.

But there had been those phone calls she'd made to him that left him wondering if maybe that night had meant more to her, too.

CHAPTER THREE

MONDAY MORNING, Devon made the dreaded first day of drop-off at the elementary school. As the line crept closer and closer to the front door area, where the teachers met the students and helped them onto the sidewalk, she noticed Conner squirming more and more in his seat. "What's wrong? Did we forget something?"

"No, ma'am. This school just looks different. It's kind of old and spooky. And what if I don't know anyone in my class?" Conner said as he stared out the window at the other children unloading and heading into the building.

"It's not that old. I remember when they built it."

"It's that old?" Conner asked, his wide eyes telling her that he must think of her as ancient.

"It's okay. I'm sure it's had a lot of renovations and it even has the internet now," Devon said as she eased another car length closer. "And I didn't know anyone in my class my first day of school when I moved to town. I'm going to tell you a secret. I was scared. I even tried to get my grandma to take me home."

She still remembered the look on her grandmother's face. Then Devon had explained that she wanted to go home, where her grandpa was, not to the home where her mama lived. She'd never asked to go back to live with her mother. After the constant moving in with one "uncle" after another, the security of her grandparents' home had been like heaven to her.

"But you know what? I made lots of friends that first day, and some of them are even still my friends," she said.

"Like Coach Bryan and Coach Hart?" he asked.

"Yeah, like your coaches," she said as she finally pulled up to the front door and one of the teachers, who looked familiar to her, opened the back passenger door. "Cassie? Cassie Long? Is that you?" She waved at the woman, then watched to make sure her son didn't forget anything as he climbed out.

"Sunshine? I'd heard you were back." Cassie glanced behind her at the cars that still waited in line then back to Devon. "Sorry, I can't talk now, but we need to get together soon. Maybe Friday, after this madness is over?"

"Sure. I'll send a note tomorrow with Conner so you can message me, if that's alright?" Devon said.

"Sounds great." And with that, Cassie slammed the car door shut. She didn't envy her friend for what this first day of school would bring as she waited for the line of cars in front of her to all move forward. Cassie had always wanted to be a teacher, while Devon had never been able to decide what she wanted to be when she grew up. She'd been lucky to find her way into health care after Conner was born, especially surgical services. She just hoped her friend was as happy with her choice as Devon was with hers.

Once she made it out of the school drop-off line, she headed back to the main highway that ran through town. The one where she'd have to decide whether to take the fork that led to the north of town, where Hart Sports Institute had been built, or the fork that led back to her home located along the bay side of the beach.

She'd tossed and turned every night since she'd left Michael at the Pizza Shack without giving him an answer to his job offer. She knew she wanted the job. Needed the job. Even though the school drop-off line was dreaded by most mothers, it was something she wanted to be able to do while Conner was young. If she took another surgical job she'd have to find early morning childcare, which wouldn't be easy. Besides, it had all been part of her plan to get to know Michael. So why was she not just accepting the job and getting on with it?

Maybe because it wasn't just Michael learning about Conner that was holding her back? Maybe because she feared that being around Michael again might start up all those old feelings she'd had for him when she was young?

Okay, that was ridiculous. She wasn't the naive girl she'd been when she'd had the crazy dream that Michael Hart, their high school star quarterback, and son of one of the richest families in town, would someday look at her and fall madly in love. She'd given up on that dream even before they'd run into each other in Tallahassee, the night she'd gotten pregnant. If nothing else, the love she'd found with Zach, a love that had grown from friendship and trust, had made her immune from all of those old, unrealistic feelings for Michael. She knew now that love was more than a kiss that curled her toes, or one single night of passion, however magical it had been.

After she'd tried and failed to get in touch with Michael, and then learned that she was pregnant, she'd needed Zach's friendship and support more than ever. When he'd first offered to marry her, she'd turned him down. But after Zach had confided in her about his diagnosis of cancer as a child and the fact that he would probably never be able to father a child due to the treatment he had received, she'd considered it more seriously. She'd made one last attempt that night to call Michael's brother and learned that Michael wasn't taking any phone calls. Once more, she had felt like the little girl who had been forgotten by her mother. Alone, unimportant, and doomed to repeat her mother's mistakes.

Yet the night they'd shared the pizza, Michael had acted like he had just heard about her calling him. If he was telling the truth, she couldn't hold him responsible for not talking to her. Still, he'd made no effort to call her the day after she'd left the hotel, either—and that was before his accident. Which had been a clear sign that the night hadn't meant anything to him. She'd been just another woman who had passed in and out of his life just as her mother had been in several men's lives over the years when Devon was growing up. She had made sure she'd never be that woman again. Now, she just needed to be sure Michael was no longer that same man.

And that was really the only thing that mattered now. It was Conner she needed to be concentrating on. Not Michael. Not her. Conner.

She got to the road that turned north. The surgical center had been built just a mile from there. She looked the other way, where the highway followed along the path of the intercoastal waterway and a bridge led across to the beach that was sandwiched between that and the gulf. She took a deep breath, prayed she was making the right decision, and took the road to the center.

A few moments later, she pulled up in front of the building and put her car in Park. She could sit there questioning the wisdom in taking this job, or she could open the car door and get out.

Someone rapped on the passenger window and she looked to see Michael standing beside her car. It seemed like it was time for her to tell him her decision. She unlocked the door, but before she could climb out, she found him getting in beside her. Her SUV suddenly felt like one of those crowded clown cars.

"Hi," she said, feeling more than a little self-conscious to have been caught sitting outside in her car staring into space.

Michael had always been large for his age when they were growing up. By the time he was in high school, he had stood over a head taller than everyone else in the school. But it hadn't just been his height that had made him stand out. Following his dream to play professional football had meant hours spent in the weight room. From the way he filled out the dark blue dress pants and white button-up shirt he was wearing today, it was obvious that he'd continued working out even after the injuries that had ended his football career. She knew it had to have been painful going through all of the physical therapy he'd had to do to recover from his injuries. Then to know that no matter how hard he worked he'd never be the athlete he'd once been? If nothing else, she admired that he'd picked himself up and done the work while some people would have just given up. And then to have gone further and pursued a career in medicine—that was more than anyone would have expected.

"I just thought I'd see if you were coming in," Michael said, turning in the seat toward her, his arm brushing against hers. "Is everything okay? Are you waiting for something?"

"Sure, everything's fine," she said, though she was beginning to feel a little breathless. It was as though just Michael's presence this close to her had sucked all the air out of the car.

"Look, I did a lot of thinking about you and this job this weekend," Michael said as his hand came up and rubbed his chin.

All of Devon's uncertainties about taking the job suddenly evaporated. Was he going to rescind his offer? Had he decided he didn't want to put up with her hesitancy over taking it? She knew she'd been lucky to be even considered for the job, and suddenly she realized she really wanted it. Why did she have to struggle with every decision she made after losing Zach? Always question if she was doing the right thing?

"I don't understand," she said. "Did you come out here to tell me that you'd changed your mind about offering it to me?"

"No, of course not. I'm serious when I say you are perfect for the job. Shalonda was in charge of recruitment and she offered you the job because your interview went well. I did have the final say, but I agreed with her decision. It wasn't because we have a past together. I want the right person in place for every job here. I don't really know how to explain it. It's just that having my family name on this place makes it so important for me to make it the best that it can be."

"I understand. In some ways this is a memorial to your parents. To what they meant to you." She had thought a lot of his parents, too. Not everyone would have let their housekeeper bring her granddaughter to work with her. But the Harts had welcomed her into their home just as they had her grandmother.

"You're right. To me, my whole career is a memorial to them. Even though they weren't there when my football career ended, I knew that if they had been, they would have believed in me. They'd have told me I was still capable of dreaming big and making that dream come true. They supported me no matter what. And I know I couldn't have done any of this without their belief in me, even though they're no longer here."

For a moment, Devon couldn't speak. Michael had always been passionate about his career, but to hear him give all the credit to his dead parents was so moving.

He rubbed his chin again, then placed both his hands down by his side. He turned his eyes away from her, and if she didn't know better she would have thought that the famous Michael Hart was embarrassed. "I wondered if maybe it was the past we shared that was causing you to hesitate about taking the job. I thought perhaps we needed to talk about that night, the one where we ran into each other at the hotel in Tallahassee. You know, the night we spent together."

So here it was. The talk that she had been dreading. But was this really the perfect time for her to tell him about Conner when they were just starting to get to know each other again?

Michael knew the fact that he couldn't look Devon in the eye right then was ridiculous. He shouldn't feel like a teenager trying to talk to his girl after they'd spent the night in the back seat of his dad's car. They were both adults. Maybe they had been too young when they'd spent that night together, but they'd both been plenty old enough to make an informed decision. The concussion he'd received when he'd been injured on the football field might have taken away some of his memories of the previous days, but he still remembered every single moment of the night he'd spent with Devon in minute detail. Not that he was going to tell her that. If anything, it would give her even more of a reason not to want work for him!

"No," Devon said abruptly, "we don't need to talk about that night. Not ever."

"Are you sure?" he said, glancing over at her to see her knuckles going white where she gripped the steering wheel. "It's not like we did anything wrong."

But he had done something wrong. Though he'd thought about it several times while he'd been recovering, he'd never called her. His head had been too messed up to do it. His life had changed so much that night when two three-hundred-pound defensive tackles had plowed through his offensive line and crushed him between them. He'd had no idea when he'd stepped on the field that night, surrounded by a sold-out crowd and television cameras, that he was experiencing the last moments of the life he'd spent years working so hard for. The sports announcers had all claimed that he had a wonderful, long career ahead of him and he'd believed them. Not once had he considered that his life wouldn't follow the path he'd set. But that night all his dreams had died. He'd thought for a short time that he might as well die along with those dreams. But then, with the help of his brother, he'd gotten his head on straight and realized there was far more to life than the game. Soon, he was dreaming a new dream. One that had led him back home.

Still, what if it hadn't happened? What if he'd never been injured that night? Would he have called Devon the next day? Or the next? Did it even matter now? Devon had gone on to marry and have a child. So why did he still feel like there was something unfinished between the two of them? "I still owe you an apology. I should have called you the next day."

"No, that's not necessary. It was all so long ago. I'm sure you had your reasons." Michael could hear the panic in her rising voice. Whether she wanted to admit it or not, he'd just touched on a tender subject. He wanted to push more to see where it might lead them, but he knew he couldn't, not when he could see that it was upsetting her.

"And I've already decided to take the job. I don't want you to think I don't understand what a privilege it is to be considered for a position here. The only reason I've been hesitant is that I've been trying to make the best decision for my son. I haven't been a single mom for long. Zach, my husband, and I always discussed things together."

"It sounds like the two of you were happy together," he said. He found himself becoming more and more interested in the life she'd built over the last few years. He knew losing her husband had to have been devastating because he still keenly felt the loss of his parents. Yet somehow, she'd been able to pick herself up and keep going.

Michael looked over at her and was relieved to see that Devon had relaxed some. He hadn't brought up the subject of that night to embarrass her in any way.

She looked back out the window to where they faced the front of the surgical center. He found himself wondering what was going on in her head. She always seemed to hold back all her emotions and thoughts as if she was hiding them away, not trusting either herself or him with them. He wished he knew which one it was.

"Your parents would have loved this," she said, then smiled. "They'd be so proud of you."

Michael let her change the subject. Maybe she was right and it was best that they forget the night they'd shared. "Thank you. I think so, too, though I'm sure it hasn't always been the case."

"What do you mean?" she asked, turning toward him. "Do you think they'd be upset that you didn't return to playing football? I'm sure they'd have been heartbroken for you, but they would have been more concerned about your safety."

"No, nothing like that. My parents were okay with

me playing football, but they also believed in me having a backup plan. They were the ones who insisted that I got a premed degree. What I mean is the way I handled everything after their deaths. They would have expected me to take care of Matt better than I did. I failed them there." When Devon looked at him questioningly, he continued. "After they passed, I should have been there for him. I was his older brother. But, as always, I only had my mind on the ball. The football, I mean."

"Yeah, you were pretty blind to everything else when we were growing up, but I think you had to be to succeed," Devon said thoughtfully. "And I think it's amazing what you've accomplished here."

"Thanks for that," he said as his hand covered hers where it sat on the console and squeezed. "And I don't think I ever thanked you for sitting with me that night on the beach after we found out my parents had been killed. So I'm telling you now that it meant a lot to me to have someone there with me."

They sat for a moment before she pulled her hand out from under his. "I guess I need to go tell Shalonda that I'm here to fill out all those employment forms."

Not wanting to give her a chance to change her mind, he opened the car door, climbed out, and waited for Devon to join him. Then they walked into the building, where they were met by the receptionist. "Good morning, Sheila. I'd like you to meet our new surgical staff manager."

CHAPTER FOUR

By the middle of her second week at the Hart Sports Institute, Devon had met all the surgical staff and started shadowing them in their duties. She'd found in her last position that working side by side with her nurses and techs helped her understand exactly what they did, which in turn helped her know what they needed to do their jobs. Very few of the staff had complaints, and she found herself being impressed with not only the staff, but also the processes that Michael and his team had put into place for the safety of their patients. From what she could see, the surgical center was being highly successful in its' mission of giving the best care possible to every patient that entered there, whether it was a professional athlete who was suffering from a sports injury, or a stock boy at the grocery store.

That night as she was getting Conner ready for bed, she was feeling good about her decision to return home. She liked her job and Conner was happy with his new friends, though there were still times when he'd climb into bed with her in the middle of the night. Her therapist had told her this was probably because he had a fear of losing her like he had lost his father, which made her worry even more about what would happen if he got too attached to Michael, and Michael wasn't there for Conner when he needed him. She didn't need her therapist to tell her that it was her own childhood abandonment issues that caused her to fear this outcome for her son so strongly.

"Did you know that Coach Hart won a Claymont Trophy?" Conner asked her as he climbed into bed. "Eric says he was the most famous football player ever."

"He was pretty good," she said as she pulled the covers up over him. She didn't mention the notebook she had full of newspaper and magazine clippings of Michael's football career that she had collected from high school until the night of his injuries. She'd never even shown Zach that notebook. She knew she should have thrown it away after she got married, but something had always held her back.

"He got hurt real bad, though. Max says he had to become a doctor because he couldn't play football anymore. He must be sad that he doesn't get to play football, don't you think? Being a doctor can't be near as much fun as being a football player," Conner said, then yawned. "Daddy said that I could be a famous football player if I worked hard enough. Do you think I could ever be as good as Coach Hart?"

Devon was used to her son's insistent questioning, but this one hit a little too close to her heart. She'd never considered whether her son would follow in his biological father's footsteps. Conner had only been five when he and Zach had attended their first college football game together, and from that moment on, her son had become obsessed with it. When she'd mentioned her concerns, Zach had assured her that it was natural for him to be interested in sports. All boys liked to kick and throw balls. But growing up, Devon had seen the way Michael had been so incredibly driven by the sport. Was it possible to pass that drive and talent on to another generation?

"Mom, are you okay?" Conner asked, then yawned again.

"I think we're both tired," she said, then leaned down and kissed her son's forehead. "I love you, Conner."

"Love you, too, Mom," he said, then turned over in his bed. She stood there for a few moments until his respirations became even and she knew he was sleeping. She had no doubts that if he dreamed tonight, it would be of footballs and trophies.

She changed into her favorite oversize shirt, one of Zach's with the United States Navy's logo stamped across the chest, and settled down for the night. She started to open her laptop and review her schedule but then decided to watch some television instead. After twenty minutes, she turned the TV off. Conner's insistent talk about Michael had her mind racing. For the last few days, she'd made a point to ask the staff what they thought of the founder of the surgical center and not once had she heard someone say something negative about him. It seemed everyone, including her son, thought the man could do no wrong. Yet there had been something she had noticed. Except for his coaching the kids' team, no one knew anything about his personal life. It was like his whole life revolved around making his career and the new surgical center a success. Which made her wonder, how would he handle suddenly having a child in his life?

Finally, she went to make herself some chamomile tea, hoping that it would help settle her enough so that she could rest. When the tea was ready, she took her cup and stepped outside, onto the porch. While her grandparents' home hadn't been built on the water, being just across the road she could still hear the waves at high tide when they came crashing against the shore. She sat down into an old rocking chair where the yellow paint was beginning to peel. It was her grandmother's rocker and it made Devon feel close to her when things were quiet. She'd had many late-night conversations there on the porch. She'd shared every heartbreak with her grandma, and there had never been a secret between them, not until the day the pregnancy stick had shown two pink lines. She'd felt terrible about not telling her grandma the truth about Conner's father, but she had known it was best that she keep it between her and Zach. Back then, her grandma had recently been diagnosed with heart failure and Devon couldn't bear to disappoint her. Having Devon turn out pregnant and unmarried, like her daughter, would have broken the old woman's heart.

So instead she had shown up one weekend at the cottage and told her grandma that she and Zach were not only married, but also expecting a baby. Her grandma had been shocked, but also excited. It seemed her heart condition was worse than she'd let on to Devon and her prognosis was poor. She had admitted to Devon that she had feared she'd not live long enough to see Devon become a mother, or to hold her great-grandchild. Devon knew then that she had made the right decision when her grandmother had passed when Conner was still a toddler.

She wondered what her grandmother would think of what Devon was doing now. Knowing her grandmother, if she was there at that moment, she'd be telling Devon to stop stalling and get on with it.

A large truck passed the house then stopped and began to back up. Devon sat up, her teacup in her hand as she prepared to head inside and defend the security of her home if she needed to. Silver Sands was a peaceful little town, but after the things she'd seen in the operating room over the years, she was always aware that bad things happened no matter where anyone lived.

The car door opened just before Devon had reached for the door handle, and she recognized Michael as he climbed out of the car.

"Devon, is that you?" he asked, his voice sounding uncertain as it carried up the driveway.

"Yes, why? Is something wrong?" she asked. She sat back down in the chair and remembered that the shirt she was wearing only hit midthigh. Well, it wasn't like she had been expecting anyone this time of night.

"I didn't mean to scare you," he said as he walked up the porch steps. "I just thought I saw a ghost for a moment."

"A ghost?" she asked, noticing that he was still wearing the clothes he'd had on at Conner's practice earlier that night.

"Sorry, it was just that I used to see your grandma sitting out on that porch when I was growing up. It's natural for me to look up at the porch when I pass by." He looked down at the scarred porch floor and she would have sworn that he was embarrassed by the admission.

"I miss her, too," she said. "Even though she would say she was just a housekeeper, she was more than that to a lot of people. Everywhere I go in town people tell me how much they miss her and how much she meant to them. They share stories about her with me and I love that." As she was talking, he sat down in the rocking chair beside her.

"The whole community misses her. I think she was more family than housekeeper to the people she worked for. I know my parents felt that way. She was more of a grandparent to me and Matt than our own grandparents," Michael said.

The two of them sat in silence for a moment, both lost in memories of a woman who'd lived a simple life, but would be remembered for that very life.

A soft breeze blew across the porch and Devon reached up and brushed her hair out of her eyes. Looking up, she saw Michael studying her too intently for comfort. Unable to help herself, she turned her eyes away from his, and stared across the street, where she could see just a sliver of the gulf between two beach houses on the other side of the road. She knew it was ridiculous, but she had this crazy notion that he could see that she was keeping something from him just by looking at her. It seemed the longer she was around him, the more guilt she felt for keeping the truth about Conner from him.

"Have you been at the football field all this time?" she asked, hoping to not only change the subject, but also drown out all her confusing thoughts.

"No, I went back to my office to finish some work. It's becoming more and more clear that I need to have someone take over the administration duties. I thought when Matt came on, that between the two of us we would be able to keep control of the center. I mean, it's our place. It seems we should oversee things. But more and more it feels like I'm becoming a businessman rather than a doctor."

"For some reason I always thought you would end up a businessman, after your football career was over, of course," she said, then winced. "Sorry, that was insensitive of me."

Michael laughed, then stretched his long legs out in front of him and sighed with what sounded like relief. She wondered if just thinking about his injuries made his body remember the pain.

"It's okay. It happened," he said. "I'm not saying that I don't still miss the game or that I don't wish it hadn't happened. I do. But having everyone tiptoe around it doesn't help anyone. And coming back here and coaching the kids has helped."

"The kids love it, too. It amazes me the way you handle it, though. So many people would be bitter about having a career they'd worked so hard for taken away so quickly. But you just bounced back and now, you've made a whole new life for yourself." Devon could still remember the way the sports channels had run that career-ending play over and over again. She'd found herself glued to social media, looking for any news about Michael's recovery.

"I didn't bounce back as easily as the media seemed to imply. For the first few months, I truly believed that the doctors were wrong, and if I just worked really hard I would be back on the field by the next season. I had to come to the realization that my body would never be the same for myself. I've learned since that every athlete has to come to that realization at some point. Mine just came sooner than expected. And it was a very hard pill to swallow when I did."

He looked over at her and she could see that no matter what he said, talking about the end of his football career bothered him more than he was willing to admit. Other than the night she'd comforted him after his parents were killed, it was the first time she could ever remember seeing any sign of vulnerability in him.

He stood and turned away from her suddenly, as if he knew she had seen the pain in his eyes. "I'm keeping you up and we both have work tomorrow."

Devon stood and watched as he walked back to his car, then froze when he turned back around. "Good night, Sunshine."

"Good night, Mickey," she whispered as he drove off.

Later, as she tried to fall asleep, her thoughts kept returning to that moment of vulnerability she had seen in Michael. For as long as she could remember, he had been the town hero. Then there had been college and he'd been the star of the football team. Had he ever been allowed to be just a normal guy?

For a moment she allowed herself to imagine the two of them being just normal people. She let herself wonder what might have happened if she and Michael hadn't spent that one night together. She'd spent so much time feeling hurt that he hadn't ever tried to contact her afterward. What if she really was just a single mom with a son who had lost his father? Would things be different between them now?

"Grr," she growled, punching her pillow before turning it over to the other side. She was doing it again. Even after everything that had happened, she still appeared to have this fairy-tale crush on the man who'd broken her heart. The same man who'd never called her, not once but twice. She knew she couldn't really blame him for not calling her after the kiss they'd shared the night he'd lost his parents. His whole life had suddenly been turned upside down…just as it had after his football injury. But she'd truly believed that, after their night together in the hotel, she'd meant something special to him. He could have reached out to her the next day, yet he'd clearly chosen not to.

She grumbled and rolled over again. None of this reliving the past was helping. She had to separate all those memories from what was happening in the present. Right now, she was trying to build a life for her son and keep her promise to Zach. The only reason she was spending time with Michael was to determine if telling him about her son was the best thing for Conner. That was all she was doing. None of this had anything to do with all those old feelings that she was remembering now.

Feeling better, she rolled over one more time, closed her eyes, and finally drifted off to sleep.

Devon had just finished restocking the anesthesia cart in operating room three when the cell phone she'd been given for work rang. She pulled it from her scrub jacket and saw that it was the recovery unit calling. She'd just made her rounds through there an hour earlier and the nurses had all been busy. If the volume of procedures continued as they had in the two weeks she'd been there, she'd need to speak with Shalonda about hiring another nurse.

"This is Devon," she said, then listened as Carolyn, one of the newer nurses in the department, explained that she had a patient she was concerned about, but she was having a problem getting the orthopedic surgeon, Dr. Morgan, to listen to her concerns. Devon had only met this particular doctor, who specialized in shoulder injuries, one time and she hadn't been overly impressed. He seemed to be one of those surgeons who thought that when he'd finished the surgery, his job was done. From what she'd learned from the staff, he never checked on his patients after they made it to the recovery area and he was typically slow to return the nurses' calls.

"I'll be right there," she told the nurse, then locked the anesthesia cart.

As she entered the recovery room, she saw Carolyn standing by a stretcher, where a man who looked like he was in his seventies lay. It only took a minute for

Devon to recognize the man as the owner of the bakery where she and her grandma had purchased donuts on Sunday mornings on their way to church. She'd only been in a couple times since she'd moved back, but Conner seemed to love those donuts as much as she had at his age.

"Mr. Waters, how are you feeling?" Devon asked as she looked at the monitors and didn't like what she saw. The man's blood pressure was extremely high at 242/112 and his heart rate was up into the 140s. Not only should the doctor have listened to the nurse when she'd called, but he also should be here already, by his patient's side.

"I've been better," the man said. "I can feel my heart racing. I have these palpitations sometimes, but they don't last this long. And I'm a bit short of breath right now. Is this normal?"

She studied the monitor a little longer. "Mr. Waters, have you ever been diagnosed with atrial fibrillation?"

"No, I don't think so," the man said. "Is there something wrong? Dr. Morgan said I'd feel some pain after the procedure, but I wasn't expecting to feel it in my chest. It must be from that anesthesia stuff they gave me."

The man seemed to grow paler as she watched him.

"David, can you bring an EKG machine over here? We need to get a twelve lead on Mr. Waters now," Devon called to another nurse and then reached over to the oxygen meter on the wall. She increased the oxygen flow as David rushed over to them with the EKG machine and began applying the electrodes. "Carolyn, is there anything else ordered for Mr. Waters's blood pressure?" she asked quietly.

"No. I explained that to Dr. Morgan. He insisted that the problem was pain control and that I wasn't doing my job properly if his patient was in pain. Then he hung up on me. I tried to call him back, but I'm just going to voice mail now. I left a message, but he hasn't returned my call," Carolyn replied, equally quietly. "And the OR just called to let me know they are bringing me another patient out now."

Devon wanted to tell her nurse exactly what she thought of doctors who blamed the nurses for things beyond their control while not addressing the problem themselves, but she held her words back. "If you'll call Anesthesia and have them come assess the patient for me, I'll take over Mr. Waters while you get the new patient settled."

As Carolyn made the call, Devon reviewed the twelve lead EKG and wasn't surprised to find that Mr. Waters's heart was in an atrial fibrillation rhythm. "Have you ever been told that your heart was in an unusual rhythm? Maybe you saw a cardiologist and they told you that you had A-fib?"

"No, I've never seen a cardiologist before. My wife sees one. A nice one. But I've never had the need for one. My ticker is as good as the day I was born."

Devon didn't want to break the news to the man that his "ticker" was definitely not as good as he thought. Instead, she pulled out the phone and sent a message to Michael, letting him know that there was a problem. In a moment, the doors opened and both Michael and

Dr. Smith, the anesthesiologist, walked into the unit. After Devon explained the situation, Michael pulled out his phone and called the patient's doctor. No answer.

While Carolyn and Dr. Smith discussed the dosage of a beta-blocker to give to bring down the man's blood pressure, Devon explained to Mr. Waters that his heart had gone into a rhythm that would require ongoing medication and monitoring. "We're going to start you on some medication now, but you're going to need to go to the hospital so that they can monitor you more closely. Do you have a preference which one?"

"The hospital? Can't you just give me the medication and let me go home? This surgery is going to be enough of a bother—I don't need this. I've had to hire help for the bakery, but I'm planning on returning next week. I'll be limited in what I can do, but I can at least help with the customers. If I go to the hospital, some doctor is going to want me to take more time off."

"I know your wife is in the waiting room. Is it okay if I talk to her and explain what is happening?" Devon asked. It wasn't going to do the man's blood pressure any good to get him more upset.

"Of course you can tell her—she's my wife." Mr. Waters stopped talking as Michael walked up beside her. "Michael, do you know they're trying to send me to the hospital?"

"I do. And I agree. Atrial fibrillation isn't something to play around with, Jim. Let me explain a little about it." As Michael explained the heart arrhythmia to Mr. Waters, Devon tried to call Dr. Morgan again. When he didn't answer, she walked out and found Mrs. Waters sitting anxiously in the waiting room. After explaining exactly what was happening with her husband and the need for him to be transferred to a local hospital, Devon returned to the recovery room.

"I still can't get Dr. Morgan on the phone, but I don't think we should wait much longer. I know it's unusual to transfer a patient without the patient's surgeon speaking with the emergency room doctor, but I don't think we have a choice," she told Michael. "I don't know Dr. Morgan, but I don't think there are many doctors who would take the news that their patient was transferred to a hospital without their knowledge very well."

"And I don't know a lot of doctors who ignore nurses' calls the way he's done today. As of now, Mr. Waters has agreed to me taking over his care and I'll be handling the transfer. If Dr. Morgan has a problem with that, he'll have to take it up with me."

As Michael pulled out his phone and made the call, Devon smiled. Over the years she had seen several doctors ignore nurses' concerns, even at the risk of their patients' well-being. She'd even seen administration side with a doctor when everyone, including them, knew the doctor was out of line. It was good to know that Michael wasn't like that. And she was pretty sure this wasn't going to end very well for Dr. Morgan.

But when she looked back at Mr. Waters, she noticed the way his hands clutched the bed railings. Looking up at the monitors, she saw that the man's heart rate was continuing to climb. She knew what had to be done, but she wasn't the one to make that call. She looked around and saw that the anesthesiologist had left the recovery room. "Dr. Hart, I need you over here."

While she waited for Michael to finish his call, she pulled the resuscitation cart up beside the bed and started opening drawers. She found the pads she knew they would need, then began to attach them to Mr. Waters.

"More of these sticky things?" the man asked, his temper starting to become short, not that she could blame him. "That nice nurse I had gave me something for the pain, but it doesn't seem to be helping much."

"The medication isn't working. He needs to be cardioverted," Devon said the moment Michael joined her. "Trust me, I've seen this before."

"You're right. I'm not a cardiologist, but I did see this before in residency. I want to have the anesthesiologist here in case we need him," Michael said, then turned to Carolyn, who'd returned. "Call Dr. Smith. Get him back in here, now. Then draw up five of morphine."

As Carolyn made the call, Mr. Waters moaned and she looked up to see that his heart rate was now in the 180s.

"Is everything ready?" Michael asked Devon. "As soon as Dr. Smith is here, I want to get this done. At these rates, his risk of going into ventricular fibrillation and cardiac arrest is just too high to wait."

"The pads are applied and I've got the machine ready. It's monophasic so I was going to set it to two hundred joules. Is that what you want?" It was funny how all that studying she'd done for her advanced cardiac life support certificate was returning now.

"We'll start at two hundred and hope that does it. If not, we'll go up to three-sixty the next time," Michael said.

The doors opened and Dr. Smith came in. Michael explained what they were about to do to Mr. Waters while the anesthesiologist listened and agreed with the plan.

"I'm not going to lie to you, Jim. It's going to be uncomfortable, but Carolyn is going to give you some morphine to help." Michael nodded to Carolyn and she began to push the medicine through their patient's IV. As soon as the medicine was in, he looked over at Devon. "We're set at two hundred joules?"

Devon nodded and hit the charging button. "Charging now. Everyone clear."

As soon as the machine told her it was charged, she looked at Michael, then hit the button. She watched as poor Mr. Waters yelled out and his body came off the bed as the shock went through him.

They all looked up at the monitor, each of them holding their breath as the heart rate recorded a spike before it returned, this time at a rate where they could see by the individual P waves that the cardioversion had worked.

"Good job, everyone," Michael said, before turning to her. "Well done."

The doors opened to the recovery entrance and the ambulance crew came in with their stretcher. As Carolyn gave a report to the EMTs, Devon put her shaking hands into her pockets and stepped away.

"That was a good call," Michael said, praising her.

"Thank you for trusting me," she said, surprised by how much that really meant to her.

"Of course I trust you," Michael said, then joined Carolyn with the EMTs.

For a moment, his words made her feel amazing. Then she thought about the secret she'd been keeping from him and wondered if he would ever trust her again after she told him the truth about Conner.

CHAPTER FIVE

DEVON WASN'T SURE when she'd become one of *those* parents. The kind who get so involved in their kids' sports that they concentrate on each play as if it was somehow going to make a difference to their child getting into a good college or gaining a professional sports contract. Maybe it was because Conner had been so wound up on the way to the football field. Or maybe it was because she knew her son would be disappointed if their team lost this game. Or maybe it was just the competitive football spirit she'd grown up around. No matter what the reason, when her son walked onto the field, she found herself holding her breath and crossing her fingers.

She watched as the center snapped the ball. Everyone in the bleachers seemed to let out a breath when, instead of the quarterback dropping the ball, as he had the last two times, he held on to it then handed it off to Conner. Devon's hand went to her chest, her heart pounding hard against her ribs. This was the play that her son had told her about. The one he'd sworn Coach Hart had picked out especially for him because he was the fastest runner. As Conner broke through the other team's defensive line, Devon knew that her son was running as fast as his little legs could take him. Then Devon saw that there was a boy from the other team playing safety, waiting to tackle her son.

"Turn, Conner, turn," she yelled as she jumped up out of her seat, sending her water bottle flying down between the bleachers to the ground. She watched as her son made the necessary adjustment to his path and then turned on the speed. The woman next to her grabbed ahold of Devon's sleeve as they watched Conner pass the ten-yard line, then enter the end zone. The sidelines burst into screams and applause as Devon and the woman next to her hugged her and laughed.

"His daddy has to be so proud," the woman said before turning to the person on the other side of her.

Devon's eyes instantly went to Michael as he ran up to Conner and slapped him on the back, almost knocking her son down. Then the two of them both looked up to where she stood in the stands, their faces wide with smiles so identical that she found herself frozen in place. Could anyone else see the resemblance? How could Michael not see it when he looked down at Conner smiling like he was right then? Didn't he see the way Conner's smile was just a little crooked, exactly like his own? Didn't he recognize those startling, light green eyes?

How much longer would she be able to keep Conner's parentage a secret when to her eyes it seemed so obvious?

She spent the rest of the game in stunned silence as the other parents and visitors screamed and cheered the home team on to victory. If Conner ran another play, she couldn't recall. All she knew, as she left the stands and headed down to where the parents met their kids, was that she had to tell Michael about Conner. She'd waited, with the excuse of wanting to make sure Michael was someone she wanted in Conner's life, but she was beginning to see that it had simply been an excuse to put off telling him. She dreaded the look in his eyes when he finally knew the truth. She was so afraid that he wouldn't understand the reason for the choice she'd made, but the longer she waited, it seemed to be more of a deception than she'd ever thought it to be.

And what about after she told him? Zach had believed that Michael would understand and that the two of them would be able to make things work, as long as they put Conner first, something she'd always thought she had done. But what about Michael? She'd watched him with the kids he coached, especially Conner, and could see that he really seemed to care about them. But could she trust him to understand that what was best for Conner was to keep his life as normal as possible? Or would he be so angry that he would fight her for custody of her son?

As she headed onto the field, she saw Michael kneeling down on the ground in front of Conner as he helped her son get his shoulder pads off, while the little boy's mouth seemed to be running ninety to nothing.

"Mom, did you see me? Did you see me make that touchdown?" Conner said as he rushed up and hugged her. Unable to help herself, she pulled him closer to her. He was hot and sweaty, but she didn't care. She held on to him as if at any moment someone might pry him out of her arms. "Mom, you're squeezing too tight."

"I think you've left your mom speechless, something I've never seen before," Michael teased as he walked up to them.

"Really?" Conner asked him as he pulled away from her. "She says I'm a jabber box because I ask questions all the time. Is she a jabber box, too?"

"Maybe not now, but she definitely was one when she was your age. I remember hearing her grandma call her that exact same thing when we were growing up. I'm afraid you've inherited it from her, so it's really all her fault," Michael said with a wink.

"You hear that, Mom? It's not my fault. Next time Ms. Jordan gets on to me for talking to Max in class, I'm going to tell her it's not really my fault."

"If I get another note from Ms. Jordan about you talking in class when you're not supposed to, you're going to lose your game system for a week, no matter whose fault you think it is." Devon's instinct was telling her to grab Conner and run to the car before it was too late.

"I was talking to Conner before the game and he asked if he could see my Claymont Trophy. I told him I'd be home all weekend if you'd like to bring him by."

"Can we go, Mom?" Conner asked, his eyes pleading with her.

"Have you already forgotten about the sleepover? You're going to Max's tomorrow night and you're going to be there most of Saturday," Devon said, glad that she didn't have to make an excuse for turning down Michael's invitation.

"But I'll be home Saturday night, right? We could go then or Sunday," Conner persisted as his hands came up and wrapped around her waist again. "Pretty please, Mom."

"Let's wait and see how tired you are Saturday night, hey? Max's dad has a lot planned for the two of you," Devon said. Then, knowing her son was not going to let this invitation go easily, she changed the subject. "How about we stop by the Burger Barn and grab a couple burgers on the way home?"

"Can Coach Hart come, too?" Conner asked, then turned to Michael before she could stop him. "Don't you want to go, Coach Hart?"

When Michael looked at her, as if to ask permission, there was no way she could not invite him without looking rude. "Would you like to join us? Unless you have other plans, that is."

She half expected him to say that he had to get back to his office to work. She'd heard through Shalonda that she was consulting with some recruiters to hire someone to take on an administrator role at the surgical center, but he was still handling everything until someone was hired.

"That sounds good. Let me help pack up our gear and I'll meet you there," Michael said, though he looked at her as if he knew she had been hoping he'd turn down her invitation.

Twenty minutes later, Devon found herself sitting across the booth from Michael and Conner. For once she was glad of her son's ability to talk nonstop as he asked Michael question after question about his football career. There was a moment of peace when their burgers arrived and all three of them bit into the juicy sandwiches the place was known for. Looking up, she saw that Michael was staring at her.

"Hold on," he said, before reaching over and wiping her mouth with his napkin. Their eyes met and something sparked between the two of them. Devon's face went hot and she looked away too quickly, causing her head to spin for a moment.

She didn't have to ask herself what had just happened. It was more than a déjà vu moment for her as she was suddenly back in high school, sitting beside a bonfire on the beach with her friends. She'd tried to ignore Michael when he'd sat down beside her. She knew that he only thought of her as one of his brother's friends. She wasn't pretty like Lisa, the cheerleader he'd just broken up with earlier that year. She was his housekeeper's daughter. Someone he'd known all his life. Self-conscious and unsure of what to do, she'd popped one of the marshmallows she'd just roasted into her mouth. She'd jumped when Michael's finger had come up and wiped some of the gooey candy off her lips. Then she'd made the biggest mistake of her young life. She'd looked up into those green eyes of his and had been totally mesmerized. She'd closed her own eyes, thinking that he was going to kiss her then. But when she'd opened them again, Michael had moved away from her. For a moment, she'd thought maybe she'd imagined it, that heated look she'd seen in his eyes. But she knew she hadn't. Just like she knew she hadn't imagined what had just passed between the two of them now. Unable to help herself, she looked back at Michael and saw the recognition in his face. He'd felt it, too.

For the rest of the meal, she kept her eyes on Conner as he continued to pepper Michael with his continuous questions, afraid of what she might see in Michael's eyes if she looked over at him. The two of them already had a complicated relationship just because he was her boss and they'd also once been lovers. Add in the fact that Michael would soon find out that he was Conner's father, and what revealing that secret would do for their relationship, and the last thing they needed was to complicate it more. So no matter how much those little butterflies were fluttering in her stomach whenever he looked at her, she had to ignore them. If not for herself, at least for her son.

CHAPTER SIX

MICHAEL SAT ON his balcony drinking his morning coffee, wondering what it would be like to not have to start his Saturday with a trip to his office. He could count on one hand the number of days he hadn't had to spend at his office since he'd opened the surgical center. What would he do with his time when he turned over all the tedious admin work that was constantly piling up on his desk? He knew he didn't really need to be the person that approved the budget increase for the center's environmental services. Devon had been right. He wasn't able to keep juggling all the things that it took to keep the place running. The surgical center was growing faster than he'd ever imagined. Next month would be the grand opening of their new physical therapy center, which meant even more work. It was all too much for one person and there were still five months until Matt finished his residency and joined him. He didn't want to admit it, but it had partly been his ego that had made him want to hang on to all those day-to-day operations that he was now drowning in. He had taken on the task of running the Hart Sports Institute and admitting that he couldn't do it was the same as admitting failure, something he was not good at.

When his football career had come to an end, he'd been at such a loss over what to do next. He'd made the mistake of building his whole life around his success as a quarterback that he hadn't done much else. He'd lived the game, avoiding anything that could pull his attention away from his goal of making it as a professional athlete. And when he'd finally made it there? He'd worked even harder to stay.

He'd ignored everything else in his life, if it could have been called a life. He'd been so self-centered that he'd let most of his friendships go over the years, as he became more and more dedicated to succeeding. He'd even neglected his brother when he'd needed him the most. The only people he'd spent time with had been just like him—driven to succeed in a career that could end at any moment. And then, that moment had come and he'd had nothing left to work for.

He sat his cup on the side table with a little more force than was necessary, sloshing the dark brown liquid onto the table. How had he not seen that he was doing the same thing again? He'd been back in his hometown for over a year now, and aside from helping out with the kids' football team and an occasional get-together with his high school friends, all he'd done was work.

He stood and looked out over the gulf waters and saw a lone surfer about to catch a wave as the high tide sent waves crashing against the shore. While a lot of his friends and his younger brother had grown up surfing, he'd only tried it a few times. He'd preferred fishing to surfing, something that he had shared with his father. But when was the last time he'd had a fishing reel in his hand? Maybe that was something he could look forward to doing when the new administrator was hired.

He looked down the beach and saw a woman walking, her head down as she studied the packed sand just outside of the waves. She was probably searching for shells that had come ashore during the night. When she stopped and kneeled down, he knew he had been right. Then she stood and held something up to the sky, her face turned up. The sunlight highlighted the copper tint to the blond waves that draped over her shoulders. He watched as the wind picked up Devon's gorgeous hair and blew it all around her, as she held her arms out and twirled around with the happiness of a child finding a great treasure.

He laughed, and before he realized what he was doing, he took the stairs down from his balcony, stepped onto the beach, and began walking toward her. He could take a few moments before he headed to the office. He was mesmerized by the happy expression he could see on her face. It was as if she had cast some spell on him, drawing her to him.

It was the same type of feeling he'd had the night they'd run into each other in the hotel. There had been something magical about the way he'd been drawn so strongly to her. From the moment he'd recognized her, those copper highlights flashing in the light from the chandelier hanging above her, he'd been held captive by the sight of her. They'd both been so surprised at seeing each other, they'd found a booth at the hotel bar to catch up. She'd explained that she was there to meet some girlfriends for a night out, but she was early and had a few minutes to spare. When those minutes had led to an hour, she'd texted her friends that she was held up. Then he'd canceled his plans to meet up with a teammate and had invited her to supper. He couldn't have been more surprised when supper and a simple good-night kiss had led to them spending the night together. Thinking about that night again made him wonder what kissing Devon now would be like. Would he still experience that wild desire he'd felt back then?

When she turned and began to walk the other way, he found himself jogging toward her.

"Sunshine, wait," he called out to her, then slowed when she turned back toward him.

"Hey there. Isn't it a beautiful morning?" she said as he caught up with her.

The smile on her face seemed to light him up inside. For a moment, he just stood there, unable to take his eyes off her. "Yes. The most beautiful."

When her face reddened, he had no doubt she knew he was talking about her, but he didn't want to make her feel uncomfortable. "Gathering shells this morning?"

She looked down at the perfectly intact pink scallop shell she held in her hands. "Just the one. It's all I need. I'll leave the rest of them for the serious collectors."

"I take it Conner is still at his sleepover," he said, knowing she'd never leave her son alone at home.

"He is, and the house was way too quiet last night without him. I sometimes give him a hard time about the way he's constantly talking and always asking questions, but I actually love the fact that he always wants to share his thoughts and questions with me."

"He's a great kid. I'm no expert, but I think he's always asking those questions because he's so smart," Michael said as he walked with her toward her home.

"I've seen you with the children on the team. You're great with them," she said. "It makes me wonder why you haven't started a family of your own. Don't you want kids?"

"I'd love to have kids. I envy what you have with Conner. I'd be happy with one just like him."

A wave came roaring toward them and he made a grab for her arm to steady her as it rolled back out, taking the sand from under their feet with it. Her hand clutched his and she held on to him until they had made it to higher ground.

"Sorry about that," she said as if embarrassed that she'd reached out for him.

"Don't be. I'd never let you fall, Sunshine." His free hand came up to move the strands of hair that had fallen around her face.

His arm came out and steadied her as she stumbled, and her sandal fell off. "Be careful. You wouldn't believe how many injuries I've seen from wearing those shoes on the beach."

"I'm fine," she said, though her voice was unsteady.

"Are you hurt? Did you turn your ankle?" he asked, bending down to check out the shoeless foot.

"No, I said I'm fine," Devon insisted, her voice still shaking as she pulled her hand from his and picked up her shoe. "It's just what you said. About envying me for having Conner."

She stood there in front of him looking at him as if

he'd just slapped her. "Because Conner's your child, Michael. He's your son."

Michael tried to comprehend what she was saying. Conner, his child? How was that possible? He'd always assumed that she was married when she had her son. Their son?

"I don't understand. How is that possible?" he asked, though he was starting to put things together. He always marked his calendar on the day he'd been injured on the football field. This year had made it eight years. Conner played on the football team of seven-year-olds, so…

A shout came from the water and they both stood and stared at where an older teenage boy, the one Michael had seen earlier riding the waves, was struggling to drag something large and dark from the water up to the beach.

"What is that?" Devon asked as they headed toward the boy.

"I'm not sure, but…" Then he realized what they were seeing. The teenager was dragging someone dressed in a diving suit out of the water.

Devon must have realized what it was, too, because they both began running at the same time, splashing out into the waves. When they reached them, Michael took the man from him and Devon helped the boy onto the shore.

"I found him out there. He was trying to make it to the beach but then he just stopped," the teen said. "And then I saw the blood. He had a spear in his hand when

I first saw him. He must have cut himself with it. He dropped it on the way in."

Michael laid the man on the ground just above the waves and began assessing the situation. He put his fingers to the man's neck and felt a pulse. Then the man took in a deep breath and coughed, a little water running out of his mouth. He needed to turn him onto his side to help with that, but he also needed to find where all the blood that was running down his suit was coming from.

"I'm calling nine-one-one," Devon said from beside him as she pulled her phone from her wet shorts. Michael could only hope it wasn't damaged as he'd been in too much of a hurry to get to Devon earlier to grab his own phone.

"Sir, can you hear me?" Michael asked as he raised the man's eyelids and saw they were equal. Michael's mind was whirling from everything Devon had just told him, but he had to block it out. Right now, he had to think like a doctor, not like a man who'd just had his world turned upside down with the news that he had a seven-year-old son.

He started down the man's wet suit looking for an injury. When he got to one of the man's knees, he saw a tear in the black suit and a stream of blood flowing out. He pulled off his shirt and held it tightly against the injury. The man groaned and pulled away from where Michael was putting pressure on, and he considered that a good sign. There was no way to know how much blood he'd lost, or how much water he'd swallowed, but his response to pain was encouraging. With Michael's other hand, he continued down the man's body, as he worked through the triage process. Though he didn't see any other injuries, he couldn't be sure until the suit was removed.

"We've got a problem," Devon said, joining him beside the man. "There's a pileup on the interstate that's blocking State Road Eighty-seven. Everyone in the county is at the accident. Dispatch says they'll send someone from the north end of the county but they couldn't give me an ETA. I told them I was a nurse and had a doctor with me and that I would call back as soon as I knew the extent of the patient's injuries."

This was the last news Michael wanted to hear, but he made himself remain calm. If they could stop the bleeding, maybe they'd be able to keep the man stable until the EMTs arrived. "The blood is coming from his knee. I think it's some kind of bite. Maybe shark or barracuda, as it sounds like he was spear fishing. We need to get him out of this suit, so I can make sure he's not bleeding anywhere else. If you'll keep the pressure here, I'll unzip the suit."

"Is he going to be alright?" the teen asked. Michael looked over and saw that he couldn't be much more than eighteen and was shaking uncontrollably.

"I don't know, but I can tell you that he wouldn't have had a chance if you hadn't gotten him out of the water," Michael said, praising the teen.

"You did good, Kyle. I can't wait to tell your mom. She's going to be so proud of you," Devon added, apparently recognizing him.

As Devon kept the pressure on, Michael worked the

man's arms, and then his legs, carefully out of the wet suit. Not finding any other injury, he went back to his right knee. "It looks like a bite. A big fish bite. Maybe a bull shark or a barracuda. I can see penetration holes to the front of the knee and it looks like there's also damage to some of the tendons, and maybe the ligaments on the side and back. Those probably happened when he was trying to get free. His pupils are equal and he responds to pain, so that's good."

"The pressure is helping, but the bleeding's still not stopped," Devon reported. Michael looked down and saw that his shirt was saturated with bright red blood.

"Yeah, I'm afraid there's a bleeder in there that needs to be tied off, but I can't do anything about it right now. If I was at the office, I'd have the equipment I needed. But here? On the beach? The best I have is a first-aid kit." Although now that he was thinking about it, there was a hemostat and a couple sutures in there that he had added. There also was a bottle of saline to be used for cleaning wounds, too.

"What about a tourniquet?" Devon asked.

"We don't have anything that would apply the kind of pressure we need." While Michael had never had the experience of doing something like this out in the field, he'd handled enough traumas during his residency that he knew what he was thinking about could be done.

"Kyle, do you see that house over there? The blue one with the big two-story balconies?" Michael asked.

"Yeah, why?" Kyle asked. "Is there someone there that can help?"

"No, it's my house. I need you to run to the house

and look in the bathroom on the bottom floor. It's on the other side of the kitchen. Open the cabinets and you'll see a big first-aid kit. It looks like a small, zippered suitcase. Grab that and a couple of towels, and bring it out here to me."

Kyle hesitated for just a moment, then he looked at the man lying on the sand, turned, and sprinted up the beach to Michael's home.

The silence between the two of them after Kyle left was stifling as they waited. Finally, he couldn't take it any longer. "Why didn't you tell me?"

"It's too complicated to discuss right now," Devon said, her hands beginning to shake from where she was holding pressure.

"Let's switch places and you can do a pulse check," Michael said. He knew she was right, yet even as he worked to keep this patient alive Devon's words—*he's your son*—kept replaying over and over in his mind.

"His pulse is in the one-tens," Devon said. "His respirations are high at twenty-four."

"The high pulse is probably because of the blood loss," he said. "The respirations are probably because of the water in his lungs."

The moment that Kyle returned carrying the supplies, Michael lifted the bloody shirt. He could see that most of the bleeding from the tearing wound had stopped. It was at the puncture site where he could see there was still blood pooling in the tissue.

Devon kneeled down beside him and laid out one of the towels as calmly as if it was a surgery towel and she was setting up for surgery. She put on a pair of gloves, then offered him a pair. She laid out several packages of gauze, opened one, and handed it to him.

"Can you call nine-one-one and see if they can give you an ETA?" Michael said as he put on the gloves. If he knew there was help on the way, he'd just pack the wound and wait for the first responders to transfer the man to the hospital.

While Devon made the call, he took the gauze and cleared out the blood so he could get a better view of the damage. Like he had thought, it looked like there was only one vessel that was continuing to bleed. If the man hadn't already lost so much blood on the way out of the water, he wouldn't be worried about it.

"Dispatch says they're still fifteen minutes out. I'm going to stay on the phone so I can let them know when I see them," Devon said.

"I can run up to the road and flag them down," Kyle said, then jumped up and ran down to the beach entrance.

Calculating the time it would take to transfer the man to the hospital, especially if they couldn't use the interstate, Michael made the only decision he could. "I can see the vessel that's bleeding. If you can keep the blood out of my way, I'm going to clamp it. We can leave the clamp on until we get him to the hospital, then I can take him to the operating room and clean the wound out and tie off anything that's left bleeding then."

Devon looked at him and, to his surprise, she smiled. "Let's do it."

With the bleeding vessel right at the entrance of the

bite mark, Michael used the tip of the clamp to maneuver it as Devon cleared the blood out of the way. With one click, the hemostat stopped the blood flow and Michael relaxed.

They had just finished applying a large gauze bandage to the site when they heard the sirens. As the first responders made their way down the beach toward them, Michael recognized one of the EMTs.

"It looks like a bite. A big fish bite. Maybe a bull shark or it could be a barracuda. There's a penetration wound to his right knee with some damage to the tendons and ligaments."

"His pupils are equal and he does respond to pain, but he hasn't been conscious. His pulse is in the one-tens and his respirations are fast," Devon added.

"We think he might have been spear fishing when it happened. Kyle saw the man trying to get to shore and then saw him go still. He dragged him in and called for help. I suspect he's got some water in his lungs, though," Michael said.

The EMT looked over at Michael as he dropped down beside them. "Oh, hey, Doc. I didn't recognize you there without your shirt on."

Then the man turned to where Kyle sat with Devon's arm around him. "Way to go, Kyle."

Kyle, still pale, nodded at him.

"This is Doctor Hart. He opened that new sports surgical center. He did my dad's knee surgery last month," the EMT said casually, as another man joined them and began to hook up all the monitors and prepare their patient for transport.

When they offered for Michael to ride along with them, he turned back to Devon, but she waved him off. "Go ahead. I'm going to give Kyle a ride home."

After climbing in beside the EMT, Michael looked back to where Devon stood, one of her arms still draped around the teen's shoulder as she spoke with him. Then she looked up and her eyes went to Michael. There was so much for the two of them to discuss. He wanted to know the reason for her keeping his son's existence from him. He had thought he knew her. But the girl he'd always called Sunshine would do never something like this.

None of this made sense. All he knew was that once this patient had been stabilized, he was going to get some answers.

CHAPTER SEVEN

As soon as Devon had gotten Conner settled in bed for the night, she had curled up in her grandmother's chair with a soft knitted blanket draped over her legs as she watched the street traffic for any sign of Michael returning from the hospital. He'd called her hours ago to tell her that the man, a chief from the local air force base, had been identified, and that he was in stable condition after receiving a couple liters of blood and plasma. He'd agreed to accept the patient and was about take him into surgery to clean out his wound and hopefully repair some of the damage.

He'd asked her about Kyle. The boy had been visibly shaken up by what he'd seen, but Devon had reassured him that he'd been okay once she'd got him to his parents. She'd told him that seeing that six-foot eighteen-year-old falling into his five-foot-nothing mom's arms, and bursting into tears, had brought tears to her own eyes.

Then he'd told her he wasn't expecting the surgery to take too long and he would like to stop by to see her on his way home. She'd wanted to put him off, but she knew she couldn't. It was time to tell Michael the whole truth about Conner.

The moment Michael had admitted how much he'd envied her for having a son like Conner, she'd known she couldn't keep his son from him any longer. Through all the years while she'd wondered about Michael and even those occasional times when she had doubts about keeping Conner from him, she'd never thought that he could be out there wishing that he had a child. His confession had hit her hard. Too hard for her to ignore it. How could she?

She'd always been able to tell herself that Michael was living the life he'd wanted. Even when he'd announced to the sports networks that he wouldn't be returning to the field, but instead would be putting all of his energy into going back to college to become the best orthopedic surgeon he could be, she'd thought she was doing the right thing. He'd devoted his life from that moment on to helping athletes, instead of being one. And from what she could see, he'd more than exceeded his dream.

Now, knowing that he'd actually envied her life with her son—their son—all along, the guilt she felt over a decision she'd made eight years ago was suffocating.

She sat up straight, her hands tightening on the blanket as a truck she didn't recognize pulled into her driveway. The passenger door opened and she saw Michael as he climbed out and waved at the driver.

She stood as he walked onto the porch to join her. His steps were slow and his normally bright eyes had dimmed. "Did everything go okay?"

He sat down hard, not waiting for her to sit. "He'll make it, but there was a lot of damage to that knee. I did the best I could, but there was extensive muscle damage. The good news is I was able to clean out the damaged tissue and it should heal well. But he'll need some time in rehabilitation and I don't know if this will affect his career as a pilot."

"I'm sure you did everything that you could," she said, but Devon could see that Michael wasn't satisfied with what he'd been able to do. "You of all people know that things happen sometimes that send us on a different path from the one we were expecting to take. His path might change, or maybe this will just be a temporary side trip."

"You're right. All of our paths change through life. My own life might not be what I had envisioned when I was younger, but now…" He paused for a moment, then ran his hands through his hair, pushing it back off his face. "After what I was able to be a part of in the OR today, knowing that I helped that man today, I honestly wouldn't change a thing."

"But we do all have things we would do differently, right? Sometimes we find ourselves at forks in the road where we have to make decisions we're not prepared for and we do the best we can." Devon certainly knew she'd been in that position several times in her life. Not just when she'd made the decision not to keep trying to tell Michael about the pregnancy when she couldn't initially get through to him, but also when she'd decided to marry Zach, knowing that they weren't in love with each other. Then there had been Zach's death and the promise she'd made to him to tell Michael about his son. She just hoped she could make Michael understand why she'd made the decision that she'd made about her son. Their son.

"Tell me, Devon. What in the world could have caused you to keep from telling me that I had a son?" Though Michael hadn't raised his voice, his words left her in no doubt of his anger.

"I don't blame you for being angry. I didn't set out to hurt you, though I can see now that I have."

"Hurt me? You just turned my life upside down. I just want to know how this happened. And what about your husband? Did he know? Were the two of you already together the night we ran into each other at the hotel?"

His words stung, but she couldn't blame him for what he was thinking when he hadn't been given any explanation.

"Yes, Zach knew. Zach… He was a good man. And, no, we weren't together, not as a couple. I met Zach during my freshman year of college. He was a computer science major and had IT geek written all over him. He was in my English composition class and when he saw me struggling with formatting for our first assignment, he offered to help. From there we became friends. The two of us and a couple other nursing students rented a house off campus our senior year." She paused, then laughed. "He said he regretted letting me talk him into moving in with us the first time he opened the refrigerator and found a dissected frog on a plate beside the ketchup."

He stood and moved away from her, and for some reason she followed him. "We were just friends then.

Good friends, but no more. Then I found out that I was pregnant."

"And you told him and not me?" he said. He turned toward her and the pain she saw in his eyes cut through her chest.

Her hands grabbed ahold of his arms and she forced herself to look him in the eye. "You never called me after our night together. But after you were injured, I called several times to check on you. Even before I knew I was pregnant I called. I wanted to hear your voice. I wanted to make sure you were okay. But Matt said you weren't taking any calls. I knew if that night we had shared had meant anything to you, you would have called me back, but still I called."

He made a small sound of distress.

"I wasn't angry. That wasn't what this was about." Yes, she'd felt hurt, but no matter how angry he might be at her about what she had done, she didn't want him to think that it had been meant as some type of revenge. "Three weeks later, when I knew I was pregnant, I called you again. Matt said that you were in a bad way. He said that it looked like your career was over and you weren't taking the news very well, and that you weren't taking any calls. When I asked him if he had told you that I'd called, he said he had. Then I asked him to please have you call me back, as it was important."

When his eyes turned away from her, she let go of him. Even after all this time, and knowing how his football injuries had affected him, the way he'd forgotten about her after that night still hurt. "I never meant for that night in the hotel to happen. But I was young and thought that what happened between us, the kind of passion I had experienced that night with you, meant something special."

His shoulders stiffened.

"When you didn't ever call me back, I knew that it hadn't meant the same thing to you. So when I found out I was pregnant and alone, I did what I thought was best for me and my child. Zach had cancer as a child and the radiation treatment he received meant he wasn't able to father children, so he offered to marry me. My grandmother was already very sick. Her finding out that I had followed in my mother's footsteps and was pregnant without a father for my baby would have killed her. The stress would have been too much."

For a moment, neither of them said anything, the roar of the waves across the street the only sound in the dark night.

"So why tell me now?" Michael asked, turning to her, his face a cold mask that she had never seen before. She was surprised to find how much more that hurt. But what had she expected? For him to suddenly apologize for not calling her all those years ago? Or for him to suddenly declare his undying love for her? When would she finally accept that she had never meant anything more to him than just being a friend with benefits?

"Because of Zach. Before he died, he made me promise to tell you." Unable to stand any longer, she sat back down in her grandmother's rocking chair.

"You should have found some way to tell me," Michael said, his voice even and his words clipped.

She ignored his words. Whether she had been right or wrong, she had made the only decision she believed she could make at the time. She looked up at the stars and prayed for Conner's sake that she had made the right decision both back then in marrying Zach, and in telling Michael now. The gulf breeze had died down and the air was heavy with humidity. The neighborhood was so quiet tonight that she felt completely alone, even though Michael stood in front of her. Her heart grew heavier with each moment that he remained silent.

Then, without saying a word, he started back down the porch steps. She stood and watched him walk away.

"Goodbye, Mickey," she whispered, as he disappeared into the darkness of the night.

CHAPTER EIGHT

THE MOMENT HE'D gotten home, he'd changed into his running gear and taken off down the beach. While his form wasn't what it had been before his injuries, he'd managed to build up his speed over the years, yet his mind still raced faster than his legs could go. Before he knew it, he was over a mile from his home.

He turned to run back, but found that he'd spent all his angry frustration and now felt empty and without the energy he needed to return. So he sat down, right there on the damp sand, and tried to make sense of everything he'd learned that night.

He'd tried his best to listen to everything Devon had said, but after her announcement that he was Conner's father, the rest had been so hard to hear. He attempted to dissect it all now, looking for something that would explain how it was possible that he had a son he'd never known about, but he couldn't seem to put it all together.

But there was one thing that had struck him when Devon had been talking that she had only hinted at. Everything that had happened from the moment she'd left that hotel room would have been different if he'd only called her and told her how much that night had meant to him. What would have happened after that, he wasn't sure. He'd been so tied up in his career and she was still in college. But he did know with certainty that if he'd made that call he wouldn't have missed the last seven years of his son's life. If he'd given Devon any hint that he wanted to continue the relationship, things would have been completely different.

Thinking of that call that had never happened, he pulled his phone from his pocket. He saw that it was after eleven and knew that his brother was probably asleep, but this couldn't wait until the morning.

"Hello," Matt said, his voice too alert for him to have been sleeping. There was the sound of a radio like those used by emergency services in the background.

"Hey, it sounds like you're at the hospital. Do you have a minute?" Michael asked. He shouldn't have called. Not until he'd had more time to think things through. To find some way to comprehend what finding out about Conner would mean to his life.

"Hold on," Matt said. There was the sound of movement and then a door shutting. "Sorry about that. They just brought in this kid riding a motorcycle that had been hit by a car. He has an open femur fracture, but they're taking him to CT first, to make sure there aren't any other injuries before I can take him to surgery."

"It sounds like you have a lot going on. I can call you tomorrow." If his brother was going into the OR shortly, Michael didn't want to say anything that might cause him to not be able to concentrate.

"Mickey, it's late. We both know you wouldn't have called if there wasn't something on your mind. What's going on?"

Michael knew now wasn't the time to discuss this, but he couldn't hold this back any longer. "You know I told you that Devon had come home. Did I tell you that she had a son?"

"I don't think so. Why?"

"Because it ends up that her seven-year-old son, Conner, is mine." As Michael said the words, he felt something settle in his chest. He'd been so shocked by everything Devon had told him that he hadn't been concentrating on the most important part. Conner, the boy he'd laughed with, and played with, and already come to care about—that child was his son.

"Okay, hold on. Didn't you tell me that Devon had been married? That her husband had died?"

"He had cancer. Apparently he'd had cancer as a child and it returned. It's all very complicated."

"I guess it is complicated since I don't even understand how this is possible. I mean, you and Devon? When did this happen? And why wasn't I ever told about it?" Matthew was beginning to sound a little annoyed now.

"If you must know, it happened a couple days before I was injured. We ran into each other when I was in Tallahassee." Michael wasn't about to go into the details with his brother.

"Well, I guess that explains all her phone calls. Not that I was surprised that she called to check on you. A lot of our friends from home called. But she was definitely calling more than the rest of them. I didn't want to be rude, but she had gotten pretty insistent about speaking to you. I had to tell her straight that you didn't want to talk to anyone, which you didn't."

The line went quiet for a moment. "Oh, wow. She was trying to get in touch with you about the pregnancy, wasn't she?"

"Yes," Michael said, "it seems she was."

"Oh, man, I'm so sorry, Mickey. If I'd had any idea that there was something going on between the two of you I would have made sure you talked to her. I didn't know," Matt said, and Michael could hear the apology and the worry in his brother's voice.

"It's not your fault, Matt. It was a bad time for both of us. Or I guess for the three of us. I have regretted for years not calling Devon after that night. I was so wrapped up in that next game, and I thought I had time." He didn't have to say that time ran out on the football field shortly afterward, and it was months before he'd felt like he had any kind of life left to live. From what Devon had said, it sounded like she would have been married by then, anyway.

"So I'm an uncle?" Matt asked. "I have to say that sounds really cool. When do I get to meet this kid of yours?"

"I don't know," Michael said. "I just found out tonight. I don't know what happens next."

"What happens next is you get to know your son. That's the plan, right? I mean the two of you don't mean to keep this from him, do you? Because that would really be messed up."

Leave it to Matt to get down to what was really important. Conner, and how they were going to handle things between them, was what was really important now. It was one of the reasons it had been so helpful to have Matt beside him during all his surgeries and rehab. There hadn't been a question that his brother didn't ask, or a possible solution to a problem that he didn't research.

"Give us some time. I need to talk to Devon and figure out where the two of us go from here," Michael said.

"The two of you, huh? Is there anything else you haven't told me? Is there more going on between you again?" Matt asked, his teasing tone returning, then disappearing again. "Seriously, bro. I don't know what happened between you and Devon, but if you still care for her at all, don't let her get away again."

"Go take care of your patient. I'll call you tomorrow." With that, Michael ended the call, then stood.

He took the walk back home slowly. His mind had finally settled and he could think more clearly now. The anger he'd first felt when Devon had told him about his son had passed for now. While he still didn't agree with what she had done, he could understand a lot of her reasoning and he was willing to accept his part in her decisions. Although it was hard for him to comprehend, he was hurt that Devon hadn't known that whatever else was happening in his life, he would have taken care of her and their son. He knew she had made several efforts to get in touch with him, but couldn't she have tried just a little harder for a little longer? If she could have waited until he had recovered from the surgeries, they would have been able to talk and work things out.

And didn't he sound like the self-centered jock he'd

been back then? Hadn't he learned over the years that the whole world didn't revolve around him?

The way he saw it, there were two things he could do now. He could choose to continue to be angry with Devon and her reasons for what she did. Or he could choose to put the past behind him and begin planning a future with his son. He knew what he would do in the end. He'd learned that the only way to move forward was to put the past behind him and look to the future.

He only hoped that he and Devon would be able to find a way to move forward from this together, so that he could be the father he wanted to be to his son.

The next morning, after much pleading from Conner, Devon called Michael to see if she could bring the boy over that afternoon to see his trophies. Though seeing Michael was the last thing she wanted to do, she felt this nagging need to make sure that he was okay. He'd been so upset the night before. He'd been angry, too, and she had expected that. But that he'd also seemed so hurt had surprised her.

"I told Max that I was going to see Coach Hart's trophies, and he was so jealous. I told him that maybe I could get the coach to let him come see them, too. Do you think Coach Hart would let him?" Conner asked as they crossed over the street to the beach, so they could look for any washed-up shells as they walked the couple of blocks to what had used to be Michael's parents' home.

"I think there's a good chance that he would," Devon said. For weeks her son had been calling Michael

"Coach Hart" and it hadn't bothered her. Now, though, it seemed so wrong. After having Michael admit his envy over her having a son like Conner, the guilt she had felt for keeping their son a secret had multiplied exponentially.

Zach had been right. She had needed tell Michael about Conner. She only wished she had done it earlier.

"I think so, too. He's real nice like that. Maybe he could just bring them to practice one day. Then everyone could see them," Conner said before rushing off ahead of her, then stopping to examine a shell stuck in the sand. When he pulled the shell out and saw that it was broken, he threw it back into the water then ran back up to her.

"Is the only reason you and your friends like Coach Hart because he was a football star and has a bunch of trophies?" Devon asked, wanting to know if it was just hero worship that was causing her son to be so taken with Michael. Though she knew that was a part of it, she hoped Conner liked Michael for more than that. She wanted the two of them to form something deeper. Something like what Conner had had with Zach, though different. She never wanted Conner to think that Michael was replacing Zach. Keeping Zach's memory alive was important for both of them.

"I think it's cool he has all those trophies and stuff and he's a really good coach, but I don't think that's why we like him. Mostly I like him because he doesn't talk to me like I'm just a kid. And when I mess up in practice, he doesn't get mad. He just explains how I can do better next time. Some coaches on the other teams yell a lot. He doesn't yell."

She stopped at the back of Michael's home and looked up. The house had been built onto pilings to protect it from the flooding that came with living in an area frequented by hurricanes. For as long as Devon could remember, she and her grandmother had used the back entrance to the home, taking the stairs up to the balcony. It wasn't because her grandmother worked for the Harts. It was because her grandmother was considered a neighbor and a friend.

But now, looking up at the balcony stairs and knowing how things had changed between her and Michael last night, she wondered if she should have gone around to the front entrance. She was considering doing just that when Michael leaned over the railing and smiled down at the two of them. "What are you waiting for? Come on up."

Before she could stop him, Conner raced up the steps, her breath catching when he almost missed a step and had to grab ahold of the railing to keep from falling.

"Conner, slow down. There's no rush," Michael said from where he now stood at the top of the stairs. "You almost gave your mom a heart attack."

As she made it up to the last step, Michael reached out his hand to her. She stood there a moment and looked at his outstretched hand. Was this a sign he'd already forgiven her? Did he understand that she had done what she'd thought was best for their son? She looked up into his eyes. There was an uncertainty there, a vulnerability that she had never seen before. She'd hurt him more than she had thought possible and her heart cracked a little. So where did they go from here?

Making her decision, she put her hand into his with the same force that she would have used to put an operating instrument into it. There was no going back now. The two of them had to work together for Conner's sake.

He squeezed her hand and something suddenly changed between them. The uncertainty disappeared from his eyes, and was replaced by an intensity so hot that it took her breath away. Unable to look away, she stumbled on the last step up and he grabbed her. His arms came around her, pulling her to him as he steadied her. Her face warmed as a flush of heat flared through her body. She forced her eyes from his and pulled away her hand before making a show of straightening the plain white T-shirt she'd worn with her shorts that day.

"These are different," she said as moved around him to the back entrance of the house. "I remember there only being a set of French doors here."

"Those doors were worn out by the time I moved back here. One of the first things I did was have the back wall removed and replaced with these doors so I could open up the whole room when the weather is pretty. They're wind-resistant and a lot more airtight when they're closed than the old doors," Michael explained as he came up behind her.

"I love them. You must have a beautiful view of the sunsets from here," she said. She'd already been nervous about seeing Michael today after all that had been said the night before. Having this… Attraction? Desire? Well, whatever it was that had just passed between the two of them, it had to stop.

She walked into the room and tried to concentrate on the other changes that had been made to the house. He'd opened up the whole downstairs with a solid wood beam placed between the family room and what had been a galley kitchen. The beam had been stained to match the driftwood mantel over the fireplace and it gave the whole room a light, airy feel that was so different from what she remembered the last time she'd been there.

"I rarely catch one, but when I do it is spectacular," Michael said. He walked toward the kitchen and her heart began to calm with each step he took away from her. "Since I doubt you really want to look at boring trophies, how about I get you a drink and you can sit outside or inside, if you prefer?"

"Mom doesn't think trophies are boring. She put the one I got last football season up on the china case so it would be safe and we could see it every night at dinner," Conner said as he turned around in a circle in the middle of the room. Her son. She'd almost forgotten that he was even there. "Didn't your mom want you to see your trophies when you had dinner?"

"My mom and dad had someone build a big cabinet upstairs for me and my brother's trophies. Let me get your mom something to drink and we can go up," Michael said, turning back toward the kitchen again before Devon reached out a hand to stop him.

"Go ahead and take him up. I'll just get a glass of water and wait for you on the balcony." Without looking at him, she walked past him into the kitchen and, without thinking, went straight to where the glasses were kept. Even with all the changes in the house, it felt familiar to her. Michael had somehow made the home more modern while still leaving it feeling like the home where he'd grown up.

After filling her glass with water and ice from the refrigerator, she walked outside and leaned on the railing overlooking the beach. The sky was clear except for a few puffy white clouds.

When Michael had left the night before, she'd gone over and over everything that she had said. She'd admitted to him that she had been disappointed that he hadn't called her. She'd even admitted that she had thought the night they spent together had meant something more than a one-night stand. It had been embarrassing in some ways to admit those things, but she'd wanted to be completely honest with him. Was that the reason for the way he'd looked at her? Was he remembering that night, too?

Or was this something different? There had been something happening between them for several days now. She'd tried to ignore it. She'd known that it was foolish of her to even want to explore it until things were settled between Michael and Conner. But now that her secret was out, did she feel any different?

She looked back to where she could see inside the second-floor window, where Michael and Conner stood. Her son was talking as fast as his lips could move, his eyes wide with excitement, while Michael stood beside him listening as if the kid's words were just as important as listening to one of his patients. She had to admit that though she'd had concerns about bringing a new parental figure into Conner's life, Michael seemed to be perfect for the job.

She knew in her heart that Michael was still angry with her. But she also knew that he was thrilled to learn that Conner was his son. Only time would tell if he'd ever really be able to forgive her.

She turned back to the beach and saw a couple had come to play in the waves. They looked no older than her and their laughing was so carefree that it made her smile. She remembered playing in those waves without a care in the world. She'd been much younger then. She wondered if her life would ever be like that again.

She didn't move when Michael stepped up behind her and casually put his arms on each side of the rail, then looked over her shoulder. "It looks like they're having fun down there."

"It does," she said, then turned to find herself almost in Michael's arms. Her body stiffened and her breath caught. Did he know he was doing this to her? "You didn't leave Conner alone with all those trophies, did you?"

As if he could feel the tension in her body, he stepped back and came to stand beside her. "He's safe in the game room. When I left him he was trying to figure out how to work the pinball machine. Apparently he's used to the virtual type of machine and hasn't ever seen one as 'old' as mine. He made me feel ancient."

"Get used to it. Some days just trying to keep up with him makes me feel old and decrepit." Her breath caught when she looked up at him. His smile was gone, his lips slightly parted, and his eyes were warm as he stared down into hers. "We need to talk. About Conner. But not here, where he could hear us."

The warmth in Michael's eyes disappeared. "He has to know at some point. You can't expect me to ignore the fact that he is my son."

"I know he has to be told, but we have to be careful to tell him at the right time and in the right way. He was devastated when we lost Zach. He's bound to be confused when he finds out he has another father."

"Hey, Coach Hart, do you have any more of those games? That one is a lot of fun," Conner called, as he thundered down the stairs toward them.

"Have you ever played the original *Pac-Man* game?" Michael asked as he stepped away from her.

"I don't think so," Conner said as he stepped outside with them.

She turned around and faced Michael first, and then her son. "How about we save that for another time? Tomorrow's a school day and I need to get dinner started."

"But, Mom…" Conner began.

"If your mom says you need to go, we're not going to argue with her," Michael said. "Unless you want me to keep Conner here out of your way and when you're ready for him I can bring him home?" he added.

She started to protest, but then the two of them smiled those identical, charming, crooked smiles at her and she knew she was beat. How was it possible that no one had noticed the similarities between the two of them?

"How about I get everything ready and when Coach Hart brings you home, he can stay for dinner?" Devon watched as Michael and Conner shared high fives before heading up the stairs. The two of them, smiling and laughing, brought a bittersweet smile to her lips.

Seeing the two of them together, she now understood what Zach had tried to tell her. Her husband had known what it was like to be a father to her son. He'd loved it and he'd always let her know how grateful he was that she'd allowed him to have that experience. But he'd also felt guilty that he was taking that experience away from another man. It didn't come as a surprise to her; Zach had always been a very sensitive man. She just wished she could tell him that she understood now. That he'd been right. She couldn't help but think that somehow he knew that she had fulfilled her promise to him.

CHAPTER NINE

MICHAEL FOLLOWED DEVON out to the porch carrying each of them a glass of the wine he'd brought with him when he brought Conner home.

"I appreciate you letting Conner spend so much time with you today. He'll talk about it for days," Devon said as she took a glass from him.

The boy was certainly a handful—his mouth and feet never slowed down. He didn't know how Devon managed to keep up with him. But Michael didn't know when he'd last had as much fun as he'd had today. The hours he had spent with Conner playing those old-school arcade games had taken him right back to his own childhood. He'd been reminded of all the time he'd spent with his brother, each competing to beat the other one, in that very same game room. "I appreciate you bringing him over. He's a great kid. You and Zach did a good job raising him."

"Thank you," she said, then took a sip of the wine. "That means a lot coming from you."

"I'm sorry I left the way I did last night. All I can say is that I needed to process things."

"I don't blame you, Michael. I know hearing Conner

was your son had to have been a terrible shock," Devon said, then repositioned herself in the chair.

"It was a shock. That's for sure. But it wasn't terrible. You have to know that finding out that Conner is my son…" For a moment, he found himself unable to go on. He didn't think of himself as an especially emotional man, but actually being able to say that Conner was his son touched something inside of him. Was this what being a father was like? This feeling of pride and humbleness at the same time? His father had always been quick to tell his sons how proud he was of them. He wanted to be exactly that kind of father to Conner.

He took a breath and cleared his throat. "Finding out that Conner is my son has to be the best thing that has ever happened to me. He is amazing and I couldn't be more proud of him. But I do have to ask why you didn't tell me the truth about him the first time you saw me at the center."

Devon walked to the old rocking chair and began to rock. "Conner is the reason I hesitated over taking this job. I was afraid that if I worked with you, somehow you'd find out about Conner before I was ready to tell you about him. Then, of course, I found out you were one of his football coaches."

"But why would you think me being around Conner would make a difference? There was no reason for me to question you about who his father was," he said with a puzzled look.

"Maybe it was just me, because I know the truth, but I can see so much of you in him. The way he smiles. The way he laughs. And have you ever stopped and looked at his eyes? They're the exact same light green as yours. The only other people I've ever seen with that color are Matt and your father."

"So you told me when you did because you thought I'd see the similarities between me and Conner and question if he could be mine?" Michael had always thought he was observant, but apparently he had been wrong.

"Maybe, a little. But then I saw the two of you together. You're so good with him, Michael. So patient. And then you mentioned that you would like to have had a son just like him. That you envied me having Conner. How could I not tell you then?" She leaned back in her chair and her shoulders sagged. He could see that the last twenty-four hours had to have taken as much of a toll on her as they had on him. "But I want to be honest with you. I think it is really important that we are honest with each other from now on, so I need to tell you all the truth."

Michael's mind tried to imagine what else she could have kept from him, but came up blank. "Okay, tell me."

"One of the reasons I applied for this job was because I wanted to make sure that you would be good for my son," Devon said, then looked away from him as if she was embarrassed by what she had done.

For a moment, he was taken back. "You thought I might be bad for Conner? Like I'd hurt him or something?" He thought she had hurt him before, but this cut even deeper.

"You have to understand that I didn't grow up in the same perfect world that you did. Things were different for me. Trust isn't something I give easily when it comes to my son." She turned her shoulder to him and he could see how much she wanted him to see why she'd done what she had done.

Yes, her words hurt, but she was right. He'd had an almost perfect life. Even with losing his parents, he knew the time they'd had together had been a gift. Though he'd heard all the rumors that had spread about Devon when she'd shown up at her grandmother's house, he didn't know what was real and what was fiction. How could he judge what she had done without knowing the real reason behind her actions?

"Do you want to tell me about it?" he asked gently. A part of him wanted to know how many of the rumors were true, but at the same time, he didn't want to cause her any more pain.

"Let's just say that my mother had a habit of bringing home men who weren't very nice to either of us. It seemed that no matter what I did, either one of them, or my mother, was mad at me. I think it was just because I was there. In some ways, the last man she brought around did me a favor by beating me. It was because of him that I came to live here with my grandmother."

Michael looked over at her and saw that she had quit rocking, and now, was staring out into the night. Was it possible that she was reliving that terrible experience right now?

The thought that the man who had beaten her could still hurt her like this made him angrier than he'd ever been. He walked over to Devon, and bent down in front of her. "I'm sorry that happened to you, but I am glad you came here to Silver Sands. Your grandmother loved you so much and she was so proud of you the last time I saw her."

His hands came up and brushed against her cheeks, and then up through her hair, and he found himself being unable to ignore the desire that was coming alive within his body. Hearing her talk about the abuse she'd experienced during her childhood made him ache to hold her. When he leaned toward her, his lips touched hers.

This wasn't the sweet kiss they'd shared as teenagers that night on the beach after the death of his parents. And it wasn't the desperate kisses they'd shared in a hotel room, knowing that in the morning they'd go their separate ways. He wanted this kiss to be protective and comforting. But even as he thought this, a fire seemed to come alight inside them both.

Her lips opened and his tongue swept into her mouth as he pulled her up out of the chair. Her arms came up around his neck and he felt her body relax into him. Though a part of him was afraid that she would regret this later, he had to taste her. Right now, with his lips on hers, their tongues tangling together, and her body pulled tight against him, he just didn't care about tomorrow or any of the tomorrows after that. There was only the here and now for them. He held her so tight that he could feel the beating of her heart against his chest, as his own heart seemed to try to match its rhythm. He pulled her even closer as the hard length of him pressed against her belly. He knew they had to stop before things went any further. They were standing on her front porch with the light shining over their heads. If anyone drove down the road, they'd see them.

He pulled his lips from hers reluctantly, but kept his arms around her.

"And then there was this thing… Something was happening…between us," she said as she tried to catch her breath.

"This?" Michael asked, his own breaths coming fast and shallow as he stepped away from her.

"Yes, this thing between us," she said. "It's another one of the reasons I finally told you about Conner. I couldn't let things go any further before I told you about him. I knew it would change things, but it's better for both of us this way. If I'd waited it would have made things even worse."

"And has it changed things for you?" he asked.

He couldn't deny that he had been hurt by the way Devon had kept Conner a secret from him. He would never have thought the girl he'd known as Sunshine, the sweet considerate girl who he remembered, could do something like that to him. But he also knew that she'd been young and scared at the time she'd made that decision. Last night, as he'd walked on the beach, he'd made the decision to put the past behind them and concentrate on the future he had with his son. But he hadn't been sure about what that might mean for him and Devon at the time. He'd hoped they could at least be friends again. Right now, he found himself wanting more.

"Because it hasn't changed anything for me," he said. Because, looking at the woman sitting in front of him, he knew that nothing that he'd discovered the night before had changed how he felt about her. He'd seen how she'd taken charge of emergency situations in the operating room. He'd seen how she was with his son. That was the woman she was now. That was the woman who he'd found himself drawn to over and over again since she'd returned.

"How is that possible? How can you forgive me, just like that?" she asked. "I still can't even say I regret my decision. It's too close to saying I regret my decision to marry Zach. I won't do that. Not that I don't feel guilty about what I did to you, as I do. But my life with Zach came to be because of my pregnancy."

"So where do we go from here?" he asked. He wouldn't push her. Not tonight. The truth was he was as confused about what was happening between them as she clearly was. He needed to take the time to get to know his son first, and then maybe he and Devon could explore things and see where they led. There were too many issues between them to complicate things any more than they already were.

"I don't know. I know that we'll have to tell Conner at some point. He has the right to know. Zach even said so. When we realized he wasn't going to beat the cancer this time, he told me that I needed to tell both of you the truth. He wanted Conner to have a father after he was gone."

"He must have been a remarkable man," Michael said honestly, his heart squeezing. How was he supposed to live up to a man like him?

"He was. That's why this is so hard. Maybe if Zach had been gone longer it would be easier. I don't expect you to understand this, but it seems almost disloyal to tell Conner that Zach wasn't really his father. At least not his biological father." She stepped away from him and he felt the emptiness of his arms immediately, something that he'd never felt before. "All I'm asking is that you give me a little time. Conner took Zach's death very hard. The two of them were so close. I just want to be careful and find the right way to tell him."

"I understand," he said. He knew he had to tread softly here for both Conner and Devon's sakes. "So how about this? The three of us continue to spend more time together, just like we did this weekend. That way, he'll get to know me better. Then, when we decide the time is right to tell him, he'll be more comfortable with the idea."

"We can do that," Devon said with a nod. "And thank you for understanding. I know you'll agree with me that the most important thing right now is that Conner feels loved and secure. He has to be my first priority."

Devon opened her front door, then turned back to look at him. Their eyes met, and once more he felt that fire inside him flare up. Like Devon, he couldn't describe exactly what it was that was happening between the two of them. Was it just lust they were feeling? Or was it something deeper? Either way, as he made his way across the beach to his home, he found himself looking forward to finding out not only what it was, but also just where it would take them.

When Devon arrived at work the next day, her emotions were all over the place. She wasn't sure if it was the kiss or Michael knowing about Conner that had her tied up in knots. Maybe she shouldn't have rushed into telling Michael the truth. Just bursting out with the fact that Michael was Conner's father on the beach had probably been foolish. But after listening to Michael talk about wanting a child, she couldn't have stopped herself. And if she hadn't told him then, when would she have? She'd been working with Michael for a month and hadn't been able to do it in all that time. So what? When would have been the right time? When Conner graduated from high school? Or maybe when she was lying on her deathbed?

She had to quit second-guessing herself. It was done now. The three of them had to move on from here. Michael certainly seemed to be ready to do so.

The truth was there never would have been a perfect time to tell Michael about his son. That time would have been eight years ago. And it wouldn't even have been perfect then, not with Michael trying to recover from his injuries. The last thing he had needed then was someone with whom he'd had a one-night stand showing up pregnant on his doorstep.

But what about that kiss? How were they going to be able to move on from that?

An alert message came over her work phone, the noise of it causing the patients and visitors in the waiting room to turn and stare as she walked by them. It only took a second for her to read it before she was running for the operating room. She stopped only long enough to grab a mask and hat as she passed the supply closet at the entrance to the operating suites. The front desk had been abandoned and the halls were empty.

It wasn't until she turned a corner that she saw several of the OR staff crowded outside operating room four, where the emergency had been paged out.

"Who's the doctor?" she asked as the staff parted to let her in.

"Dr. Morgan is doing an ACL repair on an eighteen-year-old male. It looks like the kid is having seizures," Robert, one of the OR techs, said.

Just hearing the doctor's name put her on alert. Her instincts kicked in and she made a decision that she hoped she wouldn't regret. "Call Dr. Hart and tell him I need him in here."

The tech gave her a nod and she entered the room. As Devon walked through the OR doors, she could see that the place was in total chaos as the anesthesiologist and two nurses were trying to contain the young patient, who was now shaking from head to toe, partially covered in a blue drape.

She looked for the doctor who should have been the one handling this emergency and couldn't believe what she found. Standing at the back of the room, Dr. Morgan had his arms crossed in front of his sterile gown as if he was patiently waiting for the rest of the staff to handle this emergency so that he could begin his surgery. Did he really think that they were going to continue with it?

"Let me help," Devon said as she moved to the head of the table and helped secure the boy's head.

"Thanks. I need to reverse the anesthesia and give him a dose of diazepam while we try to figure out what happened here." Devon didn't miss the scathing look the anesthesiologist gave Dr. Morgan.

"Reverse the anesthesia?" Dr. Morgan said from the back of the room. "If you'd already given him the diazepam, we could have been halfway through the surgery by now. Give it to him now and let me get started."

"He's been seizing like this for the past five minutes. There's no way that I'm going to leave him under the anesthesia," said one of the nurses indignantly. Devon looked over at her and was surprised to find that it was Rachel who had spoken up. She was a nurse who worked as a vendor representative and observed all the surgeries that their surgical devices were involved in, and Devon had liked the woman from the moment she'd met her. Then, as if needing the support, Rachel looked over at Devon. Though Devon didn't have all the facts that she needed to determine a cause for these seizures, anybody could see that the operation couldn't continue. Besides, the anesthesiologist had the right not to continue with the surgery at this point.

"Does the patient have a history of seizures?" she asked.

"It wasn't noted in his history," the anesthesiologist said. "And he didn't say anything about being on any seizure medications when I asked."

Because it was part of her job to help handle any issues that came up between the anesthesiologist department and the surgeons, she decided to be more tactful than she actually wanted to be with this particular surgeon.

"If this patient has a history of seizures, the anesthesia drugs could have lowered his seizure threshold, causing this issue. You have to agree that it's in the patient's best interest that we hold off on this surgery for now." Even as Devon had begun, she could see Dr. Morgan was going to argue with her. Not that it was going to change anything. She knew this whole room agreed with her and the anesthesiologist that the operation needed to be canceled.

"You're just a nurse. You can't make those decisions. I'm ordering you to give him the diazepam and let me do my job," Dr. Morgan said, his voice as sour as his words. The man really did need to go back to physician charm school and learn how to talk to people.

"You can't talk to her that way," Rachel objected, surprising Devon again. The look she gave Dr. Morgan said she was ready to go to war against him right then and there.

"She's not *just* a nurse. She's a nurse with a good head on her shoulders, and she's also absolutely right," Michael said from the door as he walked into the room toward the patient on the table.

Fortunately, while she'd been trying to reason with Dr. Morgan, the anesthesiologist had been reversing the anesthesia and pushing the IV diazepam. The boy's body finally relaxed and the seizures eased off.

"He's responding to the medication," she told Michael with relief, "but it was a grand mal seizure. We can't continue the surgery. He needs to be transferred to a hospital so he can be observed and have a neurologist consulted."

"I agree," Michael said, then turned to the circulating RN. "Call nine-one-one and ask for transport. Tell them we have a young man who has just experienced a seizure on the operating table before the surgery had begun."

"Wait just a minute," Dr. Morgan said. For the first time, the man stepped up to the table where his patient was lying. "You can't do that. I'm the patient's surgeon."

"That's fine," Michael said. "You can handle the transport then and call the emergency room and give your report to the doctor there. But first, I think it would be best if you and I go inform the patient's mother what just happened."

"I don't need you to go with me to talk to my patient's family," Dr. Morgan said. Then, without even giving his patient a glance, he ripped off his sterile gown, dropped it on the floor, and stormed out of the room.

CHAPTER TEN

MICHAEL LOOKED UP when Devon stepped into his office. No one would have known by looking at her that she'd just led the team through a stressful incident in the operating room. Her scrubs were spotless and her hair, which had been pulled back into a high ponytail, seemed to bounce as she walked toward him. If not for the dark circles under her eyes, she'd be picture-perfect.

"You wanted to see me?" she asked. She might have looked okay, but the slight tremor in her voice said she had been just as affected as the rest of the operating team.

"I wanted to thank you for everything you did in the OR today. I can't believe a doctor would pull something like that. Having a patient hold back information is the same as falsifying information as far as I'm concerned." He'd already sent an email to Steve Morgan stating that his rights to perform surgery at the surgical center had been canceled. And he was also reporting the doctor to the board of medicine, now that he had learned exactly how ethically incompetent the man was turning out to be.

It was only when the ambulance had arrived and they had brought the boy's mother back to see him that it had come out that Dr. Morgan had told the mother and son that they shouldn't mention the boy's seizure history because it would keep him from having the surgery in an outpatient center. Since her son hadn't had a seizure since he was a child, she'd never considered that it would be a problem. They were lucky the teenager had recovered as quickly as he had.

"I talked to the boy's mother and he's doing well. They expect him to be discharged tomorrow after the neurologist sees him." She shook her head. "Apparently, the ER doctor had a lot of questions for them once they got there. According to the mother, he seemed to have as much trouble as we did with the surgeon's actions. I have to say, you handled Dr. Morgan even better than I thought you would."

"I don't know when I've been as angry at a coworker as I am with Steve right now. I appreciate you helping to cool down the situation. See, I knew hiring you was a good idea," he teased gently.

"But do you still feel that way after finding out about Conner? I know I was wrong to take the job without telling you about him first. If you feel that it could be a problem with us working together, I'd understand."

She looked away from him, and he knew he couldn't be angry with her any longer, no matter that he still didn't understand her decision. He stood, then went over to his office door and shut it, before going back to his desk.

"Can you please sit down so we can talk," he said, motioning to the chair in front of him. "And, no, I don't think we're going to have any problem working together. This isn't about the job."

He waited until she took a seat, though he noticed she sat on the edge with her hands clasped in her lap.

"Is this about the kiss?" he asked. "Is that why all of a sudden you're so nervous around me?"

She opened her mouth and then shut it and he had no doubts that she had been about to deny it.

He understood how she felt. He'd been thinking about it since the moment he'd left her. There had been something different about that kiss from all the other ones they'd shared before. But then everything he felt for Devon was totally different from anything he'd ever felt before. Holding Devon in his arms had felt so right, as if he had finally found exactly where he belonged. It had been as if he'd come home. It had been so long since he'd felt that way. He'd lost that feeling when his parents had been killed. The only personal connection he'd felt since then had been with his brother, but it wasn't the same.

Devon cleared her throat and crossed her arms. "I don't think your office is the place to discuss this. Do you?"

Leaning back in his chair, he looked at the woman who'd just taken on a surgeon without any fear, yet here she was afraid to discuss something as simple as a kiss. Not that he really thought that this particular kiss had been that simple. It had actually been very complicated. And now, it appeared to have the power to complicate things here, in his surgical center. "So we can both agree that there will be no talking about kisses in the workplace. What about the actual kissing? Is that allowed?"

Devon's cheeks turned the color of soft pink roses and Michael couldn't help but laugh. "You know I'm kidding you. If you don't want to discuss the kiss, that's fine. But you said you wanted us to be honest with each other and I can honestly say that I enjoyed that kiss very much."

"Will you be serious for a moment," Devon said as she stood and gave him a look that would have put the fear into any seven-year-old boy. Fortunately, he was no longer seven.

"Okay, I won't mention it again. Not at work. But seriously, Devon. If you have a problem with anything between us, whether it's Conner or anything else, I want you to talk to me about it."

Her body relaxed as she stood there in front of him. "You know I will. Didn't you just see the way I handled Dr. Morgan? I have no problem speaking my mind."

After she left, Michael ignored the stack of paperwork on his desk, unable to make himself deal with it. It was much more fun to spar with Devon. If everything went well, he'd be able to hand off all of this to someone else soon, so that he could have more time to spend with Conner and Devon. It seemed like he had spent his whole life content to work toward that next big goal.

Now, he had something even more important in his life. He had a son. The fact that Devon came with the son could be complicated, though. Already, that they were feeling this attraction for each other was causing problems. He couldn't deny that he enjoyed being with her. But he worried how it would affect Conner if things between Michael and Devon went too far and then went sour.

Boys were protective of their mothers. He'd been protective of his, yet still he'd lost her because of a drunk driver. Michael knew the pain that came with losing a parent. Conner had already lost his father at a very young age. Conner would be even more protective of his mother now. And hurting Devon would hurt his son. Was he really willing to take that chance?

He thought about the kiss they'd shared. He might have teased Devon about it, but the truth was that he'd felt more passion in those few moments than he'd felt for years. There was something about her that drew him to her. He'd felt it that night on the beach, and he'd felt it the night at the hotel. Both times, other events had interceded and they'd gone their separate ways. Now, there was no possibility of the two of them doing that. They were tied together for life because of their son.

And he was already afraid that any plan he might come up with to ignore this need that they felt for each other was already doomed to fail.

For the next two weeks, Devon found herself and Conner spending each night eating dinner with Michael. On nights when they ate at Devon's place, she and Michael would share the cleanup of the kitchen and getting Conner to bed. Afterward, they'd spend an hour or so talking out on the porch together. They talked about work or something going on in Conner's life. They talked about their town and the people they knew there. But not once did Michael bring up the subject of telling Conner about Michael being his biological father. He seemed to understand that Conner needed time to get to know him better and to get used to him being a part of his life. He also made no attempt to bring up the subject of the kiss they'd shared. And he'd made no move to kiss her again.

While Devon appreciated his understanding about Conner, she had to admit that she was missing his kisses. Somehow, him not kissing her made her even more aware of his presence whenever they were alone. It was like she had some ticking bomb inside her that was just waiting for one touch from him to set it off. It was taking all her strength not to reach out and touch him, and see exactly how much damage the two of them could do to each other.

So while they'd sat on the porch, each sipping a glass of the wine Michael had brought over the night before, all she could think about was this need for him that she could feel building inside of her.

"There's something I want to ask you," Michael said as he set his glass down. "I don't have to have an answer now, though I hope your answer will be yes. It's something that I think would be good for all three of us."

Suddenly her mind went into overdrive, leaving memories of those kisses she was dreaming about behind, and jumping way too fast for Devon into thoughts of a proposal. Her hand came up to her chest as her heart began to thump too fast. Her, marry Michael?

She could see how a marriage between the two of them would be good for their son, but she'd done that once before. If she ever married again, it would need to be for the right reasons. She would never marry again unless she was in love. She'd been lucky her marriage to Zach had been such a good one. They had been friends, and later, lovers, but she wouldn't go into a marriage like that again.

"Are you okay?" Michael asked. He got up from his chair and bent down in front of her. "Are you having chest pain? Should I call nine-one-one?"

She couldn't speak. Her breaths came too fast and her ears were filled with a roaring sound. Was this what a panic attack felt like?

Maybe she'd been obsessing over his kisses recently, but she wasn't ready for a proposal. She placed her hands in her lap and, with the calmest voice she could manage, said, "No. I'm fine. But maybe it would be best if we waited before discussing anything else tonight."

He sat there in front of her for a few more moments. Then, after studying her face for several seconds and appearing to be satisfied that she wasn't going to pass out, he stood. "I don't want to rush you, but the game is next week and I don't want my friend to hold the tickets for us if you don't want to go. And if we are going, then I'll need to reserve a plane for us."

Her mind went blank. For a moment, it just stopped processing information. It was like the blood flowing up to her brain had taken a vacation and headed for her toes. Her thoughts weren't just scrambled, they had simply disappeared. It took a moment for her brain to come back online and she began to realize that she had made a grave mistake in thinking that Michael had wanted to ask her to marry him.

"A plane? Tickets for a game?" she asked, her voice higher than usual.

"Yes. It's in Tampa, so it will be a short flight, and the game is at one, so we won't be too late getting back. I get these offers all the time from the people I used to play with. I normally turn them down, but I think Conner would really enjoy seeing a live game."

"I'm sure he would," she said. The feeling was finally coming back into her arms and legs, and she was even beginning to see some humor in the situation, though she would never share it with Michael. She was just glad she hadn't made any more of a fool of herself than she had already. "How about I get back to you in the morning?"

"That's fine," Michael said, then went on to change the subject to something that had happened in the operating room that day.

He appeared totally oblivious to where her mind had gone earlier, which was a good thing for her. A proposal? She'd really thought Michael Hart was actually going to ask her to marry him? The mere thought was ridiculous.

But when he left that night, she couldn't help but feel disappointed once again when he made no attempt to kiss her good-night.

CHAPTER ELEVEN

As they made their way into the fancy suite inside the football stadium, Devon was glad that she'd taken the time to dress up a little for the game. She'd seen pictures of all the celebrity guests and famous football players' wives dressed in short dresses and boots, but she hadn't gone that far. Instead, she'd worn her nicest pair of skinny black jeans and had splurged on a new team jersey, as it had been Michael's team before he'd been injured. The only thing the least bit different from what she normally would have worn to a game were the sequins that decorated the team's name and the heeled boots she wore.

She thought she looked quite nice until they were ushered into a room filled with women dressed in clothes that would have cost her a month's income. If the private jet and the limousine ride from the airport hadn't been intimidating enough, this was almost mind-blowing. She was just a nurse from a little beach town. What was she supposed to talk about with these people?

"I'll be right back," Michael said as a man waved to him from down a set of steps where the seats faced a large window.

"Mom, you're squeezing my hand," Conner complained from beside her as he pulled against the tight hold she had on his hand.

She looked down at her son and let go of him. But when he started to step away from her, she put her hand on his shoulder. "Stay with me until Michael finds out where we're supposed to be seated."

"But can I go ask him if I can get one of those sodas over there?" he asked, pointing to where a large glass bowl filled with ice and drinks sat in the middle of a table draped in a white linen tablecloth.

"Of course you can have a soda, if it's okay with your mom," a woman said as she stepped toward them.

"I'm Lily, Darek's wife." The woman's smile seemed genuine, though it was as bright as the teardrop diamonds hanging from her ears. "You must be Devon and Conner. Darek was so happy to hear that you were coming today. He's been trying to get Michael to a game for years."

Devon looked over to where Michael was surrounded by a group of men, all seeming happy to see him. Some of the men she could picture as former players. Those were the large men who were in their late thirties or early forties, but she could tell they still worked out in the gym. Then there were others who seemed to be guests, like her and Michael. Michael had explained that Darek was the friend who'd invited them to the game, but that was all he'd told her. "It's nice to be here. Conner has been excited all week. He's big into football even though he's only seven. Michael is one of his coaches."

"And you? Are you a football fan or are you just a Michael fan?" another woman asked as she stepped up beside Lily. Devon looked at the woman, unsure how she was supposed to respond.

"Ignore Janie," Lily said, rolling her eyes at the woman.

"I guess you could say I'm both," Devon said, answering the woman even though the question seemed rude. "I've known him since I was a kid. I watched him play in high school. And now, I work for him. We're friends. Just friends."

She swallowed when Janie continued to stare at her. The woman looked Devon up and down before turning away and walking off to join another group.

"What was that about?" Devon asked Lily when she was sure the woman was far enough away that she couldn't hear her.

"Old news. She had a thing for Michael back in the day, but she's harmless. Michael never had any interest in her," Lily said.

Devon looked back at Janie and saw that she had quickly made her way over to the men, and now had her arms wrapped around Michael's neck in a hug. Devon's eyes narrowed and she had to hold herself back from walking over and pulling the woman off him.

"So just friends, huh?" Lily said. Devon looked back at her and saw her eyes sparkling with mischief. "Don't worry, your secret's safe with me. The only thing I care about is that you've somehow gotten Michael to come join us, which will make my husband a happy man tonight."

Devon didn't know what to say, so she looked around for Conner. She was surprised to see that there were other children playing games at a corner table. She'd been so busy checking out the men and women that she hadn't seen them. But Conner wasn't with the other children. Instead, he had walked down the steps to where the fanciest stadium seats she had ever seen lined a glass window that looked out into the stadium.

"Excuse me," Devon said, then headed over to where Conner stood with his face as close to the window as it was possible to be. She started to pull out a tissue from her purse to wipe his fingerprints off the glass, then decided against it.

"Wow, that's a great view, isn't it?" she asked as she stepped up to the window beside him.

"This is amazing," Conner said without taking his eyes off the field.

"What do you think?" Michael said, coming up behind them. "Are you ready for some football, Conner?"

A moment later, the teams took the field and Conner began to clap. An intercom system came on and almost everyone started to take their seats. Michael held his hand out to Devon, and she took it. But after he'd led them to their seats, he let go.

One team kicked off and the game began. In moments, the excitement of the game had filled the room. There were screams of celebration and moans of disappointment as the two teams battled on the field. By the end of the first quarter, Devon had become as vocal as the rest of the group. When Michael's former team went for a touchdown on the fourth down with one yard to the goal, everyone in the room was on their feet. As the team's offensive line pushed forward and the quarterback dived over them to score the first touchdown of the game, the room exploded with screams.

Michael turned to her, and before she knew it, she was clasped in his arms and lifted off the ground. When Michael put her on her feet, Conner was in front of them laughing at her. "Mom, why is your face so red?"

"Because the team made a touchdown, of course," Devon said and then looked up at Michael, who was laughing along with her son. Then they all took their seats to prepare for the kicker's attempt at an extra point.

For the rest of the first half, Devon found it hard to pay attention to what was happening on the field. She was wound too tight after the hug she'd shared with Michael. It seemed every few minutes Michael would touch her hand and point out something on the field. Once, he'd rested his arm across the back of her seat and she'd been afraid to lean back in case his arm touched her shoulder. She'd begun to accept the idea that Michael really wasn't interested in kissing her again. If only her body would accept it instead of reacting like some sex-starved idiot every time he touched her!

As soon as it was halftime, Devon excused herself and found the restroom. After washing her hands, she looked into the mirror and saw that her face did have a pink flush to it. She couldn't help but wonder if Michael was playing some game with her. Since the night he'd kissed her, he'd made no move toward her for anything except having contact with Conner. Yes, the two of them were growing closer, as friends, while they got Conner used to having Michael around. Was he giving her all this attention today for his friends? No, he wasn't the type of man to need a woman on his arm for his ego. So what was going on?

By the time she walked back into the suite, she'd decided that she would have to speak to Michael the next time they were alone. Even though they were spending their time together for Conner, they needed to be careful that he didn't get the wrong idea about the relationship between the two of them.

Seeing Michael across the room in deep conversation with a group of people, and Conner in the corner where the other kids were playing, she walked over to the window and looked down on the field, where the halftime performance was just finishing up.

"Devon?" a man said as he joined her. "I'm Darek. Darek Roberts."

It only took a moment to put together where she had heard the name. Lily's husband had been one of the two tackles that had slammed into Michael during the last game of his career. "I know you," Devon said. "You're one of the men who tackled Michael the night he was injured."

"I'm afraid so," Darek said. The man shook his head, and his eyes dropped to the ground. "I've relived that moment too many times to count."

Devon could tell the man's sorrow for what had happened was real. She'd watched that play more times than she wanted to count, too. There had been no ill intent on either of the men's part. "It was an accident. I'm sure Michael doesn't blame you."

The man looked up at her. "Michael is one of a kind. Even when they were loading him up on a stretcher to carry him off the field, he was assuring me that it wasn't my fault. That didn't make it any easier to bear when I found out just how bad he was injured, though. I think maybe it made it harder. The day they announced that he wasn't going to be able to play again was one of the worst days of my life."

"But you were on another team," Devon said. Seeing this six-foot-plus man who was the size of a refrigerator looking like he'd lost his best friend was almost painful. "You were just doing your job by stopping the play. I read the papers. No one blamed you or the other player."

"Didn't matter if they blamed us. We knew how hard Michael had worked to get into professional football, because we'd done the work, too. Having it all end for him right then was painful for all of us," Darek said.

"He told me that the two of you are friends, so I know there's no ill will on his part." Though she couldn't deny that she'd been angry with the men who'd caused Michael's injuries when it had first happened, she'd accepted it as something that none of the players had any control over. The anger had faded enough for her to think about it clearly. It was just part of the game and a risk that all the players took when they stepped on the field. "And look what he's done with his life. I work with him now and I can honestly tell you that he's a great doctor."

"I know. He did my knee replacement not long after he passed his boards. He thought I let him do it out of guilt, but that wasn't it."

"Then why?" she asked, knowing this man could have had any surgeon he wanted do the operation.

"Because I knew if he'd put in half the work to be a doctor as he had to be the kind of quarterback he used to be, then he would do an excellent job." The man looked down at his right knee, lifted it, and then began to swing it back and forth. "Like I said, an excellent job."

Devon smiled at this giant of a man who'd mowed down players on the field and realized he was just a great big teddy bear. "I'm glad to hear it."

"But that wasn't what I wanted to talk to you about. I came over here to tell you just how much I appreciate you getting him here today."

"He invited me," Devon said, confused about why the man thought she should take credit for Michael being there.

"I've been inviting him for years, ever since I quit playing and joined this group of broken-down ex-players. But he'd always come up with some reason why he couldn't make it. I have to believe you have something to do with why he's here now."

Devon looked around the room and found that Michael had left the group of men and was now bent down talking to Conner. "I think it's more likely that it's my son who got him here today."

Darek looked over to where Michael and Conner were deep in what looked like a very serious conversation, then shook his head. "Maybe so, but I think you had a lot more to do with it than you think."

The halftime clock ticked down and everyone returned to their seats as the teams returned to the field. For the rest of the game, Michael and Conner had their heads together as they discussed the players and the plays. Devon told herself that she wasn't disappointed when Michael didn't touch her again for the rest of the game. She was so confused, not only by Michael's actions, but also by her own reactions. She knew that Michael's interest needed to be on Conner and he had always had the power to focus on what was important in his life. He'd done it with his football career and later his medical career. Yet a part of her, a part she was ashamed to admit to, wanted some of that focus to be on her, even though she knew that was wrong.

Sitting up in her seat, she forced herself to pay attention to the field. Just then, the other team scored a touchdown, tying up the game. There were moans in the room, and one celebratory cheer from the lone home-team fan. The tension in the room was high and Devon found herself caught up in the game once again.

Michael looked over to where Conner lay curled up in his seat asleep as they flew the short distance back to the Florida panhandle.

"He doesn't look very comfortable," he said to Devon, who sat on his other side.

"He's fine," Devon said as she leaned forward and looked over at her son. "Normally, after staying up this late I'd have a hard time getting him up for school in the morning, but he's so stoked about that football Darek had all the players sign for him that I'm sure he'll pop right up."

Michael didn't want to say anything about the signing of the football. It would seem trivial to most people. It was just normal that Conner would ask for his signature, too. But maybe Devon needed to know that it had bothered him and why.

"What's wrong?" Devon asked shrewdly.

"I don't know how to explain this," he said. "It's just when Conner asked me to sign that football for him, I couldn't do it."

He wasn't sure how to explain that when his son had looked at him hoping to get an autograph from his "Coach Hart," for the first time he'd felt as if he was deceiving Conner.

"I understand," she said. "Having Conner calling you 'Coach Hart' now that you know he's your father feels wrong to me, too."

"So what do we do about it?" he asked. He knew what he wanted to do. He wanted to wake his son up and tell him the truth, but he knew that wasn't the right thing to do. "Do you think we should consult a counselor?"

"You mean like a family counselor? I hadn't considered that. I don't know. Maybe we just need to give it a little more time. You know he's crazy about you. It's bound to be a shock, though. But he's a strong kid. Just give us a couple more weeks of him getting used to you being around and then we can tell him."

"Together?" he asked.

Devon hesitated for a moment then looked back over to where Conner slept. Michael wasn't sure he agreed with them waiting another two weeks, but he did know that she only had their son's best interests in mind.

Finally, she looked up at him. "Okay. We'll tell him, together."

Later that night, after they'd arrived back at Devon's home and had gotten Conner into bed, the two of them stepped out on the porch to say good-night. Michael had made a point of keeping things light between them for the last two weeks. There had been no good-night kisses since the first one they'd shared. He was doing his best to keep his focus on his son.

Then he'd seen her in those fitted jeans and heeled boots, her hair trailing down her shoulders and her lips painted a bright red to match her jersey, and all his resolve had begun to melt. He'd known that this was bound to happen. The pull between them was too strong. But after sitting beside her at the game and then in the plane, it had been all he could do to keep his hands off her. He'd come up with reasons to show her something on the field just so that he could touch her hand. He'd held up longer than he could be expected to. It was time to throw caution to the wind. And he was about to throw it as far as he could. He just hoped that she was ready to receive it.

"So how was this for a first date?" he asked, hoping to throw her off guard.

"This was a date?" she asked, her eyes narrowing at him. "I'm pretty sure I didn't agree to this being a date."

"I asked you to the game and you agreed to go.

Therefore, it was a date." He gave her his best smile and when those lips that he had been fantasizing about all day turned up, he knew he had her. "And as we have both now agreed that this was our first date, it only seems right that we end it with a kiss."

He bent his head to kiss her and was surprised when her arms instinctively curled around his neck and drew him closer. Then her lips parted and he lost it. His tongue touched hers and his hands slid up her neck and into her hair, holding her mouth to his as he plunged deep inside. She tasted so good on his tongue, but it wasn't enough. He wanted to taste all of her. He pulled away and was rewarded with her protest. Then he moved his lips to her collarbone, just above the neckline of her jersey, and began to work his way up. After he reached the top of her cheek, he moved to the back of her ear. Her body shuddered and her breasts rubbed against his chest. He'd never forgotten how responsive she was when he'd kissed her there the night they'd spent together. Nor had he forgotten just how her responsiveness had affected him. If they didn't stop soon, they were going to be putting on a show for the whole neighborhood. They had to find somewhere new to kiss.

He pulled his mouth away then rested his chin on top of her head, which she leaned against his chest. They both were breathless and maybe a little unsteady, so they clung together for several moments.

"I have to say that was the best first-date kiss I've ever had," he said between breaths. From the way his heart was pounding, he didn't think he would have survived if it had been any better.

After a moment, Devon lifted her head from his chest. Her deep green eyes were bright, though he knew she had to be tired after the long day they'd had.

"I guess it was pretty good," she said, smiling up at him. At that moment, while she was teasing him, she was once again the girl he'd known as Sunshine.

Then her smile turned to a frown. "I don't understand. You've acted like you didn't want to kiss me, or even touch me, for the last two weeks. What gives?"

He saw the hurt in her eyes and knew he had messed up. "I'm sorry. I admit, I've been trying to keep things…less intimate between the two of us. I was afraid of what might happen if Conner started to think of us as more than friends. I don't want to confuse or hurt him."

"Okay," she said slowly. "I understand that. I'm worried about that, too. I lived in a home where men came and went on a weekly basis. I would never do that to my son. That doesn't mean that I'm never going to have another relationship, though."

The last thing he wanted to do was listen to her talk about having a relationship with any man but him. "I don't understand. You're planning on hiding these relationships?"

"Not hiding, as much as being discreet. My life would have been a lot better if my mother had been more discreet. Maybe when Conner's older and if I have a serious relationship it would be okay for him to know, but I don't see why right now he would need to know anything about that part of my life."

"So are you suggesting that it's okay for the two

of us to have a relationship as long as Conner doesn't know?" he asked. Even though he understood her reasoning, he didn't know how he would feel about being her secret fling.

She tilted her head to the side and looked him up and down, a playful smile on her lips. "How about I think about it and let you know?"

Laughing, he stepped away and started down the steps. "Good night, Sunshine."

In the darkness, he heard her laughing behind him. "Good night, Mickey."

CHAPTER TWELVE

Monday morning came too soon for Devon, so when Conner had woken her, his eyes bright with the excitement of taking his new signed football to school, her mood had not been the best. She was tired and cranky. And she knew exactly who was to blame.

She'd tried her best to sleep, but her mind had refused to shut down and her body had refused to go back into that no-sex mode it had been in for the last year. Michael admitting that he had purposely cooled things down between them because he was afraid of hurting Conner had just made her want him more.

The two of them had been concentrating on him getting to know Conner better and he'd made no effort to take things any further between him and Devon. And while a part of her had been disappointed in that, she had known that he was concentrating on his relationship with Conner.

Then…pow! He'd changed everything between the two of them again with another good-night kiss. But she hadn't let him get away with it as easily as he had thought. She'd called him on it. He couldn't keep going back and forth, from hot to cold, whenever he wanted. His concerns were legitimate, but they could be worked around.

Not that she wasn't nervous about where things could go wrong between them. She'd never admit it to him, but even after all these years, she remembered feeling so alone as she'd waited for that phone call from him that had never come.

Only this time, things would be different. Neither of them was looking for more than a good time together. They had an attraction that needed to be burned off. That was all.

Feeling better about things, she climbed out of bed and began her day.

An hour later, she arrived at work and found two people, a woman and a man, waiting for her at the front desk from the state health-care agency. As they introduced themselves and explained why they were there, she tried to make sense of it all.

"So someone put in a complaint against the surgical center?" she asked. She'd been involved in several accreditations over the years, but she'd never dealt directly with a complaint being filed.

"Yes. We actually received a complaint from a doctor who practices here." The woman handed Devon a very official piece of paper.

Devon read through the complaint and saw the patient's name listed. James Waters. The elderly man who owned the bakery, who'd had the atrial fibrillation. She should have known that Dr. Morgan would be behind this. After being denied surgical rights, he'd decided to make a complaint about the surgical center? He couldn't have thought this out very well. If he had, he would have known that this would look bad for him.

She looked at her watch, then glanced down at the surgery schedule on her desk. Michael was in surgery. She'd have to handle this and inform him later.

"I'm glad you brought this to our attention. Now, how can I help you with this investigation?" Devon asked them.

An hour later, the recovery nurses that had taken care of Mr. Waters had all been interviewed, and the chart had been reviewed. Devon had been the first to be interviewed, since she was specifically named on the complaint. She'd explained that she had been the one to request another doctor for the patient when Dr. Morgan had failed to return the nurses' calls. When the investigators had questioned why she thought the doctor hadn't called back, she'd been honest. "I can't tell you the exact reason, but it seemed to me that he felt he had done his part and we needed to handle whatever came up after the surgery. Which is exactly what ended up happening."

While the investigators didn't make a lot of comments before they left, the looks Devon had seen pass between them told her that the evidence pointed to the problem being Steve Morgan and not the care that the surgical center's staff had given the patient.

She knew that Michael saw patients in the afternoon after his surgeries, so she texted him that she had something she needed to talk to him about. When she received a text inviting her to have lunch with him in his office, she messaged her agreement. When he replied that he would handle the food, she sent him back a smiley emoji and realized she was smiling just as widely as the expressive emblem. She was in so much trouble.

By the time she got to his office, Michael was waiting for her with a delivery bag of food on his desk. "You might want to let me tell you about this first, before we eat," she warned him.

She handed him a copy of the complaint. "You don't have to worry about it, though. I've already handled it."

His eyes seemed to race over the paper, while his hands tightened and his knuckles turned white. "Tell me."

So as she unpacked the delivery bag she told him about the investigators arriving that morning and how they'd very thoroughly interviewed the staff. "I'm not sure what he was trying to accomplish, but he had to know that it would make him look bad when they investigated his complaint."

"I'm not sure he even believes he did anything wrong. I appreciate how you handled this. I just hope he's not going to make any more trouble for us. Maybe when the investigators go back to him with their findings, he'll realize that it's best to just move on."

For a few moments, they busied themselves with their sandwiches while Devon went more in-depth concerning the investigation. Though she hated that there had been an investigation, it had taken her mind off what had happened between them the night before.

It wasn't until Devon began to clean up her food wrappers that Michael changed the subject from work to something more personal. "I thought, since our first date went so well, that maybe we should give a second date a try."

She stopped by the trash can and put her hands on

her hips. "Just so there's no misunderstanding this time. You are actually inviting me out on a date?"

She watched as he leaned back in his chair and gave her that ridiculously charming smile of his. She would bet money that Dr. Michael Hart had never had to attend a physician's charm school. All he had to do was smile at his patients, at least his female patients, to make them happy.

"There's a sunset cruise that leaves out of the Destin Harbor Saturday night. We could drive down that afternoon and either drive back home that night or spend the night there."

Devon wasn't sure what to say. From the way things had ended the night before, she wasn't completely surprised by the invitation for a second date. But spending a night together? That would be moving their relationship forward faster than what she was prepared for. "The sunset cruise sounds lovely, but I don't know about spending the night. Conner is supposed to go fishing with Max and his dad Saturday afternoon. I'm not sure if he's staying overnight, though, so I'll have to check."

"It's okay if you don't want to stay the night. I'm not trying to rush you into anything," Michael said.

Devon couldn't deny that the thought of spending the night with Michael was very tempting and knew that tonight would be another sleepless night.

By the end of their second date, Michael was pretty sure it had been a success. The yacht hadn't been overcrowded. The music hadn't been too loud. The meal had been delicious. And the company had been the best. They'd almost missed the beautiful sunset because they'd been so busy talking that they hadn't noticed when everyone else had left the dining room. It had been the waiter who had reminded them—he'd explained that there was a small patio off the back of the dining room where they could see the sunset without the other diners being present. Michael had left the man a hefty tip before he'd escorted Devon outside.

Fall had finally come to the Florida panhandle, though there was very little evidence. The daytime temperatures were still warm, but at night they fell down into the sixties. As they stepped outside, the wind off the water caught Devon's hair and blew it back against him. Scents of strawberries and lemons drifted around him, stirring something inside him. He'd begun to recognize her scent and found himself missing it when she was away from him.

"It's beautiful," Devon said as she leaned against the boat's railing. "All that pink and purple mixed with the dark blue and the bright gold from the last rays of the sun. I don't stop and enjoy things like this like I use to. I used to walk along the beach every night and watch the sunset."

"I remember. I used to look out my window and see you there. I didn't understand why you did that then." He came up behind her and slipped his arms around her waist, pulling her against him. She was wearing a pretty sleeveless dress made out of a soft material that seemed to float in the breeze. A gust came up and she shivered in his arms, the motion causing his body to tighten and harden. At that moment, he was so glad he'd given up on trying to keep his hands off her.

"That's because the only thing you had eyes for then was a football," Devon teased.

"I had other interests, too. Why do you think I looked out my window? I knew when to expect you."

She turned in his arms and looked up at him. "Really?"

"Yes, really. I thought you were the prettiest girl in school back then." He bent down and kissed the tip of her nose. "Now, I think you're the most beautiful woman I've ever known."

The smile she gave him told him that she thought he was teasing her. Why couldn't she see herself as he did? Maybe because he'd hurt her before? That thought stung. He'd made her feel unwanted. He never wanted Devon to feel that way again. Instead, he wanted her to understand what it was that he saw when he looked at her. He wanted her to know how much he wanted her. So he kissed her.

When he lifted his mouth, he murmured, "I love the way your lips feel and the way they smile whenever you talk about Conner."

He kissed her nose, then said, "I love the way your pretty little nose twitches right before you let off a most unladylike sneeze."

She laughed and he kissed each one of her cheeks. "I love the way your cheeks turn pink when you're excited or embarrassed. Just like they're doing now."

She tried to bury her face in his chest, but he wouldn't let her. "And I love those beautiful green eyes of yours. They've seen so much sadness, but they still manage to sparkle with laughter when Conner is telling you a story about his day at school."

Then he smiled down at her. "Did I tell you how much I love those lips of yours?"

"I can't seem to remember if you did or not," she said, her lips turning up in a flirtatious smile. "Maybe you should show me."

And so he did.

Devon shivered as Michael drove them home. The night had been magical and she didn't want it to end. Still, she was unsure if she should take things further with Michael this soon. But whether she should or not, there was no denying that she wanted to spend the night with him. Just like always, she hadn't wanted the kisses they'd shared on the cruise to end.

As they turned down the road that would take both of them home, her to her place, and him to his own home, even though Conner was sleeping over at Max's, she made her decision. She couldn't deny that she had made some decisions in her life that she regretted, but she couldn't see how this one night could hurt anything. It was just one night.

But wasn't that what she'd told herself the night she'd spent with Michael and then come home pregnant? That was exactly what had happened. And wasn't that the reason she'd made a trip up to the store right out of town by the interstate last night, and purchased a box of condoms? She'd wanted to be prepared for whatever might happen tonight.

Making up her mind, she patted her purse where the box had been safely tucked away, then looked over at Michael. "Do you feel up to a glass of wine at your place?"

The look he gave her was smoldering-hot and she knew he understood that her question wasn't really about the wine. "Are you sure?"

She swallowed her doubt back and put on a smile she hoped was more confident than she felt. It had been a long time, over eight years, since she'd done anything like this. It had been well over a year since she'd had any physical contact with anyone. Her body had become hypersensitive since the first kisses they'd shared on her porch. Just thinking about that night had her body humming with a need she knew she couldn't deny any longer.

She nodded her head, then managed to say the words. "Yes, I'm sure."

Michael's hands tightened on the steering wheel. "I appreciate the fact that you didn't mention this earlier. Otherwise, I might not have been able to make it back here safely."

She couldn't help but laugh at his admission. "I guess it's a good thing that I didn't mention that I was carrying a box of condoms in my purse all night."

"If I'd known that, we definitely wouldn't have made it out your front door," he said as he pulled into his driveway and turned off the truck. He opened his door, then made a grab for her purse before jumping out and running over to her side of the vehicle. She had just opened the door when he grabbed her and flipped her over his shoulder.

"Michael, what are you doing?" she said between laughs.

He took the stairs two at a time, laughing as he wrapped one arm securely around her legs and patted her bottom with the other. Devon couldn't believe that he had gone all caveman on her, but she had to admit, she liked it.

He set her down at the door, making sure she was steady before punching in the alarm code and opening the door.

"I didn't realize you needed that glass of wine so badly," she joked as she walked into his living room. She looked back to find him still standing at the door, her purse hanging from his shoulder. Oh, how she wished she had a picture of this strong, masculine man wearing her glittery gold purse.

"I don't think I've ever needed anything...no, make that I've never needed anyone as badly as I need you right now." As he walked toward her, he opened his arms.

The laughter they'd shared a few minutes was gone. There was only desire in his eyes now. Desire for her. She walked into his arms and just rested there for a moment. Nothing had ever felt so perfect.

Then he kissed her and all thoughts left her brain. His lips seemed to devour hers. She molded herself against him, needing to get as close as possible. She wanted to feel him inside her. Moving, stretching her, filling her.

"Where?" she asked, her head lifting as his lips ran up her skin from her collarbone to that sensitive spot behind her ear. Her breath caught and she arched into him. He was driving her crazy with her kisses, but she wanted more.

She looked around the room where a large sectional couch sat. That would never do. His lips had moved to the other side of her neck now, and were working their way back to where the neckline of her dress cut down to a point as his hands began to work on her buttons.

When his tongue skimmed across the top of her breasts, she decided to take things into her own hands, so to speak. Moving her hands between them, she ran her fingers across the front of his pants. He was long and steel-hard, and for a second, she forgot all about finding someplace more comfortable for them to share. If nothing else, there was the dining room table nearby. She had unbuckled his belt, popped the button off his pants, and began to lower his zipper when she felt her dress slip away, leaving her standing in a tiny pair of panties and a matching bra. Once again, she felt herself leave the floor as Michael gathered her up in his arms.

"You do have my purse, right?" she said as they topped the stairs and turned toward a room at the end of the hall.

"I wouldn't think of leaving it behind," he assured her.

He pushed the door open and placed Devon on her feet once again. His hand came up and tucked her hair behind her ears. She felt the tremble in his fingers as they ran down her cheek, and then between her breasts as he slid her bra off her shoulders. "I only want one promise from you. Tomorrow, when I wake up, I want you to be here beside me."

It was such a little thing to ask and she understood that he feared, like the first time they'd slept together, she would be gone the next morning. "I promise I'll still be here."

With that promise, she removed the rest of her clothes and watched as he removed his shirt and then his pants. A moment later they were stretched out on his bed, his strong arms holding her as he teased her with his mouth and hands. Her own hands and lips explored his body, discovering scars that she knew hadn't been there the last time they'd been bared to each other. Her hands slid lower, and she wrapped her hand around the thick length of him and guided it to her entrance. He slid inside her, and she thought that she'd explode from the pleasure of him being there, finally.

For a moment they just looked at each other and an irrational fear filled her until she saw the depth of longing in his eyes and remembered that it was the same longing she'd seen once before, which had convinced her that their act of lovemaking was more than just a physical thing between them.

Then he started moving and the only thing she knew was the pleasure of his body as it thrust inside of her. She felt the tension growing, spiraling with every thrust. His lips moved to that special spot behind her ear, then he whispered, "Sunshine, come for me."

As if her body had been waiting for the command, her orgasm burst through her. He ground against her, each thrust prolonging her pleasure, until finally he reached his own release with a shout, and then the two of them sank deep down into the covers together.

She lay there beside him, her body sated while she tried to push down the fear she'd felt earlier when they were making love. She reminded herself that she wasn't the same girl she'd been the last time she'd fallen under Michael's spell. She'd grown up to become a woman. A woman who'd been through enough pain in her life. She'd told herself that she could have a relationship with a man without any expectations. And that probably would have worked with any other man except the one who was currently lying beside her.

CHAPTER THIRTEEN

MICHAEL WOKE TO find Devon beside him, shaking him. "Morning, Sunshine," he said, before rolling over on top of her to kiss her good morning.

"Morning is almost gone. I've got to get up." She laughed as he began to press kisses all over her face, then pushed against him and tried to wiggle out from between his arms. "I'm serious. I told Max's parents that I would pick Conner up before lunch. Besides, I have to do the grocery shopping and get clothes ready for the week. I should have been up a couple hours ago."

He loosened his hold and let her squeeze out from under him, enjoying the feel of her naked body against his, then got up himself. "Don't stress. We can do this."

"We? I'm going to be grocery shopping and doing laundry. I'm not sure how much help you're going to be," she said as she bent down and gathered the few clothes that had made it upstairs.

He had to pause for a moment and just take her in. At that moment, he felt like the luckiest man alive. He wanted to take her straight back to bed. Instead, he bent down and picked up his pants off the floor. He pulled out his keys and tossed them toward Devon. "Take my truck and go get changed. I'll grab a shower and be ready by the time you get back. We can pick up Conner and go out for brunch."

Not waiting for her to agree, he walked into the bathroom. A few moments later he heard his truck crank up. He looked into the mirror and saw that goofy smile that the media had always seemed to love. They didn't know that most of the time, while he was fighting his way up the ranks in college, then winning the Claymont Trophy, and eventually playing professional football, that smile had been forced. But today, it was totally genuine. There was nothing that he'd rather do than spend the day doing all those everyday domestic chores with Devon and Conner.

Several hours later, when Michael looked over at Devon as they cleaned the kitchen, he was surprised to see just how fresh she still looked. "I don't know how you do it. I was tired by the time we got finished with the groceries."

"Buying groceries would have gone a lot quicker if you and Conner hadn't decided to play games and keep putting those ridiculous items in my cart," Devon said tartly, taking the platter he'd just washed and drying it carefully. He still didn't understand why anyone would have dishes that couldn't be put in the dishwasher. "And between the two of you, I spent twice as much on groceries as I usually do."

"I tried to get you to let me pay." It had been the only disagreement they'd had that day and Michael still wasn't sure how he'd lost that argument. He had wanted to insist that it was his son that she was feeding, but with Conner beside him, he couldn't fight that battle.

"Let's not talk about it right now, okay?" Devon said as she moved between him and the cabinet where he'd just placed the last glass he'd dried. "Conner's in the shower and we have a few moments alone. Let's not waste them."

Michael placed his arms on the counter behind her and bent his head toward her. The kiss started off as playful, teasing, but it quickly heated up. Her arms circled his neck and he lifted her onto the countertop. Her legs opened to let him in closer and she wrapped them around his waist.

"What are you doing?" Conner asked from behind him.

Suddenly all the desire that had been coursing through Michael's body vanished in an instant.

Devon's legs fell from Michael's waist and her head dropped down to his chest. How was she supposed to explain to her son what he had just interrupted? She guessed she should be glad that he'd come in before things had gotten any more heated between her and Michael. She wanted to just stay there in Michael's arms and pretend that there wasn't anything unusual about her being plastered against her son's football coach's body. But she was the mom and she had to do what moms did a lot of the time. She had to improvise.

But first, she had to get Michael to let her go. Pushing against his chest, she managed to wiggle down between the cabinets and his firm body until her feet touched the floor and she stepped away from Michael. "Conner, what exactly is it you thought you saw?"

She knew Conner was very observant. That was why he was always asking questions. If he saw something that he didn't understand, he was going to ask questions until he figured it out. She just hoped this wasn't one of those times.

"I saw Coach Hart kissing you and it looked like you liked it." The look Conner gave her reminded her of that old black-and-white show when the husband would tell his wife that he had some explaining to do. "You're not supposed to be kissing."

"Uh, but sometimes people like to kiss," Michael said, coming to stand beside her.

"Mommies and daddies kiss. That's what you said, Mom," Conner said, then turned toward Michael. "Does that mean you're going to be my stepdad? There's a girl at school who says she's had three stepdads."

Michael looked at her and she could see that he thought this was the moment they'd been waiting for.

She took a deep breath and let it out. "Conner, I need to tell you something. It's about your dad. It might be hard for you to fully understand until you get older, but I want to tell you now. You see, Coach Hart isn't just your coach. He's your dad." Devon knew the moment the words came out of her mouth that she hadn't done this right. Her son would only have more questions from the lack of information she had given him.

"But my dad died," Conner said, the pain in his voice stabbing her through her own heart. "You know that, Mom. He got sick. We went to see him at the hospital. Then Grandma Campbell came and we all went to the church to say goodbye to him."

"I know, honey. And he loved you very much. But before I married your daddy, Michael and I…" She was at a loss for words. How did she tell her seven-year-old son that his mom got pregnant and then married someone who wasn't her baby's daddy? The last thing she wanted Conner to think was that he was a mistake.

"Before you were born, me and your mom loved each other and we made a baby. You. But there were a lot of complications and your mom married Zach, and he became your daddy. Does any of this make sense to you?"

"No. None of this makes sense. You're just making this up so you can pretend to be my daddy because you like my mom. That's why you've spent time with me."

"That's not true, Conner. We wanted you to have some time to get to know me better before we told you," Michael said. She could see how Conner's words had hurt him.

"Why don't we go sit down in the living room? Then you can ask all the questions you want to ask and we'll answer them," Devon said, hoping that she could find the right words this time.

"No, I don't want to talk to either of you," Conner said as he turned his tear-filled eyes to her. "You told me we aren't supposed to lie." Then, before Devon could stop him, Conner bolted away and ran out the door.

When she started to go after him, Michael grabbed her arm. "Let him have a moment. He just needs some time to think things through. He's a smart kid."

Devon wasn't sure Michael was right. He'd never seen Conner with Zach. He didn't understand how close the two of them had been, or how hard Zach's death had hit Conner.

"I'll give him a few minutes, then I'll go and check on him. But maybe it's best if you leave before I do that."

"Maybe you're right," Michael said, then leaned down to kiss her. She found herself wanting to pull away, but she didn't understand why. Michael hadn't done anything wrong. It had been her who had kept his son from him. It had been her who had never told her son the truth, though Zach had suggested it several times. And now, she had to fix it all.

She waited until Michael had left, then she went to talk to Conner. She opened the door to his room and found the lights turned out. As she sat down on the bed next to him, she noticed that the pillows were missing off the bed. An uneasiness filled her and she reached down and pulled the covers off Conner. But there was no Conner, only pillows stuffed underneath. She stood and rushed to the light switch, but she already knew what she would find. Conner wasn't in his room.

She rushed through the house, throwing open doors and calling Conner's name. She rushed out the back door, then dashed back inside and out the front door. For a moment, she couldn't remember where she'd left her phone. Then she remembered setting it down on the counter when she and Michael were doing the dishes.

Michael. That had to be it. Conner had to have gone over to Michael's house. It was a couple blocks down the road and she ran all the way. She could see the lights through the windows, then she stopped and took a breath. Conner had been hurt and angry, so he'd come to talk to Michael. She could only hope that Michael would be able to explain things better to Conner than she had been able to. She knocked on the door, then remembered there was a doorbell. She'd just hit the bell when the door opened and Michael stood there staring at her blankly.

She knew immediately that Conner wasn't there.

"How could he be gone?" Michael asked as he shoved his feet into his tennis shoes.

"I went to check on him, to talk to him about what had happened. I thought he was asleep, but I noticed that there weren't any pillows on the bed. He'd piled them up under the covers to make it look like he was there. He had to have left when I walked you out the front door." Devon followed him down the stairs to the storage room, where all the hurricane preparations were kept.

He pulled out two flashlights and checked them to make sure the batteries were still good. "Okay. So that was only about twenty minutes ago, right? He couldn't have gone far. You didn't see him on your way here—besides, I'm probably the last person that he would come to see."

"I should have driven my car here, then we could have split up." She ran her trembling hands through her hair and Michael knew that she was close to losing it.

"Look, we can't panic. We'll take my truck. We can stop by your house and see if he's come back. If he's not there, I think we should call the police. Then we can drive down to the park. If we don't see him on the road, we'll check the beach. He couldn't have gotten far. Trust me, Devon. We will find him."

They headed for the truck and Michael handed Devon a flashlight as he pulled out of the drive. "Shine it on the sides of the road as we pass. He could be hiding from us. He's probably as scared as we are."

He drove slowly, making sure that he lit up every bush and tree they passed with his flashlight. He stopped once when he thought he saw something move, but it was only a cat exploring the neighborhood.

"Wait, stop. Michael, stop."

"Hold on," he said, then swore when Devon jumped out of the truck before he came to a complete stop. He put the truck in Park, then got out to see what Devon had seen. His heart just about came out of his chest when he circled the back of the truck and saw her bent over something at the side of the road. He'd seen too many patients that had been hit by vehicles and left on the side of the road. His whole body went icy cold with terror.

"This is Conner's bicycle, I'm sure of it," Devon said, standing up and looking around. "But where is he?"

Michael's lungs expanded as he took a deep breath. For a moment, he closed his eyes and said a prayer of thanks. When he opened them, he saw that Devon was walking toward the beach, her light shining on the ground as she walked. "There's footsteps here that look small enough to be his."

As soon as they made it down the path that led to the beach, Devon started calling out for her son. "Conner? Conner, where are you?"

He shone his light to the left and started toward the

shoreline while Devon started down the other way. The boy had to be here. Unless…

"Michael, I see him," Devon called.

He turned to see her running down to the shoreline, where the tide was coming in. By the time he caught up to her, he could hear crying. He shone the light out toward the water and saw that Conner was sprawled in the sand, the water rising around him as the tide came in.

After handing his flashlight to Devon, he sprinted through the water until he got to the boy. He started to lift his son into his arms, but when he put his arms under his legs, Conner cried out in pain.

"Conner, what's wrong?" he asked as Devon dropped down beside them.

"I tripped in a hole and hurt my foot," Conner said, lifting his leg up to show them, then whimpering before he reached out his arms to his mom and burst into tears.

"Oh, honey. It's okay. It's all going to be okay. Let's get you home and we can get it checked out. Coach Hart—" Devon shook her head and corrected herself "—I mean, your dad can check to make sure there's nothing broken."

"He's not my dad," Conner shouted, the hurt child suddenly turning into the angry boy Michael had seen earlier.

"We can talk about that later," Michael said. Though Conner's words stung, Michael knew it was a sign that the boy himself was hurting. The life he'd known up until tonight had suddenly changed and been turned upside down. It would take some time for Conner to get used to the changes. "Right now, we need to get you out of these wet clothes and make sure your foot is okay."

"No," Conner protested. "I want to know the truth. I'm not going home until you tell me the truth."

Unsure what to do, the two of them looked at each other, then they both sat down beside their son in the water.

"Okay, I'm going to tell you the whole story now," Devon said. "First, I want to explain that there are two types of fathers. One is called a biological father. Michael is your biological father. And, like he told you, the two of us made a baby and that baby is you. Which is why you have the color of my hair and the color of his eyes. You've got a part of each of us inside you. But there's another kind of father, too. That's what Zach was. He was the father who helped take care of you when you were born. He loved you very much, just as much as if he had made you himself. He was every bit your dad, too. Does that help explain things better?"

Not answering her, Conner turned toward Michael. "But why didn't you take care of me when I was born? Why didn't you come to see me?"

Devon wanted to say that it was all her fault, but before she could, Michael answered him. "Something happened, and me and your mom didn't talk for a long time, not until you came here to live. If I had known that you were my son, I would have come to see you, I promise, but sometimes things happen that we can't change. I can't change that and neither can your mom. But I hope you'll let me see you now. I want to be a good father, but I don't really know how. It sounds like your other dad was a really good one. Maybe you can tell me about him and that will help me do a better job."

"I don't know," Conner said and sniffled, then turned to his mom. "Can I go home now?"

Michael stood and reached down to pick up his son, but Conner turned away from him and reached for his mother.

"No, I've got him," Devon said. Michael took her arm and helped her stand up with her son in her arms.

He started to take Conner from her when she stumbled, but she managed to straighten herself and then tightened her hold on her son. Unable to help himself, he took her arm. Though she didn't pull away, she didn't lean into him, either. It had been a long day and he knew they were all tired, but still it hurt. Badly.

Devon shifted Conner in her arms. Her back and legs strained as they made their way down the path to Michael's truck. Exhaustion was setting in and she had to force her feet to keep moving. All the emotions of the last few hours had drained the life out of her. The pain she'd seen in her son's eyes when she'd tried to explain about his father, the fear of not knowing where he was or if he was safe, then the relief when she'd found him—it had all been too much.

She'd been so foolish to think that she wouldn't have to pay for the decisions she'd made in her life. The last few weeks she'd been so happy, watching Michael and her son spending time together. She'd known that Conner would be confused when she told him about Michael, but she'd never dreamed he'd run away. She should have realized life wasn't that simple. It never had been. Not for her. Even the life she'd built with Zach had always been shadowed by the knowledge that she wasn't being honest with her son. At least that burden had been lifted now.

And Michael? Had she really thought she could have any type of relationship with him without getting emotionally involved? She'd fallen for him when she'd been a teenager and when she'd been a young woman. She should have known she couldn't escape losing her heart to him all over again.

By the time they made it back to her house, Devon knew what she had to do. After she got Conner into some dry pajamas, her son was too tired to complain as Michael examined his foot.

"It looks like you twisted your ankle and sprained it. That means your mom is going to have to put a wrap around it and you're going to have to stay off it for a while," Michael told Conner, though Devon could see that her son was dozing off even as Michael was talking.

"I'll get him into bed and then wrap it," she said, picking her son off the couch where she'd put him for Michael to examine him. "If it's still swollen tomorrow, I'll take him to get it X-rayed."

"Let me know and I can get the X-ray ordered at work," Michael said, then stood to leave.

"I'll call into work tomorrow and make sure everything is covered, but I'm going to stay home. I need to be with Conner right now." Turning back to her son, she heard the door shut behind her.

CHAPTER FOURTEEN

MICHAEL WALKED OUT the door of what he had once thought was his biggest success. Hart Sports Institute had been the culmination of all his dreams. He'd worked hard to make the surgical center a success with the same tenacity that he'd had for his dream of playing football. In fact, he'd been working toward being an orthopedic doctor and owning a surgical center for sports injuries since the day he'd accepted that his professional football career had ended. He was proud of what he'd accomplished with the surgical center. And he still looked forward to working there with his brother once Matt finished his residency. But for the first time since he'd discovered his talent and love for the game of football, he was able to see that life was about more than just a successful career.

It was about the people in his life. The ones he laughed with and sometimes argued with. The person he wanted to go grocery shopping with or do something as simple as laundry. The person he kissed good-night on the porch and then went home and dreamed of kissing again. After experiencing the last few weeks with Devon and Conner, he felt the loss of those simple, everyday things the most.

As he climbed into his truck, he saw that Devon's car was still in the parking lot. She'd started working later and only arriving in time to pick Conner up from practice. It was just one of the changes she'd made to the routine they'd established before the night they'd told Conner about Michael being his father. Since that night, there had been no invitations to dinner and no visits to Michael's office. Devon was making sure he had no doubt that things between the two of them had changed. Conner's anger at finding out that the father who'd raised him hadn't been his real father had upset both of them, but Michael didn't understand why Devon thought that meant the relationship between him and Devon had to end. Conner's anger would surely subside eventually. Michael had hoped that the two of them showing a united front would have helped him accept the change. But then, what did Michael know? He'd only been a father for a month or so. Maybe Devon had a plan that he didn't understand.

His phone rang over the car system and he answered it after seeing that it was his brother. "Hey, Matt. What's up?"

"Nothing's up here. I'm just living the harried life of a resident. What about you? Any changes in the Conner and Devon situation?" Matt asked.

"No. It's been over a week and she's still doing her best to ignore me." Michael had told Matt everything that had happened the night Conner had run away, leaving out the intimate details of the night before that he and Devon had spent together. "I'm not sure what to do. I don't want to pressure either one of them, but

I don't know how much longer I can take this. I feel like Devon and Conner are getting further and further away from me every day."

"So this isn't just about Conner," Matt said, his words a statement instead of a question.

Though Michael hadn't told his brother about the night Devon had slept over, his brother had known that the two of them had gone out together.

"You love her, don't you?" Matt asked.

Michael hadn't said he loved anyone since his parents' death. He loved his brother, but it wasn't something the two of them actually said to each other. But his parents? They'd always told their two sons that they loved them each night at bedtime, and Michael had always told his parents that he loved them. It was one of the first things Michael had missed the first night he'd gone to sleep after they were gone. He would have given anything to have been able to tell them just once more how much he loved them.

But now, there was Devon in his life and, yes, he did love her. Yet, even with everything he'd learned from the loss of his parents, he hadn't been able to say the words. And with her pulling away from him, he might never get the chance. "What do I know about love? Besides, she's made it plain that she only ever wanted a casual relationship."

"She's protecting her son. She had a bad scare and she's probably feeling a lot of guilt about not telling him earlier. And maybe she's feeling some guilt concerning her husband, too," Matt suggested.

Michael knew that wasn't the problem between the

two of them. She'd admitted that he'd badly hurt her all those years ago when he hadn't called her. Was she just as afraid of getting hurt now or messing things up between them as he was?

"I think you do love her, you're just too scared to admit it," Matt said, his voice a bit smug.

"I've hurt her before. I don't want to do that again," Michael protested. He'd gone through his whole adult life without ever thinking about falling in love. The closest he had ever felt had been that night he'd spent with…Devon. What if that was it? What if the reason he'd never fallen in love with anyone else was because he'd never felt anything that compared to that night all those years ago with Devon? Not the sex, or at least not just the sex. But the way they'd laughed and talked. He had been so happy with her that night. Just like he had that night on the cruise. And the next morning, when he'd woken up with her by his side? He'd never felt anything like that level of happiness before.

Michael turned into the sports complex and parked. He looked over and saw Conner sitting on one of the benches at the side of the field.

"If you love her, you won't hurt her. You've had enough losses in your life, Mickey, and you've fought for every win you've had. Don't stop fighting now."

Michael sat in the truck for a few minutes after he and Matt ended their call. His brother was right. He'd lost a lot in his life, but he'd never just given up. Now, the most important thing in his life, a life with Devon and Conner, was right there in front of him. He had never been one to stand on the sidelines. He'd always fought his way into the game. That had been the key to his success. So maybe it was time for him to get off those sidelines and start fighting for the life he wanted so badly.

Making a decision that he hoped he wouldn't regret, he walked over to where Conner was putting on his cleats. Michael had stayed away from the practice field until today, giving Bryan the excuse of work while actually not wanting to cause Conner any further distress. He was now starting to believe that it had been a mistake not to be around Conner. What if his son thought he was mad at him or, even worse, that he didn't want to be troubled with an angry little boy?

"Hey, Conner," Michael said, coming up behind him as he worked on tying his shoestrings.

"Hey, Coach Hart," Conner said. The boy looked up at him and for a moment Michael would have sworn that his son was happy to see him. Then, as if Conner remembered that he was supposed to be mad at Michael, his smile disappeared and his eyes dropped down.

Michael took a seat next to his son. "I don't know about you, but I'm feeling really confused and sad right now."

"You are?" Conner asked, looking up at him. "Why?"

"I guess I'm confused about what is going on between you and me and your mother," Michael said, deciding to just be honest with the little boy. "And I'm sad because I miss spending time with the two of you. I thought that we were friends."

"I thought so, too, but you were just coming around

because you're one of my dads," Conner said, his words as sad-sounding as Michael's.

"Now, that's where you're wrong. I liked hanging out with you. I'll admit that I think it's great having a son like you. I'm very proud of you. And I love the way you aren't afraid to ask questions about things you don't understand. I wish that I could tell your other dad how much I appreciate him for the way he raised you."

"You do?" Conner asked, sitting up straight now.

"I definitely do. Your mom has told me about what a great dad he was and I'm so glad you had him in your life."

"But why weren't you there? I still don't understand how you didn't know about me," Conner said.

"When your mama found out she was going to have you, she was very happy. But when she called to tell me about it, I was in the hospital. I had been really badly hurt playing football and I was all broken up."

"I know," Max said, "you had a broken arm and a broken leg and some other stuff too. She said that was why you quit football." There was no sign of the anger Conner had shown earlier. He was interested in Michael's story now. Michael only hoped that it would help Conner understand things better.

"I had a lot of injuries and my head hurt, too. I was in the hospital for a long time and it made it hard for your mom to get in touch with me. Your mom did try, though. But when she couldn't, she decided that she wanted you to have a father. So she and your father, Zach, got married. They were so happy when you were born. Then your dad got sick and had to leave you."

"I still miss him," Conner whispered. "Even if you're my dad, too, I still love him."

"Of course you love him. I want you to love him. He was a great dad." Michael saw a tear run down his son's face and he couldn't help but put his arm around him. When Conner didn't shy away from him, he pulled him closer into his side. "Conner, I will never stand in the way of you loving your first father."

"My first father?" Conner asked, sniffling against Michael's side.

"Yes, he was your first dad, right?" Michael would always regret that he had missed his son's first words, first steps, and every other first up until now, but he felt no bitterness toward the man who'd been there beside Conner for them.

"Yeah," Conner agreed. "So you're my second dad, then?"

Michael sat and thought for a moment. Having Conner call him dad at all would be wonderful. "I guess I am. Now, can I ask you a question?"

"Sure," Conner replied. "What is it?"

"What would you think if I told you that I love both you and your mother? Would that be okay with you?"

"Are you going to marry her?" Conner's sudden crooked smile couldn't have gotten any wider and it was like the sun coming out on a cold day. "Then you'll be my stepdad, too."

"You'd be okay with me marrying your mom?" Michael asked.

Conner nodded enthusiastically.

"Why such a hurry? I'm not sure she wants to see me

right now. And she might not want to marry me." His stomach twisted with the thought that his son could be wrong and Devon might turn him down. She'd said that she didn't trust easily and he'd already hurt her badly once. What if she was afraid to give him a chance? Or, worse, what if she didn't feel the same about him as he felt about her?

"But you told me that you have to ask a question if you want to know the answer. Besides, she's been crying every night after I go to bed. She thinks I don't hear her, but I do." Conner stood and took hold of Michael's hand and began pulling at him.

"Your mother's crying?" Michael said, letting Conner help pull him off the bench. He didn't like the idea of Devon crying.

"I think it's because I got mad and made you go away. It makes me feel real sad. She's at work so you just need to go find her and ask her to marry you. Then you'll be my second dad and my mom will be happy."

"It's not your fault, Conner. Your mom is just worried about doing the right thing for you." Michael thought about what his son had said. It seemed all three of them were miserable with the way things were now. As a plan began to form in his mind, he turned to Conner. "What do you say the two of us find a way to fix this?"

Devon walked down the beach gathering the shells that her son had insisted he needed right then. It had been a long day at work and she didn't feel like taking a walk on the beach, but today was the first day she had seen any excitement in her son's eyes since the night he'd learned about Michael being his father and she wasn't about to disappoint him.

She bent over to where a group of shells had washed up and began to go through them, looking for the perfect shell. Standing up again, she looked around for Conner and began to panic until she saw him several yards ahead of her. But he wasn't alone.

She stood there, unable to move, as Michael walked toward her. Even with all the injuries he had suffered, he still moved with the grace of an athlete. She'd missed him so much that she'd cried herself to sleep each night. She'd messed up everything between them. First, she'd let things go too far with him. She should have known that once she was in his arms she could never stop herself from falling for him all over again. Now, she had to find some excuse for why she couldn't see him anymore. Not like that. And then there was Conner. She'd made such a mess of that, too. Her son was so angry with Michael and none of it was Michael's fault. It was hers. She was the one who had kept Conner from his father.

"Hi, Sunshine," Michael said as he joined her.

"Hi, Mickey. Is everything okay with Conner?" She hoped the fact that her son had gone to Michael was a good sign that he was getting over some of his anger.

"Conner and I are good. He helped me plan this," Michael said, his eyes heavy with a look of longing that she knew would pull her in if she wasn't careful.

"Plan?" she asked, confused. "What plan?"

"Well, the two of us were talking and he reminded me that if you don't ask a question you'll never know the answer. And since I wasn't sure how I could get you to talk to me since you've been avoiding me, I got him to help me get you here."

"So the two of you have a question for me?" She was reminded of the time when she had been sure that he was going to ask her to marry him. That time it had turned out to be an invitation to a football game, but there was no telling what the two of them had in mind now. Not that she cared. The fact that Conner was talking to Michael was a good step forward.

"No, I'm the one with the question. Conner is here for moral support." Michael looked back to where their son still stood several yards away from them.

"Okay, I'm ready. What is it?" she asked. She didn't know how much longer she could stand there when all she wanted to do was throw herself into his arms. It had been so hard for her to stay away from him for the last week, but she knew now that it was better that she stop things between them before they went any further.

"It's very simple really. I've spent all my life working to make some dream of mine come true and now, I know that no matter how successful I am, without you and Conner in my life I'll never be happy. I want you both in my life forever. I haven't had time to get a ring, so I can't do this the right way yet, but I have to know now. Sunshine, will you marry me?"

Her eyes shot to his and her heart began to pound. Michael wanted to marry her? But was he just doing this for their son? It was like history repeating itself again. She'd married Zach and never regretted it. But this time there was a difference. This time she was in love and she didn't think she could be happy in a marriage with Michael where that love wasn't returned.

"You don't have to make a decision right now. You can take your time. I just can't go on with things the way they are now. I love you so much and I'm miserable without you."

Something broke inside of Devon hearing Michael's words. She tried to hold back the tears, but couldn't. "You really love me?"

"Of course I love you. I think I always have," Michael said. "I've spent my whole life chasing my dreams. First, it was football and then it was medical school. Then it was setting up a practice and building this place. But the last few days I've discovered that none of it matters. It's you who matters. This feeling I have for you, it's more than I've ever felt for anything or anyone in my life, because you've become my whole life. You're all I want. You and Conner. I just need to know if you feel the same way about me."

Devon brushed at the tears rolling down her cheeks, then placed her wet hands against Michael's cheeks. "Yes, I do. I love you and I always have. And, yes, I will marry you."

EPILOGUE

Devon looked down from the balcony to the party taking place on the beach below her. It was supposed to have been a small wedding. A few family members, a few coworkers, and a few close friends were all that had been expected. But when word had gotten out that the hometown football hero and the granddaughter of one of Silver Sands's dearly loved residents were getting married, the invitation list had grown, and the whole beach in front of Michael's home was filled with guests dancing in the sand with the stars and moon shining high above them.

"I can't believe they're all still here," Michael said as he came up behind her, slipping his arms around her.

"I can't, either," she said, leaning back against him. The wedding had been over for hours now. The cake had been cut and eaten, the toasts given. The live band that had been hired for the reception had been gone for at least an hour. She suspected that it had been Matt who had turned on the outside speakers and was streaming music through them. She also suspected that the woman he was now dancing with was the reason why. "Who is that woman Matt's dancing with? I can't quite see from here."

Michael leaned over her and began to laugh. "That's Rachel."

"Our Rachel?" Devon asked, stunned that the beautiful woman dancing below them could be the same one who worked as one of the surgical representatives that assisted in their operating rooms. Devon had to admit that she'd never seen Rachel out of scrubs, but the difference from how she looked at work was startling.

"I almost didn't recognize her myself. I hope Matt doesn't go falling for her," Michael said thoughtfully.

"Why? They're both single and she's always seemed very kind and levelheaded." Devon knew that Michael was protective of his brother, but what harm could come from Matt having a little romance in his life?

"She has a reputation of being a little wary where men are concerned," Michael said.

"Well, she doesn't seem to be that way right now," Devon said as she watched the woman wrapping her arms around Matt's neck as they danced off away from the rest of the crowd.

"Hmm," Michael said, his breath warm against her neck as his lips began to move downward.

Leaning back into his body, she glanced up at the stars above them. Their wedding day had been perfect. And with Conner happily going off to spend a few days at Max's house, they had the nights to themselves for a while.

"Come inside," Michael urged, taking her hand to lead her inside.

"But there's still people here. What will they think

if we leave them?" She didn't want to be rude to everyone who'd come to celebrate with them.

"They'll think I'm a very lucky man," Michael laughed as he turned her in his arms.

Devon looked up at her husband and her heart had never felt so full. "I love you, Mickey."

"And I will always love you, my Sunshine." Michael said, before leaning down and kissing her lips.

*****

*Look out for the next story in
the Sunshine State Surgeons duet*

Coming soon!

*And if you enjoyed this story, check out these other
great reads from Deanne Anders*

Festive Reunion with the Doctor
Single Dad's Fake Fiancée
The Rebel Doctor's Secret Child
Unbuttoning the Bachelor Doc

All available now!

MILLS & BOON®

Coming next month

GREEK HOSPITAL, RED-HOT REUNION
Tina Beckett

Ana shrugged, but curled her fingers around his, not quite ready to break the contact. 'When we first saw each other at the hospital, and I sensed how uncomfortable we both were, I did think it. That I would try to avoid you as much as I could. When Natalia told me I'd have to rotate through surgery, I was horrified. Wasn't sure if I could even do it.'

'And now that you've done it. Are you still horrified?'

'No. I'm actually looking forward to our next time.'

'Our next time.' Dimitry unhooked his hip from the car and took a step closer. 'Are you, Ana?'

God, he evidently felt it too. She swallowed as her senses went on high alert.

'Yes. Very much so.' The words came out as a whisper. Why had she never noticed him like this in school? Hadn't she? She could remember at least one time when she had.

Dangerous. This was moving into territory she had no business exploring. What about working on herself? Wasn't that what she was supposed to be doing?

He took another step and that muscle in his cheek bunched again. This time, though, she knew he wasn't irritated.

She had a feeling it meant something else entirely. That—like her—he was fighting his inner impulses, while being dragged slowly and methodically closer.

'What else are you looking forward to, Ana?'

'Can't you guess?'

His left hand slid behind her nape and he leaned forward until his lips were at her ear. 'Is guessing really what you want me to do?'

'No.' She turned her head so their lips were mere inches apart. 'I want you to kiss me.'

Continue reading

GREEK HOSPITAL, RED-HOT REUNION
Tina Beckett

Available next month
millsandboon.co.uk

Copyright © 2026 Tina Beckett

COMING SOON!

We really hope you enjoyed reading this book. If you're looking for more romance be sure to head to the shops when new books are available on

Thursday 21st May

To see which titles are coming soon, please visit
millsandboon.co.uk/nextmonth

MILLS & BOON

FOUR BRAND NEW BOOKS FROM
MILLS & BOON MODERN

Indulge in desire, drama, and breathtaking romance – where passion knows no bounds!

OUT NOW

Eight Modern stories published every month, find them all at:

millsandboon.co.uk

TWO BRAND NEW BOOKS FROM
Love Always

Be prepared to be swept away to incredible worldwide destinations along with our strong, relatable heroines and intensely desirable heroes.

OUT NOW

Four Love Always stories published every month, find them all at:

millsandboon.co.uk

LET'S TALK
Romance

For exclusive extracts, competitions and special offers, find us online:

- **f** MillsandBoon
- **X** @MillsandBoon
- **◉** @MillsandBoonUK
- **♪** @MillsandBoonUK

Get in touch on 01413 063 232

For all the latest titles coming soon, visit
millsandboon.co.uk/nextmonth